DUDLEY PUBLIC LIBRARIES

The loan of this book may be renewed if not required by other readers, by contacting the library from which it was borrowed.

BLEAK EXPECTATIONS

BLEAK EXPECTATIONS

Sir Philip Bin

Edited with an introduction and notes by
Mark Evans

corsair

Constable & Robinson Ltd
55–56 Russell Square
London WC1B 4HP
www.constablerobinson.com

First published in the UK by Corsair,
an imprint of Constable & Robinson, 2012

A copy of the British Library Cataloguing in Publication
Data is available from the British Library

ISBN 978-1-47210-340-6 (hardback)
ISBN 978-1-47210-341-3 (ebook)

Printed and bound in the UK

1 3 5 7 9 10 8 6 4 2

MIX
Paper from
responsible sources
FSC
www.fsc.org   FSC® C018072

For my beloved Victoria, Rosie and Georgia; for my wonderful parents; for my late Granny because she'd have loved me having written a book; and for the marvellous Mr Gareth Edwards, *Bleak* producer extraordinaire.

CONTENTS

INTRODUCTION

In my experience, many introductions to classic novels do one thing very well: they ruin the story you're about to read. If an introduction is going to discuss the plot, it should really be an afterword or appendix, but your typical academic has to stick it at the front just to boast that they've actually read the massive book, even if it does ruin it for everyone else.

This introduction will not do that.

Though I have read the book.

Honestly.

First, a word on the author. Sir Philip Bin is almost unknown outside academic circles these days, yet he was the best-selling author of the nineteenth century, selling more than Eliot, Trollope or even Dickens. Sadly, after the Victorian era his fame dwindled until he actually became the worst-selling author of the twentieth century, selling less even than some very bad writers who should never have had books published in the first place.

Indeed, by the start of the twenty-first century he was a forgotten man, and his books were thought lost to the world – until that fateful afternoon in the British Library when, full of intellectual curiosity, I was ferreting around in the book stacks, eager for a new area of study.

All right, I was actually full of a big lunch and eager for somewhere to have a nap.

Eventually I found a comfortable-looking corner in which there was a handy manuscript I could use as a makeshift pillow. The instant my head settled on it, I knew I had made a colossal literary discovery. In truth, the realization came only when I visited the lavatory after waking, washed my hands and glanced in the mirror to see imprinted on my face the inky impression of a title page: '*Bleak Expectations* Sir Philip Bin'.

I rushed back to seize the precious manuscript and decided it must be immediately reprinted. The fact that the author was long-dead and therefore the royalties would entirely come to me barely even crossed my mind.

And here it is: *Bleak Expectations*, Sir Philip's most autobiographical work, a book that, in its original 1872 printing, sold 40,000 copies – one for every person who could read in Britain at that time.

The harrowing yet ultimately triumphant story of how— Ah, no. I said I wasn't going to do that. So I won't.

But I really, really have read it, even the massively long, complicated paragraphs with words we don't really use any more and stupid Victorian syntax.

I have added explanatory footnotes throughout.[1] They appear at the bottom of each relevant page, not like some books where the notes are all at the end and you have to keep different fingers jammed in different bits of book to read it properly, usually resulting in a sprained finger or angrily thrown-away book.

If you want to tweet your thoughts while reading, don't. You're supposed to be reading. Get off the Internet.

For the same reason, you can't find me on Facebook.

Though, if you want, you can find a short clip of me on YouTube shouting, 'Get off the Internet and keep reading!'

Finally, I hope you enjoy Sir Philip's tale as much as I did.

Because, for the last time, I really have read it.

Mark Evans
The British Library
About to have a nap, 2012

---

[1] Look! A footnote!

PART THE FIRST

CHAPTER THE FIRST

In which I am birthified and
acquire a family

Whether I shall turn out to be the hero of my own life or
whether that station will be held by anybody else should be
perfectly obvious. After all, what manner of a man would set
down the story of his own life if at the end of it he came out
looking like an idiot, buffoon or wally-chops?[1] Only an idiot,
buffoon or wally-chops would do thusly and, barring one
incident involving a lack of trousers and an unnaturally
curious horse, I have never been one of those.

You, the malodorous public, know me as Sir Philip Bin:
best-selling novelist, Member of Parliament, accidental yet
still best-ever Prime Minister, scourge of the French, hammer
of the Belgians and adjustable spanner of the Italians,
discoverer of the West Pole, hider of the source of the
Nile, inventor of the Scotch egg, the Welsh roll and the Irish

---

[1] Derived from the Olde Englishe 'wolly', a fool, twit or sillyton, and 'cheps', face,
head or, in the north-east, deep-fried potatoes. See Chaucer, *Canterbury Tales*, 'The
Loss Adjuster's Tale' '. . . he weir an wally-chops of sight, all blethy and tistawint'.

bun, adventurer, explorer, philanthropist, misanthropist, xenophobe and nine-time all-England foreigner-baiting gold medallist.

But I was not always so.

Indeed, regarding my not-always-so-ness, there has recently been much speculation in the press as to my true origins: both the *Expressington Times* and the *Daily Standagraphian* have run scurrilous, fib-filled stories that have made my blood run hotter than a boiled kettle in an angry volcano. Hence this tome, my attempt to stop that speculation in its tracks like a shot elephant or a lazy train. With this book I shall set the rumour mill at rest and stop it grinding the flour of gossip, from which cometh the bread of scandal and thence the sandwich of despair, filled with the beef of misery and the mustard of grrrr.

Many clues as to my early life are to be found in my novels. *A Story of Two Towns, Miserable Mansion, The Old Shop of Stuff, Graham Grambleby, Massive Dorritt* – all my books contain hints at the truth. Apart from *Lustful Killer Bees from Mars*, which, I'll grant you, is almost entirely fictional.

But now the time has come to cast away hints, clues and obliqueness and instead present the unadulterated story of my fascinating life, with its endless progression of trials, set-backs and conveniently spaced cliff-hanger endings. For adventure has followed me like a dog follows a man with bacon trousers and beef-steak underpants; that is to say keenly, and with a good deal of slobbering.

I was born in 1806, having been conceived the year before in celebration of Admiral Nelson's victory at the battle of Trafalgar. Family tradition has it that my father,

Thomas Bin, heard the news, exclaimed, 'Hurrah for the King', then immediately donned a three-cornered hat and eye-patch before boarding my mother, Agnes, and giving her a swift broadside amidships. Whatever the truth, some months later my mother was heavy with child or, as the local poor women described it, 'all lumpy with a sex-meringue'.

I am told my birth was easy. But I did not need to be told, for I was there, and remember it as well as I remember anything of importance to me, such as my hat size (nearly clever), my shoe size (exactly one foot, obviously) and my blood group (Proper).[2] At one moment all was amniotic calm, my mother's heartbeat soothing me as I nestled on the placental pillow within her, then the next there was the dread sensation of falling as Nature's cruel but necessary process expelled me into the world. Fortunately, my birth-plummet was arrested by the pair of Dr Helplady's reinforced pregno-bloomers my mother was wearing, otherwise the first acquaintance I should have made in my life would have been with a hard stone floor, and I am quite sure we would not have got along.

As I birthed out, my mother was in the midst of a harpsichord recital for my father, but being made of stern British stuff, she bravely continued to the end of the piece before presenting me as a baby-shaped encore. Alas, the only music I could provide was a childish wailing in an utterly different key from that of the Purcell my mother had recently completed and, furious at the cacophony, my father immediately left the house to do business abroad.

---

[2] Nineteenth-century blood groups were Royal, Aristo, Proper, *Hoi Polloi*, Riff Raff and Eeurgh Negative.

My father's family name being Bin, and my Christian name Philip, my infant tongue could make of both names nothing longer or more explicit than Flip-top Bin. Over the years this was shortened to Ip, then extended once more to the far more name-worthy name of Pip. My mother, however, took my original mispronunciation personally, decided she had given birth to a twitiot and, embarrassmented, retreated to her room for a year to blush.

With my father abroad and my mother upstairs, I was raised by the housekeeper, Maggotty.[3] Ah, Maggotty. Dear Maggotty. Dear, sweet, warm, strange-smelling Maggotty. Her starched apron was my maternal bosom in those early months, her starched cap the boundary of my vision. In fact, my main memory of her is starch. She had a motto: 'If it moves, starch it. If it does not move, starch it. If it seems it has enough starch already, it hasn't, so starch it again.'

The kitchen was Maggotty's domain and hence the kitchen was my playroom. And what toys I had! Copper kettles full of boiling water, great pans of bubbling soup, pointed skewers, sharp knives . . . Among my first words were 'Ow', 'That hurts' and 'Can I have some real toys that won't hurt me, please?' Or at least they would have been, if I could talk at that age, which I couldn't. But Maggotty would just smile her strange, starchy smile and encourage me to go exploring in the hot pastry oven.

Actually, now I come to think of it, I despised Maggotty.

---

[3] *Cf* Thackeray's Wormitty in *Vanity Fair II: Judgment Day*. Maggotty and Wormitty are the Biblical twin exotic dancers who slew the Hashemidiaskanite King Zedelshratt with a pair of trained assassin-chickens. Book of Hens, 3: 4–199999.9.

Fortunately, my mother eventually emerged from her room, and Maggotty was given notice to leave. She took the news as well as would any person taking news incredibly badly, viciously attacking my young self with a meat cleaver. Alas for her vengeance but un-alas for my safety, the repeated massive starchings she had applied to my clothing had left me encased in an impenetrably hard shell and I suffered no injury. Poor Maggotty – hoist by her own starchy petard.

Actually, I don't mean poor Maggotty, I mean eeurgh horrid Maggotty, good riddance, yuk.

To my delight, after Maggotty left, my mother introduced me to the newest member of the household. It was a sister, and not just any old sister, it was my sister. Her name was Pippa, a name not dissimilar to my own name, which was Pip. In fact, it differed only in as much as it had an extra *p* at the end, as well as an additional *a* and, at the front, a silent and invisible *g*.

There were many things I wanted to know about this new sister of mine. Where had she come from? Was she from Mrs Sellstuff's village shop, like an apple, a sack of flour or a portable oik-poker? Or had she come from London like a letter, a Cockney or diphtheria? My mother shook her head, no, and told me that Pippa was the product of prayer and stern application by herself and my father. My young head cared not what 'stern application' meant, but surely my parents practised it assiduously, for some short time later a second sister joined us.

This sister, too, was mine, and her name was Poppy, again a name not dissimilar to my own, differing only enough that if, at some future point, Poppy was perhaps to be summoned by my mother, I should not make the mistake of thinking she was in fact summoning me, Pip, a mistake which, if made, might result in me inadvertently responding and consequently attending a girlish occasion such as a dress-fitting or embroidery class, despite being a boy and not a girl like Poppy, though with regard to my other sister, Pippa, at certain times when my mother summoned her the wind would blow away the final syllable of her name turning it, in its new, wind-created brevity, into my name Pip, thereby resulting in me attending an event intended for her, namely the aforementioned dress-fitting or embroidery class, thus indicating that my parents had never properly thought through the whole almost homonymous name thing, though, that said, even if the Pip and Pippa confusion did happen occasionally, there never was a Pip and Poppy confusion except once during a thunderstorm.[4]

With their desired number of children achieved, alongside his foreign businessing my father now took up the twin hobbies of cold showers and botany and my mother took up never touching him that way again. But at least my family was complete: my parents Agnes and Thomas, my sisters Pippa and Poppy, and me, Pip Bin.

---

[4] See? One of those long paragraphs with silly Victorian syntax I mentioned in the introduction. This was in fact the author's attempt on the world's-longest-sentence record, though it falls lamentably short. Even in 1874 the record was well over 20,000 words, held by a sentence in Laurence Sterne's almost unreadable first novel *Tristram Brandy*, which he later re-worked into the now famous work *Barry Brandy*.

CHAPTER THE SECOND

*Of growth and fun and
meetings of future import*

My family may have been complete in as much as I now had
as many mothers and fathers and sisters as I was ever to have
in the world, but at times it seemed incomplete, due to the
absence of my father. For he was a distant man in a very
physical sense, his place of business being some four thousand miles away in the recently discovered North Indies,
where he was a partner in the famed North India Company,
bravely exploiting indigent populations for the greater good
of God, King and Country.

I and my sisters missed our father; my mother missed her
husband; and as father and husband were one and the same
to some or the other, it meant a deal full of wistfulness
tinged with saddingtons.

Nevertheless, he regularly sent us parcels of money
and rare jewels and, though they were not he, they were a
more than adequate substitute, proving that old adage

'An absent father is easily replaced by lots of money.'[1]

We lived in a large house, Bin Manor, set in several snectares[2] of grounds. The grounds offered plentiful enjoyment for spirited young children, and we were spirited indeed. There were ponds, lakes and tiny oceans, trees and other trees and great manicured lawns on which we played games such as shuffle-hoop, bashy-bat and spong.[3]

When the weather was too ill-tempered for outside activities, we retreated inside, where there were great rooms and corridors in which we played other games, such as pointy-throw, clicky-ball and spang.[4]

Life was splendid. In a time when others less fortunate than ourselves struggled for the most basic amenities, our home brimmed with plenty. Where most folk bathed but once a year, in a festering stream or a puddle, we bathed daily – and not in disease-bearing water, but in healthy, hygienic jam. Oh, the sybaritic delight of wallowing in warm preserves! The soothing feel of the fruity goo sluicing through one's hair! The jammy delight of my mother letting me lick the bath deliciously clean afterwards!

Then there was the food, all richly rare meats and delicacies. We ate swan, otter, pig, heron, ox and natives from the colonies. For pudding there would be candied

---

[1] One of a number of nineteenth-century adages we now know to be wrong. Others include 'Men seldom make passes at girls who make vases', 'In the Kingdom of the Blind the one-eyed man has the best-looking wife' and 'Money can't buy you gloves'.

[2] In modern terms equivalent to several hundred snacres.

[3] More familiar to us as croquet, cricket and spling.

[4] More familiar to us as darts, snooker and splung.

fruits, caramelized horse or hen brûlée, often a sparrow trifle or tree cake, sometimes even mouse crumble with chicken custard.

And after these splendid feasts, we would repair to our soft, goose-down beds, beds so luxurious that the goose-down was still attached to the geese. Once, during a particularly fierce winter that bit like an angry, ice-toothed alligator, I accidentally left a window open, and before we could stop it Poppy's entire mattress migrated south to warmer climes. How we laughed! Until she turned blue with cold, at which point we stopped laughing and started crying. Little did I know then that I had just witnessed a precursor to Poppy's eventual— But no, for this is the happy part of my story, and pain and misery must wait until properly invited into the narrative.[5]

We were frolicsome children, Pippa, Poppy and I, constantly joyous and never sad. And whenever Father returned on one of his visits, his cases chock full of gifts, our joy was unrestrained as we bounced and bollibled[6] with happification.

I remember one particular paternal visit well. I had attained what seemed to me the grand old age of twelve years. Pippa was a year younger, which was a relief as a while back she had somehow been older than me for a year or

---

[5] Chapter 3 is pretty wretched. Or for truly harrowing stuff, why not try a modern-day misery memoir, like the series of horrible-relative books: *Ow, Daddy, Ow, Keep Your Hands to Yourself Uncle Lionel* and *There Were Three in the Bed and the Little One Said, 'Stop Hitting Me, Mummy'*.

[6] *Cf* nineteenth-century redcoat song: 'Oh, the sight of blown-out guts was horrible, but they were French so we did bollible'.

two, and Poppy was a year younger than her, namely ten years old, which was a relief to everyone as she had spent the past few years refusing to grow any older than two and had only recently put on a growth spurt of eight years in four months. It was a bright summer's day, and I and my sisters were returning from a morning's hard fun clodding mud at poor folk, when we saw our mother standing outside the house balanced on one leg and waving her arms like a crazed windmill, a pose she adopted whenever she was excited. To make matters more intriguing yet, she was wearing the special hat she donned only on occasions of great import: bright ribbons attached a whole hollowed-out badger to her head.

'Children! I have news!' she exclaimed exclamatorily.

'What news, Mama?' I asked askatorily.

'Your father has returned home and awaits you in the drawing room!'

We three siblings looked at each other in delight. Could it be true? We immediately ran to the drawing room that we might better ascertain the veracity of our mother's statement.

My nostrils were the first to tell me that Mother had not lied as they swiftly detected that distinctive paternal mix of tobacco, colonial sweat and repressed emotion. My eyes provided the next sensory confirmation as I entered the room and beheld . . .

'Papa!'

He turned towards us and a smile broke over his face, like a happy egg.

'Children! How good it is to see you! It has been so many years! Ah, Pip . . .' This he addressed to me.

'Papa,' I replied.

'Pippa . . .' Papa said to Pippa.

'Papa!' Pippa replied.

'And Poppy . . .' Papa said to Poppy.

'Papa!' Poppy, too, replied.

'Ah, my Pip and Pippa!' This from Papa to me, Pip, and Pippa.

'Papa.' This from Pippa and me, Pip, to Papa.

'Poppy and Pippa!' This also from Papa, but to Poppy and Pippa.

'Papa!' This from Poppy and Pippa to Papa.

'Pip and Poppy!' This from Papa to me, Pip, and Poppy.

'Papa!' This from Pip and Poppy to Papa.

'My Pip, Pippa and Poppy!' This from Papa to Pip, Pippa and Poppy.

'Papa,' we parroted to Papa, our paternal parent. Were the greetings now finished? They were. But Papa was not.

'Presents! I bring presents for my Pip, Pippa and Poppy! For Poppy a puppy!' At which point he presented a puppy to Poppy. 'For Pip a pipe!' Presently he produced a pipe for me, Pip. 'And for Pippa . . .' here he paused poignantly '. . . an anvil.'

The sudden lack of the letter *p* was like a punch in the perineum.

'Oh,' was all Pippa could say, as Papa handed her an anvil. Her girlish strength could not bear its weight and she instantly collapsed in a heap on the floor. I would have helped, but was keen to try my new pipe, which I lit immediately. Alas, it was a wooden pipe and burned to cinders within a minute. Meanwhile Poppy's puppy scampered and frolicked like a young dog, which was what it was.

'And now you must come and meet my two business partners, also recently returned from the North Indies.'

Father led us to the house's formal receiving room, the snobatorium, where my still badger-behatted mother was entertaining two gentlemen, and not in a lewd or music-hall-dancery way, but in a proper ladylike manner, which included scones and no touching.

'Gentlemen . . . may I introduce my progeny? This is Pip, Poppy and . . .'

A tortured metallic scraping sound betrayed Pippa's late arrival as she dragged her anvil into the room.

'. . . dear Pippa. Children, this is Mr Skinflint Parsimonious.'

Mr Parsimonious was a man of some height and no little depth and breadth, a man who seemed soft at the edges, like a melting cheese or velvet jigsaw. He wore a brightly striped waistcoat and pantaloons, and sported mutton-chop whiskers with a veal-cutlet moustache.

'How do you do, sir?' the three of us chimed together, like a greeting-clock. We followed it with a deep curtsy.[7]

'Dear children, how wonderful it is finally to meet you!' His voice was a deep rumble, as of approaching thunder, but warm, friendly thunder portending only good things. 'Now,' he continued, 'I understand,' he went on, 'that your

---

[7] Note that even though a boy, Pip also curtsies. Child–adult greeting etiquette was thus: if more girls were present than boys, the curtsy took precedence; if more boys than girls, the formal bow and handshake. If equal numbers of both were present, the ugliest child was sent to its room and the previous rules applied.

father has already given you gifts,' he verbally proceeded, 'yet I insist you have more for being such delightful children.'

So saying, he reached into his pocket and produced from within a handful of treats. 'See! I have toffees for Pip and Poppy and Pippa! And you must have these gaudy native baubles! And these cushions! And this painting of a lovely sunset!' He produced all these gifts from a large trunk beside him.

'Why, thank you, sir . . .' I began; but he was not yet finished.

'No! No thanks yet, thank you! For there is more to give! Money! Who wants some money? Have a sixpence, Pip. No, dash it all, have a guinea. Five guineas! And gin! All must have gin!'

He instantly produced a flask of gin and filled several pewter cups. 'Drink up! Drink up!'

The fiery liquid burned a scorching trail right down to my stomach – and yet simultaneously all was smooth and warm and good. My mind was also suddenly clear – what I believe some people call intelli-gin-ce – as I was struck with a thought that seemed terribly clever to my twelve-year-old self.

'Mr Parsimonious, I have realized something. Your name is ironic . . . for you being called Skinflint Parsimonious would imply great meanness, and yet you seem to be the most generous of men.'

He looked at me for a few seconds, with eyes like those of an inquisitive owl or curious herring, then suddenly burst into a peal of rumblesome laughings. 'Why, the boy is quite right! And to think I had never noticed! How clever he is!

And as a reward for such cleverness, young Pip, you simply must have this miniature horse!'

A small equine whinny betrayed a horse in the corner, lightly chewing the edge of a long chair.[8] It was no more than the height of a small dog or a large cat, but a horse it was, correct in every proportion save its tail, which was the length of a great shire horse's and therefore flowed out behind it like a hairy stream.[9] Poppy's new puppy immediately ran towards it with a yap of friendship and, sure enough, this small dog was exactly as high as the miniature horse, thereby proving my recent size comparisoning.

'They are to be friends! As are you and I, young Pip!' Mr Parsimonious announced. He seemed a splendid fellow or splellow.

My father clapped his hands with delight. 'Well, now that you two have met and done so handsomely, I shall introduce my other business partner. Children, this is Mr Gently Benevolent.'

This Mr Benevolent stood in stark contrast to Mr Parsimonious. Where the latter was soft and melty-edged, it was as if this other man had been precisely carved into being with a chisel, then honed on a whetstone to a fine edge. He was dressed in black from head to toe and back again, and

---

[8] What we know as a *chaise-longue*. With the Napoleonic Wars barely over, it was illegal to use French at this time.

[9] Bonsai horses had been popular since their arrival from Japan in the seventeenth century. They were bred from normal-sized horses, which, when pregnant, were housed in stables thirty times larger than normal. This change of scale made the horse think it was much, much smaller than it really was, leading to the birth of a tiny foal. Owners then often grew the tails to incredible lengths and used the animals as rudimentary equine brooms.

from beneath a fury-clenched brow, his eyes glinted with obsidian malice.

'How do you do, sir?' We three children repeated our curtsied greeting.

'I do all the better for not having to listen to your childish prattle. Speak to me again and you will find yourselves horse-whipped. With a real horse.' But we did not need a horse-whipping, for his words were simultaneously both sharp and blunt enough to cut and clout in equal quantity. He spun on his heel, not gleefully as would a dancer or giddy schoolgirl but angrily as would a thwarted cad or disgruntled navvy, then stalked to the corner of the room where he kicked Poppy's puppy and stood brooding like a sulky, eggless hen.

Alas, despite his obvious violent grumpiness, and because I was probably still a bit drunk from the gin, another clever thought struck me and I sought to impress it upon him.

'Ah, your name, too, is ironic. For Mr Gently Benevolent would imply a loving nature, and yet you appear to be absolutely horrible.'

My regret at my boldness was instant, for he whirled around, hand raised to strike me a blow that doubtless would have felled me, like a small, boy-shaped tree.

'No, Benevolent!' It was my father, leaping to my rescue. 'If there is any hitting of my children to be done, I shall do it!'

In truth, my father was not a keen advocate of corporal punishment, having beaten me only once in my young life after I had broken a vase during a vigorous game of spang. He was abroad at the time, and rather than actually beating me he had sent a long letter from the North Indies describing how he would in theory have beaten me had he been there, an experience in some ways more painful than any physical assault, but in most ways not.

Yet at my father's son-defending words, Mr Benevolent did not immediately set his hand down. Instead, he held it high and tense, a palsy of fury shaking his arm. His face reddened, purpled and puced, then finally flashed a vivid multi-coloured rainbow of rage. Veins twitched and pulsed in splenetic syncopation. Finally, he lowered his hand and emitted a tremendous snort of anger and disdain, which seemed to say, 'I loathe you, Thomas Bin, for preventing me from hitting your son and, in addition, your actions have enraged me more than the original infraction, which had already made me pretty damned angry, and you and your family will pay for it many times over indeed, yes, you will, you will, you will, yes, you will.'

Or it might just have been a sneeze.

'Besides,' my father eventually continued, 'we must hurry if we are to catch our boat.'

'You are returning to the North Indies so soon?' This from my mother, who had been quiet thus far due to her badger hat having slipped down to cover her entire head; she had only recently fought free of it.

'No, dear Agnes. For the North Indies no longer exist. We have completely dug them up and sold them for the greater glory of business and the Empire. Hence we go now to . . . the South Indies. And we must hurry if I am to get there, exploit them and return in time for Pip's eighteenth birthday in six years' time. Come, gentlemen!'

My father ushered his business partners from the room. As the still seething Mr Benevolent passed, he tried to flick me on the ear and administer a Chinese burn, but he saw my father watching and, at the last second, tried to pretend he was going to shake my hand, missed, stumbled and tripped awkwardly over a previously unseen footstool.

'I meant to do that,' he muttered, as he left the room, pausing only to take a glass water-jug from its stand and dash it shatteringly to the floor. 'Whoops.'

I did not feel his actions were entirely accidental, but further reflection was denied me as my father knelt to bid us farewell. 'I go now, dear Pip, Pippa and Poppy . . .'

My sisters immediately blubbed with emotion; I malely held my feelings inside, though I think I heard my left kidney stifle a sniffle.

'But do not be sad! For soon my business shall be complete, and I shall return for good.'

'When, Papa?' asked Poppy.

'Why, in a mere thirty or fifty[10] years. So, you see, not long at all!' With this he kissed us all goodbye, and attempted to do the same for my mother but – alas – her hat chose that precise moment to slip down again, leaving poor Papa with a mouthful of badger snout.

Oh, cruel Fate! For little did we know how much that failed kiss would haunt our mother in the future. Oh, wretched Destiny! For meetings made that day would resonate through the years ahead and not with an uplifting, cathedral-like echo but with a sinister, fearsome echo, such

---

[10] The number forty had yet to be invented.

as that in a miserable underground cavern of pain. Oh, dismal Providence! For magnificent munificence was soon to be replaced with malicious malevolence – but no, I must restrain my tremulous pen for, as I wrote before, this is the happy part of the story, and pain and misery must wait until properly invited into the narrative.

CHAPTER THE THIRD

*Pain and misery are invited
into the narrative*

A year passed. Then another, then two more, quickly followed by another seven, and I was twenty-three years old. No, wait, the events of this book take place between the ages of birth and twenty-one years old, so that can't be right.

Imagine if some of those years I have just mentioned have not yet passed, that they are fresh and gleaming with hope in an undetermined future. Imagine you have recovered some seven or so of them, and I am but sixteen years old, part man, part boy, rigid with potential and humming with possibility.

Actually, nothing much happened when I was sixteen, so forward one more year and I am seventeen, striving towards manhood with head held high and arms held low for balance. Pippa is but sixteen, blooming like a lady-rose, only without the thorns as she is a kind and generous soul. Poppy is fifteen years old, curious and questioning, all girlish enthusiasm and frills. Our mother is still our mother, our father is still abroad, having visited once in the intervening years for a period of some eight minutes, Bin Manor is still a happy house, and Britain is still great, mighty and Imperially delicious.

Now, picture a drawing room. In it is a pianoforte at which sits Poppy. She is repeatedly striking a single key: under instruction from her teacher Mr Humswell, she is learning the noble instrument one note at a time. On a sofa sits Pippa, completing her tapestry of the battle of Waterloo, a noble scene of gory patriotism. And who is that on a chair opposite her? Why, it is me, Pip Bin. And what is that I am reading? Why, it is a book entitled *Manliness for Boys*, for I am working hard towards my future man-dom. I have recently bathed, but have not dried myself properly and hence there is a small blob of jam on my ear. Not a man yet, Pip Bin! Because men do not have jam on their ears, they have hair.

You have pictured the room, imagined the people within? Good. Then we may continue.

'That note you are playing is a jolly one, Poppy,' I commented.

'Thank you, dear brother Pip. Mr Humswell insists on starting with the happiest notes.'

'Then he is a capital chap.'[1]

'Finished!' Pippa laid aside her tapestry and took up her anvil. In the years since Father had given it to her, she had ceased resenting the heavy impracticality of the gift and had

---

[1] One of a series of popular terms of acclamation ranging from 'capital chap' through 'provincial-city chap', 'market-town chap' and 'really-rather pleasant village chap', all the way down to the frankly insulting 'couple-of-cottages-on-a-bend-in-the-road chap' and 'that man is a total hamlet'.

instead embraced its purpose. She struck it with her hammer and the sharp tinking sound it made echoed round the room in counterpoint to Poppy's piano playing.

I read on in my book, studying how men shaved their manly beards and stubbles: coarse, common folk used a simple table-knife, scraping at their faces between bites of food; gentlemen used a badger-hair brush and cold steel razor; and nobility used a badger-hair brush where the hair was still attached to a live badger and a hot steel razor, which seared the top three layers of skin off simultaneously. This was to be followed by a manly splash of sulphuric acid and a spell administering a colony. I could not wait to be a man if such delightments awaited!

Pippa's metallic tinking stopped and she held up the fruits of her anvilly labour.

'Why, Pippa, you have made a tiny horseshoe!' I said, for that was indeed what she appeared to have made.

'You are wrong, dear brother Pip,' she rebutted. 'For it is not a tiny horseshoe, it is a normal-sized dog-shoe. For Poppy's puppy.'

As if it had heard mention of itself, Poppy's puppy chose that moment to enter the room with a high-pitched yap. Though it was now five years old, it was no bigger than it had been on first arrival and, indeed, was actually somewhat smaller and more puppyish. For it was that rarest of breeds of dog, the Austrian Shrinking Spaniel, an animal that, over time, grew smaller and smaller until it finally dwindled to an infinitesimal tininess and ceased to exist.[2]

---

[2] There is no evidence that such an animal ever existed. The most likely explanation

'Oh, a shoe! For my puppy. How kind of you, dear Pippa'.

'Dear sister Poppy, it is kindness that comes from a higher moral authority. For why should the horse be the only animal to have shoes? It is barbaric that other creatures go barefoot and are therefore at risk of pain from small stones, thorns and sharp grass.' She paused, panting slightly: her commitment to goodness often left her breathless.

'Thanks to you and your anvil, one day all the creatures of the world will be properly shod.'

'That is my intention. Now, come here, Wellesley.'

Poppy's puppy eagerly reacted to its name and ran to her. She took him upon her knee, and proceeded to affix his new shoe to one of his old feet. All it took was five red-hot nails being driven through the shoe and into his soft puppyish paw, and he barked and yelped with absolute delight as it was fitted. Indeed, he was so overjoyed that he fainted with doggy delight and lay in a happy, bleeding heap.

'You are so kind to the animals, Pippa. And to their feet.'

'Why, thank you, dear brother Pip. But kindness must not tarry. Could you fetch me that pile of unfinished horseshoes from the corner?'

'Of course, dear sister.'

Pippa's horseshoes were piled between a ladder and a large mirror. On top of them rested the other family pet, Bonaparte, a black cat. Alas, at that moment, dear puppy Wellesley chose to awaken from his post-shodding slumber.

---

is that over the years Poppy's puppy was repeatedly kidnapped and replaced with a smaller dog as some kind of elaborate practical joke. In those days rural British life was incredibly dull and people would do anything to break up the tedium.

He instantly spied Bonaparte and, as if their human namesakes had spotted each other, battle ensued.

The black cat raced across my path, causing me to stumble. I slid along the highly polished wooden floor, passing under the ladder and arresting my progress only by crashing into the pile of horseshoes at great speed. In a storm of clinking they plunged into the mirror behind them, instantly shattering it. I fortunately remained uninjured, though I had broken the rabbit's foot I habitually carried with me, and also pulled one leaf from the four-leaved clover I wore as a buttonhole.

'Oh, Pip, what have you done? Surely now our luck will run out and things will turn horrid!'

I had no truck with Pippa's superstitious fears. 'Nonsense,' I riposted. 'We shall remain as lucky as ever.'

At which point there were footsteps in the corridor, the door to the room burst open and there was my mother, hair wild with panic, eyes wide with shock and ears flapping with anxiety. 'Children! I have terrible news! Your father is dead!' She slumped to the floor, weeping.

My sisters looked at me accusatorily.

'Ah . . .' I began, but no more words would come. My recent acts had produced omens of terrible luck, and now this. Was it merely a coincidence?

Yes.

And yet . . . was it more than happenstance?

No.

Although . . . could it all be connected?

Definitely not.

And then I realized that nothing mattered other than

the dread news my mother had brought: my father was dead. Cold shock and hot tears fought for control of my young body, then shook hands, called it a draw, and I began to both shiver and cry.

My sisters wept, too, great gusty sobs of grief echoing round the room, the floor slickening with salty tears. But there was another sound as well, a sound not in character with the moment: it was the sound of laughter.

I looked up, and there, framed in the doorway like a malicious painting, stood Mr Gently Benevolent. It was his laughter. How could he find this funny? Perhaps he did not: perhaps this was merely a gentleman repressing his emotions so deeply that they came out the other side in an opposite fashion. His words, however, dispelled that idea, like fog in a furnace.

'I do enjoy being the bearer of bad news. Pain is so . . . nourishing. Weep, Bin family, weep. For Thomas Bin is dead and today is a glorious day!'

Now my shivering and crying ebbed as rage engulfed me, hot and red like a cross tomato. My young fists clenched and I rose to my feet . . . but grief had weakened my heart and immediately the dizzy reality of the situation made my vision go grey and my legs buckle. I collapsed into unconsciousness, the last sounds I heard being Benevolent's mocking laughter and my own voice repeating over and over again, 'Father . . . Father . . . Father . . .'[3]

---

[3] Sad, isn't it?

CHAPTER THE FOURTH

Things get even worse

My childhood until this point had been a perfectly knitted sweater of joy; now, caught on a rusted nail of misery, it began to unravel at speed.

My mother was driven mad with grief and retreated to a cupboard, where she sat wrapped in wretchedness and swaddled in sorrow. After several mother-cupboarded days, I approached, determined to persuade her out. The door opened with a squeak – though whether that was the sound of unoiled hinges or my mother's anguish within was hard to tell.

'Mama . . .'

There came no response.

'Mama, please . . .'

There came still no response.

'Mama, please . . . You have been in this cupboard for five days now.'

Response there came now some.

'That is because this is the linen cupboard, and I am a piece of linen.'

I could not let this falsehood go unchallenged. 'You are not a piece of linen! You are my mother!'

'Fie upon you, sir. I am not your mother! For I am a prettily patterned tablecloth, and my children are all naughty little napkins!'

'Mama, no, I am not a napkin, I am your son, Pip . . .'

'Pip? I see no Pips!' She covered her eyes with her hand and turned her head away from me. 'Now run along, child, for I am awaiting the return of my husband. He's a terribly dashing double-pleated curtain.'

'But, Mama!' I protested. 'Papa is dead!'

'I know. I may have quite a wait! Ha ha ha! Ha ha ha ha!'

Her laugh was not that of a sane woman. Indeed, it was that of a mad one. High-pitched and falsely ecstatic, each 'ha' was like a hyena-wielded dagger to my tender young heart. I could face it no more, and slammed the cupboard door.

'Ha ha ha! Ha ha – ow!'

I had inadvertently trapped my mother's finger in the door. It caused her but brief pause, however, and the soul-piercing laugh soon resumed, its awful sound echoing in my ears as I fled.

The rooms and corridors of our home, once so full of joy and laughter, were now full of only pain and sadness. There was no bollibling, only woement and cryification. We played no games, sang no songs, danced no merry jigs, except ironically.

Poppy had Mr Humswell teach her the saddest note he knew and she played it repeatedly on the pianoforte, bleakly striking B-miserable over and over with a grief-stricken finger. Pippa set aside her anvil – she said that striking it was too much like striking the memory of Father – and donned a bright green and purple mourning dress.[1] For my own part I decided that, now I was the man of the house, I should show no childish tears and bottled every emotion inside myself, like sad sherry.

Mr Parsimonious visited, but even his gifts of nine kinds of rare orchid, some salmon, a stained-glass representation of the battle of Agincourt, two dozen crystal wren's eggs and a funny sculpture of a bottom offered no grief-relief. Alas, accompanying him was Mr Benevolent, whose presence saddened us further.

'A dashed-darn idiot, your father, and now he's dead. No loss, really.'

'It is a loss to us, sir,' Pippa said. Poppy and I nodded our agreement.

'Cowards, eh?' Benevolent sneered, showing all the empathy of a malicious stone.

He may have been odious – in fact he definitely was – but he could at least answer something that nagged at me. I gulped like a nervous heron and asked, 'Please, sir, you were with our father in the Indies. How did he meet his end?'

A part of me did not want to know; another part needed to know; a third part could have gone either way.

'Very well. I shall tell you.' His dark eyes gleamed with delight at the dead-fathery news he was about to impart.

---

[1] In 1817 George III, the famous Mental Monarch or Krazy King, madly attended a funeral in bright green and purple robes instead of the traditional black. Rather than embarrass the King, people pretended it was a fantastic idea and adopted it as a country-wide custom. Not until some years later was black reinstated as the official colour of mourning.

'Your father had created a hotel in the Indies made entirely from monkeys.'

This unexpected building material startled Poppy. 'Sorry . . . Did you say monkeys?'

'I did. He trained them to stand on each other's shoulders, binding themselves together to form a rigid but flexible framework. It was a triumph, this monkey hotel. People came from miles to stay in it. And then . . . someone opened up a factory right next door.' He shook his head, as if this was the most regrettable and terrible thing anyone had ever done.

'What sort of factory?' I asked.

'A peanut and banana factory. The monkeys went berserk and tore your father limb from limb.'

I was astounded. 'But . . . but who would do such a stupid and evil thing?'

'No idea.' Benevolent reached into his pocket and produced a bag of sweetmeats. 'Anyone fancy a peanut and banana treat?'[2]

I was too distraught to take one of his nutty, nana-y delights, my mind filled with the image of my father trying desperately to fight off crazed monkeys and failing even unto death. I felt a hand on my shoulder and looked up to see Mr Parsimonious, his face tight with tension, yet his eyes moist with empathy. Or some sort of eye condition.

'Dear Pip . . . I am sorry . . .' It was empathy, not eye condition.

---

[2] Some academics have written about the meaning of Benevolent's offer of a peanut and banana treat and whether it is connected to the peanut and banana factory next to the monkey hotel. Idiots.

'Parsimonious, stop being weak.' Benevolent's voice acted like a scald to Mr Parsimonious's hand, and he swiftly withdrew it. 'There is business to attend to.'

'What business?' I asked.

'First, the question of your mother. And the answer to that question is: an asylum.'

Benevolent clapped his hands and two burly men entered, three, if you counted one of them twice. They went to the linen cupboard, opened it, removed my mother and carried her from the room.

She struggled and cried out, 'No! I can't go to the asylum! I haven't been ironed! And my napkin children are all stained with soup!'

Pippa, Poppy and I leaped forward to save her – but to no avail. Mr Benevolent seized us by the collar and all we could do as we were de-mothered was cry out in fear and frustration.

'Mother!'

We wept; we sobbed; we tearified. Benevolent stared at us, his face a rictus of disdain. 'Oh, don't be so nauseatingly sentimental . . .'

There was but one person we could appeal to. 'Mr Parsimonious: will you not stop this?'

Mr Parsimonious twitched with angst and guilt. Or it may have been a nervous condition. 'I am afraid I can do nothing, a fact that makes me both guilty and angst-ridden.' It was angst and guilt, not a nervous condition.

'But why not?'

'Because it is a matter of law, not conscience.'

'If I may clarify . . .' This comment came from the corner, where a bewigged and be-gowned figure had been standing silently all this time. It was my father's lawyer, a man so distinguished that his name took fully twenty minutes to say. As a lawyer, he charged by the hour; his name was his greatest asset.

'Please do clarify Mr Wickham Post Forberton Fenugreek Chasby Twistleton Montmorency Aurelius Pargordon Jezthisby Cumquatly Pobbleton Tendling . . . [text omitted][3] . . . Beastworthy Fennelham Jones.'

'It is quite simple. The estatelment of the deceased deady person including but not excluding or outcluding all chattels, listingtons, possessionaries and what we lawyers call "stuff" has devolved to the bequestified normally nominal nominee nommy-nommy-nom-nom. Nine shillings and sixpence, please.' He always added his fee to the end of every sentence.

'But, Mr Wickham—'

My father's lawyer held up his hand to stop me. 'Please. Given the circumstances we may dispense with formality. You may call me sir.[4] I shall, however, bill you for the entire name.'

'Sir, I do not understand your lawyerly talk.' How could I be expected to? I was barely seventeen: all I understood was horseplay and whittling.

---

[3] For reasons of space, the name has been edited to a fraction of its full length. The name is so long because the book was originally published in monthly parts, and at one point Sir Philip got writer's block. By having a four-thousand-word name, he could fill a whole month's pages without having to advance the story one bit. The full name can be found in Appendix II.

[4] Once the writer's block was gone, the author quickly realized he had saddled himself with quite a burden in repeating a four-thousand-word name, hence this device.

'It's quite simple.' My father's lawyer took a deep breath, then proceeded to speak more quickly than any man I had previously heard. 'Base fee, fee simple, habeas corpus, *res ipsa, ad hoc*, subtract *hoc*, divide *hoc* and drink hock, yummy. Yes? One guinea and half a crown, payable two weeks hence.'

I still did not understand, and let him know it in no uncertain terms or, to put it another way, in certain terms. 'But that is just gibberish!'

Mr Parsimonious spoke soothingly. 'No, it is the law. But close.'

'Look, you little dimwit, it's perfectly obvious.' Mr Benevolent sighed as if I was the stupidest thing he had ever seen. 'Your father's will makes me your guardian. I control you, your sisters and all of your father's money.'

'Surely, as his heir, the control and money are mine.'

'Not until you are eighteen. Which is, oh-so-unfortunately, some time away. In the meantime you are to go to boarding-school. And Poppy and Pippa will live with me until they are old enough to be married off or sold to high-class bordellos.'

At this, Poppy exclaimed loudly, 'Never! I will never leave our home!' She leaped up and ran from the room, out of the front door and thereby left our home, which was exactly what she had just said she would never do. Although I suspect when she had said 'home' she had actually meant to include the grounds as well, in which case as long as she didn't run too far she was fine.

'Let her run. It changes nothing.'

'I shall go after her and talk with her.' Mr Parsimonious stood and left, looking sadder than a penguin with a fish allergy.

'I, too, must leave. I have a case in Chancery. A no-win, big-fee case. But before I go . . .' My father's lawyer approached me. 'Your father was a close and dear friend to me, young Pip, and therefore I should like you to have this in his memory.'

He handed me a small parcel. I felt a lump forming in my throat, like undissolved flour in a badly made white sauce. This stern legal gentleman had a heart after all, it seemed. I started to open the parcel with trembling fingers.

'What is it?'

'My invoice.' I stopped opening the parcel with now angry fingers. 'Good day.'

He swept his gown behind him and left. Now it was just Pippa and I . . . and Mr Benevolent, who sneered at us sneerily and disdained at us disdainfully. 'Right, time for boarding-school, young man.'

'Already? But that is . . .' I realized I did not know what that was. I think I thought it was awful; I'm pretty sure I thought it was terrifying; I definitely didn't think it was super or lovely or beezer.

'So why don't you and Pippa say goodbye to each other? After all, you will never see each other again.'

'What?'

'Er . . . I mean, not for a while. It was a perfectly innocent slip of the murder – I mean tongue.' Benevolent looked at us for a second. 'Oh, just say goodbye and be quick about it.'

I approached Pippa, tears in my eyes. She approached me, her eyes also glistening. In fact, I had sort of assumed that I would do all the approaching and that she would stand still and wait, so her simultaneous approach caught me a little bit by surprise and we awkwardly bumped into each other. We both took a step backwards, which left us a little too far apart for a proper farewell, then finally shuffled close enough to say goodbye.

'So, dearest sister mine . . .'

'Yeah, whatever.' Mr Benevolent grabbed me and started dragging me towards the door. 'Goodbye, Pippa, goodbye, Pip, goodbye, house, goodbye, everything.'

I could hear Pippa weeping as he dragged me roughly out of the house. Poppy was nowhere to be seen, so I could not even have the briefest of farewells with her. Outside was a waiting carriage, two broad, snorty horses pawing the ground impatiently in front of it and on top a coachman with a cruel, meaty face, a greasy, high-collared coat and a long, fierce whip that he cracked in my direction.

Mr Benevolent hurled me inside, slammed the door and the carriage was away, the horses pounding down the drive, the coachman yelling and whipping and driving. I tried the door: it was locked. With no windows to open or smash, I was trapped. I pounded on the carriage walls, but no response came from the coachman, and as my new-found prison lurched from side to side on its breakneck rush, fear gripped me like an angry boa constrictor and I worried I would never see my home again.

CHAPTER THE FIFTH

*It all gets better not
one little bit*

So I was off to boarding-school, an institution I had no knowledge of, though I had once met a young pupil from Eton who had told me how much fun it all was, if you didn't mind beatings, terrible food, loneliness and abject soul-sucking misery.

Alas, I did mind those things.

And alas-er, the school I was to attend was not as soft and jolly as schools such as Eton, Rugby or Harrow. For, though I knew it not, I was on my way to the most brutal school in the whole of Britain: St Bastard's.[1]

Even today, years of plenty and happiness later, just writing those words makes me shiver. Although . . . No, it's all right, I've just realized, there is a window open in my study. It is a draught that is making me shiver. I'll shut it.

---

[1] St Bastard is patron saint of cruelty, hating small boys and, in recent times, TV talent shows. There is no record of any actual school with that name at the time. The most likely candidates for his actual place of education are Thugby School, Beaten College or St Ouch's.

Right, done that, on we go.

The journey to St Bastard's took— Ooh, no, shiver, it wasn't just the window, it was writing those words after all. I shall take a stiff brandy and a bracing sherry enema and return.

There. Much better. To proceed.

The journey to St Bastard's – ah, shudder free, thank you, brandy, thank you, sherry – took five days, though oddly only two nights.[2] Every few hours, the coachman would stop to change the horses – they had a range of different outfits – and, at each halt, he would briefly open the carriage door and hurl a morsel of food in for me. I tried to converse with him, to find out something of our destination, my eventual fate or even the capital of Peru, a fact that, for some reason in my misery, it seemed vital for me to discover. But conversation to be had was there none.

'Sir—'

'Where—'

'What—'

'Is it Lima?'

That was as long as any talk between us lasted. Eventually, I faced up to the fact that the fellow was not conversable and contented myself with the morsels he threw to me. Or, rather, discontented myself, for they were such anti-delights as gravel pie, poison bread and razor crumble and, even

---

[2] There are three possible explanations for this: the route went via the Arctic Circle during the summer months; the author was confused; or, as proposed by Britain's only professor of Quantum English, Roger Catchpole, the carriage passed through a space-time wormhole caused by rogue tachyon particles and naughty quarks. Though, as he admits, he was a bit drunk when he thought of the idea and had also just watched seventeen back-to-back episodes of *Star Trek: The Next Generation*.

though starving, at the thought of them my stomach refused, like a cowardly horse at a scary fence.

Finally the carriage halted once more, the door was flung open again, only this time instead of hurling food in at me, the coachman hurled me out at the ground. Alas, he did not miss his target.

'Ow,' I said.

'Ha,' he replied, his sadistic grin revealing a toothless mouth-maw inhabited by a grey, wormy tongue.

'Are we at the school yet, sir?'

He replied not with words but with a gesture. A meaty arm rose, at the end of it a gammony fist from which unfurled a chickeny finger. I looked to where he pointed and saw a sign: 'St Bastard's School for Boys'. His message conveyed, the coachman ruffled my hair friendlily with one hand and punched me really quite hard in the head with the other. He then turned, mounted his carriage, cracked his whip and was away.

The sounds of horse and carriage receded and all I could hear was someone crying.

It was me.

With a crack of thunder and a flash of lightning, the sky also started to cry in sympathy. Oh, empathetic English weather! Rain splashed upon me, running down my cheeks and taking a brisk walk down the back of my neck. The chill of the water stirred me, and I rose to my feet. Lightning flashed again and for the first time I saw my new school clearly.

Huge iron gates twisted and curled in front of it, and on top of them was inscribed a metal motto: 'Orando, Flogorando'.

By praying, by beating. Oh, if only it had been so gentle a place!

The school building loomed behind, foreboding, forbidding and forterrifying. Battlements ran along the top of the walls; on their edges sat gargoyles with features plucked straight from hell itself, malicious and mocking.

It looked lovely. By which I mean hideous.

Nevertheless, my school it was, and enter it I must. I took a step towards the gates, but a nearby voice startled me into stillness.

'Young Pip . . .'

Why, it was a voice I recognized; a voice I had fond memories of; a voice that belonged to Mr Parsimonious. And, glory be, it was not just his voice but it was him as well, walking towards me in the rain.

'Mr Parsimonious? What are you doing here?'

'The months ahead will be full of darkness for you, Pip. Darkness and anguish. Darkness and anguish and misery and wretchedness and despair. And probably quite a lot of actual physical pain. So I have come to say . . .'

He paused; I waited. What message of hope had he brought?

'. . . good luck with all of that. I go now.' He turned to depart, but his generous nature got the better of him. 'But before I do, you simply must have these jelly babies. And this ham. And this jewelled box will probably come in handy. And you simply must have these piglets.'

I accepted his gifts gratefully and once more he turned to go.

'And now I must leave.' Yet he turned again. 'But not

before giving you this encyclopedia and this haunch of venison. 'Bye!'

He turned yet once more again and this time did go, striding jauntily off. As I have said, he was the most generous of men.

Laden with his gifts, I walked towards the school, my heart thumping within my chest, my breath catching in my throat and my liver somersaulting nervously and thereby joggling my kidneys.

As I passed through the gates, all was ominous silence, bar the patter of rain, the sob of my tears and shrieks of woe from within the school. So it was actually quite noisy.

Now a dark-cowled figure emerged from a doorway and, with a crooked forefinger, summoned me inside. Was this Death himself come to claim me? Mr Parsimonious's piglets squealed and wriggled with fear in my arms and his encyclopedia felt heavy with dread as well as knowledge as I followed the figure through the door.

Inside was a long corridor, all dark wood and shadows. As I progressed in the footsteps of what I was beginning to fear was actually Death, I saw paintings on the wall depicting scenes from the life of the school. The first was entitled 'Hanging Day, 1807'. Small boys hung from nooses while mortar-boarded teachers danced jollily around. My fear, already great, grew a little more.

Next, a sporting scene: 'Staff v Pupils: Cavalry Battle'. The teachers were mounted on great chargers, huge sabres in their hands; the pupils seemed to ride other, smaller, pupils, who were crouched equinely on all fours, and they appeared to be armed only with blunted carrots, though it was hard to tell because of all the blood and bits of chopped-up school-boy. Now my fear swelled to a positively enormous size.

A third picture: 'School Play 1813 – live action Gladiators v Lions'. The boys had taken the roles of the gladiators, and playing the lions were some lions. There were heads and legs everywhere. My enormously swollen fear immediately fled and was replaced by a shrieking terror and a violently wobbling panic.

And now Death paused, turned and opened a door leading off the corridor, and indicated that I was to enter.

The door had a brass plaque with 'Headmaster' on it, and led to a book-lined study in which there was a leather-topped desk. I stepped in and Death followed, closing the door behind him. Then he pulled back the hood of his cloak and I saw that it was not Death, but a man. And a man whose eyes seemed to sparkle with joy and delight, whose face was lined with soft wrinkles of laughter and amusement and whose nose looked happy.

My shrieking terror quietened and my wobbling panic found its balance and was still.

'Now, you must be young Pip Bin. Welcome, welcome.'

And now my terror and panic flagged down a passing hackney carriage and left for other locations, for his voice was as rich and soothing as a caramel quilt or a custard coat. While the outside of the school and its very name conveyed horror and misery, this man – the headmaster, I presumed – suggested calm all-rightness was at hand.

'And you have brought me gifts! Some jelly babies, ham, a jewelled box, some piglets, an encyclopedia and some venison. How kind.'

He removed Mr Parsimonious's gifts from my arms and I realized he had misunderstood.

'But, sir . . .' I began to protest.

Instantly, his face changed. All gentleness, kindness and twinkly avuncularity fled, chased away by the rage and spitting fury that now filled his visage.

'Did I say speak, boy? Did I? Did I tell you directly to speak?'

He had not, and I tremulously informed him of that fact. 'No, sir.'

'You do it again! The impudence! Did I say speak? Did I, eh? Did I?'

As he seemed physically to swell with anger, the developing sense of calm his previously gentle manner had erroneously persuaded upon me disappeared. I examined the logic of the situation: my speaking out of turn had made him furious; yet when he had made an enquiry of me and I had, to my mind, spoken *in* turn, that, too, had made him furious. Given that my original crime had been giving voice, I decided to keep silent. Yet this, too, was seemingly a criminal offence, for after several seconds he assailed me again.

'I ask you a direct question and you dare not answer me, boy? Answer me clearly and simply: did I tell you to speak?'

There could be no doubt this time: I had to answer him. 'No, sir.'

Alas, this, too, was wrong.

'Again you do it! Again you speak!'

The injustice of my inescapable position stung me like an unfair wasp, and I could not help but respond. 'But, sir, you told me to!'

It was as if I had poked a headmasterly Vesuvius into

eruption, and I was the pupil Pompeii on its lower slopes. Verbal lava swept down upon me. 'Cheek and impudence the like of which I have ne'er heard! You are to be beaten, boy! D'you hear? Now, where is my cane?'

My sentence was momentarily suspended as the headmaster approached a large cupboard in the corner of the room. Inside were row upon row of boy-hurty canes. He withdrew one and slashed it about experimentally. Its thin whippiness scorched through the air with a whistle, and I could all too easily imagine the gargantuan amounts of pain it would inflict on me.

But it seemed as if those gargantuan amounts of pain were not enough for the headmaster, for he instantly discarded it.

'No, not Old Softy.'[3] He rummaged in the cupboard and removed another cane. 'Yes . . . this is more like it.'

He turned to me and I saw in his hands a small branch, gnarled and knobbly, and almost throbbing with agony waiting to be inflicted. He lifted it high and offered one final warning: 'And if I hear one bleat out of you, you shall be hanged!'

He swept the instrument down, and as it struck, an earthquake of pain exploded from the epicentre of my buttocks. Strongly desirous of not being hanged, I somehow kept the scream of agony deep within me. With a pant of exertion, the headmaster raised his weapon high again; with a grunt of satisfaction he lowered it at vast velocity. As he beat me, I

---

[3] An actual brand name for a cane in the nineteenth century. Part of the 'Cruel Irony' range of punishment instruments for children, which also included the 'Warm Your Cockles' branding iron and the 'Gentle Ben' potty-training rack.

closed my eyes and thought of many things: of my mother and father; of my sisters; of the life I had left behind; but mostly of how there was an angry man hitting me on the bottom with a large stick.

Finally, it was done. The rhythmic explosions of agony subsided into one massive throb of enormo-pain, and suddenly I heard laughter.

It was the headmaster.

I slowly raised my aching body upright and saw that the glinting twinkle of joy had returned to his face. The fury and rage had gone, and for an instant I wondered whether there were not two identical men of vastly differing tempera-ments who had somehow been changing places over the past minutes without me noticing.

'Ha ha ha . . . oh dear. You fell for that, didn't you, young man? Sorry, sorry, it's a bit of a joke I like to play on every new boy. It lets them know I'm not the type of ogre most headmasters are expected to be.'

This was unlike any joke I had ever come across in my life hithertohencely. The jokes I knew all started 'Knock, knock' or 'There were these two nuns' or 'What's the best way to kill a Frenchman?'[4] But I was perfectly prepared to believe that this beating scenario was a traditional form of physical comedy I had not yet come across.[5]

---

[4] In 1843, these three joke-forms were melded by the Queen's chief humour adviser Professor Baron Lord Robert De Monkhouse into the now famous Grand Unified Joke: 'Knock, knock', 'Who's there?' 'It's two nuns, we've come to ask what's the best way to kill a Frenchman.'

[5] A reference to the nineteenth-century German 'Comedy of Agony' (*Das Agonistische Komedie*).

'What did you think? No, really, did I fool you?'

I feared reprisal for answering; yet if it had been nothing more than a traditional prank on a new arrival, then not to respond with an honest compliment as to how genuinely he had convinced me that he was actually a psychopathic boy-hating maniac would be the height of rudeness. I took a deep breath, and ventured an answer.

'I . . .'

'You dare speak to me? Did I say you might open your mouth? Did I? Did I?'

His frothing fury covered me with grumpy spittle and I braced myself for another cane-based onslaught.

'No, actually, I did say you could speak. I remember now.' I sighed with relief, as did my buttocks. 'So . . . welcome to St Bastard's. I am the headmaster, Jeremiah Hardthrasher.[6] We have only one rule in this school, and that is "Obey every rule" and there are over eight thousand of those. If you find yourself missing home, don't hesitate to have a little cry, although if caught doing so you will be hanged. Right, that's it, you can go to your dormitory. As soon as I've administered your welcoming beating. Bend over!'

He raised his cane, I lowered my head, and the rain of pain came again.[7]

---

[6] A pseudonym for real-life schoolteacher Jeremiah Cruelthwack, inventor of the first fully automatic boy-caning machine or Beating Jenny.

[7] Some say this line is designed to convey the rhythm of a beating; others suggest the author might just have been in a hurry to get to dinner and therefore sought speed over quality.

CHAPTER THE SIXTH

Yet more misery . . . and the teensiest,
tiniest bit of hope

Thus began a period of my life so wretched I cannot put it into words. Mathematically it was like this:

$$x = 2y^4$$

Where x represents the amount of misery experienced in one day at St Bastard's and y represents the amount of misery experienced over my entire life before arriving at the school.

In onomatopoeia it was like this:

Aaaarrrggghhhh!!!

But beyond that I have not the vocabularic wherewithal to communicate my circumstances.

Although I have just realized that this is a book, so I really should have a go.

Hmmm . . .

---

[4] This number is not supposed to represent a footnote, it is meant to represent y raised to the power of four.

The dormitory I inhabited was a bleak, unforgiving place. There was a cold, hard stone floor and the only furniture was cold, hard stone stones. We used the larger ones as beds and chairs and the smaller ones as pillows.

My first night there, a pillow fight broke out: there were nine broken jaws and three fatalities.

The school routine was remorseless and cruel. Every morning at five o'clock we were awoken by being poked with sharp sticks. We were then herded at the end of some sharp sticks to prayers in the school chapel, where instead of pews we had to sit on sharp sticks. More sharp sticks prodded us towards lessons, where if we gave an incorrect answer we were poked with a sharp stick and if we gave a correct answer we were rewarded by being poked with a blunt stick, though a stick which in the greater scheme of things would still seem sharp to most people; that is to say, people who weren't used to being constantly poked with sharp sticks.

In fact, the only time we were spared the poking with sticks was when we were beaten by the headmaster, which was regularly and often. To say it made a lovely change from the sharp sticks would be a massive lie.

Lessons were rigorously streamed. By which I do not mean that selection was according to ability, but that they took place in a stream. Whenever it rained the stream was in spate, and during one Latin class alone eight boys were swept away by the torrent. If they were lucky enough to survive the watery plummet, they were sure to meet their doom at the end of the stream where it emptied out into the headmaster's shark pond.

Punishments for infraction of the eight thousand school

rules were many and varied, ranging from being sent luging bare-bottomed down the school grater to being made to don hedgehog pants then do vigorous lunges or, most feared of all, being sentenced to the school salt-mines. Once in there the salt could drive boys mad with thirst: they were often found horribly injured having tried to drink their own heads.

I myself was fortunate: I was only ever sentenced to the neighbouring school pepper-mines. This was a far less deadly place – although Chewsby-Forsdyke was once found having sneezed himself inside out.

I think the hunger was maybe the worst. After catching one of the boys smiling without permission or, indeed, reason, Headmaster Hardthrasher had banned meals for the next five months. Worse, though he had banned meals, he had not banned meal *times*. Thus, three times a day we were forced to sit in the dining hall and pretend to eat by means of whatever mime or physical theatre skills we possessed.

These were incredibly dangerous occasions. Not only would the headmaster often hang boys after being unconvinced by their efforts to eat a facsimile of a chop or a simulacrum of soup but, driven mad by pretend food, the larger boys would sometimes try to eat the smaller boys. Usually the headmaster would intervene before they had consumed more than an arm or a leg, but nevertheless one kept one's wits about one or, if one had a friend to watch one's back, two kept two's wits about two.[1]

---

[1] Sounds a bit like an owl, doesn't it? Also note that because of all the beatings they received, the boys would have been nice and tender. For further reading into nineteenth-century Public School Cannibalism, see Dr François Gourmand's *Gnawing and Knowledge: the nineteenth-century pupil as ingredient* (OUP, 1987).

We were clad in rags, unwashed and hungry, so hungry. At night the dormitory echoed with the sounds of boys trying not to weep, and often failing. One night I heard Arrowby crying. He wept for most of the night, stopping just before dawn. On investigation, we found he was completely desiccated, having cried every bit of moisture out of his young body. When I touched him, he crumbled to dust and blew away on the breeze, and I don't think there was a single boy there who didn't in some small way envy him.

And then there were games.

The headmaster took a great delight in team sports. He also had a terrible deep-seated envy of Rugby School and its now world-famous eponymous game of violence. Hence he had invented his own: Bastardball.

The object of the game was to get a ball to the end of the pitch and plunge it head first into a bucket of cold dung, for doing which you scored a Bastard.

Oh, and the ball wasn't actually a ball: it was the youngest boy in the school.

Each team was divided into five groups: the kickers, whose job it was to kick the ball; the hitters, whose job it was to hit the ball; the punchers, whose job it was to punch the ball; and the pitchforkers and shooters, whose job it was to pitchfork and shoot as many of the opposition as possible. Or pitchfork and shoot the ball.

The youngest boy in the school was unlucky indeed.[2]

---

[2] Bastardball was banned for good in 1853 after a particularly nasty international match in Sevastopol between Britain and Russia. By half-time the game was horrifically out of hand, and by full-time it had turned into the Crimean War.

The risks were not just as I have described above: in the mêlée, boys would again try to eat each other. To this day my elbow bears the scars of a desperate gnaw from Spindlesham minor. Indeed, I would have lost the entire arm to him had he not been distracted by Westington taking a huge bite out of his foot. Yet no boy bore ill-will to any other boy for an attempted eating: each part of you that was consumed was a part that could no longer hurt.

The school's mortality rate was horrific. It seemed to me just a natural consequence of the barbaric curriculum and lax approach to pastoral care; I suspected no actual machinations or scheming in the daily casualty lists. But that thought was driven from my mind one night. It may have been a night of horrible discovery, but it was also the night my life was lit up by the tiny bit of hope I mentioned in the chapter heading.

At the time, the dormitory was in shock. Earlier, Nesterton had been crying because he was homesick, so the headmaster had come in and beaten him. The beating had made Nesterton cry even more, so the headmaster had beaten him again, and Nesterton hadn't been able to stop crying so eventually the headmaster had taken him out and shot him. The shooting had proved a protracted process, for the headmaster had provided a blindfold. Alas, the blindfold was for him, not Nesterton, and it had taken him at least fifty-eight shots finally to strike lethally.

With Nesterton's tears still echoing in my ears and, worse, his sigh of relief as the fatal shot had struck home, I became aware that another of the boys was now approaching me.

'Psst! Are you still awake, New Bug?' It was a voice I did not recognize. This was hardly surprising: few of the pupils had the strength to speak.

'Yes, I am awake. Who are you?'

His face came closer, as did the rest of him – had it not, it would have been strange indeed. He was a boy of about my age, with a curled mop of hair and features that instantly suggested good humour and jollity.

'The name's Biscuit. Harry Biscuit. What's your name?'

'Pip. Pip Bin.'

His good-humoured face furrowed in thought. 'Pip Bin, eh? Pip Bin . . .' He was thinking hard indeed. 'Pip . . . Bin . . . Pip Bin . . .' He mused on, rolling my name around his mouth experimentally. 'Pip Bin . . . hmmm . . . Pip Bin . . . Pip . . . Bin . . .' His face unfurrowed as some conclusion was evidently reached. 'Pip Bin . . .' Or reached yet not. 'Pip Bin . . . Pip Bin, eh? Then I shall call you . . . Pip Bin.'

'Oh.' It seemed a poor conclusion for such long deliberation.

'For if a nickname you are to have, then it is best if it is the same as your normal name, for otherwise correspondence may go astray.'

I nodded, as this did indeed make sense.

'May I ask what brings you to St Bastard's, Pip Bin?'

I did not mind telling him and told him by telling him. 'After my father died, my mother went insane . . . and my guardian sent me here.'

'Ah! A familiar story. Exactly the same happened to me. And to Beastleham, Frobisher and Dribblington minor. In fact, every boy at the school has a father who has died, a mother who has gone insane and a guardian who has sent them here. I don't suppose you're set to inherit a lot of money when you come of age?'

'As a matter of fact, yes, I am.'

'Me too.'

'You're not—' But I could not complete my sentence before he interrupted.

'Yup, I'm Harry Biscuit of the Warwickshire Biscuits.'

'Then your father invented the biscuit!' I knew the name had sounded familiar. This was the son of the man who had finally given the nation something to eat while drinking tea. Other than cake. Or scones. Or muffins, pikelets, crumpets, bumpets,[3] warm fat Yorkshire rascals, cold thin Lancashire scamps, Spudlington garns,[4] roast lamb, trifle, tarts, flans, scoopies, jam spaniels,[5] pasties, trindlies,[6] goobershams[7] and cheese.[8]

'He did. And there's a lot of money in biscuits. It seems to me that this is a school for rich boys with no dad, a mad mum and a lot of money in trust. Now, let me ask you a question, Pip Bin: how long do you think you'll be at this beastly place?'

'Well, until I'm eighteen, I suppose.' I assumed that, at that point, I would legally inherit my father's wealth and

---

[3] Like crumpets, but made from beef.

[4] A potato scone stuffed with raisins and dripping. Famously repulsive. Not to be confused with Spadlington Gorns, a contemporary brand of fried trouser.

[5] A preserve-filled puff-pastry casing in the shape of a dog.

[6] Trindlies were a type of goobersham.

[7] Goobershams were a type of trindly.

[8] Cheese.

proceed to live a life of high-class luxury. But this Harry Biscuit soon disabused me of that notion.

'Wrong!' He seemed to invest this single word with great joy at my lack of correctitude. 'You see, Pip Bin, no one has ever left this school alive. No one. Apart from one boy, and he was dead.'

'But that's ridiculous! I know the school is dangerous but . . .'

'But nothing. If anyone ever survives to the age of eighteen, wallop – that's their lot. Think back on what you've seen while you've been here . . .'

Lying there in the darkness, I considered everything I had seen in the past weeks and realized that Harry Biscuit was right. On Thogglesden-Barclay's eighteenth birthday the headmaster had reported the tragic news that his birthday cake had exploded inside him. When Pistleton turned eighteen, the headmaster had bought him a birthday present and, seeing as it was his eighteenth birthday and he was to become a man, he had thematically bought him a man-trap. Alas, the man it had trapped was Pistleton himself, killing him instantly. Beasley's eighteenth-birthday treat had been a trip to a cannon factory; all that had returned had been a bucket of what was left of him. Grobisher had had an eighteenth-birthday fight with a tiger and lost; and Ffffffffffffforbes-Twangle had died when his giant iron birthday card in the shape of the number eighteen had accidentally toppled on him after the headmaster had given it a good shove. All dead, and all on their eighteenth birthday; yet I could not believe it was deliberate.

'But . . . it could just be coincidence,' I protested.

'If it is, it's one so big it's a Coincid-aurus Rex.'[9]

That was indeed a large and terrifying coincidence.

'The thing is, Pip Bin, I turn eighteen in two months and I don't want to die. So I'm going to need your help to escape.'

'Me? Why me?'

'Look at all the others . . . too weak and feeble to do anything.' He gestured around the dormitory. He was right. The grinding effects of the school's hideous regime had weakened nearly all the boys to a point at which they could barely carry their own bodies about the place, let alone escape. 'But you, Pip Bin . . . you're still strong.'

Again, he was right. I was weakening fast, but as yet I still had some of my youthful vigour and strength. As, it seemed, did this Harry Biscuit. He was far and away the most robust boy in the school, stout and ruddy-cheeked, oozing sap and brio.

'How come you're still strong, Harry Biscuit?'

He coughed awkwardly. 'Because when I arrived here I weighed . . . four hundred and seventy-eight pounds.'

'That is quite a lot.'

'Well, when you're the son of a big biscuit magnate, there are lots of free biscuits lying around . . . It happens.'

'But that is the size of a small cow. Or a medium-sized pony. Maybe a jolly fat uncle, or eight quite big sheep.'

---

[9] A bad anachronism, as the events of this book take place between 1806 and 1827 and the term 'dinosaur' was not coined until 1842, the first actual Coincid-aurus Rex fossil not being discovered until 1865 in a Dorset chalk-pit, along with the Flukeryx and the Whatarethechancesofthathappening-atops.

'Yes! I know!' Where his offended tone had come from, I knew not. 'But a few months of this place and I've slimmed down to the perfect size for my age.'

'Indeed you have, Harry Biscuit.' In truth, I was being kind, for he still had the heft of perhaps a Christmas pig or a big-boned Shetland pony. But beneath his massiness, I sensed a soul of profound gentleness, decency and strength, with a hint of courage, a *soupçon* of determination and a good dollop of honesty, the whole seasoned with the salt of good humour and the pepper of daring. 'And indeed I shall help you escape from this place.'

'Good man! Start planning, Pip Bin, start planning.'

'I shall, Harry Biscuit, I shall.'

I sensed at once that I had made a lifelong friend; the only question was, how long would that life be? I lay awake pondering plans, the certainty settling over me, like a steadfast blanket, that our escape should be made as soon as possible; and events the next day meant our escape became even more imperative, or imperativer.[10]

---

[10] Not a real word.

CHAPTER THE SEVENTH

A wall-based incident changes things

The next day was at least partially a Wednesday afternoon, and therefore time for artillery practice, in which the staff used the pupils as ammunition for the school howitzer.[1] They had just dressed Chokesbury as a pigeon and fired him into a tree to roost and now it was my turn.

With his trademark subtlety and wit, the headmaster crammed me down the barrel and fired me directly into a wall. Dazed, I picked myself up and noticed that my impact had created a small crack in the wall; and through that crack came a familiar sound.

Tink, tink, tink! went the familiar sound, yet I could not place it.

Tink, tink, tink! it went again and, as my head cleared, I recognized it at last: it was the sound of a hammer striking an anvil. More specifically, it was the sound of the hammer

---

[1] Most nineteenth-century public schools had artillery in case the French ever invaded or the poor got uppity. Use of pupils as ammunition was unusual, however.

and anvil belonging to my sister, Pippa. I pressed my mouth close to the crack in the wall.

'Pippa, dear sister Pippa, is that you?

Tink, tink, ti— paused the hammer and anvil.

'Pip? Dear brother Pip? Is that you?'

It was my sister Pippa! Either that or someone else who owned an anvil, sounded exactly like her, shared her name and also had a brother called Pip, who sounded exactly like me, in which case we could be about to embark on a rather awkward act of mistaken identity and concomitant grotesque social embarrassment. I quickly pressed my eye to the crack in the wall, and saw that it was indeed my sister Pippa! Or someone else owning an anvil, who sounded exactly like her, shared her name, had a brother called Pip, who sounded exactly like me and also looked exactly like her.

This, I decided, was unlikely.

'It is I, dear sister! I recognized the sounds of your anvil!'

'The only reminder I have of our dear papa . . .' There followed a sigh so heart-rending that a nearby sparrow fell out of a tree and died of sadness.

'But what are you doing here, my Pippa?'

'I am trapped in this nunnery, St Bitch's.'[2] Again she sighed, again an empathetic sparrow plunged to its death.

'There is a nunnery next to our school?' I was amazed that I had not known.

---

[2] St Bitch is the patron saint of cats, girls' sixth forms and writers with friends more successful than them. Again, it is impossible to trace an actual place of that name. The most likely candidates are St Miaow's or the Abbey of Our Lady of the Sacred I'm Going to Scratch Your Eyes Out. The latter was where the Church sent only its finest female devotees, hence its nickname 'Top Nun'.

'There is a school next to our nunnery?' She was clearly equally amazed that she had equally not known.

'Yes, it is the school Mr Benevolent sent me to. But why are you in a nunnery?'

She sighed forlornly again, a further sparrow died and the rest of the flock flew off into the sky to escape more death. Ah, how I wished I was a sparrow! Not one of the dead ones, obviously, but one of the ones that had escaped and now flew free and happy in the sky.

And then the entire flock was obliterated by another salvo of the school artillery and I stopped wishing I was a sparrow and turned my thoughts back to my sister.

'I am in this nunnery because no sooner had Mr Benevolent taken me into his home than he accused me of trying to seduce him. He called me a Jezebel and a meretricious harlot, then sent me to live here until I am eighteen, at which point he will marry me.'

'No! I will never let that happen!' The thought of Mr Benevolent marrying my sister filled me with a sick foreboding and some strongly indignant rage.

'Dear brother, if it is any consolation I think it is very unlikely to happen.'

'Phew.' The foreboding and rage left me like an unwelcome guest on a racehorse stung by a wasp, that is to say quickly, though without the whinnies of pain and shouts of fear that such a scenario would normally entail.

'Alas, not phew. For tomorrow is Joan of Arc Day in our nunnery . . .' She paused and sighed mournfully once more. There may have been no sparrows left to die of sadness, but a nearby field-mouse did shed a tear. 'And I am to be Joan of Arc.'

'Quite an honour.'

'Yes. If you like being tied to a stake and burned to a crisp.'

'No! I cannot find you again and then lose you so soon! Dear sister, I have made a friend here and together we are planning an escape. You will come with us!'

At my words it was as if I heard a church bell tolling in determined agreement with me, until I realized that it was not as if I heard a church bell tolling, I really actually did hear a church bell tolling.

'Dear brother, that is the bell summoning us to mid-late-middle-of-the-central-bit-of-the-afternoon prayers . . . I must go. But before I do, take this.'

With a metallic scraping she pushed something through the crack in the wall.

'A tiny lucky horseshoe!'

'No, a normal-sized lucky pigeon-shoe. I fear we may need it.'

'How thoughtful you are of the podiatric needs of the animal kingdom!' Such a kind soul could not be abandoned, whether 'twere my sister or not; but as this kind soul resided in and indeed was my sister, it could be abandoned even less. 'Do not worry, dear sister, I shall rescue you!'

But she was gone, away to her prayers. I hastened to find Harry Biscuit, thoughts and fears churning in my mind, like worried milk gradually coalescing into determined butter.

'Harry! I have news!'

'So do I, Pip Bin. What is yours?'

'My sister is in a nunnery next to the school but tomorrow they are going to burn her at the stake! What is your news?'

'The headmaster has moved my birthday forward by two months. I'm going to be eighteen tomorrow, and that means I'm going to die!'

This was news so dreadful it made all other news look good, even news that previously might have been seen as pretty bad.

Yet if before I had had strong purpose, now my purpose was stronger still. If my original purpose had been iron ore, which Pippa's news had smelted into iron, Harry's news was like a dose of alloy-forming carbon, hardening my iron purpose into steel. Added to my metallic strength of purpose now came a wave of determination, thrusting me forward in its briny embrace and depositing me on the beach of certainty. This school would not hold me and I would not wait for death to take me, like a scythe-bearing bully: if death did come, it would be on my terms, active and heroic, not passive and cowardly. I clenched my fists, steadied my stance and spoke loudly, clearly and, if I am honest, possibly a little too high-pitchedly to really convey the bravery and resolve I wished to exhibit.

'No! I have already lost my mother and father,' I squeaked. 'I will not now lose my sister and best friend. Tomorrow we escape from St Bastard's . . . or we die in the attempt!'

PART THE TWOTH

CHAPTER THE EIGHTH

*An unexpected aid-provider providentially
provides aid*

Alas, we died in the attempt.

Or, at least, nearly so – or else what would the remainder of this book be other than a long litany of pages made blank by the author's death many years ago? It would be a mightily short book, or perhaps a mightily long book with multiple pages devoid of ink, words, story, emotion, grammar, spelling misteaks and autobiographical anecdotage. Indeed, the last words of it would not be 'Alas, we died in the attempt' but instead 'No, look out— Eurrggh!' followed by acre upon voidy acre of this:

Trees would have been felled and paperized for naught, horses would have been boiled into book-glue for fun, not purpose, and print-setters would have lost their jobs through lack of print to set – though the publisher might have made a goodly saving on ink and, indeed, simultaneously created a new product, part book, part blank notebook, a literary-stationery hybrid that would surely have been both financially viable and vinancially fiable.[1]

I may have digressed a little. Let me now return to my life story.[2]

Trapped as I was in Britain's cruellest school, the question of how to escape was one with no easy answer, as opposed to questions such as 'Would you like a brandy?' or 'What is the capital of France?' to which the answers are clearly 'Yes, please' and 'Who cares?'

Then how lucky it was that my new-found best friend and chum-us maximus Harry Biscuit should have had plans for an escape, indeed plans he had already planned.

'I have two plans, Pip Bin. Three if you count the third one as well, which I do.'

'Four plans? But, Harry, that is brilliant!' This announcement filled me with cheer, excitement and a funny giddy feeling I recognized as hope. Or an incipient inner-ear infection.

---

[1] Now defunct phrase derived from Latin meaning 'grapes that can be made into wine'.

[2] The Great Coffee and Cake Shortage of 1867 stopped every writer in Britain being able to work for several months, just after the author had completed the first part of the book. On starting the second part some months later, he found he had somewhat lost his thread, hence the meandering nature of this section.

'My first plan is for a new method of transportation, using highly trained geese and compressed air.[3] Look, here is my blueprint . . .' He unfolded a sheet of paper with the word 'Geese?????' scribbled in blue crayon, followed by the word 'air'.

I began to leak cheer, excitement and hope, like a sad balloon or cracked joy-bottle, and it started to form a large puddle of disappointment at my feet. Yet Harry happily ploughed plannily on.

'My second plan is for a new restaurant where you dine on raw fish brought to your table by a system of continuously moving belts.[4] Good, eh?'

He said this with such delighted aplomb that I felt guilty at the strong desire arising within me to punch him for his plan-uselessness. Somehow I punched him not and merely asked, 'But, Harry, how will these plans help us escape?'

'Well, I reckon either of them could make us enough money to bribe our way out of here with ease.'

'By tomorrow morning?'

'No. Hence my third plan.'

I clenched my fists in preparation for a physical assault on his next batch of uselessness.

'A large mechanical swan on which we may fly free from the school and soar to safety.'

---

[3] A reference to Brunel's ill-fated 'Goose Rail' project, which failed because starving peasants kept stealing and eating the geese that were key to its functionality.

[4] Such restaurants existed in Victorian London, going by the name 'Good Day, Sir, Raw Fish Shop'. They saved money by having no cooking expenses, but ultimately lost more money in compensation paid to customers they had poisoned with raw fish.

My fists unclenched – this sounded like a plan that had legs and, more importantly, wings. Harry moved to a sheet covering an object in the corner of the room and, with a flourish, removed it – revealing not a mechanical swan to safety but a bare table.

'I shall build it on this. All I need is a forge, a small lathe, a plan of a mechanical swan and a large quantity of iron – and then for that iron to be lighter than air. But given those, we shall be free!'

'Aaaaaarrrrgggh!' I said.

'I knew you'd like it,' replied Harry.

Reader, I punched him.

Only lightly, for he was my best friend and best friends never punch each other with full force lest best friends they be no more or lest they hurt their knuckles. If the truth be known, my punchiness was not entirely caused by Harry's nonsensical plans, rather by frustration at the dreadful circumstances in which I found myself. Alas, circumstances have no nose, and Harry did.

'Harry, forgive me . . .'

'No need for forgiveness, Pip Bin! Indeed, I am grateful. For my nose was a little blocked, and your punch has dislodged the phlegmy obstacle so I can breathe clearly again! Or, at least, I will be able to do so once the swelling has gone down.'

To have a friend so full of forgiveness should be every man's right, though no woman's – or what would female friends gripe and grudge about? – and I knew I was lucky indeed, if you discounted the fact that I was still probably doomed to die.

At that moment the dinner-bell tolled and we hurried to the dining hall for another pointless and indeed foodless mimed meal.

But, oh, what nourishment for the soul fated Fortune was to provide at that meal!

Mr Hardthrasher intoned the traditional grace – 'For what you are not about to receive, may the Lord make you truly painful' – and we fell on the fictitious food, none more eagerly than Harry, who managed to find delight in even mock eating.

'Oh, yum, make-believe mash! And could you pass the pretend peas, please, Pip Bin?'

Over the weeks, my physical theatre skills had grown, and I was able to pass the ersatz edibles both swiftly and convincingly. Sadly, other boys were less adept, and barely had we sat down than the headmaster leaped upon poor Spittleham's latest mime-food lapse.

'You, boy! What is that you are supposed to be eating?' His voice lashed like a wordy whip.

'A meringue, sir . . .'

'A meringue? It seems more like a Yorkshire pudding. You are to be beaten, boy, as if you were the egg whites a meringue is made of.'

The headmaster might have been brutal, but his culinary knowledge was exemplary. Wielding six curved canes bent and lashed together to form a punishment whisk, he hauled Spittleham away and placed him in a large bowl, then proceeded to beat him, if not into stiff peaks then certainly into a bruised and terrified mess.

And lo! As meringuey yelps of pain came from the bowl,

fated Fortune bestowed her gift upon me. I had just slurped down the last of my pseudo-soup starter and was about to move on to my main course of fake steak and sham shallots when one of the school servants shuffled towards me.

'Mumble, grunge, mumble,' she mumbled and grunged, actual speech clearly far beyond her serving-class brain.

The servants were the lowest of the low, the vilest of the vile and hideousest of the hideous, but this crone was a particularly nasty specimen, less human being, more a human-shaped amalgamation of mud, warts and bizarrely placed hair, specifically a most unfeminine beard. And the smell! Her general odour was rank and unsavoury and her breath was not so much halitosis as Hellitosis, causing my nose to wrinkle so greatly that it nearly turned inside out, and my entire body to recoil in stenchy horror, bumping hard into Harry beside me.

'Oh, great, you've knocked over my fantasy fondue! Can someone pass me a simulated serviette?' As he knelt beneath the table to clean up a spill that existed only in his imagination, I decided that Harry might be taking the mimed meals a little too seriously.

'Mumble, grunge, mumble,' the servant repeated. But then: ''Ere, 'ave this, young 'un . . .'

Words? Actual words? This grim-perfumed, lower-class hag could speak actual words?[5] I was so stunned that I barely realized she was handing me something.

'Wh-what is it?'

'It's a dumpling.' It was indeed a dumpling. But she was

---

[5] Many servants of this low standing had their vocabularies removed as children.

not done with her handing. 'And here's a carrot.' She did not lie, it was a carrot. And still she was not done. 'And a sliver of game terrine. And a nice bit of Cheddar, couple of omelettes, slice of gammon, a mackerel salad, some stuffed mushrooms and a Wiener Schnitzel.'

Truly this servant spoke truly, for from beneath her grimy robes she withdrew all these comestibles and placed them on the table before me. I could barely believe it: food! Real food! With all its smells and tastes and stomach-filling potential. Though I don't like mushrooms.

'You'd better eat it quick, afore the headmaster sees you.'

'But . . . why are you doing this? Who are you?'

'I'm just a friend.' I had never had a grotesque crone for a friend, yet if food she had provided me with then friend she definitely was and, that food having been provided, friend indeed she had become.[6] 'A friend who's here to help ye escape. Meet me here at midnight and I shall tell ye more. Mumble, grunge, mumble.'

She grunged mumblily away, a haze of filth and rank reek trailing after her. Who was this strange creature? Why had she fed me? Would she really help me escape? And why did she not wash more or dress better? All these questions crossed my mind like an ugly man crossing a dance-floor in search of a partner, that is to say quickly and without answer.

'What a mess!' Harry had finally finished mime-mopping his imaginary spill and now sat back up at the table. Seeing

---

[6] As an experiment, the author originally wrote this sentence in Latin, then translated it back into English, hence the strange sub-clausal nature.

the food the servant had left, his eyes went wider than Queen Victoria after an all-you-can-eat sausage buffet.[7] 'Oh, great! Now it is as if I can actually see real food! Curse my gastronomic imagination!'

In frustration he banged his head on the table, thereby squashing the stuffed mushrooms and affixing them to his forehead, which was fine because, as I mentioned before, I don't like mushrooms.

'No, Harry. It is real food. Given to me. Help yourself.'

'No, it's yours. I couldn't.'

But he could, and he did, for though his words said one thing his actions said another, and as our fellow pupils simply stared, the sight of actual, edible fare stunning them into inaction, Harry descended on the food like a swarm of peckish locusts or a hungry hurricane. At length, he sat back and emitted a loud, satisfied burp.

'Oh, tremendous. That is the best and only meal I've had in ages,' he said, as a mushroom slid from his forehead and into his mouth, punctuating the meal with a savoury full-stop.

Harry and I were the only non-hungry boys in the school that day, apart from Bissington, who had eaten his own arm, and Frobisher, who had in turn eaten Bissington. But the meal had provided more than mere physical food, for the appearance of the mysterious servant meant I had also dined on the psychic food of hope.

---

[7] After the death of Prince Albert, Queen Victoria took to comfort eating in a major way. At one banquet she visibly expanded by eight inches in one hour. Stamps had to be reprinted almost daily to keep up with her hyper-inflation.

CHAPTER THE NINTH

In which good news is definitely not heard

If thoughts are like animals, which they are not, then my thoughts were now like a hectic livestock market, full of jostling mind-cows, brain-sheep and think-pigs as my head teemed with the moos, baas and oinks of potential servant-aided escape.

Yet shortly after dinner, to my mental livestock was added a ponder-horse with all its concomitant neighs and whinnies as I was summoned to the headmaster's study where a visitor awaited me. Would it be a good visitor, such as my re-saned mother, come to take me from my schooly misery? Or a bad visitor, come to offer yet more pain for my young and frankly disappointing-at-this-moment-in-time life?

Alas, it was the latter. 'An anxious gale breezes not fine silks but bad stones,' they say,[1] and they are not wrong.[2]

As I approached, I heard laughter, a sound which in that

---

[1] No, they don't.

[2] Yes, they are.

place of misery was as incongruous as a vicar at an orgy or a seagull in a waistcoat. But then I realized that the laughter was cruel, malicious and very definitely aimed at and not shared with, thereby making it far less incongruous, akin more to a vicar at a prayer-swapping party or a seagull in spats, which, as everyone knows, is a common seaside sight.[3]

On entering, I saw the producer of this laughter: my guardian, Mr Gently Benevolent, in all his sharp-featured, black-clad and slightly scary glory. He and Headmaster Hardthrasher were sharing a glass of brandy, each sipping from one side of it, which made it awkward to drink from and look a bit like they were kissing.

'Ah, young Pip. You seem well. By which I mean not yet dead.'

Though my guardian was a harsh man, he was still my guardian, and if he heard the truth of my plight surely he would, as his title of guardian suggested, guardian me from it.

'Mr Benevolent! How glad I am to see you! This school you have sent me to is intolerably cruel!'

At this, the headmaster's eyes blazed like a furious fire. 'Such insolence! You dare accuse me of cruelty? Then you must be beaten, boy. Beaten to within an inch of your life. Possibly even closer. Now bend over!' He raised his cane high, like the stick-wielding maniac he was.

---

[3] The Georgians and the Victorians tried to hold nature to human standards, including dressing animals in clothes. They put fish into striped bathing costumes, made dogs wear top hats and once dressed the elephants at London Zoo in three-piece suits – an idea abandoned when one escaped and set up his own accountancy firm, thus leading to the famous myth of the Elephant Man.

'No, Headmaster.' Mr Benevolent raised a restraining hand. 'Let us not beat him.'

'Very well.' The headmaster lowered the cane. 'We'll move straight to the hanging.' He headed to the corner, where stood his personal portable gallows, Old Noosey.

'No.' Again, Mr Benevolent raised a restraining hand.

'But . . .' The headmaster emitted a plaintive whimper, like a sad puppy or a whoopee cushion that has been sat upon by a person not heavy enough to make it work properly. He tried once more to reach his gallows, forcing Mr Benevolent, the possessor of only two hands, to raise a restraining foot, making him wobble slightly as he tried to balance.

'Time enough for beatings and hangings later. But now I wish to tell young Pip the good news.'

Good news? That was good news. And the good news that it was could surely only be one thing.

'I am to leave this school? Oh, that is a relief. For the curriculum is incredibly limited and the pastoral care practically non-existent.' Joy filled me like a sack of happy jam.

'Leave? Gosh, no. This school will make a man or dead boy of you yet. No, the good news is this.' My guardian paused, then smiled, and I sensed that the good news he brought was not good news, and that actually a huge steam train of nasty news was bearing down upon me. 'I have decided I cannot wait until your sister is old enough to marry, so instead I am to marry your mother.'

Ladies and gentlemen, the train recently arrived at Platform Pip is for Misery Town, calling at Woe City, Anguish Halt and What-the-Heck Junction.

'Marry my mother? I do not understand . . .' A sick feeling grew in my stomach. Possibly because of recently having eaten for the first time in weeks but more probably because of this news, which was as ungood or bad as I had feared.

'If I marry her then I shall have all your family's money and social standing.' His obsidian eyes glinted with malice. 'Are you not delighted?'

I was not delighted. Indeed, I was de-delighted.

'When is this to happen?'

'Tomorrow. By three o'clock, I shall have a new wife and fortune and you shall have a new papa.'

Now the sick feeling was replaced by a mix of hot anger and cold fury, like a baked Alaska of rage.

'Never! I shall never call you Papa!'

'You will call me Papa, whether you like it or not. And you will like it, whether you like it or not.' He smiled at me like a small human shark. 'Son . . .'

'No!' I hurled myself at him, fists flying, but Headmaster Hardthrasher seized me by the collar so that my fists found no Benevolenty target but instead only air. Though that air got pretty bruised, I can tell you.

'Now, here is your invitation to the wedding.' Mr Benevolent drew a beautifully embossed card from his pocket, flashed it briefly before my eyes, but then, rather than handing it over, he instead ripped it into tiny pieces, before gathering the fragments, setting fire to them and then dissolving the residual ashes in a bowl of acid. 'Whoops. How careless of me. Looks like you won't be coming. However, you may share in the wedding feast, for the headmaster has kindly agreed you may have an actual meal tomorrow in celebration. Let me fetch it for you.'

He stepped across to a bag and rummaged inside. The rummaging continued for some time, the bag evidently being capacious and hard-to-find-things-in-y.

'It's here somewhere. Perhaps in this compartment? No. Or this one? No.'

'Is that one of those new-fangled Gladstone bags, Benevolent?' the headmaster asked.

'Dear me, no, Headmaster. It is the much more fashion-able Disraeli bag,[4] which has many more compartments. For, as the great man once said, "When it comes to compartments, lay them on with a trowel." Is it in here? Nope . . .'

'Ridiculous.' Mr Hardthrasher snorted derisively. 'Bags should be like women: simple, and with one lockable opening.'

'Aha!' Mr Benevolent had found what he was looking for and turned, brandishing a tin. 'Look: special delicious soup for you.'

I could not help but feel that his soupy gift was not a generous one, for the label on the tin read 'Poison'. I informed him of that fact. 'It says "Poison" on it.'

'What? No, it says . . .' He turned away, grabbed a pen and scribbled hurriedly upon the tin, then showed me the amended label. '. . . *poisson.*'

---

[4] The author is clearly mistaken as the Gladstone and Disraeli bags were not invented until much later, in accordance with the law of the time that all Prime Ministers should have luggage named after them. Most have now fallen out of use, with the exception of the Gladstone bag and the ever popular Palmerston sack, with its two separate compartments for simultaneously transporting scrambled eggs and legal papers – the so-called barrister's breakfast bag.

By the hurried addition of a scrawled extra *s* it did indeed now say that.

'It is French fish soup?'

'Yup. Definitely. Must have been a misprint in the fish-soup factory. Tsch, the French, eh?'

We may have been opposed in many ways, but we could at least agree on the inefficiency and plain wrongness of the French, in particular their notoriously inefficient and government-subsidized soup industry. Reassured, I took the tin from him.

'So, around three o'clock tomorrow, you guzzle that down and then Bob's your uncle and Benevolent's your father. Albeit very briefly. Ha, ha, ha. Ha, ha, ha!'

He began to laugh and continued for some minutes, pausing only for breath and to motion between the tin of soup and myself before bursting into guffaws again. It was a strange sense of humour that found such fun in the idea of a boy eating soup, but then I was young and couldn't possibly know the mind of my elders. After a while, the headmaster joined in as well, his deep, mocking laughter mixing with Mr Benevolent's into a harmony of hilarity, which, despite the horror of my circumstances, I somehow found as contagious as funny cholera or chucklesome typhus, and, without really knowing why, I, too, ventured a laugh.

'Ha . . .' I began, but instantly the other two stopped, leaving me laughing into a hollow silence as they stared at me.

'Nothing funny here, boy.'

'Right.'

'Now, you run along . . . son.'

'No! Never!' Again I flew at him. Again the headmaster seized me, thus preventing my assault, only this time he also hurled me through the door of his study – which was fortunately still open or it would have hurt much more than it did, though the amount it did actually hurt was still a lot as, even though my fall was broken by a passing schoolmate, he was so thin from hunger that his boniness provided a distinctly unsoft and poky landing, possibly more painful than simply landing on the stony floor might actually have been, though I would never really know, as I did not want to re-enter the room and ask the headmaster to throw me out again only this time straight on to the corridor floor as some sort of control experiment.

As I lay on poor, uncomfortable Jaggery minor, the mental livestock began their noises again, a bestial thought cacophony that took Pippa's imminent Joan of Arc-ing, Harry's impending and deadly birthday and now Mr Benevolent's forthcoming nuptials to my mother and blended them together into one animal roar that screamed: Escape!

CHAPTER THE TENTH

In which the escape begins a bit

There are many forms of waiting. The waiting that is for a longed-for and joyous event and therefore drags on agonizingly but is tinged with anticipatory excitement; the waiting that is for a dreaded and wretched event and therefore glowers sullenly through the hours; and, of course, the waiting that is taking plates of food to people in restaurants.

My wait to visit the servant and learn what hope of escape she offered was none of those, but maybe a sort of mix of the first two. The hours moved slowly, like a laudanum-addicted sloth, or treacle that has been handcuffed to a rock.

Finally, as the clock ticked round towards midnight, Harry and I crept out of the dormitory, stepping round the sleeping forms of our schoolmates whose sleepy snores and somnolent snuffles were punctuated with whimpers of 'Mother', whispers of 'Help' and wails of 'Aaarrrgggh!'

We crept creepily towards the dining hall and, as we

arrived outside, the school bell tolled twelve – we were on time. But of the mysterious servant there was no sign.

'Hello . . . ?' I whispered hopefully into the pitch-black and dark-horse dark hall, to no response.

Harry and I took a step inside, the gloom enveloping us, and I tried again.

'Hello . . . ?' I re-whispered, again to no response.

We took a further step inside, and I re-re-whispered, 'Hello . . . ?'

Alas, as I stepped forward this time, I knocked into a pile of stacked plates, for though our food was mimed our crockery was not, and they wobbled, wibbled and in the end wabbled[1] on to the ground with a huge, platey smash, which rang out sonorously and definitely not quietly in a huge echo that seemed to say, 'We're here, we're trying to escape, someone come and catch us, we're here.'

Yet still there came no response.

Though after a few seconds there now did come one.

'Ssssh!' hissed a voice. Then a lantern flickered to life in the darkness and approached, and lit by its glow there appeared the face of the servant, a gnarled, hairy visage so dotted with warts that it was reminiscent of nothing so much as a stale Chelsea bun with a beard. 'All that noise. Do you want to escape or disturb the headmaster and die?'

'Ooh, I know this one!' An excited Harry danced around with his hand in the air. 'Is it wake the headmaster and die? No, hang on . . .'

---

[1] Olde Englishe for 'to fall'. Not that you needed me to tell you that. I mean, it's pretty obvious from the context, isn't it?

'Who are you?' I asked, a tremor in my voice for truly her ugly face was, if not impossible to behold, certainly a bit tricky to look at.

'I already told you, I'm a friend.' She swung her lantern in Harry's direction. 'And who's this you've brought with you?'

'He is my friend.'

'So he's a friend of a friend. That's good.' She stroked her beard thoughtfully.

'Do you have a name, mysterious bearded crone?'

'I have many names. There are those who have called me Bearded Brenda.' Again she stroked her beard. 'Others have called me Hairy Harriet. Others yet know me as Goateed Gretel, Whiskered Wanda or Face-fuzz Fiona.' Each mention of a name was accompanied by a beard-stroke, as if names and beard were inextricably linked, which, I realize as I write this many years later, they obviously were.

Der.

Now she took her hand from her beard and continued: 'There are also some who know me ironically as Smooth-faced Susan. But to you I am just . . .' here she paused as if on the verge of great name-revelations '. . . a friend. And I have been sent to help you, Pip Bin.'

'By whom?'

'By a friend. I am just a friend sent by a friend to help a friend and his friend,' she said friendlily.

'How do I know I can trust you?'

'Perhaps this might convince you.'

She reached beneath her filth-encrusted skirts and I felt

a shudder of fear at what possible hideousness therein she might be about to show us. Harry clearly shared that fear because he blurted out, 'Oh, God, don't let it be her pants!'

To our relief, it was not her pants. Instead she produced a gold locket – one that looked strangely familiar. I took it from her, being careful not to touch her foul hands as they appeared so flaky and diseased that I feared both personal contagion and maybe accidentally knocking one of her fingers off, and opened it.

Within there was a tiny oil painting of my mother that made me both weep with emotion and think, 'Gosh, what small paintbrushes they must have used'.

'This is my mother's locket!' I said. 'Where did you get it? Did Mama give it to you? Is she well again?'

'I was given it by a friend. Not the same friend as sent me to help, a different friend, but a friend all the same. As to your mother . . . she is quite mad.'

At this news, joy flooded me. 'But that is marvellous! She was totally mad the last time I saw her, so only quite mad is a real improvement.'

'Ah.' Did I detect a glimmer of sympathy in the crone's eye? 'I'm afraid I'm using the word "quite" as in "completely" rather than to mean "a bit". Sorry.'

This deflated me quicker than a dirigible crashing into a needle and spike factory. 'Oh. Not such marvellous news after all.' I stared at the picture in the locket, tears pricking the backs of my eyes like tiny emotional forks as I found myself adrift in a swamp of sadness, the true horror of my broken-familied plight settling on me like a forlorn fog.

Fortunately no such fog had settled on the perennially

optimistic to the point of you-worry-he-might-not-actually-understand Harry.

'Are you here to help Pip escape, beardy crone lady?'

'I am sworn to get him away from here and to safety,' the crone said, which cheered me right up again, dispersing the fog in twelve easy words, for the emotions of adolescence are passionate but shallow, like a gentlemen's all-nude bathing pond.

'And my sister Pippa? Are you to help her as well?'

'If I knew where she was, aye.'

'But she is next door to here! In St Bitch's!'

'I see. Though that is geographically convenient, it does complicate things.'

'And she is due to be burned at the stake tomorrow on Joan of Arc Day!'

'So soon? That complicates the complication.' The servant turned and started pacing up and down, frantically beard-stroking. 'To escape with both of you will not be easy. Indeed, there are those who would say it will be . . . difficult.'

'And Harry. I'm not leaving without Harry.' Though I had known him but a short time, in no circumstances could I imagine myself abandoning my best friend. Except, you know, unless I really had to. 'It is his birthday tomorrow, and you know what that means.'

'I certainly do, Pip Bin,' said Harry. 'On the one hand there will be presents – hurrah, I love presents – but on the other hand there will be almost certain death – boo, I don't like death.'

The servant stopped her pacing and stared at us. 'Three of you? To get three of you out of here is so hard it makes the people who would say that getting two of you out will be difficult look like blind optimists. Indeed, there are those who would say that getting three of you out by tomorrow is impossible. And those are people who are generally quite positive, glass-is-half-full-type people.'

'Well, if we have to leave Harr—' I began, but was cut off.

'Nevertheless, we shall try. You two wait here. For if I am to help all three of you escape, I need to get some things.'

The servant left the dining hall with a speed and grace that belied the shuffly movements I had previously seen her make – who was this mysterious woman? Who had sent her? And why had she taken her lantern with her, leaving Harry and me in the scary darkness?

Surrounded by the miserable sounds of the school, I began to fear and, indeed, think the worst: Harry and I would never escape; I would never save my sister or stop my mother marrying Mr Benevolent; and soon my ineffectual little life would end in this awful place, with me alone and weeping.

Then I felt Harry's hand on my arm and heard his voice in my ears. 'It's all right, Pip Bin, that's not going to happen. It will all be fine. And if it's not, well, how ineffectual or little can a life be that has had friendship such as ours in it?'

And so I realized that I had actually spoken my fears out loud, and that the penultimate paragraph before this one should have had the words 'I said' within it and some inverted commas.

'I'm sorry, Harry. I'm just nervous.'

'No need to be sorry, Pip Bin. And if you're nervous, would it help if I let you hit me on the nose again?'[2]

'No, Harry, of course not.' But in case it offered relief, I did hit him on the nose again. It didn't really help me, and certainly didn't help Harry, but just the thought of having a friend so loyal, decent and daft as to offer such a thing calmed me greatly.

We sat in silence, bar the odd whimper of nose-pain from Harry, and waited for the servant to return. It was a long wait. The school bell tolled many times before her return, and when a wave of smell announced her imminent reappearance, the cold grey light of dawn was starting to spread across the floor of the dining hall like grim margarine.[3] In one mottled hand she was clutching an object that seemed to me something which boosted our chances of escape enormously: a large key. How could an escape go wrong if a large key was involved?

'The key to escape is this key,' she said, moving towards the back wall of the dining hall where a heavy curtain hung down. 'Behind this is a door that leads to your sister's nunnery, locked these past decades since the Schoolboy Nun Segregation Act of 1752.'[4]

---

[2] It was believed at the time that all male emotions should be repressed and could only be relieved by physical violence. To that end, the job of 'Punch-nose' existed, men who would offer themselves as the targets of an emotion-relieving punch, an equivalent to our modern psychotherapists.

[3] Margarine was actually invented in the nineteenth century. I know, who knew?

[4] A genuine Act of Parliament. Forbidden contact with men, certain friskier orders of nuns built convents next to boys' schools on the grounds that they were not forbidden contact with boys. It was a sordid chapter in the Church's past and one only a few ex-nuns married to much younger men were proud of.

She drew back the curtain and there, as she had said, was a door, a providential portal of potential pescape. Sorry, escape. It was a huge studded thing, all thick wood and metal, with one large, solitary lock and multiple signs saying, 'Keep out', 'Go away' and 'No'. The servant inserted the key, pushed it into the lock and, with a surprisingly small 'snick', turned it.

'Now, we simply have to hope the door hasn't rusted shut over the years . . .'

It had not: as she reached for the handle and turned it, the door swung soundlessly open, revealing a long, dark corridor. But I saw it as more than that, much more, instantly knowing that it was my longed-for path to sister-saving, escape and freedom.

Or, of course, discovery, recapture and death.

Which would be much less fun.

CHAPTER THE ELEVENTH

In which the clock strikes escape o'clock

We quickly moved down the corridor and through a door at the far end, emerging into a dormitory filled with small, sleeping nuns. Conditions were not vastly different from those in the dormitory at St Bastard's, only instead of stones and straw the floor was littered with Bibles, prayer books and hymnals. The nuns themselves slept upright, kneeling on prayer mats and with their hands clasped in front of them. Above them hung banners with encouraging religious slogans, such as 'Nun's the word', 'Nun shall pass' and 'Not with a bang but with a wimple'.

'Right, let us find your sister and then get out of here,' said the servant. I hastened to do her bidding, rapidly searching the room for Pippa, but I found her not and, indeed, did not find her.

'She is not here.'

The servant tutted grumpily. 'No, of course not. Because why would it be so easy? "Get the boy out," they say, and then, as if that's not enough, he wants his sister rescued too and his best friend. I mean, blinking heck!'

I had never heard so many words from her before, and as her speech went on, her accent slipped from peasant to pleasant, even genteel, and as it did it became somehow familiar to me, but in a way I could not quite put a finger, or indeed ear, upon. She saw me staring and stopped.

'Mumble, grunge, mumble . . .' Her vocabulary disappeared once more, her accent returned to pure proletarian, and my inkling of familiarity with her disappeared. 'We'd better look harder, then.'

We passed through the dormitory and into a nunnish corridor that stretched a nunly way in each nunny direction and was lined with nunnesque doors. By now the light spilling in from the windows above was no longer the grey of pre-dawn but instead the soft yellow of actual dawn, and around us the sounds of a nunnery stirring to life could be heard: the click of rosary beads, the soft scratch of communion wafers being stacked and, from behind a door marked 'Head Nun', the quavering notes of a song that seemed to be all about climbing mountains and fording streams.

Then, amid the nunny hubbub, I heard a more familiar sound. Indeed, a distinctly anvilly one. 'Tink, tink, tink,' it went, and in return I went, 'Pippa, Pippa, Pippa,' for it was surely her. I hurried tink-wards down the corridor, Harry and the servant behind me, and when I was at the correct door I opened it to reveal . . .

'Pippa! Dear sister!' She was sitting in a large tin bath, her anvil on a table beside her. I raced across the room, relief at finding her washing over me, like hot custard over a delicious pie: sweet, comforting and oddly yellow.

'Oh, Pip! Dear brother Pip! How happy I am to see you!'

'Dear sister! If you are as glad to see me as I am glad to see you then you must be exactly as glad as I am!' How happy I was to be able to express such a balanced equation of joy.

'Glad? Oh, I am glad, so glad! So very, very glad.' But she did not seem glad, for she now commenced to weep, great salty tears splashing down her cheeks like tiny oceans of woe, or woceans.

'Dear sister, do not be sad.'

Through her tears, she spoke: 'Sad? No, not sad I. For these are tears of gladness, not sadness.' She sobbed mightily twice, then bawled, 'Aaarrggh! I am so happy!'

Dear reader, or if someone is reading this text aloud to you, dear readee, I was at a loss to comprehend this mismatch of word to deed. Though her words said she was happy, her tear-stained, snot-bubbly actions indicated the opposite. 'But you sound so sad.'

'No, not sad, glad.' At this, she let out a weepy wail that made the hairs on the back of my neck stand on end and the hairs on the top of my head lie down in fear.

I have rarely in my life felt more purely male in my utter bafflement by emotion.

'Dear sister, I admit to being confused as to the difference between tears of sadness and gladness.'

'Oh, right, it's quite simple, really.' She instantly stopped weeping and started explaining. 'These are tears of gladness: wah! Wah! Bleeeurfggh-aaarrggh-waaaaaah!'

My ears filled with the sound of an angry banshee that has just discovered it has lost its wallet and then stubbed its toe. But almost as soon as it had started, it stopped, leaving my brain throbbing with unprocessed emotion.

'Do you see? Whereas these are tears of sadness.' She breathed in and then: 'Woo-wah-glerrrrr-aaarrfggggh-boo-hoo-snaarrrrrrrggh!'

The angry, lost-walleted, toe-stubbed banshee returned, but fortunately quickly left again as once more she returned to calmness.

'See? Quite, quite different.'

As far as I was concerned the two sets of tears were as alike as two peas in a pod or a man in a hat who looks exactly the same as another man in a hat, but I knew that when it comes to shemotions, agreement is often the safest course of action. 'Ah, of course, all is clear now.' Only it wasn't. 'We have come to rescue you!'

'Oh, dear brother Pip! Wah-blarrfggggh!!!!!!!!!'[1] She started crying again with what I assumed was gladness. Baffled by her emotional fluidity, I decided to introduce her to my companions.

'The rescue is all thanks to this woman here.' I motioned to the servant standing behind me.

'Pleased to meet you, young Pippa.'

'The pleasure is all mine, hideous bearded crone.'

'And this is my new best friend, Harry Biscuit.'

'Hello!' Harry said, a little too loudly, blushing as he did so. 'Sorry, bit nervous. Don't get to talk to girls much. Or

---

[1] The author was the single greatest user of the exclamation point in nineteenth-century literature. It was the most expensive item of punctuation to print and publishers often charged its costs to the author – Sir Philip here is indicating he is so rich and successful he simply doesn't care how many he uses.

ever.' His cheeks bright red, he moved awkwardly away, as if he had slightly forgotten how to walk; I think he was quite taken with her.

'We must get you out of this bath, dear sister.' I offered a hand to help her from the tub.

'Bath? But this is no bath.'

I was baffled. It certainly looked like a bath. It was the right shape. It held liquid, and a person, like other baths I had seen, apart from the empty ones. And down the side was written the word 'bath'.

'Then what is it?'

'As you know, today I am supposed to be burned as Joan of Arc.'

A shudder ran through me at the idea of my sister being tied to a stake and burned, like a fifteenth-century French martyr.

'And to celebrate that, the nunnery will have a feast.'

Now a different shudder ran through me as I realized I was actually a bit cold.

'So this is not bathwater. This is a marinade. I am in a flavour-bath.[2] To make me a tender and tasty steak from a stake.'

'No! My own sister! Destined to be eaten!' The two different shudders now combined into one gigantic tremor of fearful, chilly fury.

'But no longer, dear brother, for you have come to rescue me!'

---

[2] Flavour-baths came in many different sizes, from tiny for marinading mice to ones big enough for an entire live cow, a size known as 'moossive'.

She reached her arms from the tub, and we hugged as only a brother and sister can, meaning I could not resist pulling her hair to annoy her and she could not resist straightening my collar and cleaning an imaginary stain from my cheek.

Our hug was interrupted by a slurping sound, and I looked up to see Harry licking a finger that he had just dipped into Pippa's bath. Fortunately, it was his own finger.

'Mmm, rosemary, garlic and olive oil. I reckon you'd have been a tasty feast, Miss Bin.'

'Why, thank you, Harry Biscuit.' Pippa smiled at the compliment.

'Hurr-hurr,' Harry stammered. 'I feel a bit giddy.' He blushed like an embarrassed tomato.

'You have come in the nick of time, for shortly Sister Cookswell is to come and squeeze lemon juice over me, then stud me with peppercorns.'

'Then we must leave at once.' The servant came over from the door where she had been checking lest anyone approach. 'It is now daytime, however, and the nuns are up and about. As a servant, they will not notice me, but you three will be more conspicuous. To that end, I have brought disguises for you, taken from the St Bastard's school-play costume cupboard.'

She rummaged beneath her dirt-encrusted skirts, then withdrew piles of clothing from within, distributing an outfit to each of us. Quickly, we dressed.

I knew that the St Bastard's school play was traditionally an incredibly violent and unusual production, but even so, the results were surprising. 'Are you sure about these disguises?' I asked.

'Yes. Why? Aren't you?' The servant bristled defensively, like an offended hedgehog.

'It's just . . . well . . .' I motioned at Harry and myself.

'Well what?'

I decided to beat about the bush of politeness no more. 'Harry is dressed as Admiral Nelson.' For indeed he was, in a blood-stained costume left over from that term's production of the *Battle of Trafalgar* in which the headmaster had shot a boy a night for a week.

'So?'

'But Nelson has been dead these past eighteen years! And now he will be discovered wandering round a nunnery.'

'Exactly. Everyone will be delighted to see him again. And who would challenge such a fine figure of authority and heroism?' The servant stared at me through her warty beardedness. 'I suppose you're not happy with your disguise either?'

'I'm dressed as a rabbit!' I blurted, for indeed I was, it being a pointy-eared, fluffy tailed costume from the headmaster's Easter production in which the boy playing the Easter bunny had been torn apart by a pack of live foxes.

At my objecting tone, the servant stared angrily at me through her warts. It was like being hated by a currant bun.

'Um . . .' Now Pippa, too, had objections. 'Perhaps I should just wear my regular nun's outfit instead of this disguise.'

The servant sighed. 'No. For there is nothing as suspicious in a nunnery as a nun.'

'Do we really think that's true?'

'If you're trying to escape, yes.' The servant sounded as steadfast and resolute as a British polar explorer determined to leave a tent against the advice of everyone else.

'So you're saying it's less suspicious if I look like a grandfather clock?' Pippa held up her disguise, which was indeed a grandfather clock, a costume left over from a production before my time at St Bastard's, but one that had gone down in school folklore, a musical written by Headmaster Hardthrasher himself called *The Beating, Shooting and Hanging of Big Ben.*

'Look, I promised to get Pip out of here. I didn't know there would be three of you and when I found out I did the best I could. You're lucky I could find any disguises at all in the middle of the night while trapped in an evil boarding-school!'

Again, as she ranted and raved, her accent mutated into something higher-born and familiar, but again as before I could not identify it. Truly, this woman was a mystery; if she helped us escape, would we ever solve her? Or like a fiendishly difficult Sudoku would she be thrown angrily away unsolved?[3]

'All I'm saying is, please trust me. The disguises will work.'

What choice did we have? Other than all the choices that involved not wearing her ridiculous disguises. Nevertheless, there was something persuasive about her tone and Pippa

---

[3] In the nineteenth century a Sudoku was not the number puzzle we know today. It was in fact a shortening of the phrase 'Super Dog Knot Undoing', a popular sport of the time where competitors would attempt to disentangle complicated knots made out of greyhounds and dachshunds.

donned her clock, I tried a tentative bunny hop or two and Harry completed his disguise by stuffing an arm inside his jacket and placing a patch over his eye.

'Actually, pretending to be Nelson is brilliant! Look at me, I'm Nelson!'

Harry's enthusiasm melted the icy atmosphere, and even the mysterious, roving-accented servant's mouth twitched upwards at the corners in a vague signal of amusement, dislodging a wart, which fell to the ground with a plink.

'Good. Now we must leave.' The servant headed for the door.

'Not without my anvil!' Pippa fondly stroked her paternally gifted anvil.

'Such an item is too heavy. It will slow us down.' There was a hint of annoyance in the servant's voice now.

'But it reminds me of our late father!' she pleaded. 'And it's not as heavy as it looks.' She lifted the anvil to prove her point, managing to hold it for a full no seconds before it plunged clangily and point-disprovingly to the floor.

'Do you not have a lighter reminder?' To the hint of annoyance was now added a pinch of peevishness.

'Well . . . there is this one-page letter he wrote me.' She held it up but, as if to prove its lightness, a breezy gust snatched it from her hands and wafted it out of the window. 'Then there is this feather. Or this paper bag full of his breath.'

'Bring those, then.' The annoyed peevishness lifted slightly.

'But only the anvil really reminds me of him. I must bring it.'

The servant now responded in a tone that could only be described as blinking cross. 'No, I forbid it.'

'But . . .' And the angry, stub-toed, pickpocketed banshee was back. 'Waarrfgggh-spphhllrrggh-wah!!!'

Why this should make Pippa glad, I did not know.

'I am so sad!!!'

Ah. It hadn't.

'Miss Bin. I shall help you carry it.' Harry stepped forward to help, thereby silencing the banshee.

'Oh, what a gentleman you are, Harry Biscuit.' Pippa leaned over and kissed Harry on the cheek.

'Hurr-hurr, girl. Kissed by a girl. And not a pretend one.' If before Harry had blushed like an embarrassed tomato, he now looked like a shy strawberry that had just fallen naked into a pot of red paint.

The blushing finally eased, and he attempted to pick up the anvil. It seemed far too heavy for a boy who had placed one arm inside his jacket to pretend to be Nelson, but Harry was committed to both disguise and anvil-carrying and, arm straining, eyes bulging and trousers ripping with effort, he somehow lifted the immense metallic block and quickly staggered incredibly slowly towards the door.

'Good. Now follow me and act just like any normal dead admiral, giant rabbit and grandfather clock.'

The servant led us out into the corridor – and immediately I saw heading towards us a group of four nuns, who were having a heated discussion in song regarding the solution to a problem with a young nun named Maria.

Was the servant right? Would our bizarre disguises work? Or was our escape over almost before it had begun?

Yet no alarm seemed to register on their nunny faces as they approached us. Indeed, they made conversation.

'Ah, good morning, the late Admiral Nelson. How nice to see you alive again,' remarked one to Harry.

'Um, yes . . . Er, Trafalgar, bloody good battle, what?' replied Harry.

To my amazement, the nuns giggled in response. 'Oh, Admiral, you're so witty.'

'Am I?' asked a bemused Biscuit.

Harry's disguise worked! They were convinced he was Nelson and were actively flirting with him, as was the law with all military heroes back then.[4]

Unfortunately, now their gaze turned to my own rabbity self. Surely I would be revealed as the fraudulent escapee I was.

'And good morning to you, Mr Rabbit.'

I struggled for a response, then remembered the servant's instructions and tried to respond as any normal rabbit would. 'Er . . . ttt-ttt-ttt?'

The nuns stared at me silently. I had ruined everything. But then: 'You're absolutely right. What an astute observation.'

Whatever astute rabbity observation I had made eluded me, but it had satisfied the nuns; I clearly spoke fluent Rabbit. Now there was only Pippa to pass the test. Without waiting to be spoken to, she boldly stepped forward and

---

[4] The Flirtius Militaris Act of 1807 made it compulsory for women to flirt when they met a decorated military man. It also compelled men to speak to them in an awestruck, slightly higher-pitched-than-normal voice, before thinking less of themselves for not being as brave and virile.

spoke: 'Bong, bong, bong, bong, bong, bong,' she clockily ad-libbed, and the response could not have been more unexpected or welcome.

'Oh! Six o'clock already! We are late for our early morning guilt-grating![5] We must hurry.'

And with a tip of the wimple, they scuttled nunnily away. We had got past them: perhaps the servant's disguises were not as strange and wrong as I had suspected.

Or nuns are very, very stupid.

'Back through here.' Now the servant led us through the dormitory via which we had entered. We had to stop briefly for Harry to sign autographs as Nelson, but soon we were at the door that led back to St Bastard's. 'Once on the other side of this door, we are but a short walk from freedom, for I know a secret exit through the school salt-mines.'

Could it be true? Was freedom really so close at hand? Could that salty place of punishment provide our route to safety? As we passed through the door back into St Bastard's, my heart soared with optimism and hope swelled inside me like a large benign cyst.

Alas, when we re-entered the school, that hope-cyst burst, spilling forth the pus of despair, as I beheld a sight that chilled me to my very marrow. I forget why I was carrying such a large vegetable. Perhaps it was part of the rabbit costume, though a carrot would have been more convincing and a lettuce leaf lighter.

---

[5] Penance in the form of a vicious scraping up and down a human-sized cheese grater.

There, in front of us, loomed the towering, terrifying figure of Headmaster Hardthrasher, a cane in his hand and a small, deadly-looking cannon by his side. I had a fleeting hope that we could bluff our way through in our disguises, but his words instantly destroyed that illusion.

'Pip Bin. Harry Biscuit. I've been expecting you.'

At that moment I knew only two things: first, that I was going to die, and second, that I had been right, and that nuns were very, very stupid.

CHAPTER THE TWELFTH

Of chases and escapes and fruit[1]

We froze in our tracks, like an Eskimo with no shoes or a frightened train. So this was it: my last day on earth.

Harry's last day.

And, once the headmaster had returned her to the nunnery to be Joan of Arc, then roasted and eaten as the Joan of Arc Day feast, Pippa's last day.

'Harry Biscuit. The ingratitude. Trying to escape when I've gone to all the trouble of getting you these lovely eighteenth-birthday presents?' The headmaster stepped aside, revealing a table stacked high with neatly wrapped gifts. 'Don't you want to open them?'

'Ooh, presents. I do love presents.'

Harry put down Pippa's anvil and headed for the present-laden table.

'No, Harry! They are almost certainly lethal!' I shouted,

---

[1] There is no fruit in this chapter. No one knows why the author wrote that. Unless he was working from notes and copied down a bit of his shopping list by mistake.

remembering the long roll-call of birthday deaths at St Bastard's.

Harry turned to me with desperation in his eyes. 'I know! But I just can't help myself.' He reached for the nearest present and gave it a shake. 'Ooh, is it a book?' He unwrapped it. 'No, it's a grenade. Now, what is this one?' said Harry, shaking another. 'Chocolates, maybe?' He opened it. 'No, it's some unstable nitroglycerine. How thoughtful.'

'And after you've opened your presents, you can light the candle on your cake.' The headmaster grinned murderously as he pointed to a distinctly untasty-looking cake.

'Ooh, is that dynamite cake? My favourite.'

Though Harry was my best friend, I am not ashamed to admit that at this moment in time I began to believe he might be . . . How shall I put this? A sandwich short of a full-house in picnic-poker? One colony short of an empire? A bit thick? Yes, that's the one.

'As for you, Pip Bin, don't you want the delicious soup Mr Benevolent left you?' The headmaster held up the tin and poured the contents into a bowl, which immediately started to melt and dissolve. 'It looks nice and spicy. Do you want me to feed you?'

He advanced on me wielding the deadly bowl and a distinctly threatening spoon. I backed away, terrified.

Out of the corner of my eye I could see the servant rummaging yet again in her manure-stained yet capacious skirts; suddenly she produced a sword and, more surprising yet, a cold, hard voice of upper-class command, which I really very nearly could identify. 'Leave the boy alone, Hardthrasher.'

The headmaster stopped in his tracks and turned to her. 'Or what?'

'Or this.' She poked him hard in the ribs with the sword – once, twice, thrice, even fourice.

He clutched at where she had struck him, his hands coming away covered with blood, or possibly some other red substance, such as ketchup, though blood seemed the likeliest, what with a sword being involved and everything.

'Ha! I have drawn blood,' the servant crowed, in her now clearly natural voice, which I really was incredibly close to being able to pin down.

'Maybe. But does not medical science tell us that drawing blood from a patient strengthens them?'[2] He licked his ichorous fingers and raised himself threateningly back up to his full height.

The servant drew herself up too, sword defiantly pointed forward. My heart beat faster: if she lost we were doomed, but on the other hand . . . sword-fight. Cool.[3] But it turned out there was to be no fight for she now yelled, 'Run! Everyone, run!'

With a final jab at the headmaster, the servant spun round and ran for the door.

'But my presents!' cried Harry.

---

[2] The medical establishment of the time insisted bleeding was a valid treatment on the basis of some incredibly dodgy statistics. Doctors would often bleed people to death but still claim a cure, claiming that the disease had technically stopped at the same time as the patient.

[3] The word 'cool' originated around this time as an acronym for 'Colossally Obvious Object of Laudability'.

'Leave them!'

'And my anvil!' cried Pippa.

'Leave it!'

'Never!'

'Your anvil must come even before my presents, Miss Bin!' Harry cried, as he abandoned the gifty table, heaved the anvil into his solitary Nelsonian arm and ran at less than walking pace through the door, which the servant immediately slammed behind us.

'There! That will hold him for a while.'

She was wrong. Unless by 'a while' she had meant less than a second and a half, for within that time the headmaster had crashed through the wood as if it was the paper it might have become had it not chosen to be a door as its timbery career, and he stood in the corridor, face studded with splinters like a man with a porcupine for a head.

'You will never escape St Bastard's!' he shouted, and advanced on us.

There were two doors nearby. Above one was written 'No Exit' and above the other 'Dangerous Exit'. The servant wrenched open the latter, revealing steps leading down into a scary darkness. Salt-tanged air rolled up from below, and not in a good way, like that from a jolly seaside, but in a bad way, like that from a deadly salt-mine, which this was: the school salt-mine.

'Down, quickly!'

She pushed us forwards; we stumbled on the top step, fell and now finally the anvil came into its own as its huge massiness provided momentum to our descent, rapidly turning it into a plummet until we landed in a heap at the bottom, where the atmosphere was already brackish and thirst-making.

Then we ran.

Not fast, obviously, because an anvil was involved. But eventually we were deep in the salty maze of the mine, and paused to catch our breath. As I panted desperately, I could already feel thirst starting to tickle my throat with its maddening fingers.

'We should be safe for a while,' the servant said. 'Hardthrasher won't dare come down here without help.'

At that there was the sound of dozens of men entering the salt-mine, for the headmaster had a huge number of wastrels, brigands, rapscallions, ne'er-do-wells, miscreants, savages, brutes, sadists and criminal scum at his disposal, whom he utilized as both PE teachers and security guards for hunting down escaped boys.

'Ah. He now has help. Run again!'

We did.

Still not very fast because of . . . well, you know.

The anvil.

The briny air filled our lungs but emptied our mouths of moisture. Thirst's fingers were now not just tickling maddeningly but clawing angrily.

'Oh, the salt!' cried Harry. 'It's driving me mad! It's making me hallucinate. I keep thinking I can see a giant rabbit!'

'Harry, I'm disguised as a rabbit,' I reminded him.

'Damn, now there's two of them!'

'This way!' The servant wheeled towards a sliver of light in the distance – could it be the way out she had talked of?

But, alas, as we approached the luminous glow of safety, a great phalanx of the headmaster's roguish battalion placed itself in our path, cutting off both light and escape, while behind us we could hear the rest of his barbaric force approaching. We would shortly be trapped between these two grim groups.

'Behind here!' the servant shouted, ushering us towards a large, salty rock, and we hurried behind it and sat still, scared and very, very thirsty. Indeed, so thirsty that Harry started trying to lick his own forehead for the sweaty moisture thereon, succeeding only in increasing his thirst and spraining his tongue.

'Where have they gone?' demanded Headmaster Hardthrasher, his frustration and rage as obvious as a large transvestite who has forgotten to shave or put on a lady-wig. 'Everybody, halt!'

Silence fell like a shot goose.

'Now, where are you, little ones? Don't you want your birthday presents, Harry Biscuit? I've brought them with me. Just for you.'

I could see a twitch of gift-avarice in Harry's eyes, and quickly clamped a hand over his mouth. 'Harry, I know how much you love presents, but we must keep completely quiet or we will die.'

Harry nodded and, trusting him like only a best friend could, I released my hand from his mouth.

He immediately starting yelling, getting no further than 'Presents! I want pre—' before I re-clamped my hand over his mouth, but the damage was done.

I stared at him. Pippa stared at him. The servant stared at

him. The anvil stared at him. Or would have done, had it had eyes. In fact, I quickly picked up two pebbles and placed them on its surface such that they looked like eyes and then the anvil did stare at him.

'What?' said Harry, all hurt, misplaced innocence.

There now came a headmasterly shout of 'Over there! Get them!' and then massed footsteps were racing towards us.

'Right,' said Pippa. 'I am going to weep now and, just to avoid any confusion, I am informing you in advance that it will be very much of the forlorn and despairing nature. Wah-blee—'

The servant cut her off. 'No! We must never give up! Never surrender!' She lifted her head and sniffed. 'Is that— Can I smell pepper?' She instantly sneezed in affirmative answer to herself. 'Of course, the pepper-mine neighbours the salt-mine!' She approached a nearby wall and touched it. 'There is a crack. Pepper is getting through. We must smash this wall down and let the pepper mix with the salt!'

'Why?'

'Just do it!'

She grabbed a piece of rock and started smashing it against the wall. The rest of us joined in, hitting the wall, tugging at it with our hands, digging as if our lives depended upon it, which they did. Finally, the wall gave way and great gusts of pepper swept into the mine, mingling with the salt and forming a blizzard of seasoning.

A lot of sneezing now started, from us, the headmaster and his approaching horde.

'We need a spark to ignite the mixture!' shouted the servant, between her own sneezes.

'Why?' I asked, baffled.

Back then, neither I nor science knew of the tremendous explosive potential of combined salt and pepper. True, most people knew of someone who had inexplicably exploded while eating soup or been found spontaneously combusted over a plate of chops, but in our ignorance we attributed such deaths to the cook using deliciously flammable ether in the consommé or to random acts of a pyromaniac God, while continuing to cause explosion after explosion by putting salt and pepper in the same shaker; only recently have we separated them on the dinner table, saving thousands of lives a year.[4] Yet somehow this servant knew what she was doing.

'We must strike a rock on something to get a spark! But what?'

'I know!' Harry cried excitedly. 'Pip's marrow!'[5]

He raised a rock and drove it hard into the marrow I was still carrying.

There was no spark.

Though there was quite a lot of splattered marrow.

'Oh, well, didn't work, we're probably going to die.' As he calmly wiped splatted marrow from his face, Harry

---

[4] This was because many people mistakenly used saltpetre instead of domestic salt. Saltpetre, or potassium nitrate, is the oxidizing element of gunpowder, and therefore obviously explodes.

[5] Perhaps the author thought the marrow was a fruit and that is what he is referring to in the chapter heading. But it's not, is it? It's a large courgette or a small hugecumber and therefore I think actually a squash.

seemed resigned to his fate, glad even. 'At least I won't have to haul this anvil around any more.'

'That's it!' I shouted, for surely I had just had the idea that would save both the day and us. 'Pippa's anvil!'

'Of course!' The servant raised a rock into the air above the anvil, and struck it a mighty, spark-summoning blow.

Nothing.

She struck it again.

Still nothing.

She struck it a third time, and that joyous phrase 'third time lucky' leaped into my mind, though only to think how wrong it was because there was still nothing.

She struck it a fourth time, and this time there was a spark.

The rest was silence.

Apart from the massive explosion, obviously.[6]

---

[6] I have just discovered that the courgette is technically a fruit and that therefore so is the marrow. So I was wrong. Apparently. But I'm not happy about it. Stupid biology and its silly Linnaean classification.

CHAPTER THE THIRTEENTH

Though an unlucky number, not an unlucky chapter

The first explosion, that of salt and pepper, was great indeed, a concussive blow of detonated seasoning, but it was what it in turn ignited that saved us. For the headmaster had been carrying Harry's deadly birthday presents, namely a grenade, some unstable nitroglycerine and a dynamite cake, and the salt and peppery blast swept these volatile substances into its ka-boomy embrace as if they were old friends met on the way to a particularly loud and destructive party, joining forces and sweeping through the mine in a gigantic storm of violent combustive relief.

Tucked behind our rock and far from the gift explosions, it seemed as if we had survived. Certainly, if I had not survived and was now dead, I was most surprised to discover that Heaven looked a lot like a salt-mine that has just been exploded.

The servant was the first to recover her boom-addled wits, clearing the rubble from us and standing. 'Is everyone all right? Pip?'

'I think so.' I felt my body for injuries and found none, though my rabbit disguise was now badly ripped.

'Pippa?'

'I am well, thank you.' Though my sister's disguise was also torn, her face etched with grime and her hair a tangled mess of stony debris, to me she had never looked more serene or beautiful, apart from maybe six or seven hundred times. 'Though I do not see my anvil.' She began searching for the beloved paternal memento among the rubble.

'And, Harry Biscuit, are you all right?'

There now came a scream of pure Harry horror.

'Aaarrggh!!! My arm! My arm's come off!'

At this I could not help but make a medical observation. 'Harry, you're still disguised as Nelson.'

Relief filled his face. 'Of course! Here it is, tucked into my jacket. Phew.' Though the relief in his face was quickly chased away by a renewed panic. 'Aaargh!!! My eye! I've lost an eye!'

'Harry, you're dressed as Nelson.'

Relief found its courage and in turn chased panic away.

'Yes, of course, you're right, here it is, under this eye-patch. Phew.' Panic suddenly returned and started a brief wrestle with relief. 'Did I have a third leg? No . . . don't think I did. I'm fine, everyone! Fine!'

Around us there was only devastation, apart from the odd bit that was simply destruction. The mine had been utterly destroyed, and it seemed we were the only survivors. But then we heard a voice, a familiar and hated one.

'What have you done to my school? You shall be beaten, all of you! Now bend over!'

Somehow the headmaster had survived and was advancing on us, cane held high, his face pocked with nicks and cuts, seemingly as indestructible as a terrifying mechanical man sent from the future with a name perhaps something like 'the Killerator', though of course such an idea is preposterous.[1]

As he neared, however, I heard a strange whistling sound, as of a large object plunging to earth from a vast height. Indeed, we all heard it, as one by one we turned our heads skywards to where the noise was coming from.

'Ah, there it is,' said Pippa. 'My beloved anvil.'

The whistling grew louder, the anvil grew closer and its trajectory became obvious: it was descending directly towards Mr Hardthrasher.

'Ah,' he began. 'Oh, boll—' he finished, in more ways than one. I will never know what word he was about to utter, possibly 'bollards' or 'boll weevil', for before he could fully syllable-ize the anvil landed, and not in a soft way, like a dove descending upon a branch or a bee alighting on a nectary flower, but in a gory, unpleasant way, like a dove landing in a threshing machine or a bee alighting on an automatic bee-burster,[2] as it struck his head with a loud, splatty crump, killing him stone, or rather anvil, dead.

'Papa's anvil helped us!' Pippa danced a jig of smug delight. 'I knew it was worth bringing.'

I nearly pointed out that without the anvil slowing us we might have got away quickly enough to need neither

---

[1] Oddly, even writing over a hundred years ago, the author seems to have referenced popular 1980s film *Driving Miss Daisy*.

[2] Bee-bursters were in common use by nineteenth-century apiarists to punish lazy bees.

explosion nor head removal but did not for, delicate rose though she was, my sister also possessed a fierce streak and a fine right hook. Besides, this was no time for recrimination for we had survived and, above us, could see the clear blue morning sky of freedom.

As we climbed from the rubble and out on to the surrounding moors, we saw that St Bastard's and St Bitch's had also been destroyed. By some miracle, no pupils or nuns had perished and now they ambled around, stunned by their freedom, many of them feasting on somewhat heavily seasoned grouse that had died deliciously in the explosion. My escape had also proved their escape, and I felt a warmth inside me, as if I had just eaten a freshly baked scone of satisfaction.

'Well, now that's all over, I can remove these garments.' The servant stood and began to disrobe, amid our desperate pleas for her not to.

'No!' 'Stop!' 'I don't want to see what's underneath!' were all things we said, but she paid us no heed, instead peeling off layer after layer like a rotten onion, until she stood clad in a woollen and leather outfit of jerkin, trousers and boots, which made her look not scrofulous, disease-bearing and old, but dashing, clean and young.

Now she attended to her face, removing warts, unscrewing a false nose, which I hoped had a real nose underneath or I was likely to feel a bit sick, taking pieces of padding from her cheeks, discarding a wig and then washing off the remaining grime and dirt in a nearby stream.

Finally she stood before us: young, beautiful and oh-so-bold; and also oh-so-familiar, her face being so known to

Pippa and me that we could not help but exclaim, 'Mother! Can it be?'

'No. Not Mother,' this once hideous woman responded. 'Just a friend. Or should I say an aunt? Aunt Lily, to be precise.'

'But . . . we have no Aunt Lily.'

'Perhaps she's my aunt Lily,' suggested Harry.

'You have an aunt Lily?' That might explain things.

'No,' he replied, moving an explanation no further into sight.

'I am your mother's twin sister, Lily. I have hidden my existence for a long while, but in time of family need I have returned.'

And suddenly I understood why her voice had sounded so familiar to me: beneath the roving accent it had been very nearly that of my mother. 'Why have you kept your existence secret?'

'Partly because of my work for the British Empire Secret Service.[3] But mostly because I can't stand family functions. Oh, the needling gossip, the drunken fights, the inevitably disappointing buffets,' she was into her stride now like a grumpy horse, 'the bickering, the tedious grudges – and don't get me started on Cousin Frank!' We didn't, but somehow she managed to start herself on the subject. 'That man does not know the concept of personal space, especially if you're a woman. And does he even own a toothbrush?'

---

[3] Founded by Sir Francis Walsingham during the reign of Elizabeth I, he named it so that its initials would form the Queen's nickname – BESS. What a creep.

She continued thusly for quite some time until I felt I had to interrupt, both because her rant was becoming slightly embarrassing and because we had to save my mother from marrying Mr Benevolent that very afternoon.

'New-found Aunt Lily,' I interrupted gently.

'And then there's Great-aunt Maud. One hesitates to use the word "bigot" but what that woman did to lovely Mr Patel—'

'Aunt Lily!' I interrupted ungently, stopping her mid-whinge. 'While your family grievances might be fascinating – though actually they are not – we must rescue our mother before our guardian, Mr Benevolent, takes her away and marries her!'

'A wedding? That's exactly the sort of occasion I'm on about. So no thanks.'

'But this is no ordinary wedding – it is an evil wedding!' I protested.

'Oh, I don't mind those so much. And matrimonial union to Benevolent could be nothing but evil.' She looked wistfully into the sky.

'You know him?'

'Vaguely . . .' There was an absent quality to her voice, but that absence itself quickly became absent and presence returned. 'Right, better go and rescue my sister. But I'm warning you, if Cousin Frank turns up I'm out of there.'

'Well, I love a wedding!' said Harry. 'So I am definitely coming.'

'Do you not wish to return to your own home and family, Harry?'

'Oh, I should like that very much. But there is no home to return to. No family. So . . . may I come to the evil wedding, please?'

He looked at me with the pleading eyes of a greedy spaniel and I could not help but yield. Besides, what use is a best friend if not for aiding you in saving your mother from a malign marriage? 'Harry, you may join us.'

'Harrumble!' he said incomprehensibly.

'Harrumble?'

'A new word I have just invented to be used instead of words such as "hurrah" or "hooray" or "hazoo", but not instead of words such as "cauliflower" or "mattress".'

'Right. Good word, Harry.'

'Thank you, Pip Bin.' And now he turned to Pippa. 'And if you're going to a wedding, you're going to need a hat, Miss Bin.' Blushing, he handed her a hat he had woven from moorland grass and wildflowers.

'Why, thank you, Harry Biscuit.' She placed the hat upon her head. It immediately fell apart, cascading bad-hattily around her face and shoulders, and I'm pretty sure I saw some sheep droppings in there, but the thought it was that counted and counted it had been indeed.

'Now, children, we must hurry to Bin Manor to rescue your mother before Benevolent can get her to a church.'

'But Mama is in an asylum. Because of her mad mentalness.'

'No, for though still fully bonkersed up, she is now back home.'

Home! Oh, we were to go home at last, even if in miserable, mad-mothered, malevolently marital circumstances.

'It's a long journey, so I have rounded up these wild moorland ponies for us.' She had indeed procured four strong, lithe-looking beasts, and now she turned and slapped them hard on their equine rumps. 'Ya! Ya! Go on, giddy up!'

As the horses thundered away, I couldn't help feeling that we should have got on them first.

'Don't worry, Pip. While you were chatting, I attached four strong ropes from the horses to your ankles. Give it a few seconds and—'

Whoosh! The ropes at our feet uncoiled and suddenly we were flying through the air, then bumping quite painfully across the ground. As the horses dragged us along, Pippa, Harry and I looked at each other, bits of grass and mud in our hair, teeth and eyes, and we smiled: we had escaped the school, freed our schoolmates, Pippa and I had gained an aunt and were off to save our mother, and though the road ahead would be dangerous – not to mention one we would be dragged along by wild horses – we had youthful hope on our side once more.

PART THE THREETH

CHAPTER THE FOURTEENTH

Of sundry sullied returns and re-meetings

The journey was long, muddy and awkward, like a dinner party in a field with shy people you don't really know that well, yet to me it seemed like only a matter of minutes before we arrived at Bin Manor.

Home!

How often had I dreamed of returning here during those grim nights at school? Lots often. That's how often. And now as the horses dragged us to a painful halt at the end of the familiar sweeping driveway that led up to the most loving assemblage of bricks I had known, I was at long last returned. I looked happily up the drive towards the familial abode, however, and was instantly startled, shocked and upset. For it was no longer the home I knew and loved: it was changed, other, different, wrong, and dear Pippa quickly realized the same realization.

'Ah, home!' she said, thus far her thoughts running the same as had mine. 'At night in the nunnery I often dreamed of returning here!' With substitution of school for nunnery, still our thoughts were matched. 'And often I dreamed of strong men in tight breeches lifting me bodily on to a heaving stallion' – here, I admit, our thoughts diverged somewhat – 'then clasping me tightly to— But hold! Home's all different!' Now our thoughts re-entwined as she saw what I had seen.

Where once the great sandstone manor had shone with happiness and gleamed with rich joy, now it glowered with misery and gloomed with woe. There were bars over the windows, and not jolly, drinks-dispensing ones but the harsh keep-people-in-y kind; a cruelly spiked fence surrounded the garden; and on the lawn where once we had joyfully shuffle-hooped, bashy-batted and spong-ed, now wild-haired and rolling-eyed people shuffled slowly around, dribbling and emitting strange sounds such as 'blurrggh', 'maaaah' and 'wib'.

'Sadly, the place has been turned into an asylum,' sighed Aunt Lily.

That at least explained the dribbling lawn-ruiners. Though actually, with hindsight, the grass probably thrived under such constant drooly watering.

'Oh, brilliant,' sarcasmized Pippa. 'Our home is full of mentalists!'

Dear reader, please forgive my sister her insulting language: it was simply the times we inhabited. In these more enlightened late Victorian days, we would never use such a demeaning word for those afflicted with mind-illness or soul-problems, preferring more sensitive, scientific terms such as 'lunatic', 'insanonaut' or 'derangeatron'; but back then we called a nutter a nutter and knew them as mentalists, whack-jobs, lady-minds, soft-heads and der-brains.

And, as Pippa had said, our home was full of them.

'How has this happened?'

'Your mother fought hard against being removed to an institution until eventually Mr Benevolent decided that if the loon wouldn't go to the asylum then the asylum must go to the loon. Hence this.'

Pippa and I had little time to digest this piece of fact-food, because just then there was the trotty-horsed sound of a fast-approaching carriage.

'Quick, we must hide! Into the ditch!'

Aunt Lily bundled us into the shallow no-no[1] that ran round the edge of the garden. From there we peeked out as the carriage pulled up outside the house, the coachman opened the door, and a familiar foot emerged. That familiar foot was attached to a lower leg I knew well, and which itself connected with a thigh I had seen many times before; the multiply-glimpsed thigh adjoined a hip I had some acquaintance with, that hip in turn abutting a torso I oddly didn't recognize at all. The neck, head and face atop the torso were, however, only too prominent in my memory, and I could not help but whisper the name of their owner: 'Mr Gently Benevolent . . .'

'Yes,' agreed Pippa. 'But why is he naked?'

Naked or not – and he eye-blushingly was – his arrival now was good news, for it meant he had not yet collected

---

[1] Where a ha-ha is a ditch to keep animals out of property, a no-no is designed to keep inferior classes of people out of posh people's gardens.

and married my mother. Despite setting off from the school a full twelve hours ahead of us, the time-sappingly meandering roads and lanes of rural England had clearly severely delayed his carriage, while we had travelled cross-country as the crow flies or, in our case, as the pony drags.[2]

The coachman handed Mr Benevolent some clothes, and, as he started to dress, a tall, angry-looking man approached him – and this man, too, seemed oddly familiar.

Even bizarrely familiar.

Indeed, impossibly familiar.

For his body, face, mannerisms and hairstyle were identical to those of the late Headmaster Hardthrasher – the same tremendous height, the same pointed nose, chisel-like in its cruelty, the same sadistic glint in his eyes. How could this be? Was I dreaming? Was it supernatural intervention? Surely the Devil himself had reanimated the headmasterly corpse, re-headed him and now placed him here to torment me from beyond the grave – it was the only conceivable explanation.

'Ah, Dr Hardthrasher,' Mr Benevolent greeted him. 'I bring news. Your twin brother Jeremiah is dead.'

Oh, a twin brother. Yes, that was a much more likely explanation.

'How did he die?'

'There was an attempted escape from the school and an explosion in the salt- and pepper-mines. He died like a steak

---

[2] Rural roads followed old, traditional tracks and were notoriously indirect. One lane in Dorset linking the two villages of Here-be-Here and There-be-There was nearly forty-seven miles long, despite the villages being only five hundred yards apart geographically.

in a bad restaurant: over-seasoned and cooked to a crisp.'
He paused briefly, then added, 'Oh, and with an anvil for a
head.'

'Ah, Steak d'Anvil, my favourite.'[3]

This Dr Hardthrasher seemed barely bothered by the
mortal fraternal news, and his next words explained why.

'I can't say I'm surprised. He was always weak, Jeremiah.
Weaker than a coward's handshake, with a milksop's heart
and a cream-twit's brain. No man at all. Whereas I, Dr
Ratched Hardthrasher, am a man's man.' He stopped and
wrinkled his brow in thought for a second. 'No, I am selling
myself short. I am a man's man's man.'

Now Mr Benevolent interjected: 'Personally, I've always
thought of you as a man's man's man's man. You're the most
manny man I've ever met.'

'Don't be such a sycophant, Benevolent.' Even my nasty
guardian flinched at this large, cruel man's verbal swipe.
'Now, why are you here?'

'I have come to collect Agnes Bin to take her away to be
married.'

At this, I could barely restrain myself from leaping out of
the ditch and yelling, 'Mother!' so I did not restrain myself
and did just that.

'Mother!' I shouted, before strong hands grabbed me
and hauled me back into the no-no, where I sat in
embarrassed, nervous silence, acutely aware of having just
behaved in a distinctly Harryish manner.

---

[3] In hard economic times many blacksmiths doubled as restaurateurs, and would
forge steaks from bits of highly heated cow, bashing them into shape and
simultaneously tenderizing them on an anvil.

Had I got away with it? Or had either of the men seen me? For a few seconds I thought I had escaped their notice, but then: 'Did you just see a giant rabbit?' Mr Benevolent asked. Thanks to the remnants of my school-escaping disguise, at least he thought I was a rabbit and not a boy.

'I did not,' said Dr Hardthrasher. 'Perhaps you imagined it. You may have caught a little dose of madness by being so close to the fruit-loops here.'[4]

'Maybe. But it said, "Mother". I heard it.'

'As your personal mind-straightener,[5] I know of your obsession with your mother and what she did to you. It is quite natural that any hallucination would say, "Mother".'

Mr Benevolent looked sceptically at the doctor, but then his face relaxed into acceptance of the frankly dubious-sounding explanation. 'You are wise as well as strong, Doctor. Like a weightlifting owl.' Reliefy phew, I thought. 'Perhaps to avoid further contagion it is best I take Agnes Bin and leave quickly.'

Alas, Pippa had clearly not learned from my own leapy-outy, shouty-mothery mistake because she now leaped from the ditch and yelled, 'Mother!' in a similar fashion to me, though in a higher voice and with less adolescent soon-to-be-man hair. Immediately and disastrously, Harry, too, leaped to his feet in sympathy and started yelling, 'Mother! Not my mother! Her mother!' while pointing at Pippa.

---

[4] The germ theory of madness was widely held until the mid-twentieth century, doctors believing it was passed on by the insanefluenza virus.

[5] Nineteenth-century term for psychiatrist. Also used were brain-bender, thought-masseur and de-mentalizer.

Aunt Lily and I quickly hauled them down, but the damage was done.

'And now I can see a grandfather clock, and the late Admiral Nelson pointing at it!' Mr Benevolent said, a tiny quiver of fear in his voice.

'Such an authority figure pointing at a clock is clearly a manifestation of your desire to hurry away.'

'Yes, of course. You are right, Doctor.'

Thank goodness for the disguises I had once derided! And Mr Benevolent's credulity in the face of a scary man with a medical qualification.

'I shall have her sent out. In the meantime, I must call the roll.' The doctor now headed towards the shambling lunatics and lined them up. 'When I call your name, answer nice and clearly.'

Though the protracted war against France was long over, there were still certain obsessions shared by the mad people of Britain, obsessions that now became obvious.

'Napoleon?' said the doctor.

'Here,' said one of the shambling dribblers.

'Napoleon?' repeated the doctor.

'Here,' answered another dribbling shambler.

'Napoleon?'

'Here.' And now another.

'Napoleon?'

'Here.' And another. Such unpatriotic lunacy these people showed, believing themselves to be a diminutive French dictator!

'Napoleon?'

'Here.'

The doctor stopped in his Napoleonic roll-call. 'If you were really Napoleon, would you not speak French?'

The derangeatron stared at him, caught out by the medical logic. But then: 'I meant . . . *ici*.'

The doctor, outmanoeuvred in the matter as if by the tiny military genius himself, sighed and continued with the next eighteen names, all of which were Napoleon, until he reached the end of his list with a satisfyingly different name. 'And Wellington.'

At last, a patriotic loon! This was a fine bit of madnessing, thinking he was Britain's greatest ever soldier. But his response did not sound brave, instead being tentative and tremulous.

'Um . . . here.'

I immediately realized the reason for such tentativeness as the Napoleons instantly all shouted, 'What? My nemesis? Here? Get him!'

Dozens of mad mock-Napoleons jumped on the wacky would-be Wellington, and a huge fight began. But then, amid the insanonaut carnage, silhouetted against the sky, I saw her: my mother.

She was calm, noble, beautiful.

And obviously still bonkers-omatic, as she talked madly to no one, arms waving crazily, a banana in each ear and what seemed to be a toast-rack on her head – she obviously still believed she was a tablecloth.

Pippa had seen her too, and now we held each other tightly, the sight of our poor, deranged mama making us both happy and simultaneously sad, a bittersweet feeling, like an emotional kumquat.

Two asylum orderlies carried her to Mr Benevolent's carriage, then threw her inside and slammed the door after her.

'And so to be married. Ha, ha, ha!' My naughty guardian now climbed up beside the driver, who cracked his whip hard, lurching the carriage into motion.

'We must stop him!' I shouted, and, springing from the ditch like a scalded greyhound that had sat on a thistle, I raced to the centre of the driveway and stood in the path of the accelerating carriage, causing the coachman to haul on the reins and drag it to a stone-scattering, hoof-skittering halt in front of me.

'Why have you stopped for an imaginary rabbit?' Mr Benevolent demanded of the driver.

'I am neither imaginary nor rabbit,' I said, stripping off my rabbity disguise to reveal that beneath it I was me.

'Pip Bin! Still alive! I thought you long dead by now.' Mr Benevolent's face was a mix of surprise and massive anger.

'No. I am not long dead. In fact, I am long alive.'

'That's not really a phrase.'

'Phrase or not, it is what I am. And I am here to reclaim my mother.' I put my hands on my hips, narrowed my eyes and pulled a heroic face.

It did not get the reaction I had hoped for.

I'd been hoping for at best a complete surrender, with Mr Benevolent handing my mother over and possibly even crying a bit, and at worst him looking a bit scared and agreeing to discuss the matter.

Instead he laughed.

'Ha, ha, ha!' he went. Then again: 'Ha, ha, ha!' And again: 'Ha, ha, ha!'

The mere repeated use of the letters *h* and *a* does not convey the Benevolent malevolence contained in the laughter; if only there were some way of recording his laugh and playing it through a device so that you, dear reader, might not imagine it but actually hear it – but, sadly, that is totally impossible and always will be.[6] Suffice to say it was nasty, bullying, superior laughter with an almost physical effect.

I felt my cheeks reddening with humiliation.

Still he laughed. My heroic face was starting to crumple into a miserable one. The laughter went on, and now my hands left my hips and swung awkwardly at my sides. He continued laughing, and though my eyes remained narrowed, it was now less with manly determination and more with trying not to cry.

Finally he finished, his cruel mockery having stripped me of all vestiges of any manliness I had thought to own.

'Reclaim your mother? I don't think so. And as for being "long alive". . .' here he paused for one dismissive 'ha' that made me feel more cowed than a browbeaten toddler or a badly teased heifer '. . . I don't think that's a state you'll remain in for long.'

He now seized the reins and whip from the coachman, snapped one and cracked the other, and the horses charged straight at me. There was no time to move before their equine bulk met my boyish slightness, and as I fell to the ground all was suddenly thundering hoofs and the knowledge of imminent, horse-footed, carriage-wheeled death.

---

[6] Sir Philip was wrong: six months after he wrote those words, the first wireless laughtergraph system was invented.

CHAPTER THE FIFTEENTH

*Involving an exciting but short chase and
then the start of a longer one*

Oh, glorious hoof ballet! Oh, wondrous horsy dance! Oh,
majestic equine prestipeditation that let me survive! For,
despite Mr Benevolent's murderous intent, the gracious
muse Terpsichore[1] didst surely inspire the horses to daintily
trot past and round my frail human body, sparing me from
injury or death.

In a matter of seconds the carriage had passed over me
and I was still alive. I was also filled with an intoxicating mix
of fury and injustice, as if I had just downed a glass of angry,
legally qualified gin, and I leaped to my feet in pursuit of Mr
Benevolent.

'No, Pip!' It was Aunt Lily, reaching to try to stop me.
'You cannot catch a coach and horses at full gallop!'

'Watch me,' I replied, as I sprang sprintily forward.

---

[1] Greek muse of dance. Other muses included Thalia, muse of comedy,
Sentimentalia, muse of greetings-card writers, Morethanmyjobsworthia, muse of
security guards and petty bureaucrats, and Graham, muse of sensible names.

My legs were as strong as mighty oaks but much more flexible; my lungs were like huge bellows; my will was as of tempered steel. My feet skimmed the ground as lightly as one of those funny beetles that can walk on water,[2] my velocity was so great that the countryside around me blurred like a rained-on watercolour painting and I was gaining on them. I could do this: I could catch them and save my mother. I knew I could!

And then I ran into a tree.

As the carriage rounded a bend my speed was too great to be able to turn in time and I skidded off into a nearby copse, striking a tree at full tilt.

Luckily, it was a young sapling, which bent springily to absorb my energy, thereby significantly lessening the impact.

Unluckily, it then rebounded to twang me straight into a fully grown oak, which had no such energy-absorbing springiness.

Ow.

Really, really ow.

Sweary, cursing ow.

And not only physical ow but also mental ow because I saw the carriage pulling away: I had not saved my mother.

'Oh, bad luck, Pip Bin,' said the ever-encouraging Harry. 'I reckon you would have caught them if it hadn't been for that tree.'

'Come on, we can still prevent the marriage!' Even tree-bruised and sapling-battered, I was not to be stopped.

'Pursuit of your mother must wait.' This unwelcome

---

[2] He means either a water boatman, skim-daddy or windsurf louse.

delaying interjection came from Aunt Lily. 'We have to free the asylum inmates first.'

'But they are just dribbling crazyators!' With the dodgy moral clarity of youth I considered their mad lives worth far less than my mother's.

'Nevertheless, would you leave them in the care of that man?'

She pointed back towards the house where Dr Hardthrasher was lining the loons up for treatment; we could hear his prescriptions from where we stood.

'Right, I've got a few theories I want to try out.' He made a Napoleonic patient kneel in front of him, then picked up a cricket bat. 'Let's see if I can't beat the madness out of you.' He proceeded to play a series of violent cricket shots using the patient's head as a ball. To give the doctor credit, his technique was excellent – head still, good foot movement, nice high elbow – but the results were awful: severe external damage to a head that was already damaged within.

'Any good?' asked the doctor, of the now unconscious patient. 'Hard to tell. Right, next theory: can I burn the madness out of you?' He wielded a can of fire-juice[3] and advanced on a group of three nutters, who had been tied together and surrounded with kindling.

At these sights, I had to agree with Aunt Lily, for this was surely the nastiest man of medicine I had ever seen, a doctor who, when he spoke the Hippocratic oath, must have rewritten it to start with the words 'First do lots of harm.' I

---

[3] Nineteenth-century term for petrol.

wondered who was the madder: the madman or the medical maniac who treated the madman.

It was clearly the latter.

He was a right old psycho, though the patients were all still tap-tap-curly-wurly cuckoo.[4] Nevertheless, they did not deserve such a Hardthrashery fate and we moved to intervene as he finished sprinkling the inmates with the flammable liquid.

'Right, it's time for a loony inferno! Anyone got a light?'

'No,' said Aunt Lily, stepping forward. 'But I have got a sword.'

To prove her point she now drew it and placed the tip against the doctor's throat, but this did not frighten him in the least.

'Ooh, is it one of those new light sabres?[5] Spark it up and we'll have flambéed crackers-brains all round!'

'I don't think so. Step away from the kindling, Doctor.' He did so, emitting a small, disappointed whine, like a kitten that has just discovered it will grow up to be a cat and not a much nobler dog. 'Children, free the maddoes.'

Pippa, Harry and I did just that and the crackpots wandered away, muttering Napoleonically. '*Austerlitz, c'était bon. Waterloo, c'était merde.*'

'Now, what are we to do with you, Dr Hardthrasher?' Aunt Lily asked.

---

[4] Other phrases for madness at the time included bonk-bonk-twisty-wisty-chaffinch and knock-knock-bendy-wendy-parrot.

[5] With criminals often using 'Got a light?' to lure victims close for a mugging, a sword with a cigar lighter on the end was invented so you could offer a light from a safe distance. And with a sword in your hand.

'You could let me go. I haven't tested half of my theories yet. This new electricity thing seems ideal for treating madness. And I'd like to stick a straw too far up a patient's nose and see if I can suck the insanity out of their brain.'

'That's not going to happen, Doctor. What shall we do, children?'

We discussed the matter briefly and decided that justice would be best served by leaving him at the mercy of his patients. On announcing this to them, they became less dribbly and much more focused, rushing to gather tools and materials, then quickly constructing a rudimentary guillotine and outfitting the doctor in a rather convincing Louis XVI costume they had run up.

Then, like the mad people they were, they ignored the razor-sharp blade on the guillotine and instead simply pushed the whole thing over on top of Dr Hardthrasher, who managed to shout, 'You weak-minded, mock-Napoleonic, pseudo-imperial—' before being crushed and emitting one final 'splat'.

Oops.

We had hoped that they might show mercy, but they had not, and now I felt responsible in some large way for the deaths of both Hardthrasher brothers, a feeling of guilt that weighed heavily upon me.

Actually, I didn't feel that bad – they had been a right pair of gits – and we merrily readied ourselves to set off in pursuit once more, with Pippa and Harry removing their clocky, admirally disguises, and Aunt Lily asking, 'Where is the wedding to take place, Pip?'

'In a local church, I suppose.'

'Yes, but which one?'

'I don't know.'

'You don't know?'

Now I noticed that my companions were all staring at me. An icicle of fear suddenly grew in my brain, instantly starting to melt and send chill drips of panic down my spine.

'I sort of assumed you knew, Aunt Lily. You seem to know everything else.'

'That's the one thing I didn't know. For some reason I thought Benevolent had told you.'

'Well, not that I remember . . .'

'Well, that's it, then, game over,' said Aunt Lily. She stalked off and sat in the grass nearby, head in hands, and with a cold, horrible certainty, I knew now we could not prevent Mr Benevolent marrying my mother and that all was lost.

CHAPTER THE SIXTEENTH

In which memory and weather take a hand

All was frowns, sad shakes of the head and incipient tears, not least in myself. Had we come so far only to fail at the last?

But then my mind tingled with the tiny, tickly fingers of a memory trying to get my attention. 'Wait a minute! Back at school Mr Benevolent gave me an invitation to the wedding!'

This re-energized Aunt Lily, who leaped eagerly to her feet. 'Where is it?'

'He ripped it up.'

'Ah.' De-energized, she once more sank down into the grass.

'But before doing so, he showed it to me, albeit very briefly. Perhaps if I could remember what it said . . .' I furrowed my brow in memory-thought. Nothing. I tried harder, pursing my lips and crinkling my eyes. Still nothing. I looked skywards, closed one eye and wiggled the tips of my ears. And still no – but wait! Now a mind-image floated before me, the invitation mentally coalescing until it was whole and readable before the eyes of my memory.

'Well?'

'It is at the church of RSVP!' I said triumphantly. 'No, hang on, that's not right. I know! The church of St Reluctant!'

'Of course! The patron saint of unwanted weddings.' Aunt Lily quickly unfolded a map. 'This is an ecclesiastical map of Great Britain. Every church is marked.' She traced her finger across the paper and stopped. 'There! It is but a few miles from here.' Now, looking alternately at the map and the countryside around us, she rotated a half-circle round, then stopped and pointed. 'And what remarkable luck – you can see the steeple from here. That way!'

But we had barely taken a step in the direction she had indicated when a strange occurrence occurred, as occurrences are wont to do. Ahead of us lay a shrubbery that bordered the adjoining property, and as we stepped forward, so did one of the bushes therein.

'Aarggh!' yelped Harry. 'A walking rhododendron!'

'Nonsense,' I corrected him. 'It is not a rhododendron. It is an azalea.'

'No, it is neither,' said Aunt Lily. 'It is a person disguised as such.'

I looked closer within the foliage where I could discern human features: an eye here, a leg there, possibly a chin, two arms and a mouth – and luckily not in that order or it would have been a freakazoidal sight indeed.

It was Pippa who first joined the limbs and features into a correct and, indeed, recognizable order. 'Poppy? Dear sister Poppy, is that you?'

Now the ambulant shrub spoke, and with Poppy's voice. 'Pippa? Beloved sister Pippa? And dear brother Pip?'

I was a bit miffed that I was merely dear Pip while Pippa was beloved, but I set aside the sibling league table of affection and simply rushed to embrace her in a hug, as did Pippa.

'Oh, joy!' said Poppy. 'I have been living wild in the countryside these past weeks, disguised as a rhododendron.'

'Told you,' interjected Harry, smugly, so I flicked him with one of Poppy's twigs. 'Ow.'

'You said that you would never leave our home, and you have not!'

'Indeed not. All this time I hoped you would return and now you have and we three siblings are reunited! Poppy, Pippa and Pip!'

'Pippa, Poppy and Pip,' Pippa echoed.

'Pip, Pippa and Poppy,' I, too, chimed.

'And Parry Piscuit!' Harry tried to join in, failing miserably. We stared at him. 'Sorry, just feeling a bit left out.'

'Poppy, this is my new best friend, Harry Biscuit,' I introduced, hoping to make him feel more left in.

'How do you do, the second Miss Bin?' Harry said, blushing much less than when he had met Pippa – perhaps he was getting used to girls.

'And, Poppy, this is—'

'Aunt Lily, yes, I know,' said Poppy, astounding me, for if neither Pippa nor I had ever heard of Aunt Lily until recently, how had Poppy? 'Mama used to sing us songs about brave Aunt Lily fighting foreigners.'

Pippa and I looked at each other, bemused. I did not remember this and clearly neither did she. 'But—'

'You two never used to listen properly to poor Mama. But I did, which is why I am her favourite child.'

Oh, well, this was fine news! Apparently Poppy was Mama's favourite child. After the recent 'beloved' and 'dear' sibling incident, it turned out I was now way down the filial affection league as well. But I clamped down on my jealous feelings, for rescuing Mama was the priority, not laying the highest claim to her affection. Though secretly I thought that if we did rescue her and I could somehow claim all the credit for it, I might yet make myself top child.

'Anyway, it's really great to meet you at last, Aunt Lily. Your adventures sound amazing! I wish my life was that exciting.'

Aunt Lily surveyed her leafy niece, then pronounced, 'That is a fine rhododendron disguise. Your skills at blendy-in-ness do you credit.[1] Skills you might perhaps one day use in the Secret Service.'

'Ooh, that sounds fun. I'd like that,' Poppy said.

'We'll see. But, first, let us rescue your mother!'

As if to underscore the seriousness of our mission, a peal of thunder now tolled across the sky, like the angry flatulence of a weather-god; perhaps today Zeus had eaten of the baked beans of Fate.

Aunt Lily pointed at the dark clouds that had gathered above us like a flock of rain-bearing black sheep. 'If it rains, it will aid us, for it will turn the rough country roads to mud and slow Benevolent's carriage.'

'Then let it rain!' I imprecated the skies, and they answered with a pit-pat of pluvial drops.

'Harrumble!' shouted Harry. 'Pip Bin can control the

---

[1] The word 'camouflage' wasn't invented until 1922 by the Russian Professor Hidin Maskirovska.

weather! Can you make it snow next, please? I love snow.'

'No, Harry. For it was not divine power, it was merely the chance confluence of my words with the enhanced statistical likelihood of precipitation in the presence of heavy black clouds,' I explained.

'That's near enough for me, Pip Bin, O rain-master.'

I shook my head in fond despair at my enthusiastic but brain-limited friend, and we re-commenced our maternal pursuit.

We had been going barely a minute when Harry asked, 'Are we there yet?'

'No, Harry,' we replied in unison.

'Oh.' He sighed in return. 'Then could someone else please carry the anvil for a while? It's really hurting my arms. I think it may have stretched them a bit as well.'

He had been carrying Pippa's anvil for a long time, and indeed his hands did now seem to swing ape-like around his knees.

'Can't we just leave it?' Aunt Lily and I asked simultaneously.

'No,' insisted Pippa. 'It has proved both useful and lucky so far. Pip, why don't you carry it?'

'But . . .'

'Oh, Pip, yes, you must carry Papa's anvilly Pippa-gift!' Now Poppy was on Pippa's side there was no choice: if two sisters jointly asked a brother to do something he was legally bound to obey.[2]

---

[2] When Edward VI inherited the throne after Henry VIII's death in 1547, his two older sisters (the future queens Mary and Elizabeth I) were so cross at being literally overruled that they passed the *Frater Faciendum* Act just to annoy him.

'Fine, I shall carry it.'

'Thanks!' Harry handed the anvil over and, with an elastic *sproing*, his arms sprang back to their normal length – though initially they twanged back a bit further so that for a brief moment his arms were ridiculously short and he looked like a small, plump dinosaur.

I immediately wished I had broken the law and said no: the anvil felt heavier than an elephant fed on lead-filled suet pudding. I plodded slowly forward, my feet squelching on the wet ground, for it was raining hard now, great splattery drops smacking into us, soaking and slowing, and the wind was picking up also, driving the liquid weather into us at speed.

As I write these words, towards the end of the glorious nineteenth century, we have tamed the climate with liberal burnings of coal, gas and liberals. But back then the weather was far more severe and eccentric. Everyone remembers the Thames used to freeze over in winter, but we forget that in summer the river Severn used regularly to boil. The people of Shrewsbury would stand on bridges and hurl tea, milk and sugar into the steamy, rushing waters, then hurry downstream to enjoy a cuppa straight from the river.

And the winds! Few people now know that Norfolk used to be right next to Somerset before a hurri-twister-phoon blew it all the way to East Anglia, explaining why Norfolk and Somerset accents sound so similar – it is not just actors being lazy.[3]

---

[3] Yes, it is.

Then there were the rains, such as the great storm which, thank God, flooded the valley between England and France, aquatically separating them for ever. And it seemed as if we were in the teeth of another such downpour, one so rain-filled that it was what we used to call an air-bath.

Rain lashed at us, like an angry sadist in an underwater lash factory. As I trudged on, my vision shrank to a few blurry feet, then several unfocused inches and ultimately a water-dimmed nothing.

'Is everyone all right?' I asked, into the rainy turmoil, and during the brief seconds my mouth was open so much rain entered that I felt briefly as if I was drowning. It caused me a momentary panic; but much worse was the panic I felt when I realized that there had been no response from my companions. I risked drowning again by yelling, 'Pippa? Poppy? Aunt Lily? Harry?'

Nothing.

I yelled again, but still nothing.

There was no sign of them. We had clearly become separated, and I was now alone – though what choice did I have other than to proceed?

Actually, I could easily have stopped, sought shelter, maybe given up entirely, abandoned my family and used the anvil to eke out a living as an itinerant blacksmith.

I chose not this last, however, instead trudging onwards, onwards and, where there was higher ground, upwards. The anvil was so heavy I was tempted to leave it, but dreaded Pippa and Poppy's wrath if I did so. I tried briefly to use it as a heavy iron hat to protect me against the rain, but that really didn't work so I simply carried it and got wet.

And I was wet indeed, so, so wet. The rain soaked me not just to the skin but to the bones and organs beneath, my gall-bladder getting so wet it got cross and became a galled-bladder, and I was just beginning to think that I could not possibly get any wetter when I realized that it was in fact not raining any more and that I had walked into a lake.

Fortunately it was not a deep lake, the water reaching only to my chest, and what was more, it offered sustenance to my now hungry self, for it teemed with fish, eels and, that most delicious of aquatic creatures, the underwater squirrel, an animal so tasty that in the past fifty years it has been eaten to extinction.[4] Alas for them, but hurrah for me, they were friendly little rodents, who quickly came to investigate my presence and, exploiting them mercilessly, I caught and ate three.

Yum.

My strength replenished, I waded onwards until I reached the far shore. I was now in an area of marshy grassland, flat, muddy and forlorn, but ahead of me I saw something that brought great cheer to my heart: a church spire. Was it St Reluctant's? Could I yet save my mother? Had Providence and an unanticipated shortcut across a lake brought me to the right place?

The spire was but a hundred yards off and I made haste towards it, albeit anvil-handicapped haste. A stone wall separated the churchyard from the marshes, but it was dilapidated and tumbly-downy, and I quickly scrambled up

---

[4] There were many more underwater versions of common land mammals before the twentieth century. Sadly for their continued existence, they were all absolutely delicious.

and over. And there amid the gravestones, wedding-rocks and baptism-boulders[5] was a sign indicating the name of the church: St Reluctant's.

I had made it!

And, better yet, there was no sign of a carriage or of any other human presence. I appeared to have beaten Mr Benevolent.

Victory might yet be mine!

I decided to check vocally the absence of presence before advancing to the church itself, and cried out, 'Hello! Is there anyone here?'

There was a short pause, and then came a reply: 'No!'

That was reassuring.

Although . . .

Hang on a minute . . .

Though the word 'no' indicated no one else was there, the mere fact of its utterance contradicted its own meaning. But before I could process the implications, a dread figure loomed up from between two gravestones, scarred and muddied, grim-faced and terrifying, and seized me in its terrible arms.

Oh, blimey.

---

[5] There was a proliferation of churchyard ornaments during the ever-commemorating nineteenth century. As well as those mentioned in the text, there were midnight-mass monoliths, harvest-festival pebbles and regular scatterings of Sunday-morning-service gravel. Eventually in 1903 Archbishop of Canterbury Erasmus Joyfree banned memorials for anything other than graves, hoping to teach people a miserable ecclesiastical lesson.

CHAPTER THE SEVENTEENTH

Of meetings of life-changing import

Aaarrggh, was my first thought; my second and third thoughts were of a similar ilk, as were my fourth, fifth and sixth. It was not until my seventh thought that I concocted a more rational mental response, and even that was 'I'm terrified.'

'Hold your noise,' hissed the dread figure, from its twisted, broken-toothed mouth, 'or I'll cut you from gizzard to guzzard.'[1]

This prospect did not seem a pleasant one so I held my noise, cupping one hand over my mouth to do so quite literally, whimpering scared sounds into it like the frightened child I was.

---

[1] 'Guzzard' was an alternative spelling of 'gizzard' so the threat is tautological. Unless it is a misprint for 'gazzard', a now disused word for the loose bit of skin on the elbow, though this would have required a level of skill with a blade more akin to that of a surgeon than an escaped criminal. Oh, hang on, just realized: the revelation that this is an escaped criminal hasn't happened yet. Oops, sorry, slight story-ruining, something I promised I wouldn't do. Don't worry, I'm certainly not going to ruin it any more by saying that this character goes on to— Ah, no, caught myself in time.

Satisfied by my silence, the figure now released me and stepped back, and I got my first unstartled look at him – for I now saw that it was a him. His face was fierce and covered with the nicks and scratches of a man who has fought nettles and briars and brambles, or is just not very good at shaving; he was shoeless, and limped awkwardly on hurty feet that were bruised and stone-bashed and flint-cut; his ankles were shackled by a leg-iron-anchored chain; and he was wearing a pristine white wedding dress.

This last, it must be said, surprised me.

'Release your noise and tell me your name, boy.'

I removed my hand from my mouth and whispered nervously, 'Pip, sir.'

'Whassat? Speak up, young cully.'

'Pip, sir,' I repeated, more strongly this time. 'Pip Bin.'

'How do, Pip Bin?' he now said, in a considerably friendlier tone than that in which all the gizzard-cutting threats had been delivered.

Emboldened by this tonal turn, I asked, 'Do you have a name, sir?'

'Aye. It's Havertwitch, Bakewell Havertwitch.'

At this I could not help my instinctive response: 'And do you, as your name might suggest, have a twitch?'

'No,' he said, a brief spasm running down the left-hand side of his face and giving the lie to his answer. 'But I do bake well. Eccles cake?'

From a muddy sack beside him he proffered a curranty treat. Not wanting to risk a gizzard cutting, I accepted it and took a great bite.

It was disgusting, thereby also giving the lie to the other

half of his name claim. Not that I mentioned that because I was still pretty scared, though I did make a mental note that his name actually should have been Bakesbadly Really-Does-Have-A-Twitch.

'Mmm, delicious,' I lied. Hoping to distract him and so be able to dispose of the repellent cake, I asked, 'Are you an escaped criminal, sir?' For surely a man in such a place and state could only be that.

'Escaped criminal? No! By heaven, no!' He seemed most offended. 'I'm an absconded wrongdoer, a fleeing malefactor, a running-away dodgy geezer or a broken-out incarcerated person of somewhat lax moral probity.' I looked at the synonymizing wastrel, and he seemed to give in. 'Yes, I am basically an escaped prisoner.'

'From the hulks, sir?' One of these vile prison ships was moored on the nearby estuary, indeed the largest one yet commissioned, a former navy frigate called HMS *Banner*, now painted bright green and known popularly as the Incredible Hulk.

'Aye. But I shouldn't have been there! I didn't do nothing wrong!'

This last phrase seemed to indicate he had done something wrong, though allowance for bad grammar could lend a more favourable meaning to his denial.

'What didn't you do wrong, sir?'

'They said I stole a loaf of bread. But I never!' He looked wistfully away, and I took the chance to flip the gruesome Eccles cake into a nearby patch of nettles. It struck one of the rabbits hopping there and killed it stone dead. 'I actually stole some flour, water, salt and yeast. But then the Bow

Street Runners got after me so I stuffed everything down my trousers and ran. Well, it wor a long chase and a hot day, and when they caught me, all that running and heat had mixed the stuff together and cooked it up into a trouser loaf . . .'

He trailed off sadly, and I thought perhaps he was not such a bad man as he had first appeared. Though he was still as bad a baker as he had first appeared, for the nasty taste of burned currants and over-larded pastry persisted in my mouth.

'And why do you wear a wedding dress, sir?' This incongruity had begged an answer since I had first seen it, and now it got one.

'I found it in the vestry of this 'ere church and I put it on because, first, it really suits me and, second, it's a good disguise. Who's going to stop a happy bride and haul her off to prison, eh? Now, if only I had some way of breaking these shackles.' He indicated the leg-irons round his ankles.

'I have an anvil, sir.' For I did. I pointed to where it had lain nearby since I had dropped it on first being surprised by him.

'That is mighty convenient.'

It was. With two mighty strikes of one of his rock-hard Eccles cakes, the chain and shackles were shattered and he was free.

'Thank 'ee, young cully.'

With that he was away, leaping over the crumbling churchyard wall and running off through the marshy surroundings, the train of his wedding dress trailing behind him. 'I'll not forget you!' he yelled back, as he ran. 'One day I shall repay your help and kindness, Mick Grin!'

'That's Pip Bin,' I corrected.

'Of course. Slip Tin, I shall remember that name!'

'No, Pip Bin,' I once more corrected.

'Got it, Drip Flim.'

'No, it's—' But it was too late: he was out of earshot and word-range, now just a speck of white on the horizon.

Then, behind me, I heard the snorts of panting horses and the crunch of carriage wheels approaching and, turning, I saw that Mr Benevolent had arrived, which meant that so had my mother-rescuing time of destiny.

CHAPTER THE EIGHTEENTH

Stop that wedding!

The carriage came to a halt and, peering out from behind a wedding-rock, I watched as the door opened and Mr Benevolent emerged and raged, 'Damnable storm! It must have taken us an hour to replace those drowned horses.'

The storm must also have turned the local roads to quagmires, for the carriage was clotted with mud even up to the sill of the door, and how glad I was of that meteorological event and its cunctatory effects!

Now my mother descended from the carriage, singing to herself:

> 'I'm a little tablecloth clean and neat,
> Aren't I pretty, aren't I sweet?
> I'm not a bath towel or a sheet,
> I go on the table and get covered with meat.'

Alas, poor Mother, still doolally and bonkers-chops!
'Come on, you mentalist, let's get you inside and into

your wedding dress.' Mr Benevolent dragged her towards the church door and then in, the driver stomping behind them, a mute slab of grumpy-looking man-muscle – not just a coachman but evidently henchman also.

I stepped out from behind the wedding-rock ready to follow them, but a shout stopped me.

'Pip Bin!'

Why, it was Harry, come to aid me! As he entered the churchyard I clasped him in a strong, male embrace with no hint of forbidden love or anything other than strong, non-beastly companionship. 'Are the others with you?'

'We are!' came a chorus of presence-stating from Pippa, Poppy and Aunt Lily, who now also arrived in the churchyard.

'The storm took us many miles from our path,' said Aunt Lily, 'but then fortunately we stumbled into a field of Gloucestershire racing sheep,[1] the fastest creatures on six legs.' She pointed to a patch of nearby grass where the woolly beasts now grazed at high speed, their sextuple legs a blur of ovine greed.

'Plus they trampled a highwayman on the way and I got this off him.' She pulled out a flintlock pistol, which looked handy indeed. 'Now, we need a plan.'

'Ooh, I've got an idea!' exclaimed Harry, instantly. My heart sank like a cement-filled coffin in thin water, familiar as I was with the awfulness of his plans. 'How about we chop down some trees, use the timber to form a rudimentary

---

[1] By the nineteenth century, selective breeding had created this tremendous meat-bearing animal. Sadly, their offspring were often born with eight legs, therefore resembling woolly spiders, and they quickly died out as people kept trapping them under giant glasses or simply squishing them.

trebuchet and then hurl heavy objects at the church until Mr Benevolent surrenders and we can all have cake?'

We all just stared at him. He stared back, a delighted grin on his face. I thought I might punch him again, but fortunately Aunt Lily intervened: 'Yes, great plan, Harry. Why don't you stay here and work on that while the rest of us just go in and stop the wedding?'

'Ooh, nice, two-pronged attack. I shall commence the trebuchet construction!' Harry marched purposefully off to work, and I heard him say to himself, 'Now, what exactly is a trebuchet?'

We left Harry to his ill-informed device building and headed towards the side door of the church, sneaking quickly and quietly inside. We slipped into a concealing pew, but not before glimpsing Mr Benevolent at the altar where he was talking to the vicar.

'Is everything ready, Reverend?'

'It is, Mr Benevolent.'

'Excellent. My plan is nearly complete. Nothing can stop me now. Probably.' He then let fly with one of his lacerating laughs. 'Ha, ha, ha!'

But something could stop him: us. For our small Pip, Pippa, Poppy and Aunt Lily-shaped army was now creeping forwards between the pews.

'What do you think about marrying me, Agnes?' My malicious guardian addressed my mother, who stood meekly but madly nearby.

'I think if you're going to put a hot dish on me you'll need a trivet or I'll scorch and won't do for best any more!' she madly replied.

'Oh, bless the linen-based insanity of the woman. Now to wed, perchance to scheme.'

We were nearly close enough to make our move but, alas, at that moment I knocked into a pile of prayer-books, which had been stacked into the ecclesiastically mandated shape of Canterbury Cathedral. They fell with a series of booky thuds, in turn disturbing a nest of church mice within, which instantly scurried off squeaking loudly – I'm pretty sure I heard them saying, 'We're so poor.' They startled me so much that I immediately sat down upon the keyboard of the church organ and, though my buttocks had by chance settled in such a manner as to play the pleasant first chords of the hymn 'He Who Would Valiant Be', it was nonetheless what I believe is known as 'a bit of a giveaway'.

Mr Benevolent turned instantly. 'Is somebody there?'

Curse his acute hearing!

I made an instant decision, stood and walked boldly towards him: if I gave myself up, perhaps it might distract him and allow the others to have more success on the thwarting front.

'Pip Bin? Good grief, boy, can't you take a hint and die?'

'No, Mr Benevolent. For I am your ward and I am here to tell you that I think you are not conducting your duties as guardian with the propriety you ought.' Out of the corner of my eye, I could see Aunt Lily creeping forward, gesturing to me to keep going. 'You're a bad guardian! I don't think you care at all what happens to me or to my sisters!'

'Oh, in that you're wrong, young Pip. I care very much what happens to you.' This surprised me: his behaviour thus far had seemed to indicate the exact opposite. 'Because I want to ensure that only very, very bad things happen to you.' Yes, that made more sense. 'But don't worry, those very, very bad things won't last long. Because, with a bit of luck, they'll kill you. Now, have you met my eponymous henchman, Mr Henchman?' From the shadows stepped the mutely muscled carriage-driver. 'He is a very strong, very obedient man.'

Mr Benevolent had not told false, for he now said, 'Seize him,' and burly arms strongly and obediently enveloped me like a meaty vice.

But it did not matter. For I had provided distraction enough, and Aunt Lily sprang up, pistol in hand. 'Step away from the bride-to-be, Benevolent!' She held the pistol in front of her, and snicked its action back ready to fire.

'Ooh, a pistol, scary.' Mr Benevolent merely smiled at this firearm threat.

'Oh, no ordinary pistol. This is the forty-four flintlock, the most powerful handgun in the world, and at this range it could blow your head clean off. I know what you're thinking: did I fire one shot, or was it only none? In all this excitement I lost count, so you've got to ask yourself one question: do I feel lucky? Well, do ya, punk?'

Aunt Lily's speech sent tingles down my spine, even if during it she had seemed weirdly to sort of turn a bit American.

'Actually, Lily, I feel incredibly lucky.'

With that, he lunged for the pistol. Aunt Lily immediately pulled the trigger, but there was no bullety response, and her weapon was then easily taken from her as Mr Benevolent had that most modern of disarming tools, a pair of pistol pliers.

'You lucky sod!' she said. 'I could've sworn I hadn't fired it.'

'Ah, but there was all that rain, wasn't there? Should have kept your powder dry, shouldn't you?[2] Henchman, kindly seize her as well.'

The burly bully changed his grip so that he held me with just one arm and now seized Aunt Lily with the other.

'Did you come to try to stop me marrying your sister, Lily? Was it because you were jealous?'

'I'd never be jealous of you, Benevolent.'

'Still aggrieved that I never turned up at the altar all those years ago?'

What? Aunt Lily had been due to marry Mr Benevolent? This was news.

'Not marrying you was the best thing that ever happened to me,' my aunt said.

'Really? Are there no tender feelings any more?' He actually sounded slightly hurt.

'None.'

Mr Benevolent approached her, trapped in the henchman's grasp. He leaned towards her, smiling sharkishly. 'Really really? No feelings at all?'

'Well . . . perhaps there are some feelings,' she said.

'I knew it! Because I am irresistible.' Now he leaned in closer, as if he was about to kiss her.

'Yes, Gently, yes . . .' Aunt Lily said and, seemingly encouraged by her words, Mr Benevolent moved in closer

---

[2] Before the invention of cased ammunition, damp gunpowder was the primary cause of weapons not firing. Hence the phrases 'keeping your powder dry' and 'Why won't you fire, you useless wet weapon?'

still, lips pursing in osculatory readiness. 'I have feelings of hate, loathing and then some more hate.' Then without warning she whipped her head forward, driving it hard into his evil but fragile nose. 'Oh dear, how unladylike of me.'

'You'll pay for that!' He clutched his now bloodied nose and hopped round the church like an angry frog.

'At a guinea a go I'd pay to do that all night.'

I had to face it: Aunt Lily was cool.

'Grrrraaarrrgh!!!' Mr Benevolent emitted a vituperative roar of rage, kicked out in furious frustration at a nearby pew, promptly hurt his foot and fell into a choleric pile of painful-toed ire. He panted hard for a few seconds, then suddenly leaped up, seemingly in control of his emotions once more. 'Right, let's get this wedding done.'

As he stomped towards my mother, I saw something unusual for a wedding. For in front of the altar stood a coffin.

'Why do you have a coffin at a wedding?' I enquired.

'That is your mother's going-away outfit.'

'But that means . . .' The implications of his statement were great and, in so many ways, grave.

'The reverend here has kindly agreed to conduct two services today: one wedding and one funeral, all for the same price.'

'Yes,' added the vicar. 'It's what I call a buy-one-get-one-free promotion.'

'And what an excellent idea it is too,' Mr Benevolent said.

'Thank you. In fact, I'm thinking of resigning from the Church and taking it into other areas.'

'Silence, Reverend Supermarket. We have a wedding to perform. And then a bridal burial.'

'Noooooooooo!!!!!!!!!!!' I shouted, for about eight, maybe nine seconds, like a character in some grotesque melodrama.

There was a long pause. Then: 'Yes.' This from Mr Benevolent. 'And you cannot stop it. Now, let us get this bride into her dress. Reverend?'

'I'll just fetch it.' The vicar went into the vestry, but quickly returned, his face pale, his voice shaking, as if his head was a talking blancmange. 'The dress, it is gone!'

Ha! Henchman-trapped though we were, we had triumphed, and I could not resist crowing, jackdawing and generally corvidae-ing about it.

'You lose, Mr Benevolent,' I triumphantalized loudly.

'Um, how so?' he asked.

'No woman may legally marry without a wedding dress!'

There was a brief silence as everyone turned to look at me: Mr Benevolent, the Reverend Supermarket, Aunt Lily – even Pippa and Poppy briefly popped their heads up from the pew where they were hiding.

'Yes, she can. There is no such law.'

'Oh. But I thought—'

Now everyone shook their heads sadly at me, and I might as well have had a sign above my head saying 'Fool', 'Dunce' or 'Twitiot'.

'Right. Bother. Then . . . you may have triumphed.'

'There is no "may" about it. Now, Reverend, matrimonialize us.'

'Of course.' The vicar picked up his prayer-book and marriage prodder[3] and began. 'Will you Mr Gently Lovely Kissy Kiss Benevolent' – I only realized at this instant quite how ironic his name was – 'take this woman—'

'Yes, I will,' interjected the evil bridegroom. 'Blah dee blah dee yes. Get on with it.'

'Very well. Will you, Agnes Pedal Bin, take this man—'

'Yup, she will.' Again Mr Benevolent interrupted.

'I must hear it from her or the marriage is not valid.'

At this Mr Benevolent sighed so deeply that I could smell his breath even from some yards away; it had a sickly, evil odour of off-milk and celery. The vicar tried again.

'Will you take this man—'

'Yes, I will,' came a sort of half-female voice, fortunately not from my poor deranged mother but from Mr Benevolent trying to pretend to be her, which he did unconvincingly.

'No, Benevolent, the bride must say it. Will you, Agnes? Will you take him?'

'Just say no, Mama!' I yelled.

'Come on, you mad witch, say it. Say "I will"! Say it!' Mr Benevolent seized and shook my mother as if he could free the phrase from her, like word-ketchup from a speech-bottle. 'Say it!'

I could see my mother breathe in, preparatory to exclaiming something. A lump of apprehension grew in my throat as I feared I was about to gain a most unwelcome stepfather. But—

---

[3] In these days, when there were still many arranged marriages, vicars carried a spiked staff to poke reluctant couples towards each other.

'I won't. I really won't . . . go in the cupboard with the tea towels. They are beneath me. For I am a tablecloth, the gentry of the linen cupboard.'

'There, she said it! Hooray for me, now let's kiss the bride then bury her.'

'No, she did not say it. In fact, she said the opposite. She said, "I won't." There is no wedding,' the vicar declared, to my relief. 'Besides, this woman is clearly too mad to marry.'

'Ha,' laughed Mr Benevolent, weakly. 'Surely being mad is a precondition for getting married.'

'You are forgetting the recent Maddus Maddiatus Act passed in Parliament.'[4]

'Oh, cursed Parliament! One day I shall destroy that pathetic institution and— Wait! Plan B has just leaped to mind.' Now Mr Benevolent rubbed his hands together excitedly and, for an evil person, distinctly stereotypically. 'I could wait until next year when Pippa Bin turns eighteen . . . but Pippa and Poppy between them have a combined age of thirty-three, so I could marry them both simultaneously. Would that be legal, Reverend?'

'There is no reason why not.'[5]

'Alas, un-dear Gently, you shall never find them. For they are hidden safely far from your grasp.' Aunt Lily smiled a small smile of triumph.

Oh, curse my adolescent desire to impress and correct!

---

[4] By the early nineteenth century there was so much inbreeding among the upper classes that most of them were insane. This Act of Parliament was intended to prevent more inbreeding among already mad people and thereby restore the aristocracy to sanity. Did it work? You tell me.

[5] There are many reasons why not.

For I could not help but blurt, 'No they aren't. They are back there, hidden in that pew.'

'Oh, great, well done, Pip, good work.'

'Thanks very . . . Oh, sarcasm. Whoops.'

Now Pippa and Poppy rose from their pewish hiding place. 'Yeah, great, thanks a lot, Pip.'

'Henchman!'

The huge man now lugged Aunt Lily and me across to Pippa and Poppy and seized them too, pausing only to put on a pair of arm-extensions so that he could hold all four of us at once.

'Bring them here and we shall do it now,' said Mr Benevolent.

This was terrible. This awful man was about to marry both of my sisters, making him not just my guardian but also my brother-in-law squared, for marriages are a geometric mathematical function, not an arithmetical one.

And it was my fault.

All my fault.

Well, not all.

Because, frankly, if other people had—

No, no blame shifting, it was basically my fault.

Henchman the henchman now dragged my sisters to the altar, with Aunt Lily and me still clutched in his other arm, and the vicar began.

'Will you, Gen—'

'Yes, I will. Get on with it,' snapped my evil guardian and would-be sinister relative by marriage.

'And will you, Pippa and Poppy . . . I'm sorry, I don't know your middle names.'

'Wheelie,' said Pippa.

'Recycling,' said Poppy.

'Thank you. Will you, Pippa Wheelie and Poppy Recycling Bin, take this man to be your husband?'

'Think carefully, my lovelies,' said Mr Benevolent, producing a wicked-looking knife, which he held at my mother's throat. 'Wrong answer and it's bye-bye, Mama.'

'Ooh,' said my mother, eyeing the knife. 'That's tarnished. I won't have it on me, I won't!'

Who could stop this evil? Who could prevent the double wedding? There was only Harry left uncaptured, and the chances of him doing anything helpful seemed less than good. Pippa and Poppy looked at each other, then at me and Aunt Lily. What could they do? Apart from say 'yes'. Their mouths opened, and a strange whistling sound seemed to emerge.

Only it wasn't from them.

Though it was a familiar whistling sound, being one I had heard before – for that is what familiar means – a heavy, cast-iron whistling sound, indeed an anvilly whistling sound.

Then the stained-glass window above the altar, which depicted a Union-Jack-clad Jesus refusing to help a dying French sailor, shattered into a thousand patriotically Christian fragments and Pippa's anvil soared in, gloriously true in its trajectory as it headed straight for Henchman the henchman. He immediately released us and flung his hands up to catch the onrushing massy ingot, and, to give him credit, he did actually catch it, a fine take showing no little skill; but, regrettably for him, its tremendous momentum drove him across the church and into a wall, where he came to rest with a loud, injury-indicating thud, an impact lessened only slightly by the fact that, on his anvil-driven path, he had swept along with him the vicar, who now rested 'twixt henchman and wall doing a very good impression of the world's first ever two-dimensional man, so flat had he been squashed.

Good Lord. It seemed Harry's plan had worked, and now not only were we free, but Pippa and Poppy would remain unmarried, for a vicarless wedding was like an Italian man who does not wink at pretty girls, that is to say impossible.

'No!' screamed Mr Benevolent, his face a crazed, rageful rictus. 'Have you any idea how hard it is to find a henchman with the right combination of strength, cruelty and mute obedience?'

I did not have any idea, and did not care, for with my guardian distracted by his fury, I seized my mother and ran for the door.

'Careful, you'll crease me, and then what will the master think when he comes to dine?'

Having a mother who thinks she is a tablecloth may be a burden and a curse, but at least it means she is happy to be slung over your shoulder and carried like a piece of dirty linen.

'Ooh, where are we going? Is it washing time? Easy on the starch!'

I carried mad Mama outside; close on my heels were Aunt Lily, Poppy and Pippa. All we had to do now was get really, truly, properly away and life could yet be mended.

CHAPTER THE NINETEENTH,

N-N-N-N-NINETEENTH[1]

In which there is fleeing and flight

Outside we were greeted by a grinning Harry. 'Hello! Did my anvil-firing help?'

'It did, Harry, but now we must escape.'

'I gave up on the whole trebuchet thing when I realized I didn't actually know what one was, so I just twanged it in using a couple of saplings with my pants strung between them.'

He pointed at an arboreal, stretched-underwear sight I wish I had not seen but, grotesque though it was, it had saved us – at least for the moment.

'We can escape in Benevolent's carriage,' yelled Aunt Lily, unnecessarily as we were all close enough together to hear even a whisper, but then perhaps she was excited.

Alas, no escape would come from that carriagey quarter, for so tired and hungry were the two horses harnessed to it

---

[1] The author did for a time suffer from an affliction known as Writer's Stutter.

that they had each eaten the other's leg, and now slept wonkily against each other.

'Then we must cross the river!' Aunt Lily was still shouting and, being closest to her, my ears were starting to hurt. But at least she shouted with sensible intention, for there was indeed a river running behind the church, swollen and water-plump following the recent storm.

'I could use my tree-pant-apult to twang you across,' suggested Harry, with much less sensible intention.

'Yes, Harry, you could. Or we could use that,' Aunt Lily said, pointing at a small, rickety-looking bridge a little way downstream, which would be both more practical and more hygienic than Harry's device. We headed quickly in that direction, but after only a few steps, I stopped, for our aunt was not with us, having stayed behind in the churchyard.

'Aunt Lily, what are you doing?'

'I shall stay and hold Benevolent off while you escape.'

'Then I shall help you,' I said, returning to her side. I removed my tableclothy mother from my shoulder so that I might have both hands free to fight, and laid her gently on the ground.

'As shall we all!' Now Pippa, Poppy and Harry returned also.

'Children, no. This is not your fight.'

'He is our evil guardian so I think you'll find it very much is,' I said.

Pippa and Poppy nodded in agreement, and then our aunt looked at us and sighed as if giving in to a reluctant desire. 'I had not wanted to show you this until later, but you have more to live for than you know.'

She reached into her bag and removed a newspaper. On the front was a large painting of the Royal Navy's latest vessel being launched, a huge ship-of-the-line named HMS *Grrr*.

'Much as I like naval things, how is this something for us to live for?'

'Look on the dock beside the ship,' she said, pointing to the corner of the picture, and I saw what she meant.

'Papa!' For it was indeed our father, looking straight at the artist as if pleading for someone to notice him. 'He is still alive!'

'This paper is only a week old – you were not told true about your father's death. For his sake, you must flee that you may live and find him.'

As if to reinforce that notion, from where she lay on the ground, my dear, linen-crazed mother noticed the picture and whispered a distinctly sane-sounding 'Thomas . . .'

Had the picture of Papa and the knowledge of his aliveness re-saned her?

If so, it was only temporarily, for she now lay back on the ground and started placing cutlery, plates and a candelabrum upon herself, still very much in her mind a tablecloth.

Worse, the imparting of this information had taken time, and suddenly Mr Benevolent burst from the church, still furious but now in a controlled, frightening fashion as if his rage had been focused through an anger-lens to be directed at us like a beam of pure ire.

'There will be no thwarting of my evil plans today!' he shouted, somewhat hammily it must be said, then ran towards his carriage and, on arrival there, reached inside and removed a blunderbuss, that most accurate of firearms.[2]

Faced with such a deadly weapon, our fighty determination dissolved, like an over-dunked piece of shortbread or a chicken in an acid bath, and as Mr Benevolent's finger tightened on the trigger, we ran.

The report of the weapon was mighty, like a vibrant slap to the ears, and as a visible blizzard of shot rushed forth we dived desperately into cover, Aunt Lily behind a tree, Pippa and Poppy behind a gravestone, and I behind Harry because he was there and wider than me.

By some miracle, the shot missed us all, succeeding only in shredding the leaves of a nearby tree and exploding three chaffinches therein.

'Fettocks!'[3] screamed Mr Benevolent, waving his emptied blunderbuss around angrily. 'Now, if you'd just give me three minutes to reload . . .'

But we were in no mood for reloading generosity and set off at speed towards the bridge, Mr Benevolent instantly pursuiting us. I quickly realized we had left Mama behind, but as I turned to go to her, Aunt Lily pushed me onwards, shouting, 'You serve your mother better by saving yourself, Pip.'

I knew she was right, and carried on bridge-wards, though not without yelling behind me, 'We will find you, Mama! Wherever you are, we will find you and save you!'

---

[2] Though we see a blunderbuss as an inaccurate weapon, compared to other weapons of the time, such as muskets, flintlocks and guesswhereithits, it was like a modern sniper rifle. It could reliably hit an incredibly close target very nearly some of the time.

[3] Cross between fetlocks and buttocks. Popular nineteenth-century swear word, along with 'bumsnot' and 'moobwang'.

Given the circumstances, I thought this was fairly brave and suave or bruave of me, but I am not sure my mother either heard or cared, for I could see she was now happily balancing a cruet set on her stomach and a decanter on her forehead.

Our flight was swift. Harry, Pippa and I soon reached the bridge and started across. It swayed; it creaked; it wobbled; bits fell off where we trod and were swept away in the thundering rush of the bloated river below.

As bridges went, it was rubbish.

But it got us across. Or, at least, three of us – for as I arrived on the far bank of the river, I looked back to see Poppy tripping and falling as she stepped on to the fragile wooden span. Aunt Lily immediately raced back to help her re-foot herself, but was not quick enough to prevent Mr Benevolent grabbing my youngest sister by the arm.

'Mine, I think you'll find,' he sneered.

'She will never be yours, Benevolent,' said Aunt Lily, grabbing Poppy's other arm.

'Ow!' said Poppy. 'This grabbing really hurts!'

Now they started tugging her to and fro with great grunts of effort.

'Ow!' said Poppy. 'This tugging really hurts!'

An almighty tussle developed as they struggled to gain control.

'Ow!' said Poppy. 'This tussling really hurts!'

Poor Poppy. I think the whole ordeal was causing her some pain. Indeed, she seemed to tire of being fought over because all of a sudden she lunged forwards and bit Mr Benevolent hard on the arm. With a yowl he let go, and

Poppy and Aunt Lily were racing across the bridge to safety again.

Mr Benevolent seemed to gird himself for further pursuit, but then stopped, de-girded, and instead bent down and took a large fallen branch from the ground beside him with which he started pounding the wooden frame of the bridge.

The whole edifice shuddered with each blow, shedding worryingly large fragments, and then, hideously, it shattered and collapsed, plunging Poppy and Aunt Lily into the thundering waters beneath.

'No!' Pippa, Harry and I screamed, as they disappeared into the raving torrent.

'Ha, ha, ha!' laughed a gloaty Mr Benevolent, from the other bank.

For they were gone.

Swept away.

Drowned.

My aunt, whom I had known for such a short time yet loved wholeheartedly, and my sister, whom I had known a much longer time and therefore loved wholeheartedly-plus.

And where they had been was only rushing water, and an aunt-and-sister-shaped hole in my wholehearted heart.

CHAPTER THE TWENTIETH

From despair to hemi-joy to re-despair

Oh, woe of woes, grief of griefs, misery of miseries! Oh, wretchedness of wretched— No, hang on, there was an arm, shooting up from the water downstream and seizing hold of an overhanging tree branch. Even better, it was Aunt Lily's arm, and with her other she was clutching Poppy.

We raced to help her as she struggled to get ashore. The riverbank was distinctly slippery with mud, and we trod carefully lest we ended up in the water also, thereby serving no useful purpose other than as companions to the already river-trapped pair, something that would no doubt be a cheering boost to their morale but would in all other respects be completely useless.

Somehow Aunt Lily managed to manoeuvre Poppy through the waters until she was close enough to grab.

'Perhaps I should invent some form of Poppy-grabbing device,' Harry pondered. 'What with my tree-pant-apult being so successful.'

'Yes, Harry, or you could just use your arms,' I suggested.

'Ooh, clever.' He reached out with Pippa and me, and together we managed to grasp part of Poppy.

Alas, it was merely the part of her that had been disguised as a mock rhododendron, and instead of sister all we dragged ashore was bits of twig and petals. Again we tried, and this time we took hold of her sub-fake-shrub dress and hauled her to safety.

Or would have done if the dress hadn't neatly slipped off over her head.

It was as if she didn't want to be rescued.

Again we lunged for her, and this time we grabbed the long braid that was her hair.

I half expected her to be wearing some kind of wig or hair extension that would now also come away in our hands, but miraculously she was not and we hauled her from the river to safety, though not without a good deal of ungrateful whining from her along the lines of 'Ow', 'Stop pulling my hair' and 'My scalp really hurts.'

Now there was just Aunt Lily to rescue. She was dragging herself along the branch towards the bank when, with a crack, the branch broke, and she plummeted river-wards once more.

Yet, with reflexes quicker than that of a caffeinated cat, I managed to catch her, my hand grasping hold of her wrist – though her weight instantly started to drag me down the muddy bank towards the river, and I slipped and slithered helplessly to a watery doom.

She looked me in the eye with a determined gaze and said the bravest thing I have ever heard anyone say: 'Pip, save yourself, let me go.'

Well, I wasn't going to disagree with such a nobly expressed sentiment so I let her go.

Her gaze went rapidly from determined to surprised, if not a bit angry. 'What are you doing? I didn't mean it! You were meant to protest and save me, you little bas—' Her words were lost, as was she, the river clasping her to its watery bosom and taking her away for an aquatic cuddle.

Oh, cruel Poseidon, controller of watery things!

Oh, harsh Neptune, his Roman equivalent!

Oh, vicious Pariacaca, Incan god of water and rainstorms!

It was definitely their fault and only a tiny bit mine.

'Ha, ha, ha!!!' Now there came mocking laughter from across the river: Mr Benevolent. 'I wonder how you'll fare without her help. Cold, wet, hungry and lost. Good luck, Pip Bin. By which I mean bad luck, obviously. Now I shall take your mother to London and my evil and cunning plan will yet be fulfilled. *Adios, non-amigo!*'

With this bizarrely Spanish valediction, he left, pausing only where my mother lay pretending to be a tablecloth, laden with place-settings. He bent down, grabbed her ankles and, with a violent, quick tug, pulled her out from under the cutlery and crockery and, though the candelabrum wobbled slightly, everything stayed exactly where it was. It was an impressive trick and, despite myself, I applauded, eliciting a small bow from Mr Benevolent, and then he was gone.

Now I turned my attention to my remaining companions. Pippa was comforting a shivering Poppy, cold from her rivery adventure; and a short distance off sat Harry, who was staring miserably at the ground.

'Where's Aunt Lily?' asked Pippa, as she saw me.

'Um . . . the river took her. I fear it was partly my fault.'

'Poor dear brother, you mustn't blame yourself.'

'Mustn't I? That's good.' Thus absolved, the small amount of guilt I had been feeling evaporated, like a puddle on a hot day or some milk in a sauna. 'Harry, how are you?'

'I'm jolly well, Pip Bin,' Harry replied jauntily, and then he burst into tears.

'Why, Harry, whatever is the matter?' I asked, hoping it was something simple and masculine, like his foot hurting, and not something tricky, like emotions.

'The river . . . Your aunt . . . It reminded me of my own poor mother.'

Oh, cripes, it was emotions. I decided to step round them as if they were an angry bear or some putrid dog sick. 'Sorry to hear that, now we'd better get—'

My sister Pippa now interrupted, however, firmly shoving us all into the path of the ursine dog vomit. 'Why, Harry Biscuit?'

'After my father died, she went insane and took her own life.'

'How?'

'She became convinced that she was literally a biscuit, not just one in name. She believed she was a chocolate wafer called Susan.'

'What was her real name?'

'Susan. That much remained sane. But . . . do you remember an incident when the people of Shrewsbury made the river Severn into tea?' Remember it? Why, I wrote of it not twenty-five pages past, or maybe more depending on how this book is typeset. 'Well, my mother heard of it and travelled to Shrewsbury. Once there, she threw herself into the river.' Here he sniffed as a tear ran down his cheek, the sniff inhaling the tear into his nose and making him cough a little before he continued. 'She dragged herself out of the river, then threw herself in again, dragged herself out, threw herself in and did it again and again and again until she appeared no more.'

'Drowned?'

'Dunked. She dunked herself to death. Then I was sent to St Bastard's and the family fortune was snapped up my father's greatest rivals, Lord and Lady Flapjack.'

'A tragic story but—' I tried to stop him, to no avail.

'And it makes me sad!' Now Harry cried, with yelps of pain and squeaks of woe, and I didn't know where to look. He might have been my best friend, but there were limits. Quite strictly defined limits, which included no crying. Fortunately Pippa was weaker and softer than me and she pulled Harry's head to her shoulder and stroked his hair until he calmed and then leaped up shouting, 'Better now!'[1]

Harry might have been better, but immediately one of our number was worse. For poor Poppy now emitted a small whimper of distress. 'Cold . . . I'm so cold.'

'Oh, I don't know,' said Harry. 'I find you quite a friendly sort.'

'No, physically cold, so physically cold.'

---

[1] Gosh, we haven't had a footnote for a while, have we? But don't worry: I'm still here and still paying attention.

'Yes, that makes more sense. What with the shivering. And the having gone blue.'

Harry was right. Poppy had indeed turned a blue colour, indicating terrible cold. Unless the river had been full of blue dye and therefore stained her skin while she was in it, but as her teeth chattered and her body trembled with great frigid spasms, I knew that that was not the correct answer and that the river had chilled her to illness, or chillness.

'We must get her warm,' Pippa said.

We tried making a fire, but any wood we found was too damp following the recent air-bath and would not light. We wrapped her in as many items of clothing as we could, but it did no good, and we cuddled and hugged her tightly to warm her with a mixture of love and our own bodily heat, but still she shivered and remained cold-blue.

Night was falling, and up the river in the distance I could see an orange glow that was not natural and therefore must be a conurbation of some size – and I remembered the old adage 'All roads lead to Rome and all rivers lead to London.'

Surely once in the capital we would find shelter and warmth for poor Poppy.

Taking it in turns to carry her, we began to trudge towards the towny glow ahead. For long hours we walked, seemingly getting no closer, and all the way Poppy kept whispering, 'Cold, so cold,' not seeming to warm one iota, or even an omicron,[2] which is smaller yet.

---

[2] Told you I was still here. 'Omicron' is a Greek letter literally meaning 'little *o*', as opposed to 'omega', which means 'big *o*'. Similar letters include the Roman 'nano-d' and the early Cyrillic 'Ж ≤ Ж'.

Then, suddenly, an aroma assailed my nostrils, the strong scent of gin, horse manure and unwashed proletarian. This had to be London, and a shouting man nearby confirmed that fact: 'London! You're in London! Get your London here!'

It was one of the famous town criers, men paid to vocally advertise the vicinity, now sadly replaced by that most modern of inventions, the sign. I had never been to London before, and as I looked around me my first reaction was one of fear. The buildings soared two, sometimes three storeys high; everywhere you looked there were people, most of them living, some of them dead; and all was coated in a grim griminess of soot and filth.

'Gosh, London is so big and busy,' I marvelled.

'Sorry to bang on a bit, but I am cold, so cold,' Poppy whimpered.

'Dear Poppy, of course. We shall find you shelter.'

We quickly approached the nearest house, a dismal, dingy-looking place but a house no less, and knocked on the door.

The whole house fell down.

This was evidently not the most salubrious part of town.

The next house we knocked at did not fall down.

Though I did, after the owner opened the door and, before I said a word, punched me in the face.

I sent Harry to knock at the next door, and he was sent packing with a series of strange Cockney insults ringing in his ears, most of which I do not remember, though some definitely ended in 'off' and another seemed to be the word 'muppet', whatever that might mean.

Desperate for aid for poor, freezing Poppy, we ignored the houses and their unfriendly inhabitants and simply approached anyone we passed and asked them for help.

But there was no help to be had.

In some ways, I did not blame these blighted people, clearly dirt poor themselves and with nothing to spare for others, but on the other hand . . .

Bastards.

'Please help us,' Pippa begged. 'We need warmth and shelter, or money to buy those things. Please, anything you can spare.'

Again and again she was ignored or shoved rudely aside, with muttered swearings to boot. But then at last, after yet another such failed plea, we heard a deep, authoritative voice, tinged with mercy and fringed with tassels of tenderness.

'Did I just hear you children asking for food, shelter and money?'

Finally a true Christian soul to aid us! By the guttering light of the oily streetlamps I could not see the face that belonged to this voice, but surely now help was at hand.

'You did. Please, can you spare some?'

'Then you stand condemned by your own mouth!' The mercy and tenderness were now gone from the voice and all was stern and condemnatory. 'To ask for things is to beg, and by all that is holy – which in God's fine world is an awful lot – begging is sinful, anti-Christian behaviour!'

Perhaps help was not to be forthcoming after all.

'As a soldier in God's own Salvation Army, it is my duty to cleanse such heathen acts from the world. Therefore you are to be delivered to the workhouse. Take them away!'

He had several colleagues with him and, as these were the days before the disarmament of the Salvation Army,[3] we were driven at bayonet point to the workhouse a short distance away. As we went, the people who had so recently refused us help lined the streets cheering and jeering maliciously and my opinion of them sank yet further; but at least within the workhouse we might find the shelter and warmth Poppy so desperately needed.

As we entered that ghastly establishment, however, the man who had taken us up stepped beneath a lit lantern and, with horror, I saw his face properly for the first time.

'My name is Beadle Ezekiel Hardthrasher and I rule this workhouse with a rod of iron, a jane of cold steel and a freddy of discipline.'

The Hardthrashers were not just twins, but triplets! And we had fallen into the hands of the third of them, who seemed, on first meeting, to be just as fierce as the others.

'Now, I am full of Christian goodness, whereas you are full of the hideous disease of poverty. And why are you povertous? Because you lack the Christian virtues of hard work, discipline and lots of money. But by God's will we will inculcate those values in you, even if we have to hold you down and force them into you like some sort of human moral sausage!'

---

[3] The Salvation Army was disarmed and reformed as a peaceful organization in 1865 after they launched an ill-fated and ill-judged crusade to Bournemouth, killing hundreds of people they deemed not to be praying hard enough on the beach. The contemporaneous Salvation Navy was even more violent. They would sail round the colonies stealing soup and secondhand clothes from indigent populations, then distribute them to old British people.

Truly, this was a brand of Christianity so muscular that if it did one of those poses that body-builders are wont to do, it would be in danger of ripping its shirt. We were taken to a small, damp, straw-strewn cell and bundled inside. It was already crammed with sorry-looking folk, and the best that could be said was that it was comfortingly familiar; alas, that familiarity was because it reminded me of nowhere so much as the dormitory at St Bastard's, with all its concomitant misery and anguish, so I've used the word 'comfortingly' completely incorrectly.

'This is where you will sleep. And on the morrow, you shall work and we shall begin scouring your souls free of poverty. Now, do you have anything to say for yourselves?'

'I'm cold, so cold . . .'

'What's that, girl?'

'Cold, so cold,' repeated Poppy.

'We fear she is extremely unwell,' said Pippa.

'What is wrong with her?'

'We think it might be a cold,' said Harry.

'It is as if the icy waters of the river have entered my soul and I shall never be warm again.'

'Please, help our sister. She is freezing to death,' I begged, brutally aware that time was short for dear Poppy.

'Help her? Why should I help her?' asked the beadle.

'Because it is the Christian thing to do!' There was desperation in my voice, as I had begun to fear the very worst.

'Nonsense. If she is near to death then she is near to the kingdom of Heaven. What Christian could begrudge a fellow human such a glorious event?'

'But see how she shivers with cold . . .' I protested.

'No, she does not shiver with cold, but with excited anticipation at her imminent meeting with the Lord Himself.'

'Please, help me . . .' Now Poppy's voice shook desperately.

'You will be warm soon, young lady, warm in the Lord's
embrace.'

'I'd rather be warm here . . .'

'No, you go to God. Frankly, I envy you.'

'Please, do something to help her!'

This I yelled at the beadle, and he now wheeled on me,
pushing me up against the wall viciously. 'To stand in the
way of God's will is blasphemy, boy. Do you blaspheme? Do
you?'

I did not answer. I could not. For a fury was growing in
me so great that mere words could not express it, only acts
of incredible physical violence to this dreadful man whose
religious beliefs were set to kill my sister.

'I can't feel my legs . . .' The fear in Poppy's voice replaced
my anger with gentler emotion, and I knelt beside her with
Pippa and Harry. 'Or my arms. My head is numb. All
sensation is gone from my chest. I can only feel a small bit of
my bottom.'

'And how does that feel, dear sister?'

'Cold.'

'Might have guessed . . .'

'Oh!' There was an abrupt spike of energy to Poppy's
exclamation: was this a hopeful sign? 'There are angels all
around me!' No, it was not a hopeful sign: visions of angels
are rarely a precursor to wellness, happiness and staying-
aliveness. 'Oh! And now I can see Jesus!'

The beadle twitched at this. 'You lucky dying cow.'

'He is offering me a coat. Thank you, Jesus. And now some soup, lovely warming soup. And what's that, Jesus? Some mulled wine? Ooh, thank you.'

Poppy was slipping away, and there was nothing we could do. Pippa and I clung to her chilled flesh, desperately hoping to warm her back to us.

'A toasted muffin? Yes, please. Oh, and you've lit the fire for me. What a nice man you are, Jesus. Mmm, that's good. The flames are so soothing, so hypnotic, so warm.'

She was gazing into some imagined distance, but momentarily slipped back into reality as she looked at Pippa and me in turn.

'Dear sister, dear brother, goodbye . . . I have to go now.' Tears filled my eyes, then flooded over the edges and down my face. 'I fear I am as a lot sold at auction, for I am going . . . going . . . gone.'

She smiled, then closed her eyes and, as she had said, was gone. Though her flesh had been river-cold before, now it was death-cold, the immersion heater of her soul removed. Pippa and I held her for a few seconds more, our sobs filling the grim cell, then laid her down and instead held each other.

'At least she is in a better place now.' Pippa could hardly speak through her tears, but her words were of comfort indeed.

'Hah.' The beadle emitted a contemptuous bark like that most scathing of dogs, the cock-a-snook-er spaniel.

'Do you disagree, sir?' My fists clenched, I raised myself from my knees.

'The fire imagery makes it quite clear she has gone to Hell,' said the beadle. My body was seething with unexpressed emotions of loss, but his attitude was quickly changing them to ones of fury and violence.

'But she saw Jesus!' Pippa protested.

'The Devil in a Jesus costume. He does that a lot. Your sister must have blasphemed in life and now she will burn for eternity. Serves her right.'

At the cruel awfulness of his words, I could contain my fury no longer and hurled myself at him. But before I could reach him, he slammed the cell door shut and I simply ended up pounding ineffectually on it, screaming rageful abuse at him as he walked haughtily away, smugly content in the Christian rectitude he believed was his; and then the rage turned to sorrow, the sorrow to grief, and I slumped on the floor next to Pippa, both of us staring at our lifeless sister, whose dreams and ambitions were now all just tiny nothings dissipating in the universe's cruel void of indifference, and we wept and wept and wept.

PART THE FOURTHTH

CHAPTER THE TWENTY-FIRST

OR PONTOONTH[1]

*Including a grim re-meeting and other
woeful events of misery*

A graphic and, indeed, geographic representation of my emotional reaction to recent events in my life would have rendered a Himalayan mountain range of joyful peaks lit by sunny hope and wretched troughs swathed in tenebrous gloom; and yea verily, at that moment truly did I walk through the valley of the shadow of the death of my sister.

Whereas until recently a statement of my family accounts would have read:

Self, one.
Sisters, two.
Father, one.

---

[1] A reference to the game of book blackjack, which Sir Philip played keenly with other authors.

> Mother, one (sane).
> Balance: excellent.

Now, after sundry unwanted withdrawals and unexpected bills it would have read:

> Self, one (sad).
> Sisters, one (other one dead, remaining one sad).
> Father, none (monkey-killed in Indies).
> Mother, one (utterly bonkers), held by evil guardian.
> Balance: awful.

True, I had opened a new deposit account of friendship, credited with:

> Best friend, one.

And there had been an unexpected additional credit to the kin account, namely:

> Aunt, one (recently discovered).

She in turn had added an interest payment of:

> Father, one (feared monkey-killed, actually still alive but missing).

But only a day later she herself had been debited as if by a standing order of woe:

Aunt, none (recently discovered one swept away, presumed dead).

And now I stood a mere two or three incidents away from being permanently overdrawn in the matter of family attachments; even worse, my postal address for any statements to be delivered was currently 'The Nastiest Workhouse in Britain, No Hope Street, London'.

In the moments after my sister Poppy's death, the other residents of our cramped poverty-cell crept forward to offer us comfort, arms wrapping us in compassion and human solidarity; or so I thought. In truth, their sympathetic hugs were mere disguise for attempted theft of whatever possessions we had on our persons, up to and including the very clothes we stood in. I suppose, given their own wretched circumstances, one could not blame them, but as I stood now half naked, shivering with chilly grief, I found I could in fact quite easily blame them or, rather, hit them until they gave us our clothes back.

In matters of death the workhouse did not stint in its haste, and within the hour poor Poppy was buried in a pauper's grave due to our pecuniary lack. The weather was not accomplice to our misery, it being a cheerily sunny day, so, as was the case back then, elements were matched to emotions by the deployment of the parish's metaphorical meteorology maker, a contraption of hoses, pipes and suspended colanders that allowed a mock rain to fall upon our small mourning party.[2] The pauper's service was a

---

[2] By law all nineteenth-century funerals had to take place in mood-matchingly

short one, meaning the beadle offered but a rapid 'Ashes to ashes, dust to et cetera, chuck her in,' before our beloved sister was deposited unfeelingly in a shallow, undignified scrape in the London clay, at its head a rough wooden cross with written on it: 'Another povvo, 18whatever – 18whocares'.

But I cared; sister Pippa cared; and though he had known her but a short while, my best friend Harry Biscuit cared.

And, surprisingly, the viciously religious Beadle Hardthrasher also seemed to join in with the caring as he now leaned towards us and, in a tone far from tender but much less fierce than his regular one, said, 'You may now have time to grieve.'

His Christianity might have been biceps-bulgingly muscular but at least it seemed to allow space for the weaker emotions and, thus given permission, we raised the sluice gates of grief and allowed our tears to flood out and attempt to wash away the pain of our de-sistering.

But barely had our lachrymose lament begun when the beadle struck his gold-plated staff of office on the ground and, fully re-fierced in tone, said, 'And that's enough of that!' With a flick of his hand he summoned two of his under-beadles, who seized us and started to drag us away. 'Now let us scourge the poverty from you with hard work! For by vigorous labour you may one day free yourselves and find respite in the arms of the ever-loving Jesus.'

Even to a non-euphemistically minded boy such as myself, this sounded less like worldly freedom and more like death,

---

miserable weather – hence great rain-making machines were present at all cemeteries.

and it occurred to me that the Anglican Church of the time was much nicer to people who had money.

Then, still be-teared, we were assigned to the improving tasks of the workhouse. Pippa was set to work sewing. But not usefully, oh, no – for what use for usefulness did such a cruel establishment have? She was given a piece of torn material and told to repair it; as soon as she had done so, the weaselly witch who supervised her took it up and tore it once more, then compelled Pippa to re-repair it, the whole ritual designed to inculcate Christian patience, forbearance and, presumably, massive rage.

As for Harry and me, the workhouse had an attached bottling factory to which we were taken and where I was given the job of testing the strength and integrity of the bottles.

Unfortunately, this was done by having them smashed over my head.

'Bow your head!' commanded the beadle, and I did. He then lustily swung a bottle at my skull, hitting it squarely and precisely.

The bottle shattered instantly, the impact being both painful and full of pain.

'A bottle as weak as the human spirit.' The beadle sighed.

'Ow!' I exclaimed, not unreasonably, I thought, as my cranium was now suffering from both blunt trauma and an infusion of small splinters of glass.

'What did you say, boy? Did you cry out weakly in the face of pain?' He wheeled upon me, wielding a Bible. 'Did our wonderful Lord Jesus cry out weakly on the Cross? He did not. He bore His pain stoically, reciting poetry and composing witty epigrams. If you lack such fortitude you dishonour His name and fiery Hell awaits you!'

Of course it did.

'Right, next bottle!'

This bottle did not shatter, instead merely striking me with a hollow but no less painful clunk.

'Behold! A good, strong bottle, fit for the Lord. But we must test it yet further.'

This time he hit me with it really, really hard and it shattered shardily and, I need hardly add but will anyway, with a gargantuan amount of agony.

'Alas, its faith has fallen short. But we fill find a worthy bottle yet!'

We didn't, because even if it took a good five or six goes, each bottle was eventually found wanting in its rendezvous with my skull.

Meanwhile Harry's job seemed at first to be much easier for he was assigned the task of clearing up the fragments of broken bottle, and to that end the beadle opened a cupboard full of brooms and brushes suited to that task.

'You must choose your tools as splendid Jesus would have chosen,' said the beadle.

'Ooh, well, I think Jesus would have liked that one,' said Harry, reaching for a broom.

'You chose poorly!' yelled the beadle, slamming the cupboard door closed. 'Super Jesus would not have chosen at all. For brooms and brushes are the Devil's cleaning tools, sent to tempt us into proud laziness, and by reaching for one you have surely condemned yourself to fiery Hell.'

'That's not fair!' wailed Harry, and I saw his point, particularly since the broom he had reached for had actually had 'Jesus's special broom' written on it.

'You must take a more bodily path to redemption.'

Thus it was that Harry was compelled to lick the pieces of bottle from the floor.

He didn't enjoy it.

Nor did his tongue, rapidly becoming swollen and hurty.

'Do you feel closer to our Lord now, boy?' enquired Beadle Hardthrasher.

'Yuth,' replied Harry, unleashing more Christian rage.

'You dare speak unclearly? Diction is next to godliness! By your slurring words you have surely condemned yourself to fiery Hell!'

Was there any act in this place that did not lead to fiery Hell? Though as the pain-filled hours dragged on, that Hadean destination began to seem a marginally more attractive option than the workhouse.

Eventually our shift was over and, exhausted and pained, Harry and I headed for our quarters.

All we wished to do was sleep, but that desire was flung from my mind like a badly strapped-in child from a poorly maintained merry-go-round as I heard a voice from the past, and not just a random or ghostly voice from the past, such as that of William the Conqueror or a mad old monk, but a real, friendly, much-liked voice.

'Young Pip? Pip Bin? Is that you?'

Why, it was the voice of Mr Parsimonious, once the ironically named business partner to both my father and my evil guardian, Mr Benevolent; and close behind it came the body and face of Mr Parsimonious as well. Unhappily, whereas he had once been a plumply prosperous figure, jolly-clothed and gaudy, now he was be-ragged, tatty and poor – though evidently still his old generous self.

'Dear Pip, though I wish we had met in better circumstances you must still have a gift!' This most munificent of men now patted his pockets and looked about him. 'But what do I have to give you? I know! Have this crust of bread, this hard, mouldy crust of bread . . .' He handed over just such an unappealing object. 'And this fetid water!' He now knelt and scooped a handful of gruesome-looking fluid from a puddle on the floor. 'Lice! All must have lice!' At this he scraped his hands through his hair and offered us the contents he found therein. 'And these rags, these hideous, tattered rags . . .' Now there was desperation in his voice as he tore at his clothing, rending it from his body. 'And why not share in these weird sores and bodily lesions that affect me?' By this point his words were turning into a high-pitched shriek of misery and, sinking to the ground, he began to weep. 'And these tears! Have these salty tears of shame and regret! And who wants some of my misery? I've got a lot to go round.' Now he was into a full-frontal crying fit.

'Mr Parsimonious, you must not weep . . .' This was not just an attempt at comfort, it was a statement of the actual legal situation, for at that point in Britain it was still illegal for a man to cry; if the beadle saw him doing so he could be hanged or, worse, pointed at disapprovingly and mocked in public.[3]

---

[3] The Emotional Repression Act of 1798 banned men from showing any strong

After a while, he sniffled to a halt and the threat of the law receded.

'I am sorry. It is just that to see a friendly face after such a long time . . .'

'How did you end up in here, Mr Parsimonious?' I asked.

'Sadly, my fortunes have not run fortunately. It turns out the old adage is true.'

'What old adage?'

'Annual income twenty pounds, annual expenditure nineteen pounds nineteen and six, result happiness. But annual income twenty pounds and it turns out your one remaining business partner is a colossal duplicitous bastard, result misery.'

'You refer to Mr Benevolent?'

'Aye! A name I cannot say any more!'

'Me neither,' said Harry, though he meant it in a more physical sense as all his glass-splintered tongue would allow him to say was 'thlee eeeephher', a pair of incomprehensible words I have chosen not to set down here, though I realize I just have.

'This is my new best friend, Harry Biscuit, by the way,' I informed Mr Parsimonious.

Harry stuck out his hand and his tongue in an attempt to get some clarity to his speech. 'How do you do?' he somehow managed to emit.

'Terribly. I do really, really terribly,' said Mr Parsimonious, taking and shaking Harry's offered hand, then using it as a

---

emotions. The most emotional outbursts allowed were 'I have high regard for you, dear wife' and 'Well played, sir'. Many blamed its repeal in 1885 for General Gordon's loss of Khartoum later that year.

rather literal hand-kerchief to wipe his weep-runny nose.

'We'll have no more of that wretched talk, Mr Parsimonious,' I admonished him, for his appearance had reinvigorated my own spirits. 'Pippa is here also, and the four of us together, why, surely we can overcome these dire circumstances and return our lives to happy joy once more!'

And as I said those words I truly, honestly, really, really, really believed them.

A bit.

CHAPTER THE TWENTY-SECOND

Of potatoes, pleases and prayers

Alas, in the following weeks, that bit of belief which nestled inside me, like a hopeful acorn in a squirrel's cheek, cracked open and revealed itself to be hollow for truly it appeared as if we were trapped in a real-life painting by that noted Dutch depicter of religious wretchedness Thereonymus Basch.[1]

The workhouse ran to a brutal and punishing schedule of brutality and punishment according to the dictates of the Bible – or, at least, selected parts of the Bible as chosen by Beadle Hardthrasher, including the hitherto unknown to me Book of Judgmentals and St Paul's Letter About How Poor People Are Evil And Must Be Punished.

Each day we performed twenty-three and a half hours of harsh physical labour, interspersed with bouts of grim manual toil and painful corporeal exertion, and in the remaining half-hour we were compelled to eat, sleep, perform both ablutions and short dramatic scenes glorifying

---

[1] Even more religiously violent painterly contemporary of Hieronymus Bosch.

Jesus, do chores and also say the regulation twenty-seven minutes of pre-bed prayers.

It was quite tiring, actually.

The food did not help our energy levels. At school, the problem with mealtimes had been the absence of food; in the workhouse the problem was the presence thereof.

For, oh! It was grim. To sum it up in one word: gruel. To sum it up in two words: revolting gruel, which, given that the word 'gruel' already contains an unspoken hint of 'revolting', is really saying – or, rather, writing – something. If I am allowed a third or fourth word, and I don't see why I am not seeing as I am the author of this book, I would choose 'foul', 'vile', 'gruesome', 'repulsive', 'abhorrent', 'nauseating', 'obnoxious', 'loathsome', 'vile' again, 'ghastly', two more 'repulsive's and a 'disgustivating'.

There! I actually took fifteen words, for three reasons: one, to show you adjectivally the horror of our meals; two, to prove that as author I am in charge of my own word destiny; and three, to demonstrate the excellence of my new reference book, an Other-words-that-mean-the-same-onary.[2]

Even though we were perpetually hungry, no one wanted to eat the gruel; and workhouse inmates would do anything to avoid it. Indeed, I remember one little mite – his name was Oliver as I recall – approaching Beadle Hardthrasher, bowl held up in supplicant hands, his quavering voice asking, 'Please, sir, I want some less.'

---

[2] The word 'thesaurus' was not used in the sense we used it until the twentieth century. Oddly, a thesaurus is also a giant lizard obsessed with the definite article. Or, at least, that's what it says on Wikipedia.

The beadle made him eat the entire workhouse's gruel supply for the day, including the tureen it was served from, the combination of gruesome gruel and force-fed crockery killing him instantly, or, rather, slowly and painfully.

He went to fiery Hell with terrible indigestion and literally and metaphorically a nasty taste in his mouth.

Given my recent experiences at school, the awfulness I had witnessed at the asylum my home had become and now the horrors of the workhouse, I was beginning to develop a deep suspicion of nineteenth-century institutions; and it seemed I was not alone, as Mr Parsimonious shared his fears with me one night.

We were involved in our daily chores, namely peeling potatoes. Not for consumption, but because Beadle Hardthrasher believed that unpeeled potatoes looked like the face of Satan and that they must therefore be peeled into the shape of either the cross or Jesus's elbow, which was apparently the holiest part of Him due to His having dipped it accidentally into a bowl of soup He had just blessed at the Last Supper. This night there were some ten thousand potatoes, and all the beadler had given us to peel them with was another, slightly sharper, potato.

Nevertheless, we peeled away and, though we were forbidden to consume anything, occasionally a small fragment of spud would fly through the air and land by chance on our hungry lips, a nectar of raw, tubery delight by comparison to our usual food. Then, mid-peel, Mr Parsimonious suddenly set down his peeling potato and turned to me. 'Young Pip, I very much fear that this is where our story comes to an end.'[3]

'Why, Mr Parsimonious, do not be so downhearted, for our tale has many chapters yet to run, I should guess perhaps twenty-three or even -four more, and some of them may even be happy.'[4]

'Pip, we are going to die in this place. Search your peelings, you know it to be true.'

I looked down at the potatoey fragments between my feet, and there, clearly spelled out among them in peelings, as if by some higher power who had chosen to use a weird, vegetable-based form of message system, were the words: 'It's true.'

Admittedly that was after looking for a really long time, scrunching my eyes until they were almost shut and then using quite a lot of imagination, but there they were, a stark and clear warning.

We had to escape this povertous hellhole!

I knew instantly we could not do it alone.

I decided that if a higher power had sent the peeling message, then a higher power might be the help we needed.

So I set about composing a letter to my Member of Parliament.

But I had got no further than 'Dear my Member of Parliament' when I realized I needed a power higher even than that.

I had to ask the big guy.

---

[3] It doesn't. Just look at how much book there is left.

[4] There are actually twenty-seven to go. And only three of them are definitively happy.

By which I mean God, and not Fat Dave, another rather large inmate of the workhouse.

I threw myself to my knees, and I prayed.

First I prayed that my knees might stop hurting because in my imprecatory alacrity I had thrown myself to them quite hard, and the workhouse floor was stony and ouchy.

Then I began to pray for release.

I prayed as hard as I could, harder even than a really keen nun trying to impress the Catholic Church's national praying team selectors.[5]

Over and over again I prayed, 'Please, Lord, let me escape from this place.'

After a while, I changed my prayer slightly to 'Please, Lord, let me and Pippa and Harry and Mr Parsimonious escape from this place,' because, frankly, I had been selfish in not including them before; and, besides, if the prayer worked and I did get out I'd want some friends to do stuff with.

Oh, how I prayed! I squeezed every drop of entreating juice from my supplication gland[6] that God might deliver me from the suffering I was in. As I slumped into an exhausted, prayed-out sleep on the floor, my last thoughts were ones of perseverance: I knew that, no matter how hard I had prayed, even the truly devoted must wait for a godly

---

[5] The World Praying Cup competition took place every four years. Britain's team was decimated by the Reformation in the sixteenth century and never regained its previous eminence. For forty-three consecutive tournaments the final was contested by Ireland and Italy.

[6] The medical profession at the time believed there was a gland connected to every human behaviour. It was only when they really began cutting people up in the name of science that they discovered this was untrue.

response, for our Lord has huge numbers of prayers to work through and, even though He is obviously divinely efficient at working through His admin, it would still take time; time I was prepared to wait, be it years, decades or even centuries, millennia, aeons or ages, even though, were it to be that long, I would be much lengthily dead, for the patient shall have their reward, and patience was now my watchword, middle name and creed.

CHAPTER THE TWENTY-THIRD

Thank you, O Lord, thank you!

Actually, we were safely out the next morning, which was much quicker than I had been anticipating and our lives were free and our own to live once more.

Once free, I immediately— Hmm? What's that? How? You desire to know the how of our escape from povertous punishment?

Very well.

I shall tell.

Ooh, those two lines rhyme. Take that, Thomas Hardy! You're not the only man who can write novels and poetry, you miserable grump.[1]

I woke after nearly four whole seconds of exhausted sleep to face another workhouse day with all the fun that that entailed, which was to say none. None fun.

---

[1] The author had a long-running feud with Thomas Hardy. Its origins are unclear – some say Hardy took Sir Philip's satirical novel *Jude the Obvious* as a gibe at himself; others say it was because at the AGM of the Society of Authors in 1876 they had a fight over the last mini pork-pie at the buffet.

By this time Harry and I had been moved from the bottle factory to different duties, namely the treadmill. Pacing in place, we drove a great geared belt, which turned a grindstone, itself connected to that most notorious of workhouse punishments, the pain-wheel, a horrific circle of agony to which were strapped miscreants whom the beadle had deemed to have committed sins such as being short (the sin of not striving to reach high enough to Heaven), being meek (they were destined to inherit the earth and therefore commit the sin of avarice), or being ugly (he didn't like ugly people). The wheel rotated them through a scraping, stinging mass of brambles and nettles before dunking them in a bath of lemon juice, and their shrieks of woe could be heard as far afield as nearby and really far away. As we ran on the treadmill, large men in strangely skin-tight outfits shouted at us if we slowed, utilizing phrases such as 'No pain, no gain', 'Work it' and 'Feel the burn'.

Then, over the noise of these hectoring hectorizers, I heard the phrase that heralded a change in my fortunes as great as that experienced by wily Odysseus himself when he rolled nine consecutive double sixes to defeat Circe the witch in a game of backgammon after having previously only thrown rubbish scores such as three, one and two.[2]

'Letter for Pip Bin!'

It was a representative of the Royal Postal Corps, the most noble of Britain's armed forces after the Army, the Royal

---

[2] No idea what he's on about. Sir Philip seems to have read an utterly different version of *The Odyssey* from anyone else ever.

Navy and the Royal Wish-we-could-fly Force.[3] By law, if a stamped letter was addressed to you even slightly it had to be delivered, or the postman would be locked up in the Tower of London for treason; anyone stopping you receiving your letter faced the same punishment.

Thus I was allowed to dismount the treadmill and receive my epistolary gift. The envelope it came in was marked 'Pip Bin, Somewhere'. It was a vague address, but enough to have found me, thanks to the diligence of the postman. What could it contain? It was not my birthday so was unlikely to be a missive with a birthday greeting; equally it was not Christmas, Easter or Harvest Festival, those other great card-sending holidays; true, it was the day after the Greek Orthodox *tyrine* or Cheese Sunday,[4] but I had never heard of a card sent in celebration of that curdled-milk-product feast day.

So what was within?

Could it be the answer to my prayers of the night before? Though I doubted God would actually use the post for His reply.

Despite my desperate desire to see what was inside, I gently and carefully opened the envelope – I had heard many a tale of someone tearing an envelope hastily open with excitement only to accidentally rip the stamp containing our glorious monarch's head and therefore be executed.

Inside were two pieces of paper. On one were some barely legible letters, spelling out 'Hope this helps you as you

---

[3] Founded in 1817, the RWF eventually became the Royal Flying Corps with the invention of powered flight. Until then they sat around cultivating dashing moustaches and inventing words such as 'prang', 'Blighty' and 'bally Hun'.

[4] Seriously. Look it up if you doubt me.

helped me.' Beneath was a smudged and smeared signature: 'Bakewell Havertwitch'.

The escaped convict from the churchyard whose chains I had broken with Pippa's anvil! Had my kindness to him now been repaid? I looked at the second piece of paper and saw that it had indeed.

For it was no ordinary piece of paper.

It was a note.

And not a note saying 'Buy more milk' or a musical note or any of the other sorts of note that would have been less than helpful in the circumstances.

It was a banknote.

Specifically, it was a £312 banknote.

This was more money than I had ever seen ever in my whole life ever.

My prayers had been answered; in terms of the plot of my life this was less *deus ex machina* and more *pecunia ex deo et fugiente malefactore.* Truly Bakewell Havertwitch had not fibbed or spoken untrue when he had promised one day to repay my kindness!

The news of my letter had been heard around the work-house and Harry, Pippa and Mr Parsimonious had joined me.

'Gosh,' said Harry. 'With that you could buy three hundred and twelve one-pound notes. Or a hundred and fifty-six two-pound notes. Or seventy-eight four-pound notes. Or—'

'I get the idea, Harry.' I feared if I did not stop him he would go through every possible money-changing permutation.

'Does this mean we are poor no more?' asked Pippa.

'It does. Surely now the beadle will release us for we no longer belong in a workhouse or poorhouse but in a rich-house or leisurehouse.'[5]

'Oh, such a rich note! May I hold it, Pip Bin?' Mr Parsimonious held out a hopeful hand.

'No, Mr Parsimonious. For you are a man of such generosity I fear you would only give it away.'

'It is a fair point, well made. Have my apologies. And my humble sorryments. Not to mention a hefty dollop of rueful-ness.' He rubbed his hands together and walked away from me, bowing his head like some sort of guilty solicitor's clerk.[6]

'You are generous even in apology, Mr Parsimonious. Now, let us leave this hideous place!'

But at that moment, Beadle Hardthrasher appeared and he was less pleased by the money's arrival and the prospect of our departure than we were by some considerable degree.

'Money? You have money, Pip Bin?'

'I do, Beadle. And that makes me no longer poor. Therefore I am leaving, and my family with me!' I declared.

'Oh no you are not. For money is the work of the Horned One!'

This puzzled me, as I knew not what he referred to. Harry, however, had an idea. 'Do you mean . . . a goat?'

'No! I mean Satan! Beelzebub! Lucifer! The Devil!'

---

[5] Nineteenth-century terms for luxury hotels. The deliberate echo of 'workhouse' and 'poorhouse' was meant to make the lower classes feel better; it didn't.

[6] I suspect this is some kind of literary reference but can't quite work it out. Something to do with *David Copperfield*, perhaps? No. *The Hunt for Red October*? Probably not.

'So both poverty and riches are the Devil's work?' I asked, confused.

'They are! The Lord of the Flies and Prince of Darkness is responsible for the sin of possessing both too little and too much money, leaving only a narrow range of virtuous wealth outside which you conveniently fall.' Now he strode towards me, hand outstretched. 'Besides, that money was not earned by Christian sweat, Christian toil and Christian exploitation of the poor. That, in my book, is blasphemy – and seeing as my book is the Bible, I am right!'

'But, sir—'

'No buts!'

'How can—'

'No hows, no cans!'

He would not allow me to speak; and I realized there was to be no reasoning with him.

'I will listen to you no more, sir. We are leaving.'

'No wes, no ares, no leavings! You are sinners, and must learn to be pure through hard study of the scriptures!'

'Hard study of the scriptures' meant standing in front of a large wall of bricks on which the books of the Bible had been inscribed, then having your head smashed into it by the beadle. For he believed that true Christian knowledge came only through direct bodily contact with the word of the Lord.

I was dragged to the wall and the beadle prepared to propel me head first into Deuteronomy. But I was not going to let this cruel man and his twisted religious views destroy me as he had destroyed poor Poppy, and a surge of strength-giving anger now flooded through me, a flood that the

Beadle could not avoid, even if, Noah-like, he had quickly built a flood-dodging ark.

As he drove me towards the wall I grabbed him and, twisting round so that he impacted first, we tumbled into the holy wall, which collapsed in Biblical bits. Blocks of scripture tumbled around us: Leviticus plummeted past my left ear, Numbers past my right, and, with a jerk of my head, I narrowly escaped a synoptic braining as, with the exception of John, the gospels plunged to earth.

Alas, Beadle Hardthrasher was not so lucky.

Well, I say alas, but as I looked at his crumpled, scripture-struck body, I felt very un-alas, and certainly not at all alack. For there he lay, his legs pinned by Psalms, his chest crushed by Revelation and Ruth perched on his head.

'Yay, got him!' said Ruth, for this last was not a book of the Bible, but a workhouse inmate who had come to gloat.

'Get off his head, Ruth,' I said. 'Give him some dignity in death.' For though he had shown none of us dignity in life, with his demise we could very much take the moral high ground; besides, dignity was the least I could offer, given that I had now been partially or wholly responsible for the deaths of three Hardthrasher siblings.

Then the other inmates of the workhouse came in and starting kicking his dead body and I thought, Dignity be damned, and, clutching my £312 note, I led Pippa, Harry and Mr Parsimonious out of that place of wretchedness and forth unto a life of riches, wealth, luxury, proper food, good clothes, lovely houses, servants, a box at the opera, weekends away, things you can't even remember buying you're so rich, exotic fruits, proper art on the walls . . . Oh, you get the idea.

CHAPTER THE TWENTY-FOURTH

I is loaded, innit?

As I stepped richly from the workhouse on to the streets of the East End of London, I inhaled deeply of the air of freedom.

Oh, liberty, how sweet dost thou taste?

Actually, not that sweet, because on one side of the workhouse was an abattoir and on the other an ordure refinery, but metaphorically it was yummy.

The first order of business was to find somewhere to live, so I immediately bought a massive townhouse in London's fashionable West End. Of course, back then, houses only cost about £20 each, so the estate agent was more than a little annoyed when I tried to pay with such a large note as the one I had.

'A three-hundred-and-twelve-pound note?' he whined. 'You haven't got anything smaller, have you?'

'He could just keep the change,' suggested Mr Parsimonious, as generous as ever, albeit with money that wasn't strictly, or indeed in any sense, his.

In the end I received change of two hundred pounds in cash, a row of mews houses and the entirety of that village in Wales with the incredibly long name.[1]

With a guaranteed home to return to, the next item on the rich-now agenda was a ginormous and enormiant meal, so we went to the finest restaurant in London: Snetterton's Eatatorium. The contrast to the workhouse was as stark as a dead jester in a snowdrift. All was gentility, linen and class – not a hint of gruel to be found. The menu was long and meaty, and as we surveyed it, our stomachs rumbled hungrily, like starving thunder. There was so much choice! When the waiter approached, we were so hungry it was all we could do not to eat him.

'Sirs, Madam, are you ready to order?'

'Indeed we are, my good man,' I said, though I had no idea as to his moral character at all. 'To start with we'll have the crispy deep-fried elephant.'

'An excellent choice, sir. And for your main course?'

'I'd like the roast dodo, please. Is that rare?'

'Increasingly so.' Now he turned to Pippa. 'And for Madam?'

'I'll just have an otter salad, please.' Dear Pippa, even half starved she ordered with lady-like restraint!

'What sort of dressing would you like?'

'I'd like it wearing trousers and a little hat, please.'

---

[1] He means Llongy-wongy-barely-pronounceable-pentre-cwm-y-gwyn-maes-parcio-bach-and-pant-cudd-heddlu-llyn-toiledau-ar-gyfyl-yr-Wyddfa, which translates as 'incredibly long and hard to pronounce valley village of the little white car park and hidden dip in the road police lake toilets near Mount Snowdon'. It's not as long as the other place.

'Of course.'

'Mr Parsimonious, what will you have?' I was delighted to be able to offer this munificent man some of my own generosity for once, though it seemed to make him feel awkward.

'Dear Pip, I cannot accept your offer, for it is I who should be treating you! You are merely a boy and I am a man, a generous one at that.'

'But, Mr Parsimonious, you have no money.'

'Nevertheless, I will not abuse your kindness.'

'Please, I insist,' I insisted.

'Well, I politely refuse,' he politely refused.

I am ashamed to admit that at this point my temper frayed and then snapped, as I slammed Mr Parsimonious face-down into the table, twisted his arm up behind his back and shouted loudly, 'Order some food!'

He quickly and meekly ordered a fruits-of-the-forest platter, a dish of badgers, weasels, stoats and hedgehogs garnished with saplings and dead leaves. Now there was only Harry to order – and I doubted he would require much persuasion.

'What is this multi-layered meat feast?' Harry pointed askily at the menu.

'Ah, that is the speciality of the house,' replied the waiter. 'It is an ox stuffed with a slightly smaller ox stuffed with a tiny ox stuffed with a sheep stuffed with a goose stuffed with a duck stuffed with a hen stuffed with a wren stuffed with a robin stuffed with a humming bird stuffed with a mouse.'

'Does it come with stuffing?' asked Harry, but I was more interested in the mechanics of the dish.

'How ever do they prepare such a thing?' I enquired.

'They carefully line up the animals nose to tail in size order, then startle the mouse. The mouse runs straight inside the humming bird, which is itself startled and runs inside the robin and so on and so forth until the slightly smaller ox runs into the large ox, which topples into a huge oven enabling the whole fleshy parcel to be cooked.'

'That sounds brilliant!' yelled Harry, not unreasonably, because it did. 'I want that!'

'Very well, sir.'

At that moment there came a terrible bestial uproar from the kitchen, as if a mouse, humming bird, wren, hen, duck, goose, sheep, tiny ox, small ox and large ox had just been startled. Then the kitchen doors burst open and the afore-mentioned animals sped out with assorted squeaks, cheeps, chirps, squawks, quacks, honks, bleats, lows and deeper lows, making straight for the restaurant exit and disappearing into the street.

'Ah, it would appear the multi-layered meat feast is off, sir. They obviously didn't line them up carefully enough.'

'Oh.' Harry sounded disappointed, but could rarely be kept down for long when food was in the offing. 'Then I shall just have the spaniel tartare and the porpoise dolphinoise.'[2]

To celebrate our escape, I decided to order some wine, and I could as, although I was still beneath the age of eighteen, in those less complicated times the legal drinking age was a much more reasonable twelve, or five if you asked nicely.

---

[2] Old French dish, being porpoise cooked in dolphin sauce.

'Now, to drink. Perhaps a bottle of the house red. And one of the white. And, because I am feeling patriotic, also one of the house blue.'[3]

'No need, sir. Your drinks have been taken care of.'

At this the waiter clapped his hands, summoning a pair of men bearing a vast bottle between them.

'By whom?'

'A gentleman over there insists you have this as a gift.'

It was a generous gift indeed. Bigger than a magnum, greater than a jeroboam, more size-y than even a Nebuchadnezzar, this was the largest bottle one could get: a Giganto-abrahamium. The waiter pointed across the restaurant at the giftor, and I looked his way to acknowledge the present with perhaps a manly nod of the head, a fingerly salute of gratitude or a bellowed 'Thanks a lot.'

But I did none of those things, instead feeling myself become rooted to the spot, like a human tree or a swan that has stepped on glue.

For the man the waiter had pointed out was a sharp-featured, saturnine man dressed entirely in black with maliciously glinting eyes of purest obsidian: Mr Gently Benevolent.

My evil guardian.

Destroyer of my life, ruiner of my father and captor of my mad mother; surely no gift from him could be generous or even safe. As if to confirm this fact, Harry now read the label of the wine bottle.

---

[3] Until wartime rationing, you could get wine in almost any colour, including tartan.

'Mmm, Château Cyanide . . . Sounds authentically French and delicious!'

'Harry, no!'

He went to take a sip of the wine, but I knocked the glass from his hand, spraying a nearby table with the contents. A drop landed in a gentleman's open mouth as he went to slurp some soup, and he immediately collapsed in what might have been an entirely coincidental fit of death but almost certainly wasn't.

'The gentleman sent a note as well, sir.'

The waiter handed over a slip of paper, and I began to read.

'"Dear Pip Bin, if I said I was glad to see you alive I would be lying . . ."'

I set the note down and turned to Mr Benevolent, who had silently and sinuously crept up behind me. 'Yes, thank you, I can read it myself you know!'

'Just trying to be helpful,' my evil guardian said, his tone caramel smooth yet simultaneously burned-gravy cruel. 'Now, come on, have a glass of wine.'

'No! Leave us alone!'

'No? Then how about a *digestif?* A glass of Eau de Mort, perhaps?'

'Ooh, that sounds delicious! Yes, please!' Harry could not restrain himself; but I could restrain him and did so as he reached for the almost certainly deadly liquid Mr Benevolent now offered.

'Mr Benevolent, please leave us.' I clenched my fists in preparation to dismiss him by force if necessary.

'I will not leave you,' he said, pulling out a chair and

sitting down between Pippa and Mr Parsimonious. 'Hello, Pippa Bin. You'll be eighteen very soon, and ripe for marriage.'

He reached out his hand to stroke hers but, strong and fine-spirited filly that she was, she took up a fork and started to poke him with it. 'Leave me alone, you fiend!'

'Oh, yes, poke me with your fork. I embrace its tine-y pain. Yes, you'll make a splendid temporary wife who will die suspiciously young.' He then turned to Mr Parsimonious. 'Hello, Parsimonious. Happy to be out of the workhouse?'

'You monster! It is your fault I was in there!'

'Lost your generous spirit, have you?'

'No! Have this slap to the face! And this punch in the stomach! And this grrr and this aaarrggh and this I-hate-you!' Mr Parsimonious now tried to do these things, but Mr Benevolent caught his would-be slapping, punching hands and at his fierce cries merely laughed.

'Ha, ha, ha!'

Oh, that laugh! So tri-syllabically innocent in print! So evil-toned and dismissively cruel in person!

Each 'ha' was like a spike to Mr Parsimonious's soul and he seemed to wither before the mocking onslaught, like a temperate-climate plant that has somehow wound up in the desert. He shrivelled and writhed and tears welled in his eyes until he had to hide under the table lest anyone witness his illegal weeping.

Fortunately at this point the waiting staff approached with our crispy elephant starter, and Mr Benevolent stood again, a smile of malicious accomplishment on his face. 'Seeing as we're in public and I can't do anything too evil, I shall leave you to enjoy your meal. But watch out, Pip Bin, for I shall have my vengeance on you.' He headed back across the restaurant to his table, but after a few steps turned and addressed me: 'Incidentally, your mother sends her love. Or would do if she wasn't still as loopy as a mad rollercoaster.'

'Mother! Where is she, you monster?'

'Where is she? You really want to know?'

'I do.' I thrust my chest out and squared off with him, though there may have been a touch of rhombusing off as well.

'Then I shall tell you. She is— But no! Why spoil all my fun? Goodbye, Pip Bin. See you around . . . Ha, ha, ha!'

He left, his evil laugh trailing behind him, and I stared after him with hate in my heart, loathing in my lungs and a good dose of spite in my spleen.

'And now, sir, we will prepare your crispy deep-fried elephant before your very eyes.'

The waiter clapped his hands for his assistants to start cooking. With a terrific trumpeting and huge sizzling, they toppled the elephant into a vast pot of boiling oil and, as my ears filled with the fearful, agonized cries of a soon-to-be delicioused-up pachyderm, I decided that it was very much a metaphor for my situation: surely I was as the elephant, poised delicately above the boiling oil that was Mr Benevolent.

And then I realized that it was much easier simply to de-metaphor and say: I hated Mr Benevolent, yet feared him also.

CHAPTER THE TWENTY-FIFTH

From riches nearly right back to rags again

The next weeks were a blur of activity and being rich. There was a house to furnish and a life to set in motion. I commissioned the finest furniture in London, all fine mahogany, teak and leg-oak,[1] and had fine clothes of finery made for us all: Harry and I looked quite the dandies about town with our silk cravats, brocade waistcoats, gold-trimmed trousers and pewter hats, Mr Parsimonious was restored to sartorial businessman glory and Pippa had dresses so grand and wide that I had to have special doors constructed for the house that she might fit through them.

I also used my new money to have Pippa's anvil retrieved from the church we had left it in; it was now mounted in a cabinet in the entrance hall of our house, a memorial to our father and to the help it had been in our various escapes.

---

[1] A tree that had the misfortune to grow its trunk and branches in the shape of table-legs and was therefore completely deforested in the nineteenth century, along with the bookcase elm, the washstand larch and the wardrobe sycamore.

There was also the small matter of a large celebration, for during this period I attained the age of eighteen – an age that had so recently seemed a destination I was unlikely to reach. We dined and drank and danced – all the fun *d* words basically, including those traditional eighteenth-birthday rites of passage, dog-dunking, duck-defeathering and dame-dangling.[2]

I was now free of the bonds of Mr Benevolent's guardianship and, until my absent presumed-dead-but-just-possibly-still-alive father returned, I was also the man of the family with the concomitant responsibility for our financial security, so I sought investment advice from an old friend.

'As my father's business partner, you helped him to a fortune, Mr Parsimonious. Now you must help me to invest wisely that we may all live free of the tedium of work and real life.'

'Oh! It would be an honour to serve, young Pip.' His cheeks shone with flattered glee and wobbled with financial acumen. 'You have some hundred and eighty pounds remaining to invest. What income would you like from it?'

'Perhaps fifteen pounds a year?'

'Living high on the hog and tall on the tiger indeed!' He furrowed his brow in thought. 'Hmm, I'm sure I can come up with something.'

---

[2] You were not truly a man in nineteenth-century England until you had dropped a dog in a bath, plucked a live duck and held a pantomime dame out of the window by his-her ankle. Or you could just go abroad and kill a lot of people in the name of the King.

He immediately set to work, thinking, researching and pondering.[3] But my approach to him had ruffled feathers elsewhere – though not on our pet duck as it was still completely bald from the defeathering I mentioned some paragraphs ago.

It was Harry whose feathers were ruffled – he'd got into the habit of wearing jaunty boas instead of cravats – for he felt I should have consulted him as well. 'I have so many ideas and schemes for making money, Pip Bin!'

'But, Harry . . .' In truth I was still a tiny bit cross and a big bit angry about the uselessness of his earlier school-escaping plans.

'You could buy a printing press and then we could just print more whenever we needed.'

'That would be illegal, Harry. What other ideas do you have?'

'That was the main one.' He thought carefully for a second or two. 'Though how about we let two five-pound notes get married and then they can have lots of little one-pound-note children?'

'Why, Harry, that is a brilliant idea!'

'Is it?' To give him credit, he did sound surprised at my use of the word 'brilliant'.

'No.'

'Ah.'

Fortunately, Mr Parsimonious rapidly came up with several incredibly wise-sounding investment opportunities.

---

[3] The great philosopher Jeremy Bentham was famous for his habit of thinking while pacing round a pond, or pond-wandering as he called it; this was contracted to form the word 'pondering'.

'I have discovered a Prussian mining concern that is seeking to sell shares so they may exploit a recent discovery.'

'Of what?' I asked, intrigued.

'They have discovered rich seams of mustard and custard. Basically all the yellow rhyming liquids.'[4]

'That sounds interesting.' It did. How could such a venture fail? Wherever people ate meat they would need mustard and wherever they ate pudding they would need custard. 'Anything else?'

'You could invest in property. After all, bricks and mortar never go out of fashion!'

'True, true. Tell me more.'

'A company needs stockholders for house-building bonds, which will employ a simple series of leased remortgages paying back ninepence on the capital sum with an amortized bond of seven per cent of the accrued interest in the contractual monies of the loaned stipendiary fiscalization.'

'Is that good?'

'Well . . . it sounds like proper businessy talk, so probably.' He looked at the paperwork he held in his hand. 'And the company is the reputable firm of Crookit, Ripoff and Wouldn't-if-I-were-you.'

'As solid a trio of names as I have ever heard! What else?'

'Investors are sought for a new gentlemen's club where men may enjoy smoking huge cigars in the rarefied atmosphere of newly discovered natural gas.'

---

[4] Modern Germany still has half the world's mustard reserves; the Germans' love of sausages comes from the economic need to have something to eat with the mustard. Geological custard is made when prehistoric eggs, milk and sugar are trapped between layers of rock, the pressure turning them into deliciousness.

'A fine mix of leisure and science! How clever we British are!'

'And then lastly a chap called Stephenson needs money to build a device he is calling a "steam locomotive", but that's just madness I tell you, madness.'

'Hmm . . .' My head teemed with these fascinating financial possibilities. 'I have decided! I shall invest my money equally in all of them.'

'Are you sure?'

'I am. All except that "steam locomotive" nonsense. The only money I'll spend on that is on a specially commissioned advertisement in *The Times* announcing to the world that Mr Stephenson is a fool, a dunderhead and a numpty!'

So my monetary dispositions were made; and I sat back to await the waves of cash that would inevitably come rolling in, like a glorious tide of lucre.

Oops.

For my investments did not go well. It was as if the moon had suddenly left the sky and with it its tide-creating gravity: no lucre rolled in.

Though much rolled out.

Day by day the news became worse. First came word from my mining investments. It turned out that they had not discovered actual mustard but instead only fool's mustard, looking the same but tasting of absolutely nothing;[5] and though they had found real custard it was so delicious that the workers in the mine ate it all, smuggling in crumbles, pies and sponges to have with it.

---

[5] There is a huge modern market for fool's mustard in America.

The company went bankrupt, and I lost my investment.

Next to turn rotten was the property deal. I first got a hint that all was not well when I took a carriage ride out to see the houses I had invested in being built. They were supposed to fill twenty acres of reclaimed marshland in the East End, but when I arrived I could see no houses. On looking closer, however, I did see some. Tiny ones, no more than a foot high, inhabitable by no one taller than four inches, maybe five, if they didn't mind smacking their head on doorframes a lot, and therefore, given that the shortest person in Britain at the time was music-hall sensation Miniature Michael, who stood eighteen inches high, inhabitable by no one.

I had put my money into a scheme that turned out to be a whopping great lie.[6]

The company claimed they were not technically in breach of contract as, despite their size, they had built the specified number of houses, and the courts agreed.

The company directors made a fortune, and again I lost my investment.

As I left the court after the verdict, I consoled myself with the thought that at least my share in the new cigar and gas club would pay me richly; indeed, I realized it was the opening day and hurried there for a relaxing gassy cigar.

As I approached down the great thoroughfare of Piccadilly, I heard the hiss of the gas being switched on and the immortal words, 'Gentlemen, light your cigars.'

---

[6] The area of the scheme was known as 'Whopping Great Lie Land', which, over the years, contracted and corrupted to 'Wapping'.

Then I heard a massive explosion, and in it the sound of all my money burning away.

For a third time I had lost my investment.

To cap it all, as I turned my back on the smouldering ruins of the club, I passed a news stand, where a boy was touting his newsy wares. 'Extra, extra, read all about it – if you can, which you probably can't given the appalling literacy rates in this country at this time!' He paused for breath, then continued: 'Mr Stephenson's *Rocket* breaks land speed record, invention of the railways, a mass transportation network and economic boom bound to follow! Investors will make huge amounts! Non-investors won't!'

Ah, I thought. Then: 'Aaarrgggh!!!'

I raced home to find a shame-faced Mr Parsimonious pacing frantically and babbling like the guilty man he was.

'It is all my fault! All mine!'

'Oh, come now, Mr Parsimonious. You advised me in good faith and could not have known what would happen.'

'I fear recent events of misery have addled my business brain.' He sighed deeply and regretfully. 'Once I was an expert. Now I am but an ex-expert.'

'Your advice was good, Mr P. Just a little bit the exact opposite of what it should have been. Which is a skill in itself.' I went to pour myself a stiff drink before hearing the answer to the question I was about to pose. 'Even after all these set-backs, we're still all right for money, aren't we?'

'Alas . . .' At that warning word I set aside the drink I had poured and picked up the entire bottle instead. '. . . you have lost everything.'

'Everything?' Although I was trying to maintain control, there was a definite quaver to my voice.

'Yes. You have nothing left.'

'Then I am poor again?' Now the quaver became a distinct wobble of fear.

'I am afraid so.'

'I see.' I downed the bottle in one, which steadied my voice and hardened my will. 'I tell you this: I shall not go back to the workhouse on pain of death! There must be a way out of this situation – and I shall find it!'

CHAPTER THE TWENTY-SIXTH

Up by the bootstraps, up, up and away!

Despite the fact that he had ruined us, I could hold no feelings of anger or resentment towards Mr Parsimonious. Though I did once sort of accidentally punch him.

And twice sort of deliberately.

I'd be lying if I said there wasn't a bit of frustrated kicking too.

And I called him things I am ashamed of now.

Things I shall not put down in a book that perchance families may read.

Suffice to say they were quite rude.

But he was a jolly, robust sort and, though bruised, he survived my aggrieved assaults, indeed often thanking me for them. No, really, he did.

I quickly decided that we must all find jobs, but the question was, of what kind?

'Is there money to be made by being pretty?' asked Pippa, over breakfast one morning.

At this, Mr Parsimonious and Harry coughed awkwardly

and seemed to find something incredibly interesting to stare at in their porridge.

'There is, dear sister. Sadly, I fear not in a wholesome way. Indeed, possibly only in a distinctly dodgy way.'

'As long as it made money . . .'

'I forbid it!' I slammed my hand on the table in a pretty darned manly man-of-the-family way.

'Very well. Then I shall take up my anvil once more and manufacture footwear for the animals. I'm sure they will pay handsomely for shoes.'

I knew not of any animals that would do so, having neither the pockets to carry a wallet or purse, nor the opposable thumb to open one, but it was better than the unsavoury options open to her otherwise. 'An excellent idea, dear sister. Once again Papa's gift will aid us.' Now I turned to Harry, slightly dreading what job he might have decided to do. 'Harry Biscuit, what about you?'

'Well, I have been keenly researching the job market and have made a decision.' Could it be a sensible one by any chance? 'Therefore I have decided to take to the music-hall stage with an act entitled "Harry Biscuit: The Human Swan". Fame and fortune await!'

I had been right to dread the job he had chosen and wrong to hope that it might be a sensible one, but did not want to discourage him so merely said, 'Well . . . good luck with that, Harry.'

'Meanwhile I have decided to set up as a business adviser.' This seemed rash from Mr Parsimonious, given his recent efforts in ruining me. 'I shall offer people advice and then run after them, begging them to do the opposite of what I just said.'

That seemed much more sensible, though still mad.

'What about you, Pip Bin? What are you going to do?' asked Harry.

'I have got the best idea of all of us. For I have decided that I shall become a best-selling novelist,' I announced.

There was silence in the room – doubtless caused by admiration for my clever idea – until it was broken by Harry. 'Is that going to make lots of money?'

'Of course. Bound to. Loads of people do it. How hard can it be to write a novel?'

Again there was an awed silence at my cleverness so, taking advantage of it, I left the room and retreated to my study. Brimming with confidence, I sat down at my desk, quill pen in hand, blank sheet of paper before me, and began.

'Chapter One,' I wrote.

Instantly, my confidence fled and a wave of self-doubt assailed me: was that a good start? Should it be Chapter Two? Or a prologue? Or even a preface?

I scrumpled up the piece of paper and began again, this time deciding to leave chapter numbers, prologues and prefaces out of it and just get on with my story.

Now, what to put?

Aha!

'It was the best of times . . . and so everyone was happy and jolly the end,' I wrote. I read it back. Apart from being far too short for a novel, it was rubbish.

I scrumpled up that piece of paper also, and began again once more.

'"I'm here for my papers," said Mr Pickwick.'

Nonsense!

More scrumpling and I began again once more anew.

I scratched and scribbled and came up with: 'How Ebenezer Scrooge hated Christmas . . .'

Gibberish! Who was this stupidly named Scrooge and why did he hate Christmas? How could anyone hate Christmas? Christmas was brilliant!

Scrumple; re-begin again once more anew afresh.

And so it went: write, scribble, scratch, read, scrumple, begin again.

Three days later, I was still unpublished and was also knee deep in discarded rubbish first pages of bad novels.

I was also exhausted, suffering from both writer's cramp and block, and distinctly worried that the workhouse beckoned once more.

There was a knock at the door. It was Harry, who had brought me a restorative breakfast of brandy porridge and whisky toast. 'Good morning, Pip Bin. How goes the novel writing?'

'Badly, as you can see.' I indicated the huge mass of scrumpled paper, which Harry was now wading through. 'How did "Harry Biscuit: The Human Swan" go down at the music hall?'

'Not so well, actually. I broke a man's arm, and the King tried to eat me. Ow!'

'What?'

'I just got a paper cut from one of your discarded goes at a novel. Ow! And another one!'

'Yes, it is both inconvenient and dangerous. But what can

one do?' I shrugged in rubbishy resignation. 'There is simply no way to dispose of waste and detritus other than tossing it casually on to the floor or out of the window.'

For that was the case in those messy, pre-waste-disposal days. London suffered terribly as people dumped their rubbish wherever they could: it blocked the streets; it clogged the Thames; it filled the houses, turning them into slums and driving the inhabitants rubbish-mad; it cultivated disease, filth and rot; and huge piles of the stuff would regularly topple fatally on to innocent bystanders and passers-by – waste in general killed more people per year than tigers, and back then tigers killed loads.

We even had a slogan for it: rubbish is rubbish.

And, thanks to my pathetic attempts to write a book, my room was now full of it.

Then, as I considered the discarded paper around me, it happened, as I suddenly had a glimmer of the concept that changed everything and made my fame and fortune, an inkling that grew rapidly into a notion and then into a full-blown idea.

'Hold on a second, Harry,' I said, holding my head very still lest the developing thought fall out of my ear. 'What about some sort of waste-disposal device, perhaps cylindrical, closed at the bottom, open at the top . . . into which you could put discarded paper or indeed rubbish of any variety? Yes, that could work. Though I'll need a name for it . . .'

'For what, Pip Bin?'

'Of course! Harry, you're a genius! I shall name it after

myself and call it . . .' Here I paused as if to allow Providence to turn her fate-y head and hear this word that would change the world. 'The Piperator!'

'Great name!' Harry agreed, and with that I rushed to build my idea into a real, concrete thing, though obviously not actually made of concrete because it would be far too heavy for a start.

I rushed to Pippa's room where she had been working at her anvil. As I entered, she had just finished affixing a pair of tiny metallic shoes to a pigeon's feet and was now setting him free from the window.

'There, my little feathered friend, fly free, your feet now protected from stuff!'

She released the pigeon and with a desperate pigeony coo it completely failed to fly, the weight of its new footwear instead sending it to a splatty death on the pavement below; but I cared not, for I was after the anvil.

'Pippa! I need your anvil!'

'You may not have it. For I am doing my good podiatric deeds on it.'

Try telling that to the recently deceased pigeon, I thought. But I said it not, instead instantly resorting to emotional blackmail. 'Papa would definitely want me to use it for what I'm about to do.'

At this mention of our father, she could not resist and yielded the anvil to me with only a bit of a slappy brother-sister fight.

I worked at my Piperator day and night, hammering, shaping, forging and generally metal-working like a maniac. But a maniac with a plan. Within a week, my prototype was ready, and I invited Pippa, Harry and Mr Parsimonious to the unveiling.

'Behold, the Piperator!'

'Good grief! Why, that thing must be fully twenty feet high and six feet across.'

'Well, new technology's always quite big at first, but it'll soon come down in size. Remember the first Spinning Jenny? It was the size of Manchester but now you can easily fit one into any ordinary ten-acre factory.'

They walked round it, admiring the great metallic waste-disposal unit.

'Why doesn't one of you try it out? Pippa?'

'But how does it work?' she asked.

'Do you have anything you wish to discard?'

'Why, yes. This apple core I have been carrying round for several months for want of anywhere to put it.'

'Then simply climb the ladder and drop it in the top.'

She did as I said, hesitating momentarily before dropping the apple core inside, where it landed with a small, appley thud.

'Oh!' Pippa sounded surprised and delighted. 'It seems so complicated at first, but actually it's quite intuitive.'

'What do you think, Mr Parsimonious?' I was eager to hear his opinion.

This most generous of men frowned as if in distaste. 'It is a terrible idea and will never catch on,' he said.

'That is marvellous news!' Given his recent form of being exactly the opposite of right on everything, I was going to make a fortune.

'Though the name "the Piperator" is excellent,' he added.

This was not good news, for the same reason his previous poor opinion had been good news.

'Right, I need a new name.'

'How about the Disposathon 4000?' suggested Harry.

'Brilliant name!' enthused Mr Parsimonious.

'No!' I shouted.

'Lionel?' re-suggested Harry.

'Even better!' re-enthused Mr Parsimonious.

'Aaargh!' I now said, despairing of ever finding the correct name.

'I have an idea,' said Pippa, quietly. 'It should be named for our absent parents with our family name.'

'The Bin? Hmm . . . Mr P?'

'Dreadful name.'

'Then the Bin it is. It shall go into production tomorrow. And one day I hope that there may be a Bin in every town in Britain!'

'Harrumble for Pip Bin and his brilliant eponymous rubbish-disposal device!' Harry now cheered, and I knew that the cheers were deserved and that by my invention I had saved my family.

CHAPTER THE TWENTY-SEVENTH

Of movements, motions and mobility (social)

I was wrong about my assumption that one day there would be a Bin in every town in Britain. For, thanks to those great twin drivers of the industrial revolution, science and child labour, the Bin was a success beyond my wildest imaginings.

It soon shrank in size to fit any domestic room and sales rocketed faster than a madman trying to reach the moon. They came in different colours and – perhaps my finest idea – a range of different sizes so that once one Bin was filled you could simply discard it in another, slightly larger, one.

Soon I was that richest of men, a thousand-aire.

But beyond that was the social capital I gained. For the Bin transformed conditions in Britain like nothing since the Black Death, only in a much more positive way, unless you were a rat, because they did really well in times of plague and less well when rubbish disappeared.

And it did disappear.

Before long houses were bigger from lack of rubbish; the roads of London were passable once more; and the Thames was restored to its former merely sewage-filled glory, for Sir Christopher Bagatelle's amazing system of cleaning the sewers by firing a massive steel ball through them was yet to be invented.[1]

Disease rates dropped, life expectancy rose, and the capital smelt better than it had since the Lord Mayor's ill-fated attempts in the previous century to spray its streets from huge perfume balloons.[2] I rapidly became not only Britain's richest man but also its pre-eminent social improver, which led to invitations and requests from all sorts of people, not least of whom was King George IV.

Yes, the King himself invited me to the palace for a ball.

I, who had so recently been in the workhouse, now went to the palace as a rich, respected man. Pippa, Harry and Mr Parsimonious came with me, though they were much less rich and respected than I.

'Oh, how glorious it is, like a fairytale!' Pippa was right: the opulence was stunning and the waiting staff were dressed as fairies, all diaphanous wings and antennae on their foreheads . . . though, hang on, that would make them more butterflies than fairies so maybe Pippa was actually wrong.

Still, it was pretty spectacular.

The Royal Hall was enormous and packed with people, some of whom were dancing, some of whom were talking,

---

[1] Bagatelle's invention was a precursor to Bazalgette's complete rebuilding of London's effluent-disposal system.

[2] The famous French ballooning brothers Montcricketier were hired to do this, but tried to save money by using cheaper perfume than specified in the contract, leading to London smelling, in the words of drunk playwright Drinkhard Ginsley Sherrydan, like 'a right cheap and nasty slapper'.

some of whom were taking sexual advantage of their social inferiors. Above hung great chandeliers of crystal, and all around were tables groaning with platters of exotic foods, including rare fruits such as mango, womangone, pineapples, pineoranges, dragon fruit and scary plums. Then in the centre of the room was the crowning attraction, a champagne fountain created by a small whale, which was spraying great plumes of fizzy wine skywards through its blowhole.

'I shall get us champagne!' Mr Parsimonious rushed whale-wards, took some glasses from a table and began chasing after the champagne spray trying to fill them.

'Oh, may I dance, dear brother Pip?'

'Of course, Pippa.' I offered my arm to my sister, assuming she wanted to dance with me, but instead she turned to Harry.

'Harry Biscuit, will you dance with me?'

'Me?' Harry reddened with embarrassment. 'Um . . . yes. I shall dance with you! Though I warn you, I am quite clumsy on the dance-floor.' As if to prove his point he immediately smashed into a waiter bearing a laden tray, sending both tray and waiter flying. 'Told you! Sorry – sorry, everyone!'

They made it to the dance-floor without further mishap, if you exclude the duchess Harry tripped up and the major-general he accidentally elbowed in the ribs, and began to dance.

As I watched them and, from the corner of my eye, saw Mr Parsimonious gleefully trying to catch the spraying champagne, I felt a feeling I hadn't felt in a long time: happiness.

And then that happiness fled as I heard a familiar, unloved voice.

'Pip Bin, how utterly undelightful it is to see you.'

You've probably already guessed, but I'll tell you anyway: it was my evil ex-guardian Mr Gently Benevolent, as glowering and malicious as ever. I refused to rise to his unpleasant baiting, and decided to be polite to him instead. 'Ah, Mr Benevolent. Good evening, sir.'

'Good evening? "Good evening," he says!' His face contorted into a puckered grin of nastiness. 'Let me tell you something, Pip Bin, your good evenings will not last if I have my way. One day soon I shall greet you by saying, "Bad evening," and you will have no choice but to sadly shake your head and say, "Yes, yes, it is a bad evening, they all are now." Ha, ha, ha!'

Gosh, but he did find himself amusing.

'What do you want, Mr Benevolent?'

'I want to see you destroyed, Pip Bin. I want to see you ruined, like a broken doll or shattered teapot, destitute and alone.'

'That will never happen.' Secure in my success, I believed what I said.

'Oh, won't it? It nearly happened before. How did your investments work out?'

'To what investments do you refer?'

'The mining industry, property and gentlemen's clubs.' He grinned like an admittedly well-dressed shark. 'All those companies were wholly owned subsidiaries of Benevolent Enterprises Limited.'

A chill spread through my stomach, like an instant

intestinal ice age. 'Those were your companies?'

'Yes. Set up just to get back at you. I've lured you to near disaster once, I can do it again.'

'Not now my Bin is a success!' Surely this was beyond his power to destroy.

'Yes, that does present a little . . . ruffle in my plans. But no matter, I'll think of something.' He leaned towards me and whispered, 'I will see you impoverished and broken, Pip Bin. Then I shall force your sister to marry me in order to save you, and I shall have won. Ha, ha, ha!'

The cruelly mocking tones of his harsh laughter rang in my ear as he left me, pausing briefly to turn and wave a coquettish goodbye before melting into the crowd. I was about to plunge into the social mêlée after him, determined to fight him, but my actions were stayed by the sudden arrival before me of a face I recognized all too well from stamps, coins, portraits and statues of the King, for it was the King.

'Your Majesty!' I bowed before his royal person both because it was custom and because the King's accompanying chamberlain had used a long stick to push my head down into a bow anyway.

'Mr Bin!'

The King knew me – what an honour!

Though he was a mad, lecherous, dissolute by all accounts.

'Sire, I am honoured you recognize me.'

'But of course! Your marvellous invention has changed life at the palace much for the better. We now have some-where to put leftover food and dead servants.' He gestured around him. 'In fact, this ball is your doing, because before your Bin thing, this whole room was full of rubbish!'

'I am glad to have been of service, sire.'

'Aarrggh! The pain, the damnable pain!' This non-sequitur momentarily threw me, but fortunately the King now offered an excuse for his outburst. 'Sorry, sorry, it's just this gout I suffer from. Feels exactly like a child stabbing me in the foot with a fork.'

I looked downwards and, to my surprise, saw a small child stabbing the King's foot with a fork. 'Um . . .' I hesitated. Should I tell him what I had seen? Then I decided: yes, I should, for though he be royal, he was still a man, as was I, and men talk to men as men, that is to say with honesty and reason and no fibbing. 'Sire, you do have a small child stabbing you in the foot with a fork.'

The King looked at his foot, then back at me. 'Yes, I know that. The gout is in the other foot. The child is to equalize the pain across both feet. My doctor ordered it.' He gestured at a medical man behind him, who looked me in the eye, winked and put a finger to his lips.

'Aaarrggh, the pain, the damnable pain! Sorry, it's just this child stabbing me in the foot with a fork. Feels just like gout. Aaarffggh!!!'

I looked down at his feet: one twitched goutily and the other was being stabbed by the fork-wielding child.

'Aaarggh, the gout! Aarrgh, the child! Frankly, Mr Bin, my life is hell.'

'I'm sorry to hear that, sire.'

'Oh, mustn't grumble,' he said regally. 'I do have lots of money and palaces. And I can get away with almost anything with the ladies, you know. Watch this!' He suddenly turned, spotted an attractive woman in the crowd, then ran and leaped on top of her. As his attending retinue moved to surround the couple and shield the monarchical shenanigans from public view, I could still hear his royal voice. 'Sorry, it's just that I'm the King and I can get away with this! Don't worry, I'll make any dodgy offspring a duke or something!' Now the circle of retainers was closed and I could thankfully see and hear no more.

I had just met the King!

And he was barking mad and as fine an argument against hereditary entitlement as I had ever come across.

But still . . . the King!

What other fascinating meetings awaited me this night?

I decided to seek out Harry and Pippa to tell them of my kingly meeting. They were still on the dance-floor, Pippa all elegant pirouettes and spins, Harry all disastrous flails and malcoordination.

'Sorry!' yelled Harry, as he gyrated madly and clumsily, elbowing a dowager duchess in the face, bruising a marquess and, judging from the upper-class shouts of pain, quite possibly breaking an earl's leg.

My watching was interrupted by a tap on my shoulder. I turned to see a man clad in an admiral's uniform and thought, How splendid, another interesting person to meet, but that thought died as I looked at his blunt, cruel face and its terrible familiarity. And then he spoke, and I sensed that the party might be over, at least for me.

'Pip Bin? My name is Admiral Horatio Hardthrasher. You killed my brothers – prepare to die.'

CHAPTER THE TWENTY-EIGHTH

Of death preparations and a short reprieve

I immediately did as Admiral Hardthrasher said, grabbing a passing lawyer and starting to dictate my will, but my estate-devolving speech was interrupted by the ferocious naval officer bellowing with laughter.

'Gotcha! Oh, you should see your face.'

And so that I might indeed see my face, he produced a small mirror and held it before my eyes. I looked shocked, pale and unamused.

'Prepare to die? No, prepare to be thanked, for I detested them,' he said, to my great surprise. 'Terrible brothers, weaker than baby's gin and softer than a month-old apple. And they never bought me birthday presents.'

Like his brothers, he was a large, fierce-looking man, but unlike them, this Hardthrasher was evidently the veteran of many wars: his face was grimly scarred with powder burns and his uniform was covered with medals, including the highly prized I ♥ Nelson badge given to those who had served at the battle of Trafalgar; and as I shook his offered hand of greeting, I noticed that it was hard to the touch.

'Forgive my wooden hand. The fact is, after the number of body parts I've had blown off in battle I'm made mostly of wood. You see this leg?' He gave the left one a tap and it resounded woodenly. 'Teak. The other's made of balsa – helps me float if I fall overboard. My right arm's poplar and the left's made of willow and doubles as a cricket bat. I'm literally a left-handed bat.' Now he took a fork from a nearby table, ran it prongily down his side and a pleasing musical scale came in response. 'That's my ribs. Pure mahogany, cut precisely to xylophonic proportions. My kidneys are elm, my liver sycamore and, as a good sailor, I have a heart of oak. Oh, and my hair is chestnut.'

Truly he was a man of his wood; a small deciduous forest in human form.

'And did you sail here tonight, sir?' I asked jokily, for we were far from the sea.

'Yes. My ship is currently moored in Piccadilly Circus.' This was unusual, but did at least explain the traffic jam I had encountered earlier that evening, as well as the mast and sails I had seen. 'I never like to be more than a few hundred yards from her so I had my crew drag her out of the Thames and moor her there. But tomorrow HMS *Grrr* shall return to Portsmouth.'

Suddenly my heart beat faster. For the picture of my father that Aunt Lily had shown me in the newspaper those weeks ago was of the docks in that fine naval town – and the ship he had been in front of was this admiral's very own

HMS *Grrr*. Perhaps this was my chance to go and investigate further.

'I have always wanted to visit Portsmouth,' I said non-chalantly, twirling a piece of hair round my finger as if the thought had only just occurred to me and was of no consequence at all.

'It would be an honour to have such a distinguished inventor on board. Why not come down for lunch tomorrow?'

'I should like that very much, Admiral.'

'Then tomorrow it is. Now, excuse me, there are people I need to see.'

The rest of the evening passed in a giddy blur, all champagne, dancing and excitement at the potential discoveries I might make the next day. I remember brief images – Harry and Pippa dancing together amid the human wreckage created by Harry's dangerously uncoordinated movements; Mr Parsimonious yielding to his innately generous urges and pretending to be a waiter so he could give people things; and Admiral Hardthrasher walking past Mr Benevolent and seeming to wink collusively at him – but the party was no longer the most important thing, that status now being held by my imminent trip to Portsmouth.

Indeed, as soon as the clock struck midnight and announced the arrival of a new day, I boarded a carriage to the south coast, found my way to the docks by following the night cries of desperate prostitutes, and as dawn broke over the Channel I was knocking on the front door of HMS *Grrr*.

'Too early?' I asked, as the admiral himself answered it.

'It's never too early in the navy. We've been up for hours swabbing and swibbing the decks.[1] Come aboard and let me show you round.'

The ship was a mighty chunk of oaky magnificence, a four-decker and nine-master, with a hundred and forty-seven cannon – it should have been a hundred and forty-eight but the admiral was an enormous snooker fan. We stood on the pointy bit at the front[2] and surveyed the fleet at anchor.

'Look at all those marvellous ships.' The admiral sighed happily. 'Let me tell you their names. We have HMS *Aarggh*, HMS *Eeeurggh*, HMS *Anger*, HMS *Take-that-you-French-swine* and HMS *Take-that-you-British-swine*, which we captured off the French. Ah, my ships, my lovely violent, cannony ships . . .' He looked lovingly and longingly at them, shuddered briefly with joy, then snapped himself from his passionate naval reverie. 'Now I shall show you below decks.'

We went down to the next deck, the so-called throat of the ship, the remaining two decks being the stomach and bowels.

'This is the officers' mess, so-called because it is traditionally a terrible mess.' Nearby the ship's band was practising and I now heard a small drum-roll and cymbal-clash. 'Of course, your invention's changed that, so we'll probably have to call it the officers' neat from now on.'

---

[1] Swabbing technically refers to the vertical strokes of a mop, swibbing to the horizontal; they are equivalent to the warp and weft in weaving.

[2] He means the prow. With tight deadlines and the absence of Wikipedia, nineteenth-century authors often just ploughed on if they couldn't think of the right word.

We moved on through the ship and entered a vast chamber with large pieces of terrifying-looking equipment on the walls.

'These are the punishment quarters,' said the admiral, proudly.

'It seems the largest compartment on board.'

'Yes, well, we do a lot of punishment in the navy.'

'The cat o' nine tails?' I said, trying to sound knowledgeable.

'Cat o' nine tails? A pathetic tool. You might as well attack the men with a feather-duster. Which we do daily, of course, to keep them free of dust.' Now he approached a fearsome chunk of metal on the wall, and stroked it fondly. 'No, we use the dog o' ten spikes, the rabbit o' twelve punches and a very angry biting weasel. Proper punishments.'

Though he may have appeared to like me, clearly this Hardthrasher was as violent and cruel as his three late brothers.

'And if those punishments are not enough, the men go down here into solitary confinement.'

He opened a hatch in the deck, revealing a dark, wretched space. I shuddered at the claustrophobic horror therein.

'What sort of crime would see a man sent down there?'

'Only three things: cowardice in battle; being rude about the King; or murder. So in you go.'

Without warning, he shoved me hard in the back and I toppled forward through the hatch with a shout of alarm and a squeak of fear. I landed hard at the bottom and looked up to see the admiral glaring down at me.

'When I thanked you for killing my brothers, I thought you had only disposed of Jeremiah and Ratched. But in the meantime it has come to my attention that you were also responsible for my brother Ezekiel's demise.'

Ah. The beadle.

'I was not! Technically it was several blocks of stone with the Bible written on them that killed him!' I protested. Weakly, it has to be said.

'I don't care. I may have hated the other two, but I loved that man like a brother. Because he was.'

'But . . . how did you find out?'

The answer came not from the admiral, but from a new, familiar arrival whose face now loomed over me framed in the hatch.

'He found out from me.'

'Mr Benevolent!'

'Yup, me again. Thank you so much for helping me with my little problem, Admiral.'

'My pleasure.'

'What are you planning to do with me?' I asked fearfully.

Mr Benevolent grinned down at me, his teeth tiny white shards of malice. 'To use the vernacular your Bin invention has given us, the admiral is taking out the trash. Now, forgive me, but I must hurry back to London to woo your sister. For I am going to make her my bride, just to upset you. Even if you are dead when it happens. To upset your ghost, perhaps. Not that I believe in that sort of supernatural nonsense. But the principle stands.' He came to a slightly awkward halt. '*Aaaa*nyway, that's what I'm off to do. Goodbye, Pip Bin. Goodbye for ever.'

He waved at me, blew a kiss and then the hatch slammed shut. I could hear footsteps and evil laughter as he walked away, his horrid cackle dwindling to nothing.

'Ha, ha, ha, ha, ha, ha!'

All was briefly silence, but then I heard the sounds of the ship preparing to depart.

'Haul anchor and hoist the mainsail!'

'Middentrops to puncty and splice the shimmie-shangles!'[3]

With creaks and groans the mighty vessel set off, its destination unknown to me, my fate unknown to me, the square root of eight hundred and twenty-one unknown to me, though after a few seconds' rough calculation I reckoned it was just under twenty-nine, possibly about twenty-eight and three-quarters.

Fear gripped me as I stared at the confining walls of my shippy prison; terror wrapped its sinuous fingers around my throat, and panic began to tickle me under the arms, making me jitter and shake nervously.

What hope of escape was there for me now?

Or indeed for Pippa, whose future would involve a lot more Mr Benevolent than anyone might wish. True, she had Mr Parsimonious and Harry to protect her but . . . well, you know, they were both a bit rubbish.

Only I could protect her; and it seemed as if I could not protect even myself. For even if I could escape from this confinement – and it seemed as if I really could not – then I

---

[3] Sir Philip may have made up these supposedly nautical terms. I have never come across them in any other literature, and I've read at least two Patrick O'Brian novels.

would have to fight my way off the ship, which again seemed incredibly unlikely, and even if I managed that I would be adrift alone in the ocean with all the dangers that entailed.

Despair set in; and though I was now eighteen I felt nothing other than a boyish misery and the strong desire to shed bitter, illegal tears of woe.

So I did.

PART THE FIVETH

CHAPTER THE TWENTY-NINTH

Doom-despair to hope-happiness and back again

I slumped tearfully against the rough wood of the ship, as miserable as that most woeful of fish, the saddock.[1] All my money, success and fame as the inventor of the Bin meant nothing, for I was trapped and doomed to die, leaving behind a mad mother, a still missing possibly dead father, a daft best friend and an imminently Mr Benevolent-seduced sister. But as I rested my forehead despairingly against the coarse planks that encased me, I realized that the wood was not just rough from nature but from design – someone had scratched writing on it.

The near darkness of my captive space prevented reading, so I traced the letters with my fingers and read: 'Tnqneg 8lm'.

Alas, it was just nonsense. Or I'd got it wrong, accustomed as I was to reading with eyes not fingers.

Squinting in the dim, lazy light, I tried to make out the

---

[1] Basically a haddock with a frown. Probably sad because its name is a pun.

letters by more conventional ocular means and, over a period of some hours, my eyes gradually adjusted until I could read two sensible, non-nonsense words, which together formed a name, and not just any name, but a morale-boosting name of great import.

That name was Thomas Bin.

My father.

He had been on board this vessel! Admittedly in the hellish prison I now found myself in, but it proved that he was alive, or at least had been back then and might indeed be so still if in the meantime no deathy circumstance had waylaid him; though given that I had not heard from him in ages I was less than optimistic on that front, being perhaps only nano-hopeful or pico-positive.

Nevertheless, his name and that eency-weency teeny-tiny bit of hope was enough to fill me with both resolve and a resolution: I was going to get off this ship if it was the last thing I ever did.

Which was a bit of a silly resolution, actually, for if getting off the ship *was* actually the last thing I ever did then I might as well not bother, as other than some sense of satisfaction at having achieved that nautical escape, I would have gone no further to saving my family and would still be dead.

I re-resolutioned thusly: I was going to get off the ship and make sure it definitely was not the last thing I did, instead making sure that I went on to do more things, such as de-maddening my mother, finding my father and saving Pippa from Mr Benevolent's saucy clutches.

With that purpose in mind, I began to formulate a plan. Within an hour, I had got one. It was bold and ambitious, and required a tin of gunpowder, a small trampoline, seven yards of silk ribbon, a pineapple, a large trampoline and five highly trained parakeets, none of which I had to hand, so I abandoned it and started planning again.

But I had got no further than reformulating my original plan so that it needed only four parakeets, no ribbon and just the small trampoline, when the hatch above me opened to reveal the sadistically grinning face of Admiral Horatio Hardthrasher.

'Out you come, young swabbo!'

Two sailors reached down and hauled me out of my tiny, solitary compartment. They smelt of rum, seawater and gunpowder.[2] It was quite pleasant, actually, manly and mildly intoxicating. They threw me on to the deck in front of the admiral, and left, holding hands. Not each other's, just some hands they happened to have with them.

'So, just you and me, Bin. Before I send you down to Davy Jones's locker to fetch Ryan Jones's kitbag,[3] I thought I'd make you pay for killing the brother I loved.' The admiral was holding something out of sight behind his back, and I trembled at what horrific punishment it might be. 'Say hello to the rabbit o' twelve punches!'

I flinched in painful anticipation of this no doubt monstrous device, but instead the admiral merely produced a glove-puppet of a fluffy, sweet-looking rabbit, an

---

[2] This was the original scent of popular gentlemen's aftershave Old Spice, which was first sold in the nineteenth century as New Spice.

[3] Nineteenth-century nautical slang terms for the sea-bed and therefore drowning. Oddly, in recent years the phrase 'Ryan Jones's kitbag' has become a Welsh rugby slang term to denote general excellence.

object that seemed designed to make me say 'aw' rather than 'ow'.

'Why is it called— Ow!'

The admiral rapidly punched me twelve times, thus physically explaining the device's name, and I realized I had been wrong. For while the rabbity exterior might elicit coos of sweetness, the massive fist within was definitely meant to hurt, and it really, really did.

But it also unleashed a ferocity within me I had not known existed. Before the admiral could reload his punching bunny – by which I mean hit me again – I charged him and tackled him to the ground as if I was playing Bastardball, the hideously violent game taught me by one of his own brothers, though the irony of that fact was lost on me as only aggressive thoughts filled my mind.

As the admiral tried to get up, I hurled myself atop him and, seizing his wooden left arm, I pushed it hard against his wooden right leg and desperately began to rub the two together. My frantic efforts soon bore fruit as tendrils of smoke issued forth and then – glory be! – a spark followed by a small flame. I blew gently and encouragingly on the tiny fire, and it grew, spreading rapidly until every wooden part of him was aflame.

'No!' he shouted, staggering flamily around the deck. Where he touched, the ship too blossomed into fire, which raced pyromaniacally across the walls, ceiling and floor until I was surrounded by flickering menace.

It seemed as if I had leaped straight from an admiral-shaped frying pan into a fire-shaped fire, for I could see no way out. Then I espied a potentially life-saving axe on the wall, grabbed it, started hacking desperately at the walls of the ship and, after several splintering blows, a great rent appeared and seawater flooded in – surely this would now extinguish the fire.

It did.

It also sank the ship.

And so, mere minutes later, I found myself adrift in the English Channel. Alone. Wet. Cold. Frightened. But free.

CHAPTER THE THIRTIETH

Regarding rescues and returns

I quickly realized that my freedom from the ship might very soon be converted into a different kind of freedom, that is to say freedom from life, for the salty chill of the Channel rapidly began to suck the warmth from my body, like an aquatic vampire. There seemed no chance of survival as I was far from land and entirely at the mercy of the capricious tides; for this was still some years before Professor Wilkie Swim invented his famed method for propelling oneself through the water without the aid of a sail or a well-trained fish.[1]

And as I bobbed helplessly, feeling the cold sap my life-force, I saw a terrible sight in the form of a large, floating sign: 'Warning: you are about to leave the Channel and enter La Manche.'

I was drifting towards France.

---

[1] Wilkie Swim (1807–78) spent years perfecting Wilkie-ism or, as we know it, swimming, after witnessing an accident at a party where two men fell into a giant punch-bowl and drowned.

'Help!' I began to cry, as the watery border approached. 'Help!' Yet no help came, and I knew that within minutes I would have to shout, '*Au secours!*' to attract aid, a thought that made me sick to my incredibly British stomach.

Though it also occurred to me that if the cold waters continued their effective work at driving me towards death I might not actually live to face that French fate, in some ways a positive, but on balance a distinctly mixed blessing.

'Help!' I cried again, though more weakly than before. 'Help,' I now merely said, weaker still. 'Help . . .' I whimpered, my strength nearly gone.

I closed my eyes, and prepared to yield to the briny embrace of the sea. The river had claimed my aunt Lily; now its salty cousin was going to claim me. In fact, here from her watery afterlife, as if to guide me Charon-like[2] into the next world, was my late aunt, for I now heard her voice.

'Pip! Open your eyes, Pip!'

I did, and there she was before me, my brave, noble aunt Lily appearing to stand on the waves like a sea-nymph or Channel-elf.

'Are you come to carry me over to the other side, dear aunt?'

'What, France? No, I'm here to take you home.'

Home? I suppose in some ways the afterlife is a final home to all of us.

'Now grab this rope and let's get going!' She sounded cheery at the prospect of my death, and I have to admit this

---

[2] Charon was the ferryman who took souls to Hades across the river Styx in Greek mythology. Since the demise of ancient Greek belief systems, he is believed to have worked offering underworld booze-cruises.

made me a little cross. Then a wet rope hit me in the face and I was a lot cross. What place in spiritual death journeys did a wet rope in the face have?

Unless I wasn't dying and she was real.

I looked a little closer, and indeed she was real, tangible and alive, not standing on the water but on a small raft, and a distinctly corporeal, non-spiritual raft at that.

'Come on, grab the rope.'

I did as she said and she hauled me aboard her vessel.

'But I thought you were dead!' I exclaimed, hugging her equally from affection and for her bodily warmth. All right, maybe eighty-twenty in favour of the warmth. But I was much fondly glad to see her.

'The river swept me out to sea where I was trapped on a sandbank for weeks,' she explained, 'though I used the time constructively to capture and train this fish we are on.'

'Then this is not a raft?'

'No, it is a tuna.' Indeed it was, a mighty fish spread out beneath our feet.[3] 'I was just heading back to land when I saw you departing on HMS *Grrr*. Well, I thought I'd tag along, see what transpired, and isn't it lucky I did?'

'It is indeed. Thank you, Aunt Lily.'

'Now, let's get you home. Yah, go on, yah!' She snapped the fish reins she held in her hand and we were away, the tuna emitting a surprisingly horse-like whinny as it leaped forward through the waves.

As the noble piscine bore us back to Britain, I told her everything that had happened since I had last seen her,

---

[3] Probably the now extinct dinghy tuna.

especially of Mr Benevolent's naughty machinations and his avowed intention to marry Pippa.

'I fear that awful man will not rest until he has married a daughter of our family.' Aunt Lily sighed, and I remembered that she had once been engaged to my evil ex-guardian herself.

'Why were you going to marry him, Aunt Lily?' I was eager to hear how such a state had come about; it seemed as if the tuna was, too, as he now turned his head to look at her.

'I was once young and naïve. And Benevolent was handsome and charming. Alas, that charm was an illusion and the good looks concealed bad thoughts.'

'What happened?'

'He wooed me. He used all the seductive tricks a girl might fall for – flowers, pleasant letters, tips of the hat, a funny nickname, pretending to care about my womanly opinion, being nice – and I did indeed fall for them. We eloped to marry without the knowledge of our families, but it turned out he was merely after the money my father had left me; he took it and then abandoned me at the altar. I was too ashamed to admit what had happened so I ran off and started my life of adventure.'

'But why does he persist in persecuting our family?'

'I do not know. I heard that a friend of Benevolent's did a similar thing to a woman named Havisham and it drove her insane. Perhaps my refusal to collapse similarly made him angry. Or maybe he needed a family to hate and randomly picked ours from the telegram directory.[4] Whatever

---

[4] Forerunner to the telephone directory.

the reason, it has been a long and complex act of sustained malice.' She stopped and pointed forwards. 'Aha! We are nearing the shore!'

Indeed we were: looming ahead of us I could see the great cliffs of Dover, which were much more patriotic back then, being not just white but red and blue as well. Soon Aunt Lily pulled the tuna alongside the dock in the small Kentlesex port of Narrowsteps and I stepped off on to good old English soil once more.

'I am afraid, dear Pip, that I cannot come with you to thwart Benevolent.'

'Why not?' I feared that, without her aid, defeating my evil ex-guardian would be beyond my callow self.

'I am required on a mission by the Crown.'

'What mission?'

'I'm not really meant to say but . . .' She pulled me close and whispered, 'We're going to go and steal a Channel Island and bring it closer to Britain. Such larks, eh, Pip?'

'And jolly moorhens too, I should imagine, Aunt Lily.'

'I will return as soon as I can to help you.' She looked me in the eye and smiled. 'But I think that now you are a grown man you will not need such help.'

At her words my self-doubt melted away and I felt my chest swell with pride, which ripped my shirt and popped a button off my waistcoat. The button pinged into the dock, striking the tuna on its dorsal fin. It reared up with a startled sea-whinny, then raced off, Aunt Lily barely managing to cling on.

'Good luck!' she yelled.

'And to you!' I yelled back, and she was gone.

As it turned out, my luck to her helped, for she was a successful part of that great, sneaky British accomplishment the theft of Jernseyark, the largest remaining French Channel Island that was towed across to England and renamed the Isle of Wight.[5]

And her luck to me helped also, for on my return to London I had the good fortune to— But, no, that is for another chapter, which is coming up . . .

---

[5] This is officially the greatest practical joke in history, a gigantic operation involving seven thousand ships, thirty-eight miles of rope and an absolutely enormous spade. It was overseen by legendary secretary of state for pranks and pranking Sir Jeremy de Beadle.

CHAPTER THE THIRTY-FIRST

In which I am love thumpd and passion punched

. . . now.

I immediately hired a coach and four to take me to
London, though two of the horses had a limp and one of
the wheels was square so it was a brutally uncomfortable
trip. To make matters worse, halfway there one of the
non-limping horses broke free of its harness, thereby
making us a coach and three and, directionally imbalanced,
we went round and round in a wide, bumpy circle until,
mercifully, the driver managed to shoot another of the
naughty equines and we could continue in a more direct
direction.

On entering London's hectic streets we came to a
halt, along with what seemed to be every other vehicle in
the capital. There was a street-sweepers' strike in progress and consequently the roads were piled high with
impassable piles of unswept horse ordure: movement
was being prevented by movements, motion by motions.

The whole city was one gigantic traffic chutney.[1]

Realizing that walking would be quicker, I paid off the driver, dismounted the carriage and remounted Shanks's pony, that is to say my feet; and to make the journey home both faster and less blocked by equine faeces, I decided to cut through Indigo Park, part of the newly constructed ring of so-called spectrum parks around inner London.[2]

I was barely seven or so steps into the park when it happened.

For there, crossing a path ahead of me, gaily twirling a parasol and giggling lightly, was the most beautiful creature I had ever set eyes on; and when I say creature I do not mean a squirrel, pigeon or other such parkland beast, I mean a woman.

And oh! Such a woman I had never seen!

I instantly fell in love with her perfect mix of beauty, radiance, prettiness, gorgeous-osity, loveliness, allure, tiny kissable nose-iness, elegance, charm and pure good looks.

In the vernacular of the day, she was hot; in Latin she was *puella phwoarissima*; and in comparison with characters from ancient polytheistic societies, she made Aphrodite look a bit of an old munter.

She was a stunner – quite literally, for one perfect glimpse of her and my entire body stopped working and I

---

[1] The phrase 'traffic jam' did not enter common parlance until the twentieth century. Until then people used the phrases 'traffic chutney', 'traffic ketchup' and 'traffic-shire sauce'.

[2] Most have been built over since the nineteenth century, the only ones left to us being Green Park and the invisible Ultraviolet Park.

collapsed on the ground in a smiling, dribbling heap of lovestruckness.

As I lay there, I noticed a gentleman nearby crouched behind some bushes, and as soon as the power of speech returned to me I asked if he knew who this goddess was.

'Why, sir, the whole of London knows who she is! For she is noted beauty Miss Flora Dies-Early. And I am definitely not hiding behind these bushes to spy on her.' I had thought no such thing, but as he continued, his voice a rising crescendo of defensiveness, I began to think exactly such a thing. 'Nor am I using these binoculars to look more closely at her. And this notebook I am carrying is certainly not full of obsessively logged details of her every waking moment together with various lewd yet imaginative drawings. How dare you accuse me of such behaviour, sir?'

With that, he stalked haughtily off. And I suspect my use of the word 'stalked' is more than apposite. But at least I now had the name that was to live in my heart, and, as I lay in my lovestruck state, I whispered it to myself over and over.

'Flora Dies-Early . . . Flora Dies-Early . . . Flora Dies— Ow!' This last syllable emerged as a large man tripped clumsily over my still prone body.

'Sorry, old chap, didn't see you down there.'

I was about to get incredibly cross with the galumphing oaf, but suddenly realized I had recognized his voice. 'Harry? Harry Biscuit, is that you?' I asked, for the careless heffalump was indeed my best friend.

'Pip Bin! What a joy!' he exclaimed in reply.

'Dear Harry, how glad I am to see you, old chum!'

'Not as glad as I am to see you, I wager.'

'Well, I am very glad to see you, Harry.'

'Then I am . . . a lot very glad to see you much.'

Now that the amount of gladness all round had been established, I offered him my hand and he helped me to my still love-wobbly feet.

'So, how are you, Pip Bin?'

'Tremendously well, thank you, Harry. For I am in love!' As I said the words my heart skipped giddily and stars of joy swam before my eyes.[3] 'Have you ever been in love, Harry?'

'No, Pip Bin, I have not. Though I have been in Hove. Is that similar?'

'Possibly,' I replied. 'But love has no pier and fewer old people.'

'Well, it sounds great, as long as it still has the ice creams and funny seagulls.'[4]

'What are you doing in the park, Harry?'

'Oh, I am taking a walk. Because Mr Benevolent popped round to see Pippa and I thought I should give them a bit of time together.'

'Harry, no! Have you not learned how evil Mr Benevolent is? He has pledged to seduce her – we must save her!'

---

[3] It seems as if he may have been suffering from a love-related heart condition known as *ding-dongycardia.*

[4] Seagulls are never funny. They are all terrifying. This is not just personal prejudice because a seagull once attacked me in Aberystwyth when I was younger, it is a true fact of science. Ask Richard Dawkins. About the science. He wasn't there when I was attacked.

'Oh, ruddy cripes,' said Harry, his face reddening. 'What have I done? Pippa!' he cried, and set off running across the park.

'Wrong way!' I yelled after him, starting to run myself, but in the correct direction, namely towards my house, with only one thing on my mind: saving Pippa from Mr Benevolent's potentially lewd clutches.

CHAPTER THE THIRTY-SECOND

Get your hands off her, you damned dirty ex-guardian

Actually, there were two things on my mind, for I could not forget Miss Flora Dies-Early, and the combination of the two simultaneous mind-thoughts made my face alternate between a soppy look of wistful adoration and one of sister-saving determination as I ran.

But as I approached the large West End townhouse I shared with Pippa and Harry, thoughts of Flora fled and my priority became sister protection as from inside I heard the silken, malevolent tones of my evil ex-guardian.

'So, Pippa Bin, your brother is nowhere to be found. Perhaps he has abandoned you, maybe even been lost at sea, cast into the oceans by an evil admiral from a ship called HMS *Grrr*. That's just a for-instance. A guess. You can't tie me to it.'

Now I had reached the front door – but it was locked. I frantically patted my pockets for my keys as his sinuous tones continued within.

'No young woman should be left alone, lest saucy and fiendish things happen to her.'

'But I am protected by true virtue, Mr Benevolent,' replied my steadfast sister.

He snorted in response. 'True virtue? Pah! You'd be better off with a pair of lockable metal pants.'

My keys, where were my keys? I could not find them in my pockets and feared they had been lost on my recent adventures. I turned to see Harry approaching, still some distance off, and prayed to Heaven that he had his keys on him.

'Now, let me woo you.' Mr Benevolent cleared his throat and began. 'First of all I have brought you some flowers. I have also written you a letter, which you may find pleasant. And now, look, I am respectfully yet suggestively tipping my hat in your direction.'

With horror, I realized he was using the seductive tricks Aunt Lily had said he had used on her all those years ago. How could my poor, innocent sister resist them?

'Tell me, Pippa-poo, what do you think of the Corn Laws?'

Now he had combined two more of the tricks, giving her a nickname, though an uninventive slightly scatological one, and asking her womanly opinion; and as Pippa began to answer I could hear him saying, 'Uh-huh,' as if he was listening to her and actually caring what she thought. My blood ran cold: all he had to do was be nice to her and surely his seduction would succeed!

Now Harry had arrived and – thank Clortho the keymaster – [1] he had his keys in his hand. I seized them from him and

---

[1] An ancient Sumerian deity. This is one of only two known references to him in modern literature, the other being in F. Scott Fitzgerald's novel The Great Ghostbusters, later adapted into the film of very nearly the same name.

started to work on the lock, as Mr Benevolent moved to the final stage of his wooing.

'A valid opinion, well expressed.'

'Oh, why, thank you . . .' Pippa giggled. She giggled! At this most evil of men!

This was not good.

'And may I say what a lovely dress you're wearing.'

He was being nice to her! The end was nigh. And the lock was proving fiddly. I removed the key and tried again.

'Now, I have wooed you with sweet words and blandish-ments so I think I deserve a kiss.' Through the window I could see him lunge at Pippa with lips pursed; fortunately she stepped out of the way and he ended up kissing the mantelpiece, which blushed.

'Mr Benevolent! That is no way for a gentleman to behave!'

Bless my morally strong sister, resistant to the wooing that would have seen so many women already kissed, if not fully naked.

'Oh, come on, just one kiss. Or maybe a touch.' I could see him advancing on her as the lock finally turned. 'Let me touch your foot. Or ankle. Or your calf.'

Now a small, frightened moo came from the house.

'You leave that calf alone!'

Pippa moved protectively to the young orphaned cow she had taken in as part of her charity work for animals, and I at last opened the door and rushed inside.

Pausing for only a minute or so to check the post on the table in the hallway – I had been away a while and you have to keep on top of these things – I at last made it into the drawing room to hear: 'One day, Pippa Bin, I shall marry you, take your family name and money, then divest you of your virtue and discard you like a bad book or a used hen.'

Until this point, my blood had been running cold; now it inverted its temperature and ran piping hot, like grumpy soup.

'No! Enough of your malicious and seductive verbiage, Mr Benevolent!'

I quickly interposed myself between my ex-guardian and my sister, who clasped me in sororal relief.

'Oh, look, it's Pip Bin. The richest young man in Britain, hurrah for him. Not.' Mr Benevolent stared at me with his glinting obsidian eyes. 'And still alive. Which is surprising. And inconvenient.'

'Get out of my house, Mr Benevolent.'

'No.'

'Please?'

'Still no.'

'Damn! Then we have a stalemate.'

And as we stood there, eyeing each other beadily, like jealous crows, it seemed as if we did indeed have such a situation. But I had reckoned without Harry, who burst into the room, his face purple with rage, like an angry grape.

'Get away from Pippa, you fiend! Or I shall attack you both violently and with violence!'

Only now did I noticed that Harry was wielding a weapon, which he thrust in Mr Benevolent's direction: it was a stuffed badger, taken from the house's taxidermatorium,[2]

---

[2] Until 1854 by law all houses of rich people had to have a room full of dead, stuffed animals, preferably shot or strangled by the owner themselves.

its teeth bared in an angry, pre-stuffing death rictus.

This was an unusual choice of weapon, but surprisingly effective, as Mr Benevolent instantly flinched and cowered before Harry's threats.

'No! How did you know about my fear of the largest British mustelid?'[3]

Though I hated him, I did have to admit a little admiration for his knowledge of mammalian taxonomy.

'Um, lucky guess, really,' Harry admitted, jabbing the badger Benevolent-wards once more, forcing him to back away.

'The mere threat of that striped beast, even though dead, is enough to make me leave.'

I took the badger from Harry and used it to drive Mr Benevolent out of the room and from the house, though as I shut the front door on him he jammed his foot into the jamb and sneered at me. 'I will overcome my badger-fear and return, Pip Bin. For you can only stop me so many times before your luck runs out or mine runs in. And then your sister will be mine. Ha, ha—' He stopped mid evil laugh, his nostrils wrinkling. 'Incidentally, you smell of fish.'

'I have been riding on a tuna.'

'That would explain it, then. Now, what was I saying? Ah, yes. Ha, ha, ha!'

He laughed cruelly at me, but for the first time it instigated no cowering fear for, as Aunt Lily had said, I was a man now, indeed a rich man who had survived all this evil

---

[3] From the Latin *mustela* meaning 'weasel'; yes, the badger is related to the weasel. As are the otter, the wolverine and the polecat. Biology and evolution are interesting, aren't they?

fellow had thrown at me thus far, and I was certain I could survive anything.

He continued laughing ineffectually for some seconds, then noticed my lack of response and came to a slightly embarrassed halt. 'The laugh's not really doing it any more, is it?'

I shook my head at him, I like to think slightly patronizingly.

'Hmm. I'll work on a new and improved one. Good day, Pip Bin, whom I hate and will destroy.'

He tipped his hat at me, withdrew his foot from the door and I slammed it in his face, then went to see how my poor, nearly seduced sister fared.

She was sitting on a chair, gazing out of the window, as custom dictates troubled womenfolk should do, and Harry stood in the equivalent male pose, leaning thoughtfully against the mantelpiece with a whisky in his hand.

'Pippa, are you all right?' I asked, hastening to her side.

'Yes, thanks to you, dear brother, and Harry, dear friend.'

'That must have been a hideous experience.' I placed a consoling hand upon her shoulder.

'Oh, yes, it was. Although . . .' She turned to me, her eyes oddly shining.

'There can be no although!'

'Yes, of course, you are right.' She resumed her fenestral gaze. 'The idea of being touched by a man makes me shudder. In a sort of ambiguous way . . .' Now she shuddered ambiguously with excitey-horror.

'There can be no ambiguity!'

'Again you are right, dear brother.' She ceased shuddering and resumed gazing.

'Mr Benevolent has designs on you, dear sister, and not noble designs such as those for a cathedral or a lovely dress, but vile, lascivious designs that would leave you tainted and soiled.'

'Ooh, crikey!'

This word sounded entirely too excited for my liking and I responded strongly. 'No, not crikey! Nor cripes, tish or ooh-la-la. This calls for bah, aaarrggh and "Get your hands off my sister." You must be protected. But how?'

'I know, Pip Bin!'

'Yes, Harry?'

As Harry leaned on the mantelpiece, whisky in hand, he looked so sensible and manly that for a minute I genuinely believed he might have a proper solution.

'We could build a very big wall around her.'

'Harry . . .'

'Or we could make her a dress out of copper and then pass modern electricity through it meaning that anyone who touched her would be electricked to death!'[4]

'Harry . . .'

'Or what about a highly trained guard-swan—'

'Harry!' I cut him off with a bolt of verbal violence. Despite his sensible, manly, whisky-wielding demeanour he had once again been an utter twit. 'I have made a decision.

---

[4] The sterner Scottish Presbyterians actually utilized such dresses as anti-lust devices. Unfortunately, though protected from men, the wearers were not protected from the rainy Scottish weather, leading to several nasty cases of short-circuiting and electrocution.

Pippa must go and live abroad for a while; only then will she be far enough away from Mr Benevolent's clutches.'

Harry nodded in agreement. 'A fine idea, Pip Bin. Of course, she will need a chaperone. Someone of a noble and faithful temperament, loyal beyond doubt, brave and strong and dedicated to Pippa's protection.'

'You are right, Harry. And I know just the person for the job: Mr Parsimonious.'

'Actually, I was talking about— Oh, never mind.'

For some reason Harry now went to the corner of the room and angrily kicked the skirting board; perhaps he had seen a mouse.

I immediately summoned that loyal friend Mr Parsimonious and, on his arrival, explained the situation to him. He agreed with my proposal, and even had a suggestion as to a safe destination for Pippa protection. 'We shall head to France,' Mr Parsimonious said.

At mention of this destination a shudder ran down my spine. 'Is that wise? Will it not be fearfully unpleasant?'

'Exactly. No Englishman would willingly choose to go there, so even if he found out where we were, Benevolent would not follow.'

I understood the logic, but liked it not.

'Besides, I am to protect Pippa's virtue, am I not?' Mr Parsimonious continued. 'And Frenchmen are surely too cowardly to come near any woman. For the same reason we shall head afterwards to Italy.'

Again, I could not fault his logic, but still liked it not. Nevertheless, in fear of Mr Benevolent's seductive return, plans were set in motion, bags were set in pack, a coach and horses was ordered up, and by teatime Pippa and Mr Parsimonious were ready to leave.

As I stood with Harry on the doorstep, waving them off on their journey, I knew that Pippa's virtue would now be safe, and I felt a burden of responsibility lift from my shoulders and a heavy package of obligation lift from my head.

'I shan't miss her, you know,' said Harry. 'I shan't miss her sweet nature, her angelic presence and her beautiful face.'

This surprised me, as I had always thought Harry was rather fond of Pippa. He quickly surprised me again, as with a thick snuffle he began to cry.

'Are you all right, Harry?'

'Yes, fine, all fine, thank you.'

'Are you crying?'

'No. Yes. But because I just remembered a sad story I once read. About a poorly child. And a dead dog.'

'Those are the saddest stories.' Indeed, to this day the saddest story I know is the tale of *Consumptive Colin and his Late Lamented Labrador.*[5]

'Oh, Pippa!' Harry now wailed. 'The dog was called Pippa. I'm crying about the dog in the story, not your sister.'

'I understand, Harry.'

'Excuse me. I'm just going out for a walk. Or I might go and join the army. To forget.'

Harry, still crying, left the house, and from outside I heard another great wail of 'Pippa!'

---

[5] A book that was finally banned in 1927 after making too many children cry.

It really must have been a good story to have affected him so deeply, and I made a mental note to ask him to lend it to me when he returned; but for the moment, I had other things on my mind. For my thoughts had turned seriously to love, and I had decided that I must begin planning my campaign to woo Miss Flora Dies-Early.

CHAPTER THE THIRTY-THIRD

Woos that girl

Early the next day, I headed to Indigo Park, where I had first seen the gorgeous Flora, for it was the custom of the time for young ladies to gather there of a morning to exchange girlish gossip and tinkling lady laughter.

The weather was glorious: clear blue skies, the gentlest of tickling breezes and the temperature warm but not sweat-inducingly hot – a meteorological ideal to match my perfect love.

On my way, I stopped and bought a bunch of flowers, the first weapon in any wooing war. As I emerged from the florist's, however, I had an unwelcome meeting.

'Ah, Pip Bin, off wooing, are we?' It was Mr Benevolent, as smoothly malicious as ever, like a buttered snake. 'You won't get far with those flowers. They are awful. Mine are much better.' He, too, was bearing a bouquet of floral flattery. 'These are for your sister. She will yield to me eventually.'

'Ha!' I decided a small gloat or klid was in order. 'You'll

have to find her first. For I have hidden her far from your reach!'

At this piece of news, Mr Benevolent's face spasmed with thwartedness, but he quickly recovered his poise. 'I won't be needing these flowers for wooing, then, will I?'

'You will not, sir.'

'So I may as well put them to a better use. Have at you, sir!' He suddenly sprang into a sword-fighting pose, raised his bouquet as if it were a sabre, and began slashing at me with it. I had no option but to fight back, parrying his blows with my own flowers, and this floral fencing continued until both bouquets were ruined, beheaded of their pretty blooms and reduced to mere tattered stalks.

'You won't be wooing anyone with that, Pip Bin!' he crowed triumphantly. He was right; he had won a tiny, petty, woo-ruining victory.

'Yes, but neither will you with yours, Mr Benevolent,' I retorted somewhat lamely. 'Besides, you'd have to find Pippa in France to even attempt to woo her.'

With hindsight, letting slip Pippa's location was a rash thing to have done, as the next chapter will inform you. But at the time I thought nothing of it as Mr Benevolent instantly grinned with evil happiness, then hailed a passing carriage and boarded it, shouting, 'Coachman, take me to Dover so I may find a ship to France!' for I was merely glad he was gone and I could continue my quest for love.

I stuffed the broken fragments of flower into one of my Bins – London was now full of them – proceeded to Indigo Park and for the second time I saw Miss Flora Dies-Early. This time I was prepared for the majestic sight of her, and did not collapse in a dribbling heap, though my heart beat faster, my breath breathed shallower and my knees wobbled excitedly. Nearing her glorious radiance, I raised my hat and said my first words to the woman I knew I was destined to love for ever.

'Excuse my boldness but—'

I got no further before a colossal, black-clad figure tackled me from the side, piling into me and driving me to the ground.

'How dare you talk to Miss Dies-Early? How dare you even look at her?'

I raised myself painfully from the ground and addressed this huge person. 'I beg your pardon, sir. I merely—'

Again I was interrupted, though this time fortunately with words, not violence. 'Sir? You call me "sir"? Is it not obvious I am a woman?'

I looked the massive figure up and down. 'Um, well . . .' For it was not obvious. True, 'she' wore a dress, and had a feminine hairstyle that looked like a hairy loaf of bread stuck to 'her' head, but then 'she' also appeared to have stubble, and certainly possessed the strength and physique of a man, and not just any old man but a somewhat strapping, beefy one at that. Plus, 'her' voice was a little deep for a lady.

'Because I am a woman! I am Miss Dies-Early's governess.'

Delicate politeness fought with truth-seeking directness, and the latter won. 'And you're sure you're a woman?'

'As sure as I am sure that I have a womb, which I do.'

Despite the manly-seeming evidence to the contrary, that statement clinched it: no man could possibly have said such a feminine word as 'womb' without either laughing or dying of embarrassment, and I decided to remove the inverted commas from my thoughts on the matter, 'her' swiftly becoming her.

'Then I apologize for my wrong-gendering, Miss . . . ?'

'Miss Chastity Hardthrasher.'

Ah. That explained the strange familiarity I had sensed in her, as well as the distinctively frightening height, cruel nose and grumpy eyebrows – she was clearly the sister of those monstrous brothers, and would therefore doubtless prove a formidable obstacle to my wooing of Flora. But love drove me on, as if I were an incredibly determined, much-whipped horse.

'Allow me to introduce myself. I am—'

'I know who you are, young man.' This might not be good for me, if she knew what I had done to her brothers. 'You are Mr Pip Bin, inventor of the Bin.'

Phew. That was the context she knew me in.

'And murderer of my brothers.'

Oh. And that one.

'Luckily for you, I hated them. Oh, we got on fine while children but then as we grew and I became a woman they said I was a weakling and a coward who clearly hadn't tried hard enough, otherwise I'd have become a man like them.'[1]

She sniffed a little, and did I see a memory of pain in her eyes? Certainly they glistened with something, possibly tears – or maybe she'd got some make-up stuck in them, as often happens to women. I chose to believe it was a painful

---

[1] It was a common theory of the time that women were just men who had suffered from weakness of spirit in adolescence.

memory and that this woman had emotions her brothers lacked; and that therefore if I showed my love was pure and honest and true I might have a chance.

'Miss Hardthrasher, may I walk and talk with your charge?'

'No!' Her voice tolled like feminine thunder. 'For she is no slattern or morally slack trollop!'

'But—'

'If you wish to talk to Miss Dies-Early you may apply in writing for a tea appointment, as etiquette demands.' She turned and began to usher her charge from my sight. 'Good day, sir.'

'And to you, tall madam.' I respectfully doffed my hat in her direction, then instantly rushed home and did as she had suggested, using nice notepaper, my best handwriting and a substantial bribe to persuade the postman to deliver my tea-requesting missive as soon as possible. I received a reply by return of post; the appointment was for later that week.

My heart skipped, my liver twirled and my kidneys did a tango: I was going to meet Miss Flora Dies-Early, and our life of love together could begin.

CHAPTER THE THIRTY-FOURTH

Of love and letters

On the morning of the longed-for tea appointment I received a letter from my dear sister Pippa:

Dearest brother Pip,

We have arrived safely in France and, much to my surprise, it is fantastic or as they say here '*fantastique*'. Last night at dinner I discovered a local dish called '*cheval*'. Alas, it turns out '*cheval*' means 'horse', and you know how I despise cruelty to animals of all sorts, so imagine my dismay when it turns out that horse is delicious. Really, really yummy. I am ashamed to admit that gastronomy won out over ethics and I had two helpings of horse pie and three of sticky pony pudding. I felt so bad! Yet so full. Must dash, as we are shortly to continue our journey.

Your loving sister, Pippa

This was a relief, as I had feared after my accidental mention of France to Mr Benevolent that he might have followed her there. But, as I was about to set off for tea with Flora, the second post brought a more worrying sisterly missive.

Dear Pip,

I am writing again so soon to tell you that we have been forced to stay another night in this hotel as our beloved coach-pulling horse has apparently fallen ill. Still, at least I have another chance to enjoy *cheval* for supper, and I'm sure he'll be better soon and we shall be on our way.

Lots of love, Pippa

PS Thought I saw Mr Benevolent skulking in some shadows but I'm sure I didn't really.

This was less of a relief to me, but I sort of didn't care because I was in love and about to meet the target of that love for the very first time. I arrived precisely at the requested time, and was shown into a room where Miss Hardthrasher awaited me.

'Mr Bin, you are prompt. That is good. What is that you are carrying?'

'Flowers. For Flora. For does her name not mean "flowers" in Latin?'

'Flowers!' Her voice was a curious mix of shrill and deep. 'Flowers are the vegetation of that most lustful of creatures, the satyr!'

'Eh?'

'They are lusty plants of immorality! With their stalks nestled within unfolding petals! And their nectar! They are wicked, symbolically saucy things, and must be burned lest they taint the moral atmosphere!'

She was panting as she finished this moralizing speech, her stubbly face flushed, and she seized the flowers from my grasp, hurled them into the fireplace, then slumped into an armchair with an audible groan of satisfaction.

'Might I ask when Flora will be joining us?'

'She will not.'

'But I thought we were to have tea together?'

'And so you shall. But in the same room? No!' Now the governess raised herself from her chair and towered scarily over me. 'For she is no slut, strumpet or gaudy Jezebel-like harlot!'

'No, of course not.'

'Miss Dies-Early is in another room.'

'Next door?' I gestured at the wall and the room beyond.

'In Scotland. If today goes well and you comport yourself with dignity, grace and not a trace of lust, then you may soon have tea in the same country. If that goes well, then we shall remove the *r* and you shall tea-ize in the same county. Then in the same town and eventually in the same house.' How exciting this all sounded! I was so close to actually seeing Flora! 'But not unaccompanied in the same room until you are married, lest bawdiness ensue. After all, she is no panting scullery-maid desperately hoping to catch the young master at his ablutions with all the consequences that might imply.'

'Heaven forfend such a thought.'

'Hmm, Heaven. That is a moral word, therefore I deem

our tea a success. You may return another time.'

Oh, joy! The path to true love was set out before me like a shining, many-treaded staircase that would take ages to climb – but I had taken the first steps, and I knew nothing now would stop me.

Other matters, however, were not so reassuring, for on my return home I found that the ninth post – there were fifteen daily deliveries back then – had brought another letter from Pippa.

Dear Pip,

All is not well. It turns out that it was Mr Benevolent skulking in the shadows earlier. He has somehow discovered that we are in France and even as I write he is hammering at my very door. Oh, Pip! He is through the door and is advancing across the room towards me almost faster than I can write this! I must stop now and call Mr Parsimonious for help.

Hope you are well,

Love, Pippa

Then the letter continued in a different hand:

Dear Pip,

Just writing to reassure you that I heard Pippa's cries for help, have entered the room and seen Mr Benevolent advancing on her, and as soon as these brief lines are finished I shall stop him.

All good wishes,

Mr Parsimonious

Though the reassurance that his note provided was short-lived as the letter now continued in a cruel spidery hand:

Dear Pip Bin,
   Mr Benevolent here, just letting you know that that old fool has put down the pen so it is mine now, mine! And soon your sister will be too. Ha ha ha! Ha ha—

Here there was an inky squiggle as if someone had wrenched a pen off someone else, and then the writing changed to the reassuring script of Mr Parsimonious:

Dear Pip,
   I've got it back! And I—

Again there was a pen-wrenched squiggle and now the cruel, evil writing reappeared, though it lasted only two words:

   Mine again.

Before, in a differently coloured ink, my sister's writing reappeared:

Dear Pip,
   I have found a spare pen! Help us, Pip, help us!

Now there came a swift flurry of differently written intercessions, first Benevolent:

Dear Pip Bin,

Just a quick line to let you know that I am about to tell Pippa to put that other pen down or I shall kill Parsimonious.

Yours etc . . .

Then Pippa:

Just to let you know I'm going to do that then.

And, worryingly, the final lines were in a hand all too familiarly nasty again:

She's done that and I've said 'good'. I have them now and there's nothing you can do about it.

Yours sincerely,

Gently Benevolent esquire xxxx[1]

I was concerned by this latest missive, but also in love. And love triumphs concern every time. I decided that they would probably be fine. Or not. Anyway, what could I do about it? Apart from going to help. Which I wasn't going to do while I was wooing Flora. And at least there was also a cheering postcard from Harry:

---

[1] It's all gone a bit epistolary, I'm afraid. I'm sorry if it reminds any English-literature graduate of being forced to read those interminable chunks of dullness *Pamela* or *Clarissa*, or even Richardson's longest and dullest such novel *Letters to and from my Accountant.*

Dear Pip Bin,

In the end I did go and join the army. I wish I hadn't. It is awful. For starters, it turns out I have a terrible fear of the colour red, which is not ideal, what with the uniform, all the blood and the rations being mostly tomato soup. And they made me kill two men. With my bare feet. Which was horrid.

Yours ever,

Harry

PS I did see a funny pigeon though. Hilarious!

At least it seemed as if Harry was having fun, though I admit I may not have read his postcard all that carefully.

Because I was in love.

Did I mention that?

Ah, love!

It filled every fibre of my being and every morsel of my soul. My love for Flora made life so much deeper: colours were brighter, noises were louder, tastes were stronger. I could not sleep, could not eat, could not sit, could not stand, could barely kneel without thoughts of her rushing in and crushing all else, like a massive, lovely mammoth.

And I hadn't even met her yet.

But I worked assiduously towards that moment, over a series of more and more geographically proximate teas with the forbidding governess Hardthrasher, until at long last it was the day I was due to actually meet the glorious object of my affections. Really, actually, truly, properly meet her for real, like.

CHAPTER THE THIRTY-FIFTH

More love, more letters

On that most glorious of days, I entered the woo-atorium[1] and, directed by Miss Hardthrasher, sat incredibly carefully in the suitor's seat, a high-backed chair with a threatening spike protruding dangerously between my legs towards my gentleman's special region.

'You have prepared as I ordered, Mr Bin?'

'I have.'

'You took a cold bath for three days?'

'Yes.'

'You are wearing ice-filled underwear?'

'I am.' I shivered with discomfort; but if that was the lust-denying price of meeting my beloved, so be it. I would have done anything to meet her properly: chopped off my right hand, eaten my own eyeballs, even sung 'La Marseillaise'.

Actually, no, not the last.

Or the other two, come to think of it.

---

[1] Special room for courting.

But ice-pants and a three-day cold bath, fine.

'Good. Then I shall make final preparations.'

Now Miss Hardthrasher took a hammer, nails and several planks of wood and rapidly built a fence around my chair. 'Do not move beyond the fence. For my charge is no naïve debutante stumbling across a sweaty stable-boy stripped to the waist and wondering why she's suddenly gone all hot downstairs.'

'I never thought she was.'

'Very well. I shall fetch Miss Dies-Early.'

As I waited for my beloved's arrival, I was nervous. Now our meeting was actually real, fears and worries crowded into my mind like dodgy relatives at a family function, unwelcome and frightening.

What if we had nothing to say to each other? True, that is the case in many relationships, but usually becomes so only some time after marriage – with good luck, years afterwards, with bad luck, minutes. Or what if in the weeks since I had last actually seen her she had got moosey and munterish? Maybe grown a spot on her nose, or developed some kind of repellent facial tic, even cut her hair. All these things could destroy our love, even though it was obviously strong, true and not shallow.

I need not have worried.

As she approached the room, I began to feel quite strange.

When the door opened, I swear I could hear my heart beating, like a well-struck drum; and as she stepped into the room, it was as if the air was filled with uplifting choral music.

Then there she was: serene and beautiful.

And with a choir and a drummer behind her.

'Miss Dies-Early likes music when she enters a room,' said Miss Hardthrasher.

'It is the least her beauty deserves,' I flattered, because, blinking heck, she was a cracker.

She glided across the room like a well-oiled swan, and sat in a chair in the manner I imagine an angel would have sat, though with fewer wings, that is to say none.

Miss Hardthrasher seated herself on a stool between us, less like an angel, more like a navvy in a dress.

'Now, you may have intercourse.'

Hello!

'In the traditional, old-fashioned sense of the word.'

Oh. That sort of intercourse.

'Of course. I thought nothing else,' I lied. 'So, are you well today, Flora?'

'How dare you address her so informally and directly! She is no leather-clad Dutch lady-of-the-night beckoning through the steamed-up window of a house of ill-repute!' Miss Hardthrasher pulled out an anti-lust pokerizer[2] and prodded me hard in the ribs. 'All conversation will go through me!'

'Of course. Forgive me. Would you kindly ask Miss Dies-Early if the day finds her well?'

The governess repeated my question to Flora, who answered with a shy, coquettish giggle that almost made me burst with loveful joy.

---

[2] Essentially a rather grandiose term for a stick.

'Miss Dies-Early says . . .' Now Miss Hardthrasher repeated the giggle.

It really wasn't the same.

Where Flora's trilling happiness had filled every part of me with a tingling sensation, her governess's version left me feeling as though I had been filled with wet suet, then hit with a clay hammer, so lumpen and heavy a version of my love's laugh it was. Nevertheless, I pressed ahead with my intercoursing.

'Perhaps you might now pass my compliments on to Miss Dies-Early on her dress.'

'No! That is enough of your lustful advances for one day. For she is no drunken floozy seeking to earn the money for a holiday by means of paid debauchery. The staff will dismantle your fence and show you out.'

Miss Hardthrasher now led Flora from the room; at the door she stopped and, without using the governessy intermediary, my beloved waved quickly at me and was gone.

Never had I known such intimacy with another human!

Our relationship now proceeded apace, though at all stages obeying the Byzantine romantic rules of the day.[3] At our next meeting I was still behind a fence, but there was a gate in it; at the following meeting the gate was actually opened. Next, I was allowed out through the gate, though Flora was kept safely out of my reach by being hoisted high off the floor in an anti-debauchery harness. Eventually, we were going for walks with each other, though tied to opposite

---

[3] These were officially codified in nine incredibly dense legal volumes. Romance lawyers made a lot of money in the nineteenth century.

ends of a twelve-foot wooden pole to prevent us getting too close to each other; the pole got shorter with each visit until finally we were walking hand in hand – though, alas, not with each other, I holding Miss Hardthrasher's right hand, Flora her left.

Then, after long, frustrating weeks of wooing, our relationship took a turn for the physical.

It happened as we sat on a courting bench, the governess between us, trowel in hand as she built a small, touch-preventing wall. Flora suddenly leaned towards Miss Hardthrasher and whispered something in her ear; in response that doughty chaperone's eyebrows rose in surprise so greatly that they momentarily disappeared beneath her hair.

'You are sure, Flora?' she asked, disapproval filling every word.

Flora nodded and giggled sweetly – could this creature of Heaven ever do anything ugly? – and tiny spots of blushing red grew on her perfect cheek. Miss Hardthrasher sighed and turned to me. 'Miss Dies-Early would like you to touch her—'

'Get in!' I yelled ecstatically, and possibly with less decorum than was appropriate. But the governess had not finished, for now she added a final word to her sentence.

'—shoe.'

Oh. Well, still, it was something, a pure gesture of love, and what I believe the cruder youth of the time referred to as 'getting to first base'.[4]

---

[4] This is not the baseball term used in modern sexual vernacular. The nineteenth-century version derived from military vocabulary, first base referring to the primary encampment of an invading British army.

I bent down towards Flora's foot, a sensation of excited love tightening my throat, but suddenly all was blinding agony as Miss Hardthrasher smashed me over the head with her pokerizer.

'Not while she still wears it! Do you think she is some sort of painted Italian courtesan leaning out of a window shouting, "Fifty lire a touch, a hundred to go all the way"? Do you?'

'Absolutely not,' I replied, massaging my hurt head.

'She will remove the shoe, I shall hand it to you, and only then shall footwear tactility commence.'

That is what now happened, and as I touched Flora's delicate, perfect shoe, I felt an electrical charge of unadulterated passion surge through me. It lasted but a second as the governess snatched the shoe back and wiped it with a pine-scented cloth.

'I am disinfecting the shoe of lust, and shall now place it back on Miss Dies-Early's foot.'

She did so, and the small red spots on Flora's cheeks blossomed into a glorious facial sunrise of joy.

'Oh, I am quite overcome with passion!' she said breathily, and then her eyes rolled upwards into her head and she fainted, first slumping against the courting bench's arm-rest, then sliding forward and plunging to the ground with a loud thud.

'Miss Dies-Early has fainted,' Miss Hardthrasher informed me, somewhat unnecessarily, 'for she is unused to such behaviour, not being a lapsed nun seeking to make up for years of abstinence by touching any man she can get near.'

'Evidently not.'

'Now, after such intimacy, the law dictates you must marry her.'

Oh, wondrous feeling of love-joy and joy-love that now exploded within me like a mighty, amorous burp! Oh, miraculous sensation of infatuation rewarded! Oh, sublime sentiment of future marital bliss! Oh, imminent weddingy ecstasy!

CHAPTER THE THIRTY-SIXTH

Weddingy, weddingy, woo!

It is a truth universally acknowledged, that a single man in possession of a good fortune must be in want of a wife – but I was shortly to be in want no more and, even better, the wife I would have want of no more was both astoundingly good-looking and one I truly, deeply adored.

My spirits were raised further by receipt of another letter from the continent:

> Dearest Pip,
>
> Mr Benevolent still has us captive but I have managed to find a pen and paper and am writing this secretly. If we can— Hold on a bit, Mr Parsimonious wants to write something.
>
> Bye for now,
> Pippa

The familiar cheery hand of Mr Parsimonious now took over:

Dear Pip,

Do not worry, I have protected your sister's virtue thus far and we are planning to try and ow ow ow! Mr Benevolent has just come in and caught me writing this and is now twisting my ear with some tongs. Ow, ow, ow!

Yours ever,

Mr Parsimonious

PS Ow.

Inevitably, given those words, the next hand was not cheery, but menacing and cruel:

Dear Pip Bin,

What's this I have found? A secret letter? Pathetic! Ooh, must dash as a mysterious figure is leaping through the window.

Yours despicably,

Gently Benevolent

The letter continued over the page in a more jaunty and heroic hand:

Dearest nephew Pip,

Have just dramatically smashed through window, wrestled Mr Benevolent to the floor and rescued Pippa and Mr Parsimonious. That villainous wretch has run away like the coward he is, and we are all now safe and well. The weather continues fine for the time of year.

Lots of love,

Aunt Lily

Oh, thank you, noble and fearless Aunt Lily! Now Pippa was under her protection I felt truly relieved, though there was also a mildly unnerving postcard:

Dear Pip Bin,
Though that pesky ex-fiancée of mine might have foiled me I will destroy you yet and shatter your sister's virtue like a moral vase that has been attacked with a naughty hammer.
Lots of hate,
Gently Benevolent
PS Ha, ha, ha!

But even that could not shake my jolly mood as I approached the final hurdle in my quest to marry Flora: I still had to ask her father for marital permissioning. He was an important man indeed, Lord Backhander, a Member of Parliament and secretary of state for expenses, corruption and petty larceny.

'So you want to marry my daughter, eh?' He did not look at me as he spoke, instead concentrating hard on something he was writing; later I discovered it was a forged receipt for eighteen fake carriage trips on state business, an otter-house, which was apparently necessary for the defence of the realm, and a completely fictitious second castle in his constituency.

'I do indeed, sir.'

He stopped writing and looked me fiercely in the eye. 'And you think just because you are Britain's richest young man you can flash your money in my face and then waltz off with Flora?'

'No, sir, of course not,' I protested.

'Hmm. Still, might be worth a try, eh?'

'Um . . .' My head spun with the implications of his words. 'Are you suggesting I offer you a bribe, sir?'

'What? No! How dare you, sir? How dare you?' He stomped about indignantly for a while, to my mind a little unconvincingly. 'I am merely suggesting we make the marital process easier with a little . . . palm-greasing. Eh? A bit of forearm-oiling or elbow-buttering. Take my meaning?'

'I think so, sir.'

'Although I want to make it quite clear that my daughter is not for sale!'

'No, sir.'

'But I would be prepared to offer a ninety-nine-year lease on her. More tax efficient. Say, ten thousand pounds, cash or cheque, payable now?'

So this was how grown men of politics and power did things! What an enlightening and inspiring life lesson! I quickly wrote out a cheque for the bridal amount and handed it over.

'Thank you. You may marry Flora with my blessing. As soon as the cheque clears.'

Marital permission was granted! I skipped and danced and jigged all the way home, light-headed, light-hearted and heavy with happiness.

Sadly, Pippa, Aunt Lily and Mr Parsimonious could not make it back from their travels for the wedding, but I gladly bought Harry out of his army commission and he returned to be my best man. On his arrival home, he immediately threw himself to his knees and hugged my legs gratefully.

'Thank you for saving me from military service, Pip Bin. It was awful!'

'Oh, come now, Harry, it cannot have been that bad. Surely it has at least made a man of you.'

'Yes. A very traumatized man.' He stopped hugging me, stood up and looked around in a seemingly casual manner. 'By the way, is Pippa back yet?'

'I am afraid not.'

'Aaargh!' Harry shouted despairingly. 'Sorry, bad army memory. Or maybe a bit of dust in my brain. Definitely not upset at Pippa's absence. Still, you're getting married to someone you love so I suppose it's all fine.'

He was right: it was all fine. Better than fine. It was marvellous, splendiferous and fantastigreat.

The marriage was to take place in the famous London church of St Wedding, with its towering, triple-layered, cake-like spire, and even though it was set for the next Saturday, on the Tuesday before I decided I could not wait that long and so, taking my future father-in-law's example, I persuaded the authorities, with lots and lots of money, to swap the two days that week. So Tuesday became Saturday and I was to wed four days earlier.

The morning of the wedding was the most glorious morning I had ever seen. Even though it was raining. And the pollutive smog of London was sitting thick upon the streets. And all I could hear was the sound of consumptive paupers coughing their last. But to me the rain was the softly falling dew of love, the smog was a shimmering mist of passion and the retching wretches were a heavenly choir singing of my besotted ardour.

I barely remember anything leading up to the ceremony: all was just a blur of excited anticipation. I do recall the bachelors of London pelting me with horse-dung as Harry and I walked to the church, so envious were they of me marrying Britain's hottest unmarried hottie, but in my joy their ordure assault seemed only a compliment; and soon I was standing in front of the altar, brushing manure from my coat and watching my beauteous bride come down the aisle towards me.

Her father had refused to attend the service unless someone 'made it worth his while' – such a fine, sensible man of business! – and so Miss Hardthrasher gave Flora away, standing for the last time between us. The vicar commenced his marital work, and soon we were at the crucial moment, my heart fluttering like a happy butterfly.

'Will you, Pip Put-that-in-the Bin, take this woman to be your wife?'

'I will,' I said.

'And will you, Flora Moribund Dies-Early, take this man to be your husband?'

'I will,' whispered Flora.

'She will,' echoed her ever-protective governess.

'Then I now declare you' – here it came – 'husband' – getting there, my bit at least was said and done – 'and' – the glorious conjunction was now said and done also – 'wife.' Yes! I was a married man! Married to an absolute belter! And with that came certain instant benefits. 'You may kiss the bride.'

I had been waiting for this moment for so long, and in a pure, honest, true way, and not in a sordid, physical, lustful way at all. I pursed my lips – I had been taking osculation lessons – and moved towards my glorious Flora, closing my eyes and leaning forwards.

It was a rougher, more stubbly kiss than I had imagined and, on opening my eyes, I saw why.

'All kisses must go via me,' said Miss Hardthrasher. She smiled at me. I didn't like it. She turned and went to bestow my kiss on Flora, but I had had enough and seized her by the arm.

'No, Miss Hardthrasher. For though you be her governess, I be her husband. And I will kiss my wife.'

So I did.

Was anything ever more soft, sweet and delicious? No. Apart from maybe a really good profiterole. Truly that kiss was a taste of Heaven. When it was finished, I smiled at Flora, and she smiled back, her hand to her chest.

'Oh, I feel quite, quite giddy,' she said, and collapsed in a wifely heap at my husbandly feet.

'Harrumble for Pip Bin and Flora, who has fainted!' shouted Harry, and the whole congregation erupted into cheers and applause as I picked up my unconscious bride and carried her down the aisle and out of the church.

Yet as I prepared to pass through the doors of the church and into glorious married life, I felt a shadow fall over me and, looking upwards to the choir loft and organ attic above, I saw a cloaked figure duck out of sight. The choirmaster or organist, I thought, but then I heard a laugh, echoing sinisterly, a familiar yet, as he had promised, new and improved 'ha, ha, ha,' and I knew it was no musical member of the church staff but the worst ex-guardian in the world, Mr Gently Benevolent, and I wondered what evil, happiness-ruining plan he had in store for me now.

CHAPTER THE THIRTY-SEVENTH

Of married life and married . . . ?

None, it turned out.

At least at first.

For our married life was blissful, joyous and super-duper-James-Fenimore-Cooper.[1]

Flora and I rewarded Miss Hardthrasher for her support and diligence by sending her on a Church-sponsored tour of the bordellos of Europe where she could give full rein to her vast moral disapproval. I did not envy the bawdy ladies of the continent, but it gave Flora and me time together, time to get to know each other.

We took long, unaccompanied walks arm in arm and chatted about every subject under the sun, two minds in perfect harmony.

'Ah, what a glorious day,' I remarked, as we stepped out

---

[1] Nineteenth-century version of the popular 1970s phrase 'super-duper-Henry-Cooper'. James Fenimore Cooper's *The Last of the Mohicans* was the most popular American novel in Britain at the time, though the sequel *The First of the Mullets* sold less well.

one morning and, though every day was glorious merely by dint of Flora's existence in it, this day was particularly so, the skies above us being blue and dotted with idyllically fluffy clouds, the trees around us being particularly lush and leaf-full and the flowers in the meadow we walked through being open and bright and petally.

'Oh, but it is glorious, my dear Pippy.' Flora had many new nickname variants of my true name; each time she used one my heart soared a little more. 'Look at the pretty clouds in the sky. I do so like clouds!'

'I too like them, dearest.' In truth, I had no opinion about clouds, but if my beloved liked them then so did I.

'You like what?' my perfect Flora asked.

'Clouds.'

'Oh, what a silly thing to say, Pipling. Who could possibly like clouds?'

'But you just said you did.'

'Oh. Did I? I am sure I did not.' Her brow furrowed in confused thought. 'Or maybe I did. I do not know. For my brain is occupied with making me pretty, not clever. Oh, I fear I must be very vexing to you, dear Pipply-chops!'

'No, of course not, my love.' For such a creature could never vex me!

Now she suddenly changed subjects. 'I have had an idea! We should get a kitten! Two kittens! No, three. Oh, please say we might, Pipsy-wipsy!'

'An excellent idea, my sweet.' For any idea so gorgeous a girl had could not fail to be excellent, even if it were an idea such as 'Let's cut our legs off' or 'Why don't we make Britain talk French?' 'Why, we shall get them this very day!'

'Get what, Pippington-pipple?' Again her brow furrowed, making a tiny wrinkle so adorable I wanted to fill it with cream, which I would then lick off.

'Get kittens. Like you just suggested.'

'Ooh, no, I cannot stand kittens. Why would I want kittens?'

'Dear Flora—' I began, but she cut me off.

'Oh, I vex you so! Please, do not be vexed with me, my Pipsa-Poodle-Pansy! For am I not pretty?'

Though I was loath to admit it, a tiny part of me had found her capricious conversational about-turns a little vexatious, but as she smiled at me and asked me to consider her prettiness such cross thoughts disappeared, like a street urchin threatened with a bath. 'You are pretty, dearest. So very pretty.'

'Then forgive me and kiss me, Pipsarama Pipply-poo!'

I did forgive her, and I did kiss her.

'Ooh, giddy again!'

Then, just as in the church, she slumped unconsciously and adorably to the ground.

Indeed, over those first weeks of marriage, every single time I kissed her she became giddy and collapsed. Initially I put it down to two things: her joyful girlish excitement at being married to me and my evidently incredible swoon-arousing ability as a kisser.

Alas, it was neither of those.

Though I really am an excellent kisser.

As time passed, her fainty collapses began to be provoked by smaller and smaller incidents, any even mild excitement seeming to cause another turn: the sound of my key in the door as I returned home; the arrival of a meal; catching sight of herself in a mirror; a sudden breeze; the smell of baking bread; even breathing a little too deeply – all caused her to go giddy and collapse in a beautiful heap.

It was becoming a worry, and after a trip to the British Museum when a tweeting bird startled her and she collapsed, taking the entirety of an incredibly rare and expensive vase collection with her, it was becoming costly. Though she did once faint in a music shop, her fall into a display of xylophones creating musical noises so tuneful that she received a spontaneous round of applause from the other customers.

But it was not all impromptu xylophone sonatas. Mostly it was just collapsing on to the ground, which caused her great bruises and contusions, so I paid for a bed to be wheeled round after her just within fainting range. But, one day not long after, she swooned into the bed and could not get out again as she was so weak; and so she became bedridden.

'Oh, my beloved Pipsington-poodle,' she whispered weakly to me. 'I am sorry I am so silly. So weak.'

'You are not silly or weak, my love,' I assured her, though I feared she was both. 'We shall make you strong again. For I shall summon the finest doctors in the land!'

I did exactly that. After long research of asking a couple of people in the street, I discovered that the greatest medical mind in Britain was a Dr Anthony Curesomebychance. Though his reputation preceded him – he sent ahead a summary of all his cases in a large box before he arrived – I insisted on establishing his credentials for myself before I let him near my feeble, extremely attractive wife, so when he arrived I poured him a sherry and asked him several piercing questions.

'Doctor, where did you train?'

'In Edinburgh. Where I learned absolutely everything there is to know of medicine in this day and age.'

'A long process, I imagine.' I marvelled at anyone being able to have such vast knowledge.

'It's about a fortnight. The first week is the medical knowledge, and the second is elocution lessons to learn the Edinburgh accent so vital to reassuring patients.'

He did indeed possess a soft and rolling burr of a Scottish accent, soothing and calm.

'So that is not your original voice?'

'No. My native accent was far more high-pitched, nasal and, in a medical context, unnerving.'

'And are you a good doctor?'

'Yes.'

'Well, Doctor, you have convinced me of your excellence. I only hope you can aid my wife.'

'I must examine her as soon as possible. There is no time to waste in cases such as this!'

To that end, we quickly finished our sherry and hurried out for a very rapid gentlemen's dinner lasting only nine courses, before returning home and sharing but a solitary bottle of port. After a brief eight-hour sleep, a visit to his barber and lunch at his club, he was ready to examine Flora.

While he was in the room with her, I paced up and down outside, the legally required action for a man with a sick wife. I could hear soft murmurs from within, then footsteps coming towards the door and the doctor emerged. I stopped pacing and addressed him.

'Well, Doctor?'

'I have completed my examination and—' He stopped, then took me by the arm and steered me towards a chair; this was unlikely to be a good sign. 'Actually, perhaps you should sit down before I tell you.'

'Perhaps you should tell me what's wrong with my wife.'

'Only if you sit down.'

'I'll sit down if you tell me what's wrong with her.'

'Very well.' He looked me in the eyes, frowned sympathetically, and with the brogueiest Edinburgh brogue he could summon, he told me, 'I'm afraid your wife is suffering from a condition called Non-specific Weakness.'

I had promised the doctor I would sit down if he told me, but I had no choice in the matter as my legs now buckled beneath me with shock.

Non-specific Weakness!

It was like a death sentence. For this was a disease that had claimed so many lives over the years, a fearsome medical foe indeed.

'I know what you're thinking, Mr Bin, but rest assured, this is a curable condition. Medical science has come on in leaps and bounds in recent years, like a very clever rabbit, and I tell you this . . .' Here he paused, placed a comforting hand on my shoulder, looked gravely at me and said: 'I will save your wife.'

Never had I been so reassured by a combination of eye contact and accent! The doctor now turned away and spoke rapidly under his breath into his hand. 'Terms and conditions apply, the health of your wife may go down as well as up.'

'What's that, Doctor?'

'Nothing, nothing. I shall return tomorrow and the treatment shall begin.'

And so it did. The doctor came every day for weeks, applying his knowledge, utilizing his skill and striving to defeat the dread disease. News of Flora's condition quickly spread and soon we were inundated with gifts and cards from well-wishers. Pippa, Aunt Lily and Mr Parsimonious sent a card from the continent:

> Dear Flora Pip's wife we haven't yet met,
>> Hope you get well soon!
>> Lots of love,
>> Your new sister-in-law, aunt-in-law and close-friend-of-the-family-in-law

I showed it to her and it made her so, so happy.

'Oh, how lovely they are to me despite not knowing me! Why it makes me quite faint—'

Though only for a short while as she almost instantly collapsed again. There were also other, less welcome, cards:

> Dear Flora Pip Bin's wife,
>> Hope you get well never and therefore make him miserable. Ha, ha, ha!
>> Yours spitefully,
>> Mr Gently Benevolent

I did not show poor Flora that card. Well, not twice anyway. Not after it upset her so much the first time.

Miss Hardthrasher found out about her former charge's plight and cut short her holiday casting aspersions at European harlots, returning to be Flora's constant helper; and I too had a constant helper, indeed a Harry-shaped helper, for it was Harry. The nervous pacing and deep worrying I did made me too tense and tired to do anything for myself, and during those long, dreadful times, he was a great source of comfort to me, often literally as I would fall asleep mid-pace leaning on his plump frame. He made sure I ate and drank, and even bathed me, stripping me bare, helping me into the water then washing my entire body – and all without once looking me in the eye. Such a true friend!

Alas, the treatment did not go well.

In these more advanced medical days of the late nineteenth century, the doctor could have used ether, opium or cocaine, possibly even a deliciously curative radium sandwich. But back then the palette of treatments was sparser and less refined.

The doctor tried every weapon in his medical armoury: lotions, potions, tinctures, unguents, emollients, ointments, salves, balms, rubs, liniment, embrocation and creams both medical and dairy.

None of it worked.

He tried other methods: opening all the bedroom windows, praying, giving Flora a good shake, crossing his fingers and hoping it all got better, shouting at her to pull herself together, and that wonder-drug of wonder-drugs, beef. He even paid a man to stand next to her bed saying 'beep' now and then.

None of that worked either.

Until one terrible night that will remain etched on my heart for ever, he emerged from Flora's room, downhearted, downcast and un-upbeat. He looked at me with serious eyes and shook his head sadly. 'Mr Bin, I am afraid that the disease is winning. Your wife is dying.'

My legs buckled again – they'd done a lot of that in recent weeks – and only Harry quickly dropping on to all fours and turning himself into an impromptu stool prevented me from falling.

'Is there nothing more you can do?'

Oh, aching, breaking heart, let him say there is something!

'There is only one remaining chance. But a very dangerous one that might kill her.'

'If Flora is dying anyway, how dangerous can it be?'

'True, true.' He sighed deeply and began to pace up and down. 'There is a new medicine in development, still only at the experimental stage, but one there are high hopes for. I have certain . . . contacts who might be able to get their hands on a sample.'

'What is it, Doctor?'

'Perhaps you have heard of a medical advance known as the tablet.'

I had indeed heard of that most modern pharmacological innovation. 'The new method of medicine delivery? Yes.' The tiniest drop of hope dripped into my anxious heart. 'Is that what will save Flora?'

'No.' The doctor pulled the plug from my heart and the

hope drained away. 'But have you heard of a similar invention called . . . the pill?'

'I have,' I said, for I had. 'Will that save her?' The hope tap began to drip again, yet once more the doctor swiftly yanked on the plug-chain.

'No.'

I quite wanted to hit the doctor at this time for his evasive questiony meanderings, but I did not. Instead, I shouted at him. 'Just tell me what this miracle cure is!'

'It is a mix of the two, known as pablets.'[2] Even in the face of my shouty anger his voice remained medically calm and Scottishly soothing. 'Very new, very experimental. And very expensive.'

'Expense matters not!' I would have spent a small fortune to save my Flora; and fortunately, thanks to the Bin, I had a large fortune. 'Just get the damned thing and cure my very comely wife!'

'I shall see what I can do.' He gave me a reassuring nod, turned and headed off to track down the potential cure. I composed myself with a few deep breaths and two large brandies, then entered Flora's room, where she lay guarded by Miss Hardthrasher.

'Please, I wish to be alone with my wife,' I told the stern, matronly figure.

'Of course. But no hanky-panky!'

I was in the mood for neither hanky nor panky, let alone both, and was about to snap thusly at her, but as she left, this

---

[2] Its companion drug, the 'till', never found a medical use, being far too big to swallow, but did find a role in shops as something to put money in.

harshest, most masculine of women placed a concerned hand on my arm and looked me in the eye with a nod of empathetic sympathy, and all malice towards her fled.

I settled into the armchair next to poor Flora's bed and took her sleeping hand. She stirred, and I soothed her back to somnolence by stroking her beautiful face. As I did, she sighed, 'My lovely Pippy-nippy-woo,' and I felt as if my heart might burst.

I could not lose her!

But I was really worried that I might.

For the next hour I could hear frantic footsteps outside and hushed, urgent conversations, until eventually there came a ring on the downstairs doorbell – the pablets must have arrived. I stood, went to the bedroom window and, pulling the curtain back, looked down to see a figure handing over a parcel to the doctor. It was a cold, wet night and the deliverer had on a hooded cloak against the elements. As they turned to go, they looked up at the window in which I stood, and though I could not see their features properly, I saw the white teeth of a wide smile; whoever that person was, it seemed they wished me well.

As I let the curtain fall back into place, I could hear the doctor rushing up the stairs; he slowed outside the room and entered at a calm, reassuring pace, Harry and Miss Hardthrasher with him, and in his hand a box marked 'pablets' – would these cure my astonishingly attractive ill wife?

'There is little time. I must administer them immediately,' he said, with an urgency in his voice I had not heard before.

'What will they do?' Though the doctor's voice was urgent, mine was distinctly scared.

'I do not know. They may do nothing, or there may be dangerous side-effects. All we can do is give them to her and hope.'

The doctor moved towards the bed, but Miss Hardthrasher put out her arm and stopped him. 'Wait! As her one-time governess and now constant helper, I must test them first. At least that way we may discover any potential dangers.'

The doctor looked at me; I looked back and nodded.

'Very well.' He removed two of the pablets from their packaging and handed them to the governess, who swallowed them down with a glass of water. There seemed no obvious instant effect, but then . . .

'Ooh, I'm feeling something. I think they're starting to work. Ooh, oh, yes, that feels good. It is like a great warmth spreading through my body.' She wiggled about slightly as she spoke, an unnerving sight in such a tall woman. 'Actually, I feel better than I have done in years. All my aches and pains have gone, my breathing feels clearer than ever – I feel wonderful!'

She sounded jauntier and less disapproving than I had ever heard her, and as if to prove the wonderfulness she felt, she danced a jig on the spot, then grabbed Harry and whirled him round the room in energetic pirouettes of joy.

But she was not the only joyous one: on this evidence, the pablets worked. If they could do this to Miss Hardthrasher, they would surely cure my Flora! The doctor clearly thought the same, because he now moved towards her bed, pablets in hand.

'Oh, this is marvellous!' shouted Miss Hardthrasher, as she danced on. But then she abruptly stopped, put Harry down, set a hand to her head and said, 'Actually, no, hang on, I think I'm going to die.'

She collapsed where she stood, and the doctor stooped to examine her. 'She wasn't lying. She is dead.'

Joy turned to anguish. The cure had turned out to be no such thing, indeed the very opposite of a cure, and would only kill my beloved even quicker than the disease.

'Flora shall not have the pablets!' I declared, my heart filled with despair.

'It might not have been their fault,' protested the doctor. 'It might have been coincidence. She might have been about to die anyway.'

'Or maybe a snake bit her,' suggested Harry. 'Or a poisonous mouse.'

'No, I am decided, she will not have them!'

But then there came a heartrendingly weak voice from the bed: 'Please, dearest Pippy-wippy-ping-pong-poo . . . Let me take them. They will make me better, I am sure . . .'

I rushed to my gorgeous wife's side. 'No, dearest, no. It is not wise.'

'But I am not wise. I am pretty.'

She had a point. For she was pretty – so, so pretty!

'They may have a very different effect on me from Miss Hardthrasher. For I am much better-looking than she was, and God takes the ugly people first because He feels sorry for them.' She had a point, albeit a theologically tenuous one. 'The pablets are my only chance. Please, Pip, for me.'

Maybe it was the pleading tone of her voice; maybe it was

because I knew she was dying anyway; or maybe it was because for once she hadn't called me by one of her frankly irritatingly twee nicknames, but I yielded to her wish. 'If you insist, dearest heart.'

I nodded to the doctor, and he administered the pablets, Flora washing them down with a glass of medical gin.

And we waited.

And waited.

And wai—

All of a sudden, with a glorious burst of energy, my beloved Flora sat up in bed, something she had been too weak to do for a long time. Was the cure working?

'Oh, I feel much stronger now . . .'

'That is good, my darling.' I held her hand encouragingly, all too aware that Miss Hardthrasher had suffered a similar pre-death energetic surge.

And, alas, it seemed as if my fears were to be fulfilled as poor Flora turned frantic and yelled, 'Help! I cannot see!'

'No! She is blind!'

But blindness was just the start, and things rapidly got worse.

'And I cannot hear!'

'No! She is deaf!'

And worse.

'And I cannot speak!'

'No! She cannot— Hang on, no, that can't be right,' I said, for I had distinctly heard her saying, 'I cannot speak,' which indicated that she could.

'Or maybe I can still speak but cannot hear it because I cannot hear.'

That would explain it.

'Wait! I can see again! And hear! And speak!' Her words filled me with hope, but it was sadly temporary as she then slumped and muttered, 'Though I am feeling weak once more . . . so weak . . .'

She slid down into the bed again, and now it was as if she began physically to shrink, my wonderful wife growing smaller and smaller, melting away before my very eyes.

'Oh, I am weaker than ever,' she gasped. 'I have not the strength to lift a flower, even a light flower . . . or some flour, which is even lighter in small quantities.'

'Mr Bin, I fear the weakness is taking her . . .' the doctor whispered to me.

'No! She will be strong again! She will live!' But my words were filled with false optimism, for deep in my mind, where the worst whispers of truth lie, I knew she was dying.

'I fear I shall never be strong again, darling husband . . . for I think I can see Heaven above me.' I looked upwards to where she pointed with a single, weak finger, but could see only ceiling; she was looking beyond, to the infinite afterlife, and I was losing her. 'Oh, and Heaven is filled with angels and lovely friendly spaniels with waggy tails – and chocolate, so much chocolate! And, oh, it looks such a fun, happy place!'

Her body was racked by a spasm of coughing, and I knew the end was near; as did gorgeous Flora, for she turned to me, a resigned sadness in her eyes. 'I fear I must now leave you, dear Pip. Goodbye, lovely husband. Farewell. *Auf wiedersehen. Dosvidaniya. Arrivederci* . . .' She was rambling foreignly now. '*Adios, sayonara, au revoir*, whatever the Welsh for goodbye is and . . .' Struggling for breath, she reached out and touched my face, then, with a final 'Toodle-oo,' collapsed backwards into her pillows, and was gone.

My beloved wife was dead.

Or so I thought.

For suddenly she sat bolt upright and said cheerily, 'Actually, I feel fantastic! Anyone fancy an arm-wrestle?'

'Dearest, you live yet!'

She turned to me with a rueful smile. 'Sorry, false alarm, I'm afraid. Really dying this time. Eeeurggh!'

She collapsed backwards once more, and was gone, this time for good.

Or so I thought.

And, sadly, this time I was right.

I slumped on to the bed and held my poor, deceased wife, who even in death was beautiful, so beautiful. I kissed her over and over again, and it was as if she seemed to be crying from beyond our mortal realm, because each kiss had the salty tang of tears to it; and then I realized that they were my tears, splashing down on her in a woeful drizzle of melancholy.

I felt Harry place a supportive hand on my shoulder, and could feel true friendship coursing into me from him, but it did little to assuage my misery and nothing to fill the aching gap that had opened in my heart and would remain there eternally, for my wife was gone, my beloved Flora was dead, my adored soul-mate was with the angels, and that triplicate sum of grief now sat like a huge dark cloud in my soul.

PART THE SIXTHTH

CHAPTER THE THIRTY-EIGHTH

Of woe, gloom, sorrow and worse

The hole in my heart left by Flora's death soon filled with a shard of purest, darkest grief that pierced my very soul, then infected the wound with woe and caused a great festering boil of misery to grow inside me, throbbing and pulsing with the agony of bereavement.

On the day of her funeral, I paid for it not only to rain over the entirety of London, but for that great city to be silent, apart from the sounds of lamentation. A million souls wept with me, but it comforted me not, partly because I'd paid them to do so, but mostly because Flora was still dead.

There was no catharsis for me in the ritual of her burial at the church of St Late-Hotties;[1] I found no solace in the vicar's hollow address of spiritual condolence; and the buffet afterwards was dreadful, all cheap sausages, warm white wine and the muttered commiserations of people who could not possibly understand the depth of my agony.

---

[1] A church where they only allowed especially beautiful people to be buried.

For truly no one had ever suffered as I was doing now.

I burned to the ground the rich West End house Flora and I had shared, not wanting to have memories of our brief time together thrust into my mind at every turn, and I purchased a new, sparse, dead-wife-reminder-free property.

Then I decided that actually I missed those memories, began to regret my house-burning decision and had the original house reconstructed to the finest detail.

It did not help.

Despair gnawed at me, like a discouraging rat. Colour drained from my life, and all became black. I had my house painted black, my clothes dyed black and my face coloured black – though that verged on the dodgy, heading towards the full-blown racist, so I quickly abandoned that particular strand of woe. I ate only black, being served food such as charcoal pie, coal soup and really, really old bananas. I had a pair of spectacles manufactured with black-tinted lenses so that I might see literally how I already saw metaphorically; in doing so I inadvertently invented sunglasses and made myself an even greater fortune, but I now cared not for money and spent the profits on a gigantic statue in memory of Flora, a five-hundred-foot-high model of her in all her gorgeous beauty, which some years later the government was forced to tear down because it was so winsome that it was attracting perverts from all over the world to come and be unsavoury within its vicinity.[2]

In short, I was sad; and I remained that way for a considerable time.

---

[2] Built on Highgate Hill, it was known as 'the fit lady of the north'.

CHAPTER THE THIRTY-NINTH

Of ongoing wretched, woeful misery

A month later, and I was still sad.

CHAPTER THE FORTIETH

Of more misery yet

Two months later, and I was still definitely despondent.

CHAPTER THE FORTY-FIRST

Of . . . oh, you get the idea

Three months later, and I hadn't cheered up one little bit, remaining forlorn, desolate and bigly broken-hearted.

CHAPTER THE FORTY-SECOND

Of false hope and optimism

Four months on from Flora's death, and I felt the tiniest shoots of potential happiness forcing their way up through the soil of misery, but it turned out it was just wind, and after a large burp I was wretchedly woeful once more.

CHAPTER THE FORTY-THIRD

Of mood-changing events, though not for the better

Then, one day, as I sat in a black mood in my black chair in a black room in my black house, there came a knock at my black door.

It was a visitor.

Though not an expected or welcome one.

For it was Mr Gently Benevolent.

'Ah, Pip Bin, I heard that your wife would rather die than live with you.'

At this I felt a spasm of theoretical anger, but in my depressed state I could not act on it, instead simply staring at the floor and responding flatly by saying, 'You have come to mock my anguish?'

'No, no. For though I find your pain nourishing, like a hearty broth of woe, I come to impart news.'

'What news?'

'That I have been forced to shut down my latest business venture, Benevolent Pharmaceuticals.'

'I don't care.'

'Oh, but you will.' A predatory grin twitched at the corners of his mouth. 'The business failed because its new medicine never succeeded. Unfortunately, it killed rather than cured. A pity, I had such high hopes for pablets.'

Now my mind stirred from its depressed torpor. 'Pablets? Your company manufactured pablets?'

'Yes. I'm surprised you didn't know. After all, I did hand-deliver them to you . . .'

I thought back to the figure I had seen leaving my house on that fateful night; the features hidden by the cloak; the smile I had interpreted as supportive but which now took on a whole new meaning. 'That was you? You are responsible for my wife's death?'

'Well, the weakness would probably have taken her anyway. I just . . . made sure.'

Now my torpor was swept away by a mighty wind of rage surging through my soul, and I stood angrily to confront this most hideous of men; though after months of stationary mourning, my muscles had wasted to virtually nothing, and I only succeeded in falling helplessly to the floor like a drunk toddler.[1]

'Oh dear, is the weakness taking you as well, Pip Bin?'

He stepped closer to me to gloat, and I desperately lashed out from my prone position, trying to strike him. 'You monster! You killed her! You killed my Flora!'

---

[1] A common sight in nineteenth-century Britain. People would often soothe whining children with alcohol, such as infant whisky, child gin and small-person beer. The problem went undetected for a long time as, with their constant dribbling, lack of speech and wobbly gait, most toddlers seem to be drunk anyway.

'No use crying over spilt milk or dead wives.'[2] My pathetic blows came nowhere near hitting him and I slumped pathetically, tears flooding my eyes. 'Oh, and before I forget, I have brought you this.' He threw a fat envelope down in front of me.

'What is it?'

'A court summons. You are being sued over your invention of the Bin.'

'I don't understand . . .'

'By an American gentleman who thinks you stole the idea from him. His name is Mr Harlan J. Trashcan.'

'But that's a lie!'

'Is it? I reckon the courts might think differently.' He leaned down and spoke quietly and maliciously. 'You're going to be ruined, Pip Bin. And when you're no more than a penniless widower begging on the streets and dying of poverty, the last thing you shall see will be me wedding your sister and ruining her life via the sanctity of marriage.'

'No!'

'Oh, very much yes. Perhaps I'll be in court to see the start of your humiliation. Maybe I'll bring your mad mother so that she can witness your destruction. But until then, farebadly, Pip Bin.' He strode to the door and left, but then popped his head back in. 'Oops, nearly forgot. Here's the new laugh I've been working on.' He cleared his throat and now emitted the most vile, depraved sound I had ever heard. 'Nee-yah, ha, ha, ha!'

---

[2] An expression dating back to the Great Plague, when people would often go through up to nine spouses in a month.

I had conquered my fear of his old one, but this was harsher, crueller, more demonic, and I could not help but cower before it. He had obviously been practising, and it had been worth it as, syllable for syllable, it was the most unnerving thing I had ever heard, even more unsettling than the phrase 'Just pop your underpants off and we'll take a quick look at the problem.'

Laugh complete, he spun on his heel and departed. I lay there on the floor, weak of body and mind, and wondered if this was how it all ended: with nothing but a dead wife, a dishonoured sister and humiliation in the courts to show for a life that until recently had seemed so promising.

CHAPTER THE FORTY-FOURTH

In which determination is renewed

I lay on the floor for some hours until Harry came in and discovered me slumped in a cold puddle of my own tears, sobbing with fury and despair.

He tenderly helped me back into my chair, where I continued to sob for some time, and he stroked my hair soothingly, as if I were a distressed spaniel or miserable best friend, the latter of which I most assuredly was, until at long last I ceased my weeping, having wrung every tear from my wretched body.

And as I sat there in a small salty lake of my own creation, a tiny fragment of determination grew in my mind, as if all the tenacity and purposefulness that had been dissolved by Flora's death had formed a super-saturated solution within my soul into which had now been dangled the thin, crystallizing thread of Mr Benevolent's visit, around which the dissolved determination was beginning to coalesce, growing into a great lump of staunch intent.

I was going to destroy Mr Gently Benevolent.

For so long he had threatened, menaced and hurt my family, and finally I had had enough and vowed to myself that I would stop him, if possible by legal means but if not then by violent, blood-soaked means, such as stabbing him, shooting him, beating him to death with a cricket bat, tying his limbs to wild horses and having them rip him apart, forcing him to eat a pie with a grenade in it, replacing his blood with oil and then offering him a lit cigar, coaxing him beneath a waterfall where the water had been replaced with strong acid, making him wear a shirt with 'Eat Me' written on it and then sending him into the East End, using a blunt razor to peel him like an apple, pretending to mistake him for a trampoline then bouncing on him to death, coating him in peanut butter and letting squirrels nibble him to a slow, painful demise, clipping his ears to a crane and then raising him up so fast that his head came off, or simply punching him until he stopped working as a viable life-form.

You get the idea.

With that vow, I began to reassemble the shattered fragments of my life. I started to eat, drink and move again, gradually regaining my strength. I took control of my business once more, increasing Bin production so I might gather funds for my fight. I wrote to Aunt Lily on the continent, urging her to keep Pippa safely away from Mr Benevolent until I had finished destroying him; and lastly I took the still agonizing grief I felt over Flora and set it aside in a mental box where it lay, always with me, but now a motivating force, not a crippling one.

Eventually, after weeks of effort, I was strong again in both body and mind, and ready for the avenging fray, but before I could turn to Benevolent destruction, there was the matter of the court case against this mysterious and litigious American, Mr Harlan J. Trashcan. I knew my invention was mine and mine alone, with no hint of impropriety, theft or plagiarism about it, but would the courts agree?

CHAPTER THE FORTY-FIFTH

Of the law, legal matters and the assiness thereof

I needed a lawyer and could think of no one better than my father's one-time legal adviser Mr Wickham Post Forberton . . . Oh, you remember the fellow, the chap with the name that took fully twenty minutes to say.[1] For, though he had been a harsh man, he had always struck me as knowledgeable and scrupulously honest.

With him at my side, I felt great confidence in the unassailability of my position as I entered the famous Courts of Potluckery[2] in all their grim legal glory.

The corridors were panelled in a dark wood that seemed to absorb all light;[3] candles made from paraffin-soaked mice with their tails as wicks burned by the dozen but the weak

---

[1] See Chapter Four, footnote three, and Appendix II.

[2] Closely related to the Courts of Chancery. Chancery dealt with matters of equity, as opposed to common law; Potluckery dealt with both, its cases being randomly selected by a celebrity drawing them out of a hat in the weekly legal lottery.

[3] Possibly wood from the Singularity Tree, whose surface was dotted with tiny black holes.

flames barely caressed the darkness, let alone banished it. All around were the screams of convicted felons, plaintiffs who had lost and clients shouting incredulously at their lawyers, 'You're charging me how much?' Yet none of this shook my confidence.

Stepping into the court itself revealed more horrors. The walls were lined with the stuffed and mounted heads of criminals, a salutary taxidermal warning to miscreants; the judge's bench was fully thirty feet high and distinctly terrifying to behold in its loftiness; and over everything towered a statue of Justice herself, blindfolded and holding in one hand a noose and in the other a noose. Yet still my confidence remained solidly in place.

'The court will rise!' an usher declared, banging his staff of office hard on the floor and even harder on the head of an innocent bystander, who instantly collapsed.

We stood, and the judge entered. He was an enormous man, tall, broad and deep, clad in sweeping black robes and with a vast white legal wig perched atop his head, each side trailing down some thirty or so feet to end in a live sheep.[4] Owls nested in the wig's higher reaches from which they gazed beadily down, suggesting both great wisdom and an ability to eat a mouse in one gulp.

At the sight of such an imposing, frightening figure, I am not ashamed to admit that my confidence wobbled a tiny bit – but I still felt it was fundamentally solid, like a tall building that shakes in the wind not due to weakness but because

---

[4] On appointment each judge was given a pair of sheep from which to grow their own wig. The longer the wig, the more senior the judge.

flexibility is actually an inherent engineering strength in such a structure.

'The court is now in session. Judge Buford Hardthrasher presiding.'

At the mention of that name and the sight of yet another set of familiar Hardthrashery features, my confidence began to crumble, as if the foundations of that recently mentioned strongly flexible building had been laid by a sub-contractor who had cut corners and therefore not adequately done the job.

To come up against yet another Hardthrasher sibling – could life be more unjust?

The judge banged his enormous, sledgehammer-sized gavel, and the case began.

'So, the case of Trashcan versus Bin, eh?' The judge peered down at me from his mighty perch. 'Are you Bin? Pip Bin?'

I could not deny it, for I was. 'I am, Your Honour.'

'So at last I meet the man responsible for the deaths of my four brothers and one sister.' He stared hard at me, and I felt as if I was shrinking beneath his accusatory gaze. But then he broke off that gaze and even smiled. 'Luckily for you, young man, I am an excellent and impartial man of the law and will in no way let those deaths interfere with my judging of this case.'

My confidence grew again, as if the sub-contractor for the foundations had been contacted, informed of their inadequacies and had promptly returned to make good the work at no extra cost. Thank the Lord for the unbiased excellence of the British judicial system!

Though as the judge turned away and looked back at his notes, I was pretty sure I heard him mutter, 'You're a dead man walking, Bin.'

'I'm sorry, Your Honour?'

'Nothing, nothing. Now, who represents the defendant in this case?'

'I do, Your Honour,' my lawyer intoned pompously, simultaneously handing me a note, which read, 'You already owe me three guineas.'

'Please state your name for the record.'

'Of course. My name is Mr Wickham Post Forberton Fenugreek Chasby . . .'

As my lawyer began his enormous name, I looked across the court to see if I could spy my opponent in the case. He was a heavily bearded man sitting by himself with no lawyer in evidence and clad in a suit made from the bestarred and bestriped American flag; he also wore a hat on which was perched a stuffed American bald eagle.

He certainly looked American.

My perusal was disturbed, however, by a spluttering noise from the judge as he turned crimson with anger, rage clearly building within him. His mood affected the sheep and owls in his wig and they baaed and hooted angrily as he got redder and redder until, barely three minutes into my lawyer's name, he snapped.

'Enough! How long is this absurd name of yours?'

'Twenty minutes, Your Honour. Forty if I choose to repeat it. Which I might.'

'I will not have it! You will approach the bench.'

He did so, and I could only watch in horror as the judge

reached up to the statue of Justice behind him, took one of the nooses from her hand, lowered it around my lawyer's neck and began to haul on the other end.

'I will not have such a ridiculous name in my court! You are to be hanged for contempt of court!'

My lawyer struggled hard, desperately trying to free himself as his face purpled breathlessly, but it was no good: the judge was fearsomely strong and determined, and soon he had carried out the sentence and my lawyer lay dead on the floor of the court.

My first thought was of horror at what had just happened; my second was of how I needed a new lawyer; and my third was of how difficult it was going to be to find a gravestone big enough to fit the late man's name on.

'Now, does anyone else have a name that lasts longer than five seconds?' The judge looked scarily around the court; no one dared move a muscle or speak a word. 'Good. Then I suggest an adjournment for lunch. Administering justice always makes me hungry.' He raised his gavel, ready to end the morning's proceedings, but paused. 'Oh, and, Mr Bin . . . I'm afraid to tell you that for the duration of this case I have frozen all your financial assets. Attempt to access any of your funds and I will have you hanged for contempt of me. Obviously this action is entirely in line with legal precedent, and nothing personal at all, Sibling-killer.'

'But how will I afford another lawyer?'

'You won't, I imagine. Lunch declared, case adjourned!'

He smashed his gavel down and the court began to empty. I left with my confidence in tatters – how could I win the case without a lawyer? No lawyers in London would act without at least a massive payment up front.

I realized I had no choice: I would have to represent myself, which would not be easy. With all the laws and obfuscatory legal language to be learned, the traditional training for a lawyer lasted six years, and I had just one lunchtime.

CHAPTER THE FORTY-SIXTH

In which there is a turn very much not for the better

I returned home via the library, where I borrowed every book on the law I could, and I began frantically to study; though I was barely eight pages into the seventy-four thousand I reckoned I had to read to stand a legal chance when I was disturbed by my dear best friend Harry returning.

'Pip Bin! Hello! How goes the case?'

'Not well, Harry. I have been forced to become my own lawyer. Now, please leave me, I must study.'

'Right-o.' Harry headed for the door, but did not make it there, instead stopping and turning. 'Ooh, quick question, though. Can I borrow some money to invest in a brilliant business I'm starting up?'

'No, Harry.'

'At least let me tell you about it. For if you lose your case – which I'm sure you won't, but you might – and therefore lose all your money – which again I'm sure you won't but you might – then for a tiny investment in my business now you might still remain rich.'

'Harry, I am sorry, but I have no money to give. My assets are frozen.'

'I can light a fire.' He moved stupidly towards the grate.

'No, financial assets. What is this business anyway?'

'I have noticed that there is lots of money to be made from selling vintage wines. And I thought, What about other vintage things? To that end, I have set up a vintage meat emporium.'

'A vintage meat emporium?' I asked, barely concealing the baffled contempt in my voice.

'Yes! Brilliant, eh? I can't imagine why no one's thought of it before.' He looked contemplatively into the distance. 'Just imagine, huge cellars of maturing meats getting more and more valuable every year.'

'But, Harry, meat rots.'

'No, it matures. Look, here is a steak I have been maturing for the past two months.'

He produced a cloche-protected plate. A loud humming came from within, and as he proudly removed the cover, the source of the noise became clear as hundreds of flies flew forth. 'The flies are a natural by-product of the process. Like sediment in wine. But with wings. Now, go on, have a taste.'

He thrust the plate towards me. I quickly turned away, but not before I had seen a festering piece of green filth that looked less like a steak and more like deadly food-poisoning about to happen; to that was added a repugnant smell that burrowed its way up my nose and into my brain, an odour so pungent that it made my already fraying temper snap with a twang of anger, or twanger.

'Harry, this is the most ridiculous idea I have ever heard!' I raged. 'Even if I could invest, I would not!'

At this, Harry's face went from one of proud, grinning expectation to a surly frown. 'Are those the words of a best friend, Pip Bin?'

'Harry—' I started to explain, but he cut me off.

'I ask for a small investment – no more than seven hundred and twelve pounds, eight shillings and sixpence[1] and you refuse me. Me! The man who has always been there for you, the man who held your hand and stroked your hair when Flora died, the man who looked after you. I gave up my dreams and ambitions for you, and now I want to do this one tiny thing for myself and you won't let me!'

'Harry—'

'No! I will not hear a thing you say unless it is "Sorry, Harry, here's the money." Is it going to be that, Pip Bin?'

'Harry, I cannot. For the idea is ridiculous, and I have no money.'

'Then you also have no best friend. For you are a friend to me no more, Pip Bin.' Head held high, he proudly marched from the room, the effect lessened only slightly by the fact that he had got the wrong door and consequently walked straight into a cupboard. 'I meant to do that!' I heard from within. 'I'd rather be in a cupboard than be with you!'

Now he emerged from the cupboard and marched across the room again. 'You are still a friend to me no more, Pip Bin!' He left, slamming the door behind him.

---

[1] About twenty-three million pounds in today's money.

The door to the billiards room and, again, not the way out.

'Aarggh!' He came back in. 'I'm confused! I don't know which the right door is any more. So I shall just use the window.' He went to the window, opened it and sat on the sill, legs dangling outside. 'For the final time I say: you are a friend to me no more, Pip Bin.'

With this solemn declaration, he jumped, landing below with a thud, and I heard him say, 'Ow! I think I've broken my ankle! But you are still a friend to me no more, Pip Bin!'

I went to the window and looked down to see him hobbling away, and sadness now filled my heart for I had lost my best friend – but I had not the time to worry about the matter for I had to study the law and, looking at my watch, I realized I had but four minutes to do so before the court was back in session.

CHAPTER THE FORTY-SEVENTH

Of sundry disasters and rubbish happenings

Four minutes was not a long time. Oh, true, a man may achieve a lot in four minutes – run nearly a quarter of a mile,[1] sire several children, establish a small colony,[2] look at the minute hand on his watch go round four times, even five if the watch is rubbish, beat Italy in a war twice –[3] but to learn the law, well, it was pushing it a bit. Or a lot.

Indeed, it was impossible, and though I tried as hard as I could, by the time I returned to court I had got no further than learning how to talk while holding the lapels of a legal gown, and had only just begun work on a condescending lawerly sneer.

---

[1] In the nineteenth century the world record for running a mile stood at seventeen minutes, slower even than a brisk walk – it was deemed ungentlemanly to hurry and any man of high breeding caught running in any circumstance other than racing after a saucy scullery-maid was liable to be sent to prison.

[2] The quickest colony ever established took three minutes and was Burkina Fast-o.

[3] The famous Minute War of 1795, which, after a two-minute truce, was followed by the even shorter Thirty-second War.

I feared that might not be enough.

As I re-entered the court, I reassured myself with one thought: at least thus far Mr Benevolent had not arrived to gloat at my misfortune, and I glanced up at the public gallery to ensure his continued absence. To my surprise, it was completely empty, when before lunch it had been packed with the usual audience such cases brought. What is more, apart from my opponent Mr Trashcan, Judge Hardthrasher and the usher, the entire court was now bereft of people – even the jury box was deserted.

An explanation was quickly forthcoming.

'Over lunch I made a decision,' the judge said. 'The verdict will no longer be decided by a jury but instead by me alone. Juries are so inconvenient and messy.'

'Your Honour—' I gripped the lapels of my legal gown firmly, but he cut me off, which was lucky as I didn't really know what I had been intending to say.

'I know what you're thinking, Mr Bin. But do not worry, I am a scrupulously fair man who despises partiality, and your slaughter of my siblings shall have no bearing on my judgment. The case will be conducted in line with the noble British tradition of being presumed guilty until proven dead.'

'Surely Your Honour means innocent until proven guilty.' I was pleased at being able to display at least this minor piece of legal knowledge.

'I know what I mean, young man. Now, let us begin.' He banged his mighty gavel hard and turned to me. 'Mr Bin, did you invent the Bin?'

'I did, Your Honour.'

'I see.' The judge turned to the star-spangled American plaintiff, who had removed his eagled hat to reveal hair that looked unnaturally wiggy, and was itching awkwardly at his beard, as if unused to its hairy facial presence. 'Mr Trashcan, did you actually invent it first?'

'Yes, sirree, Your Honour, I surely did.'

'Oh, well, that is most convincing. And incontrovertible. I find for Mr Trashcan. Pip Bin, you are guilty on all counts and I sentence you to—'

This had not gone well, and not gone well at a much quicker rate than I had expected. I quickly rose to my feet to protest.

'Wait! Your Honour, I wish to question the witness.'

'Really? You're only delaying the inevitable, you know. Inevitable impartial judgment, I mean.' The judge rolled his eyes and sighed. 'But very well. Justice must at least be pretended to be done.'

The usher escorted Mr Trashcan to the witness box. He stumbled on his way, an act that caused his hair to dislodge and fall over his left ear, and I instantly thought how odd it was that he wore a wig, given that I could clearly see a full head of glossy black hair beneath.

How eccentric were the ways of our ex-colonial cousins across the Atlantic!

In scrabbling to reattach hair to head, he now caught his beard on the large signet ring he sported, and it came momentarily unstuck, revealing bare chin beneath. There was a brief flash of familiarity to that chin, but I dismissed it – for all men have chins and therefore all chins are familiar.

'Place your right hand on the Bible and take the oath, please,' the usher said.

Mr Trashcan cleared his throat, then said, 'I swear to tell the truth, the half-truth and something a bit like the truth, so help me, God.'

I instantly knew this was not right and turned to plead with the judge. 'Hang on. He said—'

'It sounded fine to me. Get on with it, Bin.' The judge banged his gavel angrily.

'Sorry, Your Honour.' I refocused my attention on my American accuser. 'Mr Trashcan, you claim you invented the Bin yourself.'

'I do.'

Now I had him! He had fallen into the complex legal web I had woven for him, and there was no way he could extricate himself. I steadied myself lest I seem too obviously excited and asked my deadly question.

'Is it not the case, Mr Trashcan, that when you say you invented the Bin first you are lying?'

'No.'

'Damn! I was hoping you'd say yes.'

I slumped to my seat, my brilliant strategy in tatters, like a battle-plan that has been attacked by a scissor-wielding cat. But, from nowhere, inspiration struck, and I leaped to my feet again.

'Are you sure you're not lying?'

'As sure as I am that my name is Mr Gentl—' He stopped and consulted a bit of paper he held in his hand. 'I mean, Mr Harlan J. Trashcan. Which it is.'

His words pushed doubts into my mind. Was this Harlan

Trashcan all he seemed? Or was he slightly more? Or less, even? Who was he really? Where had he sprung from with his convenient accusation? Could he even be an agent of the dastardly Mr Benevolent, sent to legally ensnare me?

'Are you even American?' I asked, suspicious.

'What? Yes. Of course. Y'all. As American as a breakfast platter of hominy grits.'

'Hmm.' I had no idea what hominy grits[4] were, so could find neither truth nor falsehood in his answer, but immediately thought of another way to test his Americanness. 'If you truly are American, then you will be able to name all the states of your fair nation.'

'Of course. There's Virginia. West Virginia. And, um . . .' He looked baffled and uncertain, but then rallied geographically. 'North Virginia, South Virginia, East Virginia, South-east Virginia, mid-Virginia, Virginia-Virginia and Texas.'

Alas, I myself did not know what the states of America were, but he sounded jolly convincing and I decided he was probably right, even though it did sound as if there were a few too many Virginias in there.

'I have had enough of this tiresome questioning. It is my turn now.' The judge turned to the witness box. 'Mr Trashcan, in your own words, please tell us why Mr Bin is guilty as charged.'

'Of course. I, Harlan . . .' Now I noticed something strange: his American accent temporarily disappeared and a

---

[4] A porridge-like dish of coarsely ground corn. Not as delicious as it sounds, and it sounds horrible.

smooth British accent, with oily undertones of evil, briefly took its place. 'Ah, damn, lost the accent . . . I *Haaar*lan, *Haaaar*lan, I Harlan J. Trashcan' – here the accent gained traction again – 'invented the Bin a whole month before this gosh-darned varmint. Which is American slang from America, by the way.'

The British accent had seemed tantalizingly familiar. But whose was it?

'Do you have proof of this?'

'I surely do, Your Honour.'

'Excellent. Case proved. I find Pip Bin guilty—'

'May we at least see this evidence?' I was not going down without a fight, even if it was a rubbish, hand-slappy, hair-pulling, playground-style fight.

'Oh, if we must. Mr Trashcan?'

'The proof is this newspaper, containing a story about my invention of the Bin or, as we call it in America, the Trashcan. Someone has circled the story in ink and written "Great idea, must steal, lots of love Pip Bin." You can see it quite clearly.'

He waved the newspaper about the courtroom and there was a shocked intake of breath from everyone watching – or, at least, I am sure there would have been had there been any spectators.

'What newspaper is it?' I asked.

'The *Philadelphia Fictional Times*. There is no more accurate journal in America.'

'And when is it dated?'

'Hmm, let me see. When did you invent the Bin?'

This was a date burned on my memory with the intensity

of any life-changing experience, and I proudly told him. 'Why, the tenth of May, last year.'

'Really? Then this newspaper is dated . . .' He now turned away so that the newspaper was out of sight, removed from his pocket what appeared to be a small ink-pad and date-stamping kit, took that from view also, fiddled around briefly, then triumphantly brandished the newspaper saying '. . . the tenth of April last year.'

'May I see that to confirm it?' asked the judge.

'Of course, Your Honour.' Mr Trashcan handed over the newspaper as the judge reached for it. 'Though be careful, the ink is still wet.'

As he leaned towards the judge, a host of things came together in my mind regarding this bizarre American: the way he had sounded when his accent had slipped; the way he had looked when his wig and beard had slipped; the way he had moved when, on his way into the witness box, he himself had slipped. These parts added up to a recognizable and entirely horrifying whole: this was no Harlan J. Trashcan, this was one Mr Gently Benevolent.

'Your Honour! There is about to be a terrible injustice!'

The judge turned to me with curious eyes, that is to say eyes full of curiosity, not eyes that were themselves curious, though as I think back on it, one of his eyes was green and the other brown, so in fact they were curious in both senses.

'How so, young man?'

'That is not an American called Harlan J. Trashcan. It is an evil Englishman by the name of Mr Gently Benevolent! He has brought this invented case to destroy me.'

'Nonsense.' The judge's eyes now turned from curious to

angry, though, as recently established, with their bi-coloured nature they remained in at least one sense curious. 'For I know Gently Benevolent and he would never do such a thing. Would you, Benevolent?'

This protestation would have held more weight had he not just addressed himself directly to the disguised Mr Benevolent in the witness box; even the vile fiend himself seemed somewhat taken aback and knew not how to answer.

'Um . . . er . . .' he floundered.

'My mistake,' said the judge, trying desperately to recover. 'Thought I saw him there. But I didn't. Because he's not. Anyway, it's judgment time. I find you guilty on all counts, Pip Bin. You forfeit all rights to the Bin and all monies deriving therefrom. Furthermore, you are guilty of industrial theft, a heinous crime against society.'

A bitter, burning sense of injustice rose in me, like badly digested flambéed lemons; this whole trial was a fraud, and I was about to suffer for it.

'But before I pass sentence I want to emphasize that, whatever I say, my decision has in no way been prejudiced by Mr Bin being responsible for the deaths of my entire family. I simply cannot stress that enough.' He banged his gavel savagely. 'The sentence for industrial theft is five years' imprisonment.'

Five years in gaol! This was more than I could bear. To think that after so much recent personal emotional agony I had now also been falsely accused, convicted and imprisoned.

'No! That cannot be!' I shouted, emotions seething within my chest.

'And nor shall it be.' Was the judge about to show

lenience? As it turned out, only if it was sarcastically. 'For I deem your crimes much more serious than that and sentence you to be hanged by the neck until dead a week hence. Yes! Take that, you murdering scum. Not that it's personal, of course.'

I could not help but feel it might have been a tiny bit personal, but that was of scant comfort to me as officers of the court now entered, chained my hands and feet and dragged me out. As I passed through the door, Mr Benevolent raised his disguising wig as if it were a hat raised in farewell, and then laughed, the scornful triumph of his evil cackling seeming to follow me down the corridor, outside the courthouse, all the way to prison, and thence to death.

CHAPTER THE FORTY-EIGHTH

Despair, and all who sail in her

They hurled me into a prison cell and threw away the key. Then they realized that later that week they had to let me out of the cell to get hanged and also that in the meantime they'd need to put other prisoners in there with me, so they immediately started to look for it again.

My cell was grim, grimy and gruesome, but I cared not. For I had given up all hope. My vow to destroy Mr Benevolent was forgotten, for he had destroyed me first, his fiendishly fake plan having succeeded beyond his wildest dreams and my wildest nightmares. I was spiritually broken; and after a week I would be physically broken too.

But now I welcomed death, for either the priests were right and I would be reunited with Flora in Heaven, or the scientists were right and I would simply dissolve into blissful oblivion.

Either way, the pain would be gone.

While the guards continued their search for the key, I had the cell to myself. Huddled in the corner, I stared without seeing, and my mind wandered. It roamed around my happy childhood, so carefree and family-filled, the reverse of my now care-filled and family-free situation. I remembered the giddy laughter I had shared with Pippa and Poppy, laughter we would never share again, for Poppy had gone to the grave and, if Mr Benevolent had his way and married her, Pippa would probably never laugh or be happy again. I thought of my mother before the madness had taken her, the cuddles, the hugs, the kisses, the constant flow of unadulterated love and affection that had helped make my childhood so glorious. Paternal memories came next, of my father's reassuring masculine presence that had made the world seem such a safe place when I was little, and of how his love had been less overt than Mama's but had still always been there, like a background bass-line of devoted emotion, his long absences on business only so that he might provide a plentiful and joyous life for us; and I wept, thinking back to the time, moments before I had heard of his supposed death, when I had tripped over the family black cat, slid under a ladder, smashed a mirror, spilled a pile of horseshoes and broken the rabbit's foot and four-leaved clover I had had on my person. Pippa had said then that all our luck would run out and I had scoffed; yet she had been right, for soon afterwards the uncomplicated joys of childhood had been washed away by a cruel, adult world, full of malice and misfortune.

Next I thought of Harry, dear Harry Biscuit, from whom I had parted on such bad terms, and I wished there was some way of telling him I hadn't meant it, that he was the best friend I had ever had, the best friend any man could ever have, true, loyal, decent and just stupid enough never to doubt you, a friend who had helped me escape from that dread school, had aided me in all my trials and adventures since and had been the only comfort I had had in the wake of my wife's death.

And that led me, of course, to Flora, dear, sweet, beautiful Flora, whose existence had brightened my life like a glorious sun, a sun, alas, destined to burn brightly but shortly – and she had burned so very, very brightly.

Everything and everyone I had ever loved was gone; and soon I would be too. I sat alone and wretched, holding the metaphorical cards that God had dealt me, a Benevolent-trumped hand that had brought only pain.

Thus I mused for the days before my execution.

Finally, my last night on earth arrived. The guards brought me my last meal, but I did not eat it, as I had already mentally consumed a bowl of Regret Soup, followed by a slice of Rueful Pie, and for pudding, Wish-it-had-all-been-different Crumble.

As darkness fell, I turned to the wall and attempted my last, bitter sleep.

But barely had I done so when I was disturbed by the guards arriving with another prisoner. They swung the door open and hurled the felon inside. He was a huge, wide mass of a man, and he landed with a mighty, bone-jarring thud and let out a yelp of pain.

'Ow!'

It was an 'ow' I recognized, as familiar to me as one of my own.

'Harry, is that you?'

'Pip? Pip Bin?'

'Yes, it is I, old friend.'

'Hmmph. You are a friend to me no more as I remember.'

He turned huffily away from me; I was evidently still unforgiven. But I remembered how in the past days I had dreamed of setting matters right with him, and knew that even if God had treated me cruelly – and, oh, how He had! – at least now He had sent me this last chance to do a tiny bit of good with my remaining earthly time.

'Harry, it is true, I was a bad friend to you. I did not value you as I ought to have done.' He still did not look at me, though I sensed a stiffening in his body that indicated he was at least paying attention. 'But know this: you are the finest friend I have ever had, and if you can find it in your heart to forgive me, it would cheer me greatly in my final hours.'

For a few seconds there came no response. But then: 'No.'

I had had my hand stretched out towards him in hopeful anticipation of absolution and reconciliation, and at this single negative syllable it dropped, as did my spirits, which is really saying something, as they were already right down in the basement of my soul. Barely a second had passed, however, before I heard more cheering words.

'Oh, all right, then. I forgive you.' Bless Harry and his fickle swiftness of mood! 'You are a friend to me some more again, Pip Bin.'

'Harry, you do not know how glad I am to hear that!'

I offered my hand and he shook it, then enfolded me in a huge, affectionate embrace that reminded me of why it was good to be alive, which was a shame, what with death so imminent.

'So how is it that you are in this vile place with me, old friend?' I asked, keen to make the most of these last hours of human company.

'Well, much as I hate to admit it, my vintage meat emporium was not a success.'

'No, how could that be?' I said unconvincingly. 'What happened?'

'I poisoned seventy-four people.'

This only surprised me in as much as the figure was so low. 'So that is why you are here. For committing meat-slaughter.'

'Not entirely. You see, I only set up the emporium because I wanted to be a success. To be famous. To stand out. Like you, Pip Bin.'

'But, Harry—'

He put out a hand to stop me, actually pinching my lips shut with his fingers. 'No, you must hear this. You and your Bin were my inspiration. To achieve something so amazing! Why, I was honoured to be your friend. And I thought my vintage meat idea would see me lauded and loaded as you were. When it failed, I knew I had to do something else impressive and unique. So I decided to make myself the best in the world at something and, to that end, set out to become the fastest man on earth!'

'A noble if strange ambition. How did it go?'

'Badly. It turns out I am very, very slow. So I changed my

ambition again, but not by much, because I vowed to become the fattest man on earth. Only one letter's difference, you see.'

'And how did that go?'

'Pretty well, actually. You may have noticed I've put on a few pounds . . .'

'No, no . . .' In truth, I had noticed. Indeed, when the guards had first brought him to the cell, I had thought him to be three prisoners with but one head, a sort of human reverse Cerberus. 'I mean, you are looking . . . prosperous. Very . . . healthy. Rubenesque, even.' I could suddenly think of no more polite euphemisms and snapped, 'All right, fat! You're looking massively fat! Fatty, fatty, fat-fat!'

I am not proud of my outburst but, after so many days of navel-gazing misery in my own company, I was simply glad to be able to talk to someone else, even if that talking ended up being incredibly rude.

'Yes, it turns out I am really, really good at getting fat. I only have to look at a piece of cheese and I put on half a stone.'

By the size of him, Harry had clearly been looking at a lot of cheese.

'Sadly, I was nowhere near the fattest man on earth. That is a man called "Big" Jeff All-lard.[1] No matter how big I got, he was bigger. I needed to make one last effort to top him

---

[1] A famously huge man who earned a living in the freak shows of the nineteenth century. He died after eating a ton of apples for a bet; the apples fermented inside him and the expanding gases exploded him in a massive fountain of cider. After his death he was discovered to be in fact not a man, but a small, pale hippopotamus in a suit.

on the scales, but I didn't have the money to buy enough food, so I . . .' Here he paused, reddened and looked awkwardly at the floor. 'I am ashamed to admit that I went to a food-lender.'[2]

'Harry, no!'

'I borrowed two geese and a big pie. When the time came to pay him back, I couldn't. Because I'd eaten them. The interest was eight per cent, but I didn't realize that was per second. It turned out that by the end of the week I owed him more geese than actually exist and a pie the size of the entire universe. Obviously I couldn't pay, so he sued me and won, and with the seventy-four poisoned people taken into consideration as well, I was sentenced to be hanged and here we both are.'

This was a tragic fate, though I could not help thinking an utterly avoidable one.

'Harry, you must not blame yourself,' I lied, because it was so obviously his own daft fault. 'At least we shall die with each other tomorrow. As friends.'

'I suppose you could say it's our last chance to hang out together!' Harry tried to laugh, but it rapidly turned into a weepy bleat of sorrow, and I comforted him with another manly man-hug, sober and virtuously masculine.

'Oh, that is so sweet . . .'

Our hug was interrupted by the oily tones of the man I hated more than anything in the world, more than spiders in baths, more than France, more than people not saying

---

[2] Like money-lenders but for food. Obviously. Food-lenders originated in medieval Italy, and the biggest grew to become the Gourmand Banks we know today. Or would do if they existed.

'thank you' after I had held a door open for them, more even than salad:[3] Mr Gently Benevolent.

'What are you doing here?' I broke off my Harry-hug as this most hated of figures appeared at the cell door.

'Just popped round to say BBFE.'

'BBFE?'

'Bye-bye for ever. Oh, and to deliver this letter.'

He pushed an envelope through the bars. I recognized Pippa's sisterly handwriting on the front and tore it open with fear in my heart.

> Dearest brother Pip,
>
> I heard about the court case against Mr Trashcan. What a horrid man he sounds! And for you to be condemned to death is so unjust. To set that injustice to rights, I therefore wrote to Mr Trashcan asking if there was anything I could do which would see him drop the charges with posterity and thereby free you.
>
> He said there was.
>
> Oh, Pip! I can hardly write this, but must. For he said if I agreed to marry him then he would ensure that you were freed.
>
> In consequence, I have agreed to the marriage. So that you might be free. Doubtless it will be hideous, and every time his rough American hands

---

[3] A survey of Sir Philip's domestic accounts shows that in his entire adult life he never bought anything remotely resembling salad. Indeed, he hated it so much that while in his country-house retreat he invented the sport of clay-salad shooting, where lettuces were fired from traps and shot at with bullets made from meat.

come near my soft English bosom I shall shudder,
and not in a good way, but if it saves you from death,
it must be done.

    Your ever-loving sister,

    Pippa

The letter fell from my trembling fingers and fluttered to the floor – though given the gravity of the news it bore it should have plummeted.

'But – but this cannot be!'

'Oh, it can and will be. Tomorrow she will marry Mr Harlan J. Trashcan, and the instant the deed is done it's wig off, beard begone and goodbye accent, and she will realize who she has truly married. Me. Your worst enemy. Shacked up with your sister. For ever! Nee-yah, ha, ha, ha!'

Truly his new laugh was a despicable thing, like being verbally shot, stabbed and punched simultaneously.

'But at least I shall be free!' It was a small comfort to me, but better than none.

'No, you won't. Because as she is saying, "I will," you will be saying, "That rope's awfully tight – eeeeurrrrfgggh."'

'So the deal you offered was false. You lied to her.'

'Well, duh. Of course. Oh, and incidentally, just to rub it in, the marriage will take place in the church of St Wedding.'

'You besmirch the place where Flora and I swore our love!'

'Yes. Yes, I do. And one final thing . . . It's always nice to die as a family, so you might as well have this. I have no further use for it.'

He beckoned to two guards who dragged a sorry-looking

figure into sight: my mother. They opened the cell door and threw her in.

'Ooh, is this the new linen cupboard? Hello, I'm Agnes the tablecloth. You must be a towel. How do you do?' She offered me a mad hand and I shook it, glad to feel my mother's touch, no matter how crazed; but it was not a long touch, for she now turned to Harry. 'And goodness me, you must be the fattest bed-sheet I have ever seen!'

'She will hang with you tomorrow.' Benevolent's eyes glistened with happy malice.

'Why? What has she done to deserve such a fate?'

'Nothing. I simply tired of her. Judge Hardthrasher condemned her to death as a favour. Right, well, that's that. Enjoy being dead, Pip Bin. It's not been a pleasure knowing you.' He tipped his hat at me ironically and left.

But he had lit a fire within me, a fire I had thought long extinguished, and I now ran to the cell door and yelled after him, 'Mr Benevolent! Mr Benevolent!'

He stopped and turned back to face me. 'What? Do you have some pathetic last words of futile resistance?'

'No. I just wanted to tell you something. By bringing my mother to be hanged and threatening to marry my sister you have made a huge mistake.'

'Have I? Feels pretty right to me.'

'You're wrong. Because, for the first time in a long while, I have a reason to live. And that reason is to save them, save myself and then kill you, Benevolent. No force on earth can stop me, for my name is Pip Put-that-in-the Bin, husband to a murdered wife, son to a maddened mother, brother to a soon-to-be-defiled sister . . . and I will have my vengeance, in this life or the next.'

The corridor outside the cell was only dimly lit, but I swear I saw Mr Benevolent's face blanch at my words.

'It'll have to be the next, then, won't it?' he retorted, but though his words were bold, his tone was shaken, and I knew I had frightened him. I watched him leave with my spirits returned, my courage high and just one problem: I had not the first clue as to how to go about wreaking the vengeance I had promised.

CHAPTER THE FORTY-NINTH

Day of destiny; ending of endings

I had told Mr Benevolent that no force on earth could stop me, but in the end the cell door did a pretty good job, for it would not yield, no matter how much I pounded and bashed at it. I even got Harry to lean on it with his newly massive bulk, but it merely creaked under the strain and held fast.

Dawn arrived all too quickly. Inside the prison I could hear the sounds of London waking outside, sounds once commonplace but now special, for they were among the last things I might ever hear.

I racked my brain for escape ideas; none came.

As the time grew nearer to my date with a noose, I could hear people arriving in the prison courtyard – for it was to be a public execution – and the merry chatter of the touts outside offering tickets.

The supporting act was two floggings and a man in the stocks being pelted with animal excrement, and the cheers and excitement of the crowd were great indeed, sadistic, ordure-throwing voyeurs that they were. As their cries of delight dwindled, it was time for the main attraction.

Us.

Or, to be more specific, Harry, my mother, me and three nooses.

We were led out to great baying and howling from the bloodlusty horde of onlookers. Ahead of us was the scaffold, three ropes hanging down and swaying ominously. Around it stood soldiers drafted in to keep the slavering crowd in check, and to one side was a table where Judge Hardthrasher sat, his eyes wide with eager anticipation.

I held my mother's hand tightly, desperately trying to squeeze even just one word of sanity from her before we died. Alas, it seemed as if it was not to be.

'Ooh,' she said. 'Is it washing day? Are we to be hung out to dry?'

'Sadly, Mama, we were hung out to dry a long time ago.'

'Do the fat one first,' shouted the judge, over the noise of the crowd. 'I like seeing a fatty hanged. And bring me food! All this justice is making me hungry.'

A minion scurried to do as he said as the prison executioner, a surprisingly affable psychopath named Gibbet Geoff,[1] manoeuvred us to beside the nooses, each of which had our names embroidered on it in gold thread.

It was a nice touch, actually.

---

[1] Based on either the long-serving chief executioner of England, 'Noosey' Nick Nasty, or the infamous amateur vigilante hangman String-them-up Simon Scaffold, both of whom were apparently lovely men who just happened to enjoy hanging their fellow humans.

Gibbet Geoff placed the noose around Harry's neck; this was it.

'Goodbye, Harry Biscuit.'

'And goodbye to you, Pip Bin. See you in Heaven, I hope.'

His dignity was great, as was his size. He shed no tears, but stood nobly, straight-backed and calm, as the executioner released the trap door beneath his feet.

Harry plunged downwards, the rope tightening around his neck and the wooden scaffold creaking under the strain of his bulk. If only it would break, freeing him! But it did not.

To make the spectacle last longer, hangings back then strangled rather than the more modern method of neck-breaking, and my poor best friend swayed and swung chokily, his face going red, the breath being throttled from his body.

Above the cheers of the crowd, I could hear the judge gloating. 'Ha! Look at the swinging fatty!' He was truly enjoying himself, and where a decent, moral human might have been sick to the stomach at the sight, he was hungrily stuffing food into his drooling, hate-filled face, great chunks of pie and cheese.

Cheese.

There was a tingle at the back of my brain as Harry dangled desperately.

It was something about cheese, something Harry had said – and then I remembered, and at last saw a possible way out for us.

'Harry! Look at the judge! Look at his cheese!'

A now purple-faced, half-throttled Harry managed to turn himself to look at the judge and his curdled-milk-product snack.

'Ooh, cheese, delicious . . .' Harry managed to croak.

He said no more, but it did not matter: the cheese had worked its weight-gaining magic for, as Harry had told me, on looking at it he had instantly gained half a stone. Those extra pounds did the trick, the straining scaffold now giving up the unequal fight against his destructive mass, cracking and splintering and ultimately collapsing in a heap of shattered timber.

'I'm not dead!' cried Harry, joyfully.

'Oh, but you will be,' shouted Judge Hardthrasher, foaming with furious spittle. 'Guards!'

The soldiers surrounding the now ruined scaffold unslung their muskets and ran threateningly towards us; and another thought tickled my brain, a memory of something else that could help us, an event in a dock on the Kent coast some months back involving a rogue button and a startled tuna.

'Harry!' I shouted. 'You must breathe deeply and strain!'

'What?' He looked briefly baffled, but then his face lit up in understanding. 'Oh, nice, I get it.'

He took a deep breath, puffed out his stomach and chest and strained. While putting on all that weight, he had clearly never found the time to replace his clothes, and consequently they were far too tight on him, bulging and almost bursting with excess flesh, the buttons pulled tautly to breaking point. His straining efforts now took them past that breaking point and they popped off with a ping, their dense, brassy weight skimming through the air at huge velocity straight into the path of the oncoming soldiers, striking and stunning them in their tracks. The crowd ran for cover to avoid the ricocheting missiles, and our path to freedom was clear. I picked up my mother, shouted to Harry, 'Run!' and then, obeying my own instruction, ran myself.

We raced across the emptied yard and had nearly attained the exit-y safety of the unattended gate when Judge Hardthrasher stepped into our path, his personal noose in his hand, his face twisted with violent hate, spittle-flecked and furious.

'I don't think so, Bin. I mean to have a hanging, and I will have one!'

He quickly slipped the noose around my neck and started to pull. I dropped my mother and tried desperately to free the chafing, choking rope from my throat, managing to whisper a pleading 'Harry . . .'

As I scrabbled to get my fingers between rope and neck, I could hear Harry breathing in and straining once more, followed by the ping of his one remaining trouser button firing. To my distinct and potentially deathy disappointment, it missed the judge, who happily kept trying to strangle me to death.

'Damn!' said Harry. 'I am out of ammunition.'

'But I am not!' cried an approaching voice, which was accompanied by the sound of thundering hoofs, and suddenly there was my aunt Lily, flintlock pistol in hand, appearing as if by magic from nowhere or, more likely, by horse from round the corner. She now fired with a precision almost unimaginable, her bullet striking the rope in the judge's hands and severing it.

I fell to the ground, spots of air deprivation before my eyes, and at last pulled the noose from my neck.

'Aaargh!' screamed Judge Hardthrasher in frustration and, turning, he let fly an almighty, rage-filled punch that caught Aunt Lily's horse on the jaw. He was a huge, angry man and the blow felled the beast in its tracks, an incredible and terrifying sight for anyone to behold, but probably for no one more than the horse itself. 'Why does everyone keep spoiling my hanging fun?'

Aunt Lily had rolled free of the falling horse and bounced to her feet ready to fight. 'Run, Pip, go and save Pippa.'

'But—'

'No buts. She is your priority. I shall deal with this judge.'

I stood and picked up my mother from the ground beside me.

'Oh, I've got smudges on me now. I'll need a good wash.'

'And you shall have one, Mama, as soon as we have saved Pippa.'

'Ooh, I once had a little napkin called Pippa . . .'

Was this a sign of imminent re-saning? There was no time for pondering the matter, however, as the ferocious judge had now re-gathered his bullet-shortened noose and was advancing on us again.

'Go!' Aunt Lily thrust herself into the judge's path as I started to run, Harry behind me, slowed by having to hold up his now buttonless trousers. 'For it is a far, far better thing I do now, than I have ever— Eeeurggh!'

I looked back to see the judge slipping his noose around

her neck and pulling – but Aunt Lily swiftly kicked him in his uniquely gentlemanly parts[2] and he let go again with an agonized 'Oof.' I suspected that somehow she would be all right in this battle, and I even pitied the judge a little.

Actually, of course I didn't, my only regret regarding him being that I would now not be the one who killed him and therefore I would not bag the complete set of dead Hardthrashers.

I could see the spire of St Wedding's soaring high above the roofs and I hurried down the narrow streets of the East End in that direction, Harry right behind me. Our escape had been noted, however, and as we ran, a platoon of soldiers appeared in pursuit. We rapidly got closer to the church, but the soldiers rapidly got closer to us; surely I could not fail and be thwarted so near to my objective! Fortune herself seemed to agree with me, in the form of Harry, for as we raced out of one particularly narrow alley I noticed he was no longer with me.

'Harry! What are you doing?'

'Giving you a chance, Pip Bin.' The soldiers were nearly upon him, but Harry stood where he was, nearly blocking the passage completely with his gigantic bulk. There was a cheese shop nearby and he started looking repeatedly in its window, each glance expanding him more and more until he was tightly jammed between the walls of the alley, or walleys. The soldiers ran into him, bouncing off his massy solidity, unable to shift him. 'Now go, Pip Bin, go and save

---

[2] Do I really need to explain this? Because I don't want to have to write the word 'testicles'. Though I just have.

Pippa. And . . .' he paused, looked briefly at the ground, then up at me, sincerity and certainty filling his face '. . . tell her I love her.'

'What? You love Pippa?'

He nodded. 'With all of my heart.'

That explained a lot about his weepy behaviour in her absence; and I was instantly certain that Pippa would reciprocate his love. If he lost a bit of weight first. Not that she was shallow and obsessed with physical looks but, you know, Harry was really, really, person-crushingly big.

I said no more, simply gave him a nod of thanks, respect and friendship,[3] and, saved by the Harry, I ran onwards, the church so close now and the only question being: would I reach it in time? Barely a minute later and I was there, and as I approached the door I could hear the wedding ceremony beginning inside.

'Who gives this woman to be married?' I heard the vicar ask.

'I do,' Mr Parsimonious replied, standing in for our still-missing-feared-dead father.

'Good, good. And now let us confirm who is to be married. You are Mr Harlan J. Trashcan?'

'Sort of,' came the hated but disguised voice of Mr Benevolent in response.

'And you are Pippa Wheelie Bin?'

---

[3] In those repressed times when men were forbidden to express emotions verbally, a whole language of nods existed. There were over three hundred different ways to nod at another gentleman, from the simple tip of the head, all the way up to incredibly complex manoeuvres that looked more like cranial ballet, or a serious neurological condition.

'I am . . .'

Poor Pippa! She sounded so reluctant, so alone, so scared! I readied myself to burst in and stop the proceedings, but hesitated, because if I was right, I would soon be able to do so in a manner that had real style to it.

'First I must ask whether any persons here know of any lawful reason why these two should not wed.'

That was what I had been waiting for, and now I pushed the doors open and stepped in with a bellowed 'I have a reason!'

There: that was much more dramatic.

The disguised Mr Benevolent turned to me with a spasm of disgust; Pippa turned with a look of surprised hope; and the vicar gazed at me with curiosity and excitement – I think all clergy secretly hope that someone will burst in at that point in the marriage ceremony.

'And what reason might that be, young man?'

'She is my sister!'

'That's not exactly a lawful reason for them not to wed, is it?'

Vicars could sound so condescending.

I put my mad, tablecloth-minded mother down in a pew where she set about trying to fold herself neatly, and marched towards the altar.

'Then how about false identity, false representation and false . . . false . . .' I could not think of a third false thing, but then with a flash of inspiration I did, reaching out and pulling the wig from Mr Benevolent's head. 'False hair!' In fact, I now thought of several more false things. 'And a false beard!' I ripped the false beard from his chin. 'And a false arm!' I grabbed his arm and started to pull it off.

'The arm is real, you imbecile,' said Mr Benevolent, in his true voice. Both Pippa and Mr Parsimonious gasped in horror.

'No! Mr Gently Benevolent! To think I nearly married you.' Pippa placed a horrified hand over her mouth and buried herself in the safety of Mr Parsimonious's pseudo-paternal embrace.

'You still shall marry me. Once your pesky brother is dead. On guard!'[4] My evil ex-guardian drew a huge sword from a hidden scabbard and slashed at me. I managed to leap swiftly backwards and he cut only air, but he advanced on me, cutting angrily, and I was gradually pushed further and further down the aisle to avoid his blows. I searched desperately for a way to fight back as I retreated, but all too soon there was no further I could go, as I hit the cold, unyielding stone of the church's wall.

'Nowhere to run, Pip Bin,' said Mr Benevolent, raising his weapon high for a killing blow – but I had deliberately aimed for that part of the wall and now desperately scrabbled with my hands to reach what I knew was mounted on it, and as he swung down at me, I found it.

The church's communion sword.[5]

I pulled it from the wall and managed to get it into the

---

[4] No Englishman of the time – even an evil one – could have said the French '*en garde*' without arresting himself for mild treason.

[5] Since the sixteenth century all Anglican churches had contained considerable amounts of weaponry to fight off potential Catholic assaults. As well as the communion sword there was usually a christening sabre, an anti-Mass musket and an Easter cannon.

path of Benevolent's down-rushing blade. They collided with a great metallic clang, sparking and scraping.

'Dammit!'

Not only had he lost his chance to kill me, but he was destined to lose. For strength had flooded into me like muscly water, strength derived from all the injustices I had suffered, all the losses, all the happiness I had been deprived of and, as I had promised him back in my prison cell, now no force on earth could stop me.

I smashed at him again and again, and he backed away, terror on his face.

'Go on, Pip!' shouted Pippa and Mr Parsimonious, encouragingly.

'What, no one shouting for me?' whined Mr Benevolent.

'Go on, Mr Benevolent,' the vicar said, but received such a look from Pippa and Mr Parsimonious that he instantly changed his mind. 'Go on and lose, I meant. Hurray for Pip!'

My violent assault had pushed Mr Benevolent into a corner of the church that was piled high with prayer-books, hymnals and Bibles, and there was nowhere left for him to go. I smashed the sword from his hand and slashed onwards, my vengeance nearly at hand. Desperately, he picked up a book and threw it at me, but I easily caught it on the point of my sword, skewering it straight down the middle. He threw more and more, and I merrily stabbed them from the air until there were none left.

'Aha, you are out of books!' I said, stepping forward to administer a killing blow . . . but there was no fear on his face, not even resignation. Instead he seemed strangely, smugly certain.

'And you are out of sword, Pip Bin.'

I looked at the weapon in my hand, and discovered that he was correct in his statement: I had caught so many books on the tip that it was now less sword and more word-kebab – there was absolutely no pointy, cutty, stabby bit left.

'Oh.'

'Yes, oh.' He leaped forward, quicker than a startled cheetah or espresso-addicted rattlesnake, and regained his own sword.

Now it was my turn to retreat, my theological library on a stick being useless for fighting.

'I shall soon be rid of you, Pip Bin, and then my incredibly complicated plan to destroy your family will have succeeded.'

Slash, slash, he went. Stumble backwards, stumble backwards, I went.

'I have worked on my plan for so long . . .'

Slash, slash, stumble back, stumble back.

'Since Aunt Lily?'

More slashing, more reverse stumbling.

'She was just the start of it. You are the end. And that end is . . . now.'

He abruptly stopped slashing as I took another backwards pace and tripped on an unexpected step, falling helplessly to the floor. Mr Benevolent loomed over me, sword in hand, hate on face, murder in mind.

'Ha! You have tripped over my special step! Many years ago I funded the building of this church and had that step incorporated for just this eventuality. That is how complicated my plan was.'

Though I was about to die, a part of me had to hand it to

him: he had played the long game and had clearly really thought things through.

'Now die, Pip Bin, die!'

He raised his sword and prepared to plunge it into me. I refused to close my eyes and instead stared hard at my evil ex-guardian, determined to meet death openly, bravely and with a manly handshake.

It turned out I had no need to. For at that moment the church doors swung open and with a cry of 'Mine!' Aunt Lily hurled herself into the path of the down-rushing blade, taking its full force into her own body, saving me but seemingly mortally wounding herself.

'Aunt Lily . . . why did you do that?'

'I wasn't going to let that swine kill you, Pip Bin.'

'But he has now killed you instead.'

'Yes. Bit of a drawback that. But I'd take a sword for you any day, Pip. That said, if I'd known it would hurt this much, I might not actually have done it. Still, all done now. Ow. Really ow. Earn this, Pip. Make it count.'

Then, with a trickle of blood from her mouth and a brief sigh, she collapsed, and was dead.

And I was angry. Worse than angry. I was livid. Enraged. Furious. Incandescent, apoplectic, fuming, seething and incensed.

In short, I was blinking cross.

I stood, pulled the sword from poor Aunt Lily and ran at Mr Benevolent screaming, 'Take that, you fiend!'

He looked at me, baffled. 'Take what?' Then he glanced down and saw what I had given him. 'Oh. A sword in the guts. Ruddy heck.'

And with those underwhelming last words of mild sweariness, he slumped to the floor in death.

I had finally triumphed over him, but there was no sense of glory or fulfilment, only a sick, empty relief that left me shaky and weak, for at what cost had victory come?

'Oh, Pip . . .' Dear Pippa, now safe from Benevolent's marital attentions, rushed up and threw her arms around me.

'Good work, young Pip.' Mr Parsimonious, that most generous of men, shook me heartily by the hand. 'You must have my thanks, my well dones and my admiration.' He looked around for more physical gifts. 'And these wafers . . . this hymnal . . . and this bottle of communion wine.'

He handed me these things, and I gratefully uncorked the last and took a great swig. 'Thank you, Mr Parsimonious. After all that I need a drink.'

As I glugged down the welcome wine, I heard the doors slam open and then a familiar voice. 'It's all right, I'm here! Nobody move!'

It was Harry! Alive and well.

And stark naked.

'Sorry about my nudiness, everyone, but I hadn't got any buttons left and so my clothes all fell off as I ran here.'

'How did you escape the soldiers, Harry?'

'Bit of luck, actually. There's been a colonial rebellion somewhere in Africa, and they all got summoned to go and fight that, leaving me to come here and help.'

'Thankfully, Harry, there is nothing left for you to do.' I gestured at Mr Benevolent's body, and swigged at the bottle of wine again, shaky weakness retreating and a calm satisfaction settling upon me.

'Oh, but there is one thing I must do.' Harry turned to Pippa and knelt nakedly before her. 'Pippa Bin . . .'

'Yes, Harry Biscuit?' Her voice quivered with anticipation.

'Will you marry me?'

'Oh, Harry, of course I will! Yes, yes, a thousand times yes!'

'Harrumble! I am to marry Pippa!' Harry danced ecstatically around the church, knocking things over and creating general joyous havoc.

'And we may all be happy again,' I said, joining in with his dance – but that merry dance was interrupted by a weak though still distinctly evil voice.

'Not if I've got anything to do with it . . .'

No! Mr Benevolent yet lived! Pale and blood-stained, he raised himself from the floor, in his hand a small flintlock pistol he had clearly had concealed upon his person.

Then he fired, and it was as if time slowed, dramatically and terribly.

Harry was closest to Mr Benevolent and made a desperate lunge for him as the rest of us dived for cover; but it all seemed too little, too late, as the pistol belched fire and sicked up its deadly load.

Then normal speed resumed, and I could see Mr Benevolent no more, for he was buried beneath the colossal, fleshy mass that was Harry.

'Is everyone all right? Did he hit anyone?' I asked, hoping that the answers to my two questions were 'yes' and 'no' respectively.

Fortunately, those were the answers; it seemed we had escaped, both wound and dead-person free. But then I noticed that Pippa was pointing at my chest with a trembling finger, and I looked down to see a great red stain spreading across my shirt.

'Oh . . . I am hit.' Yet I felt no pain. Was this the numbness of approaching death? The others ran to me and opened my jacket. Beneath it, all was blood. There was a strange smell in my nostrils, potent but calming, what I assumed to be the Heavenly smell of the hereafter. I could feel my vision fading and my strength going, but at least I knew I had defeated Mr Benevolent and saved what parts of my family I could; in the end, it had been worth it. 'Then I must bid you farewell. At least I shall be with dear Flora soon. Promise me that you will live and love well in my name, dear family. For I love you all more than I can say. Goodbye . . .'

I fell back on to the cold stone floor of the church and closed my eyes, ready to be received into Paradise by the angels of the Lord.

I was dead.

'Hang on,' said Harry. 'That isn't blood . . . it's wine.'

What? Not blood? Wine? That would explain the smell in my nostrils, for on reflection it was not Heaven's scent but that of fermented grapes. When Mr Benevolent fired, I had still been clutching the communion wine Mr Parsimonious had given me, and the bullet must have struck that. It *was* blood, but only symbolic Jesus blood and not the actual blood that ran in my veins.

My strength came back and my vision returned.

I was not dead!

But I was quite embarrassed.

'Ha, had you going,' I bluffed, but I need not have done so for people were simply glad I was alive and I was now surrounded by love and hugs and happiness. 'Are we quite sure Mr Benevolent is dead this time?'

'Yes,' replied Harry.

'Absolutely certain?'

'Well, I am sitting on him, and I weigh forty-three stone. And I'm naked, so the embarrassment alone would be enough to kill him.'

It seemed as if my vicious ex-guardian was definitely gone this time; and now evil had departed, we needed joy to take its place.

'Reverend, I am assuming there is still a wedding that has been paid for?'

'There is.'

'Then let us see Harry and Pippa married this day!'

Amid cheers, jolliness and harrumbles, we quickly assembled at the altar and the vicar prepared to maritalize.

'First, I must once more ask whether any persons here know of any lawful reason why these two should not wed?'

I smiled as I remembered that I had recently waited outside the door until after just this sentence, the better to make my entrance, but surely no one would object this time.

I was wrong.

For someone else had a similar dramatic sense of timing to mine as the doors now opened and a deep voice boomed, 'I know a reason!'

We turned to see who it was, but this person's next words revealed all before we saw it with our eyes.

'For no girl should be wed without her father to give her away!'

It was Papa! Alive! And returned! Pippa and I rushed to him and smothered him with embraces, kisses and other affectionments.

'Oh, Papa! Where have you been?'

'It is a long story, and one for another time. Suffice to say, Benevolent faked my death and hid me away, keeping me quiet by making me become addicted to opium.'

'How terrible!'

'Oh, I don't know, the opium was pretty good, actually.' He caught himself and coughed. 'Um, I mean, yes, it was awful. Really, really awful. But thankfully your aunt Lily found me and set me free.'

We bowed our heads in memory of that marvellous aunt.

'We all owe her a great debt.'

'It was my pleasure . . .' came a weak voice from where Aunt Lily lay dead, somewhat indicating that perhaps she was not as deceased as we had thought. We rushed to her side – she was still alive! 'Did no one think to check whether I was actually dead or not?'

'Sorry . . . sort of slipped our minds,' I admitted.

'Doesn't matter. Help me up, someone. If Pippa and Harry are getting married, that's a family function I'm happy to be at.'

We helped her up and returned to the altar. On the way, Papa stopped and knelt next to his poor mad wife, my poor mad mother, where she had sat in a pew through all these events, trying to iron herself with a Bible.

'Agnes, dear Agnes, what has happened to you?'

She looked at him with the glassy eyes of madness, but they quickly cleared as if someone had washed them with the soap of sanity.

'Oh, hello, Thomas. Not dead after all, then.'

'No, my love. And you are no longer mad.'

'Gosh, no. I never was. I was just pretending to be mad as part of a very clever plan to defeat Mr Benevolent.'

'Really? Are you sure?' He quite reasonably sounded sceptical at this claim.

'It worked, didn't it? Unless that's not him lying dead over there.'

'Um, right . . .' He looked as if he did not know what to say in the face of Mama's patently ludicrous suggestion, but the exigencies of marital harmony won out over the truth. 'Yes, well done, dearest. You beat him, all right.'

'Clever me, eh?' Mama now turned to Pippa and me. 'Aren't you going to give me a hug, children?'

'Of course, Mama!'

We rushed over and hugged her, and I felt the warmth of a restituted family growing inside me, like an expanding loaf of happy bread. For not only was my family as mended as it could be, it was about to be enlarged by the addition of a new brother-in-law.

Our small group of re-happied people gathered before the vicar and he proceeded to join Pippa and Harry in holy and wholly deserved matrimony.

'Will you, Harry Chocolate Wafer Biscuit, take this woman to be your wife?'

'I will.'

'And will you, Pippa Wheelie Bin, take this man to be your husband?'

'Oh, I will.'

'Then I declare you to be husband and wife.'

'Harrumble!' we all cried delightedly, and as Harry kissed Pippa, the church erupted in joy.

My father was returned; my mother was re-saned; Pippa and Harry were wed; and Mr Benevolent was at last conquered and dead. True, there would be the bumps and scrapes of any life still ahead of us, and me in particular, for this is my book, by me, about me, and there are more tales to tell, more stories to write.

But for now let us leave my younger self in that church all those years ago, with joy and optimism restored; let us come to a happy end, ignoring the tiny detail that on leaving the church for the weeks of happy celebration that ensued, my younger self noticed that Mr Benevolent's body was suspiciously absent, strongly hinting at the possibility that he was not dead and might one day be back for vengeance; let us leave the woe and misery behind, the betrayals, back-stabbings and front-punchings; and let us shortly set the book aside, take up a bracing glass of post-reading brandy and toast the fact that, at that point in time, all I could see was a clearer, brighter future stretched out ahead of me, like a glorious carpet of happiness, a future of love, family and friendship, a future of rich experience and high adventure, and, above all, a future in which finally all my expectations were far from bleak.

APPENDIX I

There is no Appendix I.[1]

---

[1] It was removed from the novel after it suffered a bout of book appendicitis.

APPENDIX II

The full name of Pip's father's lawyer – which is reputed to contain the author's acknowledgements hidden in a supposedly uncrackable code – is as follows:

Mr Wickham Post Forberton Fenugreek Chasby Twistleton Montmorency Aurelius Pargordon Jezthisby Cumquatly Pobbleton Tendling Hampton Barderby Flumsome Incoborant Nonwheely Williams Wibbler Crabton Insecuritant Farneilly O'Reilly Q'Veilly Ooh I Have Just Realized That This Might Be An Ideal Chance To Insert The Acknowledgements For The Book So Let Me Now Do That And Here We Go Because There Are Plenty Of People To Thank Probably Starting With The People Who Made It Happen Such As Jo Cantello For Shoving Me In The Direction Of Mister Ben Mason Gentleman Literary Agent Of The Finest Pedigree Who Said He Would Sell The Book And Only Blinking Well Went And Did Just That Indeed Sold It To James Gurbutt Who Took A Crazily Deadlined

Chance So Thank You For That James We Seem To Have Done It In Time And Thanks To Everyone Else At Corsair For Their Mighty Efforts And Pleasant Politeness And All Round Excellence Though They Do Not Actually Dress As Corsairs Which I Think They Ought To Given The Company Name Anyway Those Thanks Would Include Sam Evans Clive Hebard Sarah Castleton And Colette Whitehouse And If I Have Missed Anyone Sorry It Might Be Just Because I Had Not Yet Met You When I Wrote This Bit Anyway Moving Outside The Company Itself I Want To Say Thanks To Angela Martin For Making People Aware Of The Thing And Hazel Orme Who Really Knows Her Commas And Saved Me From Some Egregious Errors Of Style Grammar And Punctuation And Then I Would Like To Say Thanks To Nick Ranceford Hadley At Noel Gay For Graciously Letting The Book Head Elsewhere And Also To Everyone At That Fine Agency For Their Lovely Excellence Over The Years With A Particular Shout Out For Charlie Olins And The Now Departed Claire King And Holly Nicholson And Also To Anyone Else There Who Has Helped And Been Great And Whose Names I Have Almost Criminally Excluded By Mistake Honestly And Not On Purpose I Will Buy Anyone Who Objects To Their Omission A Cake To Say Sorry If They Would Like And Now On To Those People Who Helped The Former Incarnation Of The Material The Original Radio Series Bleak Expectations Because Without Them I Would Be Nothing I Tell You Nothing Just A Miserable Hack With Some Unperformed Drivel On My Laptop Not That There Isn't A Lot Of That Anyway But Here Goes Firstly Thanks To Paul Schlesinger For Much Support And Fighting

On The Show's Behalf Caroline Raphael At Radio Four For
Commissioning It And To Mister Paul Mayhew Archer Guru
And Supporter Of The Finest Sort And Of Course The
Radio Cast Who Are Uniformly Brilliant Richard Johnson
Tom Allen Tony Head Sarah Hadland James Bachman Susie
Kane Geoffrey Whitehead Are The Ever Presents And The
Often And Sometimes Presents Include Laurence Howarth
Perdita Weeks And Of Course The Majestic Brilliance That
Is Celia Imrie And The People Up In The Box Of Wizard's
Tricks Like Roger Danes And Jill Abram And In Earlier
Series Gary Newman Not That One Another One Plus The
Wonderful Ann Osborne And Lyndsay Fenner And Tamara
Shilham And Sundry Guest Stars Such As Raquel Cassidy
And Jane Asher Who Didn't Bring One Of Her Excellent
Cakes But Was Brilliant And Lovely Anyway And Do Not
Think I Have Forgotten The Severally Appearing David
Mitchell Who Was Always Excellent As The Reverend Ripely
Fecund And That Leads Me To Robert Webb Who Was
Jedrington Secret Past In The Sadly Cancelled The Bleak
Old Shop Of Stuff And The Rest Of The Cast And Crew Of
That Deceased Show Who Were All Great And I Am Sorry I
Let Them Down By Writing Something That Not Enough
People Watched But Go On Everyone Buy It Online Or On
DVD Because I Need The Royalties As I Am Having Some
Building Work Done At The Moment Oh Hang On No That
Is Not The Point The Point Is The Acknowledgements So
Let Me Return To Them With A Familial One Which Is
Thanks To The Marvellous John And Hilary For All Round
Brilliance And Loveliness And For Helping Look After And
Distract The Girls While I Was Under Enormous Deadline

Pressure And Thanks To All Those Who Have Read The Book Or Parts Thereof At Different Points And Been Encouraging Such As David Wolstencroft For Example Or Will Maclean Or Professor Yes That's Professor Simon James Who Really Knows His Dickens Or Tim Kevan Who Will Be Knee Deep In Nappies Soon So Good Luck With Working From Home While That Is Going On And That Might Be It But I Am Pretty Sure I Must Have Sent It To Mister Robert Thorogood At Some Point Though I Might Not Because He Has Been Incredibly Busy In Recent Years Doing The Fabulous Death In Paradise For BBC One And It Gets Over Five Million Viewers Blimey That Is Impressive And Way More Than I Have Ever Got And I Might Have Sent It To Toby Davies As Well But I Forget Because I Am Past Forty And Have Two Small Children So The Memory Is Not What It Was And Then I Must Also Include A Thanks For Some Etiquette Advice To Molly Hawn And Yes For Fans Of The Radio Show She Is The Model For Mrs Hawn Of The Cutlery Collecting Society In Series Four Episode One But She Knows It Is Meant Fondly And That Might Be It For Acknowledgements Actually But I Am Sure I Will Have Missed Someone Out For Example In Case Anyone Is Thinking I Have Excluded Gareth Edwards Esquire Then Look At The Dedication At The Beginning Of The Book Because He Is In That Along With Other Folk Not Mentioned Here Not That This Is The Second Division Of Thanks But You Know Gareth Needed To Be Up Front Because Without Him There Would Be No Bleak Expectations And He Is A Brilliant Brilliant Producer Who Has Made Me A Better Writer And Together With The Cast Has Made The Show

Better Than I Could Have Imagined So It Turns Out He Is
Mentioned Here After All But Anyway Now It Is Time To Say
To Everyone I Have Forgotten To Include On This List I Am
Sorry And The Cake Offer From Earlier On Still Stands So
If You Think You Should Have Been Acknowledged We Will
Put It Through An Arbitration Process And Then If It Turns
Out You Should Have Had A Thanks You Can Have A Free
Cake And If You Really Really Persuade Me An Erratum Slip
In The Book Or Maybe Your Name In The Next Edition If
There Is One Because You Never Know Do You This Might
Only Sell A Copy Or Two But I Really Hope Not Because
That Would Make Me Feel Awkward And A Little Embarrassed
So Anyway That's The Acknowledgements Done And I Have
Still Got A Couple Of Thousand Words Of Silly Name To Go
To Make It Up To The Full Twenty Minutes So Let Me Get
Back To Writing The Names By Writing Wasby Grimbleton
Spelunkist Robertsina Taylorizer Burton Bisby Von Rasping
Ambrose Wispy Beardiness Oh Good Grief Why Did I Saddle
Myself With Such A Long Name I Don't Quite Know How I
Will I Fill The Entire Three Thousand Or So Words Of It
But I Will Try I Really Will So Let Me Do A Bit More Now
With Names Such As Chibberton Frankton Monty Randall
Brearley Hendrick Old Botham Boycott Ooh I Seem To
Have Slipped Into A Late Seventies Early Eighties Cricketing
Name Riff So I Might As Well List Some Of My Favourite
Cricketers Starting With Childhood Hero David Gower
Followed By In No Particular Order Certainly Not Batting
Order Ha Ha Weak Cricket Joke Anyway Here Come Those
Names Marcus Trescothick Phil Edmonds Malcolm Marshall
Adam Gilchrist Brian Lara Virender Sehwag Shane Warne

Andrew Strauss Because What A Good Captain He Was And I Must Not Forget Jeff Dujon The Cricketer Whose Last Name Is Nearest To A Mustard Obviously Apart From Phil Mustard Of Durham Whose Name Actually Is Mustard And Though He Is Not One Of My Favourite Ever Cricketers I Think The England Selectors Were Very Harsh On Him But Then They Often Have Been With Wicketkeepers Such As Chris Read And Particularly Steven Davies Who I Think Has Been Messed Around Chronically Though Who Am I To Question Andy Flower One Of The Great Keeper Batsmen Himself Sorry I Am Digressing A Bit But Hang On Actually This Cricketer Thing Has Got Me Thinking That Maybe I Could Fill Quite A Lot Of This Interminable Name With Lists Of A Few Of My Favourite Things To Go All Sound Of Music For A Bit Which Is Not An Unusual Thing For Me To Do As You Might Have Noticed If You Have Read The Book So Let Me Continue The Sports Theme By Listing A Few Of My Favourite Rugby Players And Obviously I Have To Start With Jonathan Davies That's The Dual Code Legend From The Nineteen Eighties Not The Current Welsh Centre Though I Am A Big Fan Of His As Well And I Actually Worked On Jiffy's Welsh Rugby Chat Show A While Back And He Was Great To Work With Where Was I Oh Yes Favourite Rugby Players Ieuan Evans Because As Well As Excellence He Bore More Than A Passing Resemblance To Bruce Willis In Die Hard Neil Jenkins Because Of His Golden God Full Back Heroics In South Africa In Nineteen Ninety Seven And Because He Bore With Stoicism The Traditional Criticism Of Welsh Fly Halves Who Are Not Barry John Or Phil Bennett And For A Similar Reason I Love Stephen

Jones Though I Do Remember In The Grand Slam Of Two
Thousand And Five Against France He Made A Clean Break
Of About Fifty Yards Ooh Yards That Dates Me Anyway He
Made The Break And Looked Round For Support But There
Wasn't Any Because Everyone Else Was Sort Of Startled By
Him Having Done It Not Least I Think Himself And Also
Ryan Jones Who In Two Thousand And Five In A Midweek
Game After His Late Call Up To The Lions Performed The
Most Single Handed Winning Of A Match I Think I Have
Ever Seen And He Seems To Be Just An Excellent Player
And Person Who Even Has A Footnote In The Book
Dedicated To Him And Just To Show It Is Not Just Welsh
Players I Shall Now Add Jonny Wilkinson Who Is Exactly My
Height A Fact I Know Because I Deliberately Backed Myself
Into Him At The National Television Awards One Year To
Find Out Jeremy Guscott Was Pretty Good To Watch And I
Always Enjoyed Michael Lynagh Who Was A Complete Gent
When I Met Him Many Years Ago On A Radio Five Sports
Quiz Well That Has Got Through A Few More Words So
Perhaps It Is Now Time To Include My Favourite Crossword
Clue Which Is This Gegs Nine Four Answer Later Though
You Might Already Know It Because It Is A Pretty Famous
One Oh Good Grief I Have Still Got Loads To Go Though I
Suppose I Could Just Now Cut And Paste What I've Already
Got And That Would Fill The Word Count But That Would
Be Cheating Wouldn't It So I'm Going To Push On With
This Silly Long Name With More Actual Name Style Words
In Here Such As Bosworth Sinky Westerton Pommel Nesby
Van Dismorterton Buswibbler Tranquist O'Condor Esserty
Normanside Pushpuller Cooky Biswas Nowparry Colander

Basket Sumsplinky Incidentally I Discovered While Working On This Book That I Enjoy Writing In A Hat Not A Special Hat Just A Baseball Cap I Bought On Holiday But One Day When I Was Struggling To Concentrate I Thought If I Put The Hat On It Will Help And It Did Because All Of Us Need A Touch Of Strange Ritual In Our Lives I Think And Sometimes My Writing Ritual Included Starting The Day With A Bit Of Inspirational Music Such As Ron Goodwin's Main Theme To Where Eagles Dare Or Bruce Springsteen's Born To Run A Track I Used Many Years Ago As My Start Writing Music When I Did An Unusual Ghost Writing Job Under Great Time Pressure Actually Music While Working Is An Interesting Topic Because Sometimes I Find I Just Can Not Listen To Anything And At Other Times It Is Vital For Example On This Book I Listened To Bach's Cello Suites A Lot And Quite Often Some Beethoven Symphonies And Also A Lot Of Film Soundtracks Such As Crimson Tide And Jurassic Park And Also The Batman Films By Which I Mean The Recent Hans Zimmer And James Newton Howard Batman Begins And Dark Knight Scores And Not The Still Excellent Danny Elfman Batman Score From Nineteen Eighty Nine Which I Now Realize I Need To Buy Because It Seems To Have Disappeared From My Collection And As We Are In The Area Of Film Perhaps I Should Slip In A List Of Some Of My Favourite Films That Should Fill Some Space So Here We Go With In No Particular Order Back To The Future Raiders Of The Lost Ark The Life And Death Of Colonel Blimp The Shining The Godfather Apocalypse Now Die Hard Star Wars The Empire Strikes Back Where Eagles Dare The Ipcress File Robocop All The Toy Story Films

Brazil Airplane Dirty Harry Fight Club Aliens Terminator
Two Anchorman Dodgeball The Jerk All The Monty Python
Films Casablanca Out Of Sight The Long Kiss Goodnight
Kiss Kiss Bang Bang Saving Private Ryan Almost Famous
Annie Hall Some Like It Hot It's A Wonderful Life When
Harry Met Sally Jurassic Park Full Metal Jacket Sense And
Sensibility Silence Of The Lambs The Good The Bad And
The Ugly The Elephant Man Because Of Anthony Hopkins's
Amazing Performance As Dr Frederick Treves In Fact I Have
To Say Hopkins Is One Of My Favourite All Time Actors For
All Sorts Of Things But As A Standout The Moment In The
Remains Of The Day When Emma Thompson Catches Him
Reading A Romance Novel And The Look On His Face
Breaks Your Heart And Also All The Seventies Films He Did
Where He Was Still A Bit Of A Drinker And You Can Play
The Is He Pissed In This Scene Game I'm Thinking
Specifically Of The Film Of All Creatures Great And Small
In Which He Plays Siegfried Farnon To John Alderton's
James Herriot And There's A Scene Where Alderton Is
Getting Something From The Dispensary Probably
Something For Tricky Woo If You Get The Reference And
Anyway Sir Anthony Leans In To Tell Him Something And
Has A Close Up And You Think My Goodness Those Are
Drunk Person's Eyes Though He Is Still Excellent Right
Back To Some More Name Style Names Like Huggins
Jaffraptor Yellbibby Tamsk Norbington Thompson
Frisbeenudge Goshawk Falcon Chaffinch Sparrow Swan Oh
I Seem To Have Started Doing Types Of Bird Well Why Not
Thrush Bluetit Swallow Swift Marlin Hang On That's Not A
Bird That's A Fish But I Could Do Some Fish As Well

Especially Fish Like Pollock Which Is Both A Fish And Also A Surname As Is Salmon And Of Course John Dory Is A Whole Name In Itself But Back To Other Names Like Retwisty Pease-Watkin Bamfield Baker Barker Cleaver Gallimore Roe Just A Few Teacher Names There For Anyone Who Went To My School Perhaps A Pleasant Reminder Or Perhaps Not Because You Know It Was School Wasn't It And Some People Don't Have Fond Memories Hazelhurst Bontempi Squatly Diddlecombe Masterton By The Way The Answer To The Crossword Clue A While Ago Which Was Gegs Is Scrambled Eggs And Blimey I Am Well Over Half Way Now And I Am A Little Tempted To Cheat By Saying That The Lawyer Spoke His Name Very Slowly Making It Much Shorter In Terms Of Words But No I Am Going To Plough On And Do A Full Four Thousand Plus Words Which I Am Taking As The Correct Length For A Name That Would Take Twenty Minutes To Say I Suppose I Could Go Back Into The Text And Edit It So That The Name Only Took Fifteen Or Even Ten Minutes To Say But It Was Always Twenty Minutes In The Radio Version Which Makes It Sort Of Canonical Plus There Is The Fact That Twenty Just Seems The Correct Funny Number For Some Reason Even Though It Is Not A Prime Number And Worse Is An Even Number Because As Everyone Knows In Most Circumstances The Prime Number Is Funniest And Odd Is Always Funnier Than Even For Example Seventeen Is A Funny Number But Eight Is Not Although Now I Write It Down The Blunt Directness Of Eight Is Somehow Amusing So Maybe My Rules Of Comedy Numbers Are All Wrong Oh Well Let Me Think Of What Else I Can Put In Here Maybe Some Namey Name

Type Names Like Waspington Splincoln Stopnastington Oh
I Know This Is A Book So I Should Maybe Put Some Of My
Favourite Books In So I Shall Start By Saying That For A Very
Long Time My Favourite Book Of All Was The World
According To Garp But I Reread It A Few Years Ago And
Discovered It Was A Book Of My Younger Days That While
Still Admirable And Excellent I Do Not Quite Love As Much
Now Meaning That My Favourite Book As An Adult Is
Probably Tinker Tailor Soldier Spy A Book I Think I Have
Read Five Times In Eight Years Other Favourite Books
Include The Great Gatsby Why Evolution Is True By Jerry
Coyne A Slimmer More Elegant Book Than Mr Dawkins's
Equivalent Works Red Storm Rising Day Of The Triffids
Great Expectations Adventures In The Screen Trade The
Stand And The Quincunx Which I Suppose In A Tiny Way
This Book Is A Very Silly Less Clever And Complex Version
Of Incidentally For Those Who Are Interested I Didn't Read
English At University As You Might Imagine But Actually
Read Classics It's Just There's No Real Market For Books In
Ancient Greek Or Latin These Days Not That I Could Have
Written One Because My Prose Composition Was At Best
Decent Just Ask Any Of My Poor Long Suffering Teachers
Over The Years To Whom I Would Now Like To Apologize
For My Slackness In Their Classes Teachers Such As The
Late Great Mr Buckney Mr MacLennan Mr King Mr Barlow
Mr Siviter And Later On Dr Patterson Dr Hardie And Dr
Sedley Ah That Worked As Some Actual Names Within This
Long Name So In An Attempt To Get Even More Names In
Let Me Ask If You Have Ever Done That Thing Where You
Have To Say Which People From History You Would Most

Like To Be Which Is A Longer Term More Personal Version
Of The Fantasy Dinner Party Guest Game Well Anyway I
Would Most Like To Have Lived The Lives Of The Duke Of
Wellington Winston Churchill And Even Though He Is Not
Historical Michael Palin Who Is One Of My Comic And All
Round Heroes And Possibly I Might Add WG Grace To That
List Just Because He Seems To Have Led A Pretty Bonkers
Life Full Of Lots And Lots Of Cricket And Ooh I Love
Cricket And Do Not Get To Play Anywhere Near As Much As
I Would Like To Any More But You Know It Is A Time
Consuming Game And I Have A Young Family To Think Of
But I Do Miss It And Will Play Again At Some Point And Try
And Get That Elusive Century That I Have Never Made As
My Highest Score Remains Ninety Two A Score I Have
Actually Got Three Times Would You Believe One Of Them
Not Out For Oswestry Under Thirteens Back In The Early
Eighties But The Other Two I Was Dismissed At That Score
As I Refused To Compromise My Attacking Approach As I
Neared The Century Or More Likely Had Simply Lost Count
Of How Many Runs I Had Got I Have Also Scored Eighty Six
Twice In My Batting Life The First Time Going From Forty
Six To Eighty Six In Ten Balls Including Being Out That Was
A Good Day And Even Though It Was Nearly Twenty Years
Ago I Can Still Remember The Six I Hit Over Long On Off
A Relatively Fast Bowler As For Bowling Figures My Personal
Best Is Eight For Thirty Four But My Favourite Bowling
Figures Were When I Played For My School Under Elevens
And My Analysis Read Eighteen Overs Sixteen Maidens Six
Wickets For Two Runs Need I Say The Opposition Were
Both Bad And Timid Left Arm Spin In Case You Were

Wondering And I Also Bat Left Handed So It Is No Wonder
My Cricketing Heroes Feature Several Left Handed Batsmen
Okay That Has Been A Long Digression So Back To Some
Names Such As Jartwell Discusmus Ruction Tarpaulin
Lozenge Platyhelminth Warp Oh Dear Now I'm Just Listing
Words I Think Sound Nice Like Mattress Concomitant And
Splosh Which The Spellchecker Doesn't Think Is A Real
Word Even Though It Is And Here's A Thought Back In The
Nineteenth Century When This Was Supposedly Written Do
You Think They Also Had Spellcheckers Who Were People
Who Watched You Write Things Down And Then Leaped In
With A Red Pen To Underline Anything You Got Wrong
Actually I Might Use That In The Fifth Radio Series Which I
Was Writing In Parallel With This Book Gosh I Am Getting
Along With It And Really Crunching Through This Insanely
Long Name Though I Realize Now As I Write Towards My
Final Deadline That I Really Should Have Just Done It In
Small Bits As I Went Along Rather Than Remembering At
The Last Minute That I'd Put In A Footnote Saying The Full
Name Can Be Found In Appendix Two And Then Humming
And Hawing Thinking I Could Just Ask The Publishers To
Take That Footnote Out But Then Deciding That No It Had
To Be Done Because I Think It's A Joke That At Least Shows
Commitment And Then Trying To Write It All In One Go
Anyway Nearly At The End Of This Ludicrously Long Name
Which Isn't Really A Name At All Now Is It Instead Having
Become A Strange Discursive Ramble Through My
Subconscious All For The Sake Of A Stupid Joke But Then
Sometimes You Just Have To Commit To The Joke And
Really See It Through Don't You And I Jolly Well Am Going

To Do That With This Just Keep Typing Until I Get There And Actually Looking At The Word Count I Have Very Nearly Done It So Here Goes Into The Last Few Words Nigelton Crumbarton Mintybitson Spilling Wangerator Tubripley Gonwester Highty Jinstamatic Nurker Habiston Beastworthy Fennelham Jones.

APPENDIX III

A Chronology of Sir Philip Bin

1806   Philip Put-That-In-The Bin born to Thomas and Agnes Bin of Bin Manor, Little Itchingham, in the county of Kentlesex.

1806–27   The events of this book take place. They shall not be spoiled here. Or, if you've already read it, they shall not be recapped here.

1828   Mysteriously, no trace of Philip Bin's activities exists for this year. Though in other events it is a leap year, the Duke of Wellington becomes Prime Minister, Andrew Jackson is elected President of the United States of America, Henrik Ibsen is born, London Zoo opens, Jöns Jakob Berzelius discovers the element thorium, Ányos Jedlik creates the world's first electric motor, Mary Anning finds the first pterosaur fossil in Lyme Regis, the MCC changes the Laws of Cricket to allow round-arm bowling, Dresden University of Technology is founded and the Treaty of Turkmenchay is signed.[1]

---

[1] I love Wikipedia.

1829   Wins All England Foreigner Baiting Competition for the first time, defeating 'Rude' Jem Sawbridge in the final.

1830–31   Adventuring abroad and at home; conquers the West Pole and discovers the fabled North-West passage from London to Manchester.

1832   Becomes Member of Parliament for the constituency of Poverty-St-Mary and Dreadfulness North. Refusing to join either Whig or Tory party, sets up his own combination of the two, the Twig party.

1833   Marries second wife Miss Ripely Fecund, seventeenth daughter of Reverend Godly Fecund, nine times voted the Church of England's most muscular Christian.

1834–47   Has innumerable children, like the Victorians often did.

1834   Knighted by Queen Victoria after rescuing her from kidnap by Mr Gently Benevolent – Bin's former guardian.

1835   First novel *Bleak Expectations* published. Rapidly becomes best-selling book in British history, after the Duke of Wellington's *How to Hate a Frenchman Vol II.*

1835½   Bin sued by a Mr Gently Benevolent over portrayal in *Bleak Expectations*. Argues it is a travesty of his actual character.

1836   Bin loses libel case against Mr Gently Benevolent. Forced to pay damages of £150,000, financially destroying him.

1837   A sequel to *Bleak Expectations, Bleaker Expectations* is published to try and restore his financial standing. It sells even better than the first book, and Sir Philip becomes rich again.

1838 Sued for a second time by Mr Gently Benevolent over portrayal in *Bleaker Expectations*. Benevolent wins, damages again ruin Bin.

1839 Publishes *Bleakest Expectations* in attempt to re-restore fortunes once more. Succeeds, as book becomes bestseller.

1840 Sued yet again by Mr Gently Benevolent, loses, huge damages, new book, sued again, loses again etc, etc, etc – this cycle continues for the next five years.

1845 Bin spends all year sulking and writing rude letters to lawyers.

1846 Mr Gently Benevolent attempts to take over world with help of evil undead army, Bin leads army to defeat him; on the basis that his attempt to conquer the world was a truer representation of his character, Mr Gently Benevolent's libel victories are reversed and Sir Philip is awarded the money back with interest.

1847 Now the richest man in history, Sir Philip retires from public life.

1848 Bored, he reappears in public life. Publishes first true fiction book, *Graham Grambleby*. Critics hate it, but it still sells well.

1849 Publishes *A Story of Two Towns*, set in the fictional Prussian revolution. Critics love it, but it only sells five copies.

1850 Founds monthly magazine *Storymuncher*, weekly magazine *Mr Dingle's Narrative Bag* and daily magazine *Words & Ting*.

1851 Adds hourly magazine *All The Hour Round*. The effort of publishing twenty-four times a day is too much, and he uses his powers as a Member of Parliament to introduce a bill redefining the hour as seven hundred and twenty minutes. The bill passes. The British economy almost instantly collapses, as most workers are paid by the hour and therefore wages are reduced by a factor of twelve. It takes the abolition of the bill and a small war with France to mend the economy.

1852   Publishes out of character 'entertainments' *Riff-raffles the Proletarian Thief* and *Lustful Killer Bees From Mars*; the latter is banned for obscenity until 1960 when the famous Lustful Killer Bees Trial is won, resulting in the first publication for over a hundred years.

1853   After Charles Dickens's *Bleak House* becomes best-seller, Bin publishes his own *Miserable Mansion*, which instantly becomes a worstseller.

1854   Furious with Dickens for outselling him, Sir Philip retires from public life for the second time.

1855   Returns to public life with series of readings from new novels *Dombey and Daughter* and *Massive Dorrit*. Hugely popular – but each sells two copies fewer than Dickens's latest works, plunging Bin into fury.

1856   After drunken political evening in Downing Street, Sir Philip accidentally becomes Prime Minister for three hours, during which he declares war on France, makes cats illegal, replaces income tax with a reverse-lottery where the winners have to hand over all their money to the government, introduces the vote for farmyard animals but still not women, bans trousers in pubs and renames March Sirphilipruary. Reluctantly resigns with highest ratings of any Prime Minister ever.

1857   Publishes three new books, all of which are entirely blank. Claims it is a joke on the literary mores of the time; later admits he'd just forgotten to write them.

1858   Sir Philip took the year off, and did nothing. Absolutely nothing. Seriously. He just sat in a chair for a year, staring, broken only by a twelve hour sleep every night.

1859   Reinvigorated by his year of rest, starts quest to destroy Charles Dickens for taking his place as Britain's most loved novelist. In July is arrested for breaking into Dickens' London home and balancing buckets of water on top of doors and giving him an apple pie bed.

1860   Dickens moves out of London to Gad's Hill Place near Rochester. Sir Philip gleefully claims responsibility.

1861   On publicity trip to America accidentally starts US Civil War when visiting Fort Sumter and jokingly asking, 'is this cannon loaded?' It was.

1862   Publishes final volume of autobiographical fiction, *Even More Bleakerest Expectations*. Widely accused of making it all up.

1863   Tours Antarctica giving series of readings to icebound explorers, penguins and massively lost polar bears.

1864   Publishes seasonal tale *A Christmas Quarrel*. Though he claims it is fiction, it is widely held to be a syllable for syllable transcription of a family argument over how to cook the turkey.

1865   Bin causes railway accident at Staplehurst, believed to be attempt to nobble Dickens.

1866–70   The 'disguise years'. Spends bulk of fortune on make-up, costumes, false beards and hats to appear as different person at every public reading Dickens does and heckle viciously.

1871   Is drunk for the whole year in guilty celebration of death of Dickens the year before. Publishes cheap cash-in book *The Dickens I Hated* and is reviled both critically and popularly.

1872–80   Disappears from public life once more, with only occasional appearances to be rude about other writers.

1881   Briefly reappears drunk and naked to claim he has invented a new type of cheese called Choddar. It turns out to be just Cheddar painted orange.

1882–91   The lost years – including divorce, remarriage, redivorce, re-remarriage, re-training as a marriage guidance counsellor, addictions, depression, pessimism, weight gain and bitterness. So a normal writer's life, then.

1892   Death of second wife Ripely. After being seen publicly to shed a tear at her funeral is condemned for weakness by every male in the British Empire. But receives two million offers of marriage from women desperate for a man who might express at least a tiny bit of emotion.

1893   Marries two million women in world's largest ever wedding ceremony.

1894   Divorces all two million new wives after eleven months and three weeks on realizing that imminent purchase of so many wedding anniversary presents will financially ruin him.

1895   With late burst of creative energy, re-emerges into public life. Sets up the Post-Raphaelite Brotherhood, dedicated to showing the beauty of crayons and finger-painting in art. Also composes fifteen symphonies, writes eight plays, tickles two trout, and produces thin volume of sonnets and massively fat volume of abusive poems about Arthur Conan Doyle, George Gissing and Rudyard Kipling.

1896   After publication of *Jude the Obvious,* a thinly veiled parody of *Jude the Obscure,* the ninety-year-old Sir Philip has a fist-fight with Thomas Hardy – the culmination of a long-running feud which Hardy was previously unaware of.

1897   Sets up home in Worcestershire with one-time mortal enemy Mr Gently Benevolent who is now well over a hundred years old but thanks to dabbling in the dark arts looks no older than forty-five or so.

1897–1914   Further lost years – there is no trace of Sir Philip in any records of the time. He and Mr Benevolent are rumoured to have travelled the pan-dimensional universe, though they may just have stayed in Worcestershire really, really quietly without anyone noticing.

1915   At the age of one hundred and nine, Sir Philip wins the Victoria Cross for leading a British charge against the German lines at the second battle of Ypres. He later admits he thought he was charging the French lines.

1916   Sir Philip dies in an incident involving a swimming pool full of brandy and forty-eight semi-naked dancing girls: a post-mortem reveals that at the age of a hundred and ten in such circumstances he simply smiled himself to death.